PENGUIN  C1

T0249121

# THE FIDDLER OF T.
## AND OTHER STORIES 1888–1900

THOMAS HARDY was born in a cottage in Higher Bockhampton, near Dorchester, on 1 June 1840. He was educated locally and at sixteen was articled to a Dorchester architect, John Hicks. In 1862 he moved to London and found employment with another architect, Arthur Blomfield. He now began to write poetry and published an essay. By 1867 he had returned to Dorset to work as Hicks's assistant and began his first (unpublished) novel, *The Poor Man and the Lady*.

On an architectural visit to St Juliot in Cornwall in 1870 he met his first wife, Emma Gifford. Before their marriage in 1874 he had published four novels and was earning his living as a writer. More novels followed and in 1878 the Hardys moved from Dorset to the London literary scene. But in 1885, after building his house at Max Gate near Dorchester, Hardy again returned to Dorset. He then produced most of his major novels: *The Mayor of Casterbridge* (1886), *The Woodlanders* (1887), *Tess of the D'Urbervilles* (1891), *The Pursuit of the Well-Beloved* (1892) and *Jude the Obscure* (1895). During the same period he published three volumes of short stories: *Wessex Tales* (1888), *A Group of Noble Dames* (1891) and *Life's Little Ironies* (1894). Amidst the controversy caused by *Jude the Obscure*, he turned to the poetry he had been writing all his life. In the next thirty years he published over nine hundred poems and his epic drama in verse, *The Dynasts*.

After a long and bitter estrangement, Emma Hardy died at Max Gate in 1912. Paradoxically, the event triggered some of Hardy's finest love poetry. In 1914, however, he married Florence Dugdale, a close friend for several years. In 1910 he had been awarded the Order of Merit and was recognized, even revered, as the major literary figure of the time. He died on 11 January 1928. His ashes were buried in Westminster Abbey and his heart at Stinsford in Dorset.

KEITH WILSON is Professor and former Chair of English at the University of Ottawa, and an Honorary Vice-President of the

Thomas Hardy Association. He has published widely on nineteenth- and twentieth-century British literature, Victorian and Edwardian music hall and the contemporary British novel. His work on Hardy includes *Thomas Hardy on Stage* (1995), a study of Hardy's plays, dramatic adaptations of his own fiction and relationship with the theatre, articles on the poetry and drama, and contributions to *The Oxford Reader's Companion to Hardy* (2000). He has also edited Hardy's *The Mayor of Casterbridge* for Penguin Classics.

KRISTIN BRADY is the author of *The Short Stories of Thomas Hardy: Tales of Past and Present* (1982) and of *George Eliot* (1992), as well as numerous articles on Hardy, Eliot, Nathaniel Hawthorne and feminist theory. She also edited Hardy's *The Withered Arm and Other Stories* for Penguin Classics. Educated at the University of Toronto, she was Professor of English at the University of Western Ontario, where she taught in the Department of English and in the Centre for Women's Studies and Feminist Research. Kristin Brady died in 1998.

PATRICIA INGHAM is General Editor of all Hardy's fiction in the Penguin Classics Edition. She is a Fellow of St Anne's College, Reader in English and *The Times* Lecturer in English Language, at the University of Oxford. She has written extensively on the Victorian novel and on Hardy in particular. Her most recent publications include *Dickens, Women and Language* (1992) and *The Language of Gender and Class: Transformation in the Victorian Novel* (1996). She has also edited Elizabeth Gaskell's *North and South* and Thomas Hardy's *The Pursuit of the Well-Beloved and The Well-Beloved* and *The Woodlanders* for Penguin Classics.

THOMAS HARDY

# The Fiddler of the Reels and Other Stories
# 1888–1900

*Edited with an Introduction and Notes by*
KEITH WILSON *and* KRISTIN BRADY

PENGUIN BOOKS

PENGUIN BOOKS

Published by the Penguin Group
Penguin Books Ltd, 80 Strand, London WC2R ORL, England
Penguin Putnam Inc., 375 Hudson Street, New York, New York 10014, USA
Penguin Books Australia Ltd, 250 Camberwell Road, Camberwell, Victoria 3124, Australia
Penguin Books Canada Ltd, 10 Alcorn Avenue, Toronto, Ontario, Canada M4V 3B2
Penguin Books India (P) Ltd, 11 Community Centre, Panchsheel Park, New Delhi – 110 017, India
Penguin Books (NZ) Ltd, Cnr Rosedale and Airborne Roads, Albany, Auckland, New Zealand
Penguin Books (South Africa) (Pty) Ltd, 24 Sturdee Avenue, Rosebank 2196, South Africa

Penguin Books Ltd, Registered Offices: 80 Strand, London WC2R ORL, England

www.penguin.com

Published in Penguin Classics 2003

009

Introduction and Notes copyright © Keith Wilson, 2003
Appendices copyright © the Estate of Kristin Brady, 2003
General Editor's Preface and Chronology copyright © Patricia Ingham, 1996
All rights reserved

The moral right of the editors has been asserted

Set in 10.25/12.25 pt PostScript Adobe Sabon
Typeset by Rowland Phototypesetting Ltd, Bury St Edmunds, Suffolk
Printed and bound in Great Britain by Clays Ltd, Elcograf S.p.A.

ISBN 978-0-14-043900-7

www.greenpenguin.co.uk

# Contents

## Short Stories

# Acknowledgements

This edition, the second in a two-volume selection of Thomas Hardy's short stories, was originally to have been prepared, like the first, by the late Kristin Brady. Professor Brady's death in December 1998 deprived Hardy studies of one of its most respected scholars, and her colleagues and students of a dearly loved friend and teacher. My main debt is to her, without whose initial work the edition would not have been completed in its present form. She is the sole author of both Appendix I and Appendix II. At the time of her death she had drafted part of an Introduction and started preparing some of the Notes. While in their final forms both Introduction and Notes are inevitably different from the ones she would have completed, products as they are of a different cast of mind and in some ways a different sense of Hardy, elements of her work are reflected in all components of the editorial apparatus. I trust, therefore, that while this is not the same edition that Kristin would have produced she would have found it one to which she would have been happy to have her name attached. My thanks go also to Kristin's husband and colleague, Richard Hillman, who was instrumental in collecting and forwarding her research materials and preliminary drafts.

Several libraries granted either Kristin or me, and in some instances both of us, access to materials in their keeping: thanks go to the staff of the Robarts Library and the Thomas Fisher Rare Book Library at the University of Toronto; the Morisset Library at the University of Ottawa; the D. B. Weldon Library at the University of Western Ontario; the British Library; the Bodleian Library; Cambridge University Library; and the Dorset

County Museum. I thank my colleagues Ina Ferris, April London, Seymour Mayne, David Rampton, David Shore and Nicholas von Maltzahn for various kinds of assistance and advice. Michael Millgate, whose scholarship has made unrivalled contributions to so many areas of Hardy studies over the last thirty years, has been his customary generous self. And I am most grateful to Laura Barber, Lindeth Vasey and Sarah Coward of Penguin for both their professionalism and their patience.

Keith Wilson
*University of Ottawa*
March 2002

# General Editor's Preface

This edition uses, with one exception, the first edition in *volume* form of each of Hardy's novels and therefore offers something not generally available. Their dates range from 1871 to 1897. The purpose behind this choice is to present each novel as the creation of its own period and without revisions of later times, since these versions have an integrity and value of their own. The outline of textual history that follows is designed to expand on this statement.

All of Hardy's fourteen novels, except *Jude the Obscure* (1895) which first appeared as a volume in the Wessex Novels, were published individually as he wrote them (from 1871 onwards). Apart from *Desperate Remedies* (1871) and *Under the Greenwood Tree* (1872), all were published first as serials in periodicals, where they were subjected to varying degrees of editorial interference and censorship. *Desperate Remedies* and *Under the Greenwood Tree* appeared directly in volume form from Tinsley Brothers. By 1895 ten more novels had been published in volumes by six different publishers.

By 1895 Hardy was sufficiently well-established to negotiate with Osgood, McIlvaine a collected edition of all earlier novels and short story collections plus the volume edition of *Jude the Obscure*. *The Well-Beloved* (radically changed from its serialized version) was added in 1897, completing the appearance of all Hardy's novels in volume form. Significantly this collection was called the 'Wessex Novels' and contained a map of 'The Wessex of the Novels' and authorial prefaces, as well as frontispieces by Macbeth-Raeburn of a scene from the novel sketched 'on the spot'. The texts were heavily revised by Hardy, amongst other things, in relation to topography, to strengthen the 'Wessex' element so as to suggest that this half-real half-imagined location had been coherently conceived from the beginning, though of course he knew that this was not so. In practice 'Wessex' had an uncertain and ambiguous development in the earlier editions. To trace the growth of Wessex in the novels as they appeared it is necessary to read them in their original pre-1895 form. For the 1895–6 edition represents a substantial layer of reworking.

Similarly, in the last fully revised and collected edition of 1912–13, the Wessex Edition, further alterations were made to topographical detail and photographs of Dorset were included. In the more open climate of opinion then prevailing, sexual and religious references were sometimes (though not always) made bolder. In both collected editions there were also many changes of other kinds. In addition, novels and short story volumes were grouped thematically as 'Novels of Character and Environment', 'Romances and Fantasies' and 'Novels of Ingenuity' in a way suggesting a unifying master plan underlying all texts. A few revisions were made for the Mellstock Edition of 1919–20, but to only some texts.

It is various versions of the 1912–13 edition which are generally available today, incorporating these layers of alteration and shaped in part by the critical climate when the alterations were made. Therefore the present edition offers the texts as Hardy's readers first encountered them, in a form of which he in general approved, the version that his early critics reacted to. It reveals Hardy as he first dawned upon the public and shows how his writing (including the creation of Wessex) developed, partly in response to differing climates of opinion in the 1870s, 1880s and early 1890s. In keeping with these general aims, the edition will reproduce all contemporary illustrations where the originals were line drawings. In addition for all texts which were illustrated, individual volumes will provide an appendix discussing the artist and the illustrations.

The exception to the use of the first volume editions is *Far from the Madding Crowd*, for which Hardy's holograph manuscript will be used. That edition will demonstrate in detail just how the text is 'the creation of its own period': by relating the manuscript to the serial version and to the first volume edition. The heavy editorial censoring by Leslie Stephen for the serial and the subsequent revision for the volume provide an extreme example of the processes that in many cases precede and produce the first book versions. In addition, the complete serial version (1892) of *The Well-Beloved* will be printed alongside the volume edition, since it is arguably a different novel from the latter.

To complete the picture of how the texts developed later, editors trace in their Notes on the History of the Text the major changes in 1895–6 and 1912–13. They quote significant alterations in their explanatory notes and include the authorial prefaces of 1895–6 and 1912–13. They also indicate something of the pre-history of the texts in manuscripts where these are available. The editing of the short stories will be separately dealt with in the two volumes containing them.

Patricia Ingham
*St Anne's College, Oxford*

# Chronology: Hardy's Life and Works

**1840** 2 June: Thomas Hardy born, Higher Bockhampton, Dorset, eldest child of a builder, Thomas Hardy, and Jemima Hand, who had been married for less than six months. Younger siblings: Mary, Henry, Katharine (Kate), to whom he remained close.

**1848–56** Schooling in Dorset.

**1856** Hardy watched the hanging of Martha Browne for the murder of her husband. (Thought to be remembered in the death of Tess Durbeyfield.)

**1856–60** Articled to Dorchester architect, John Hicks; later his assistant.

**late 1850s** Important friendship with Horace Moule (eight years older, middle-class and well-educated), who became his intellectual mentor and encouraged his self-education.

**1862** London architect, Arthur Blomfield, employed him as a draughtsman. Self-education continued.

**1867** Returned to Dorset as a jobbing architect. He worked for Hicks on church restoration.

**1868** Completed his first novel *The Poor Man and the Lady* but it was rejected for publication (see 1878).

**1869** Worked for the architect Crickmay in Weymouth, again on church restoration.

**1870** After many youthful infatuations thought to be referred to in early poems, met his first wife, Emma Lavinia Gifford, on a professional visit to St Juliot in north Cornwall.

**1871** *Desperate Remedies* published in volume form by Tinsley Brothers.

1872 *Under the Greenwood Tree* published in volume form by Tinsley Brothers.

1873 *A Pair of Blue Eyes* (previously serialized in *Tinsleys' Magazine*). Horace Moule committed suicide.

1874 *Far from the Madding Crowd* (previously serialized in the *Cornhill Magazine*). Hardy married Emma and set up house in London (Surbiton). They had no children, to Hardy's regret; and she never got on with his family.

1875 The Hardys returned to Dorset (Swanage).

1876 *The Hand of Ethelberta* (previously serialized in the *Cornhill Magazine*).

1878 *The Return of the Native* (previously serialized in *Belgravia*). The Hardys moved back to London (Tooting). Serialized version of part of first unpublished novel appeared in *Harper's Weekly* in New York as *An Indiscretion in the Life of an Heiress*. It was never included in his collected works.

1880 *The Trumpet-Major* (previously serialized in *Good Words*). Hardy ill for many months.

1881 *A Laodicean* (previously serialized in *Harper's New Monthly Magazine*). The Hardys returned to Dorset.

1882 *Two on a Tower* (previously serialized in the *Atlantic Monthly*).

1885 The Hardys moved for the last time to a house, Max Gate, outside Dorchester, designed by Hardy and built by his brother.

1886 *The Mayor of Casterbridge* (previously serialized in the *Graphic*).

1887 *The Woodlanders* (previously serialized in *Macmillan's Magazine*).

1888 *Wessex Tales*.

1891 *A Group of Noble Dames* (tales). *Tess of the D'Urbervilles* (previously serialized in censored form in the *Graphic*). It simultaneously enhanced his reputation as a novelist and caused a scandal because of its advanced views on sexual conduct.

1892 Hardy's father, Thomas, died. Serialized version of *The*

*Well-Beloved*, entitled *The Pursuit of the Well-Beloved*, in the *Illustrated London News*. Growing estrangement from Emma.

1892–3 *Our Exploits at West Poley*, a long tale for boys, published in an American periodical, the *Household*.

1893 Met Florence Henniker, one of several society women with whom he had intense friendships. Collaborated with her on *The Spectre of the Real* (published 1894).

1894 *Life's Little Ironies* (tales).

1895 *Jude the Obscure*, a savage attack on marriage which worsened relations with Emma. Serialized previously in *Harper's New Monthly Magazine*. It received both eulogistic and vitriolic reviews. The latter were a factor in his ceasing to write novels.

1895–6 First Collected Edition of novels: Wessex Novels (16 volumes), published by Osgood, McIlvaine. This included the first book edition of *Jude the Obscure*.

1897 *The Well-Beloved* (rewritten) published as a book; added to the Wessex Novels as vol. XVII. From now on he published only the poetry he had been writing since the 1860s. No more novels.

1898 *Wessex Poems and Other Verses*. Hardy and Emma continued to live at Max Gate but were now estranged and 'kept separate'.

1901 *Poems of the Past and the Present*.

1902 Macmillan became his publishers.

1904 Part 1 of *The Dynasts* (epic-drama in verse on Napoleon). Hardy's mother, Jemima, 'the single most important influence in his life', died.

1905 Met Florence Emily Dugdale, his future second wife, then aged 26. Soon a friend and secretary.

1906 Part 2 of *The Dynasts*.

1908 Part 3 of *The Dynasts*.

1909 *Time's Laughingstocks and Other Verses*.

1910 Awarded Order of Merit, having previously refused a knighthood.

1912–13 Major collected edition of novels and verse, revised by Hardy: The Wessex Edition (24 volumes). 27 November:

Emma died still estranged. This triggered the writing of Hardy's finest love-lyrics about their early time in Cornwall.

**1913** *A Changed Man and Other Tales*.

**1914** 10 February: married Florence Dugdale (already hurt by his poetic reaction to Emma's death). *Satires of Circumstance. The Dynasts: Prologue and Epilogue.*

**1915** Mary, Hardy's sister, died. His distant young cousin, Frank, killed at Gallipoli.

**1916** *Selected Poems*.

**1917** *Moments of Vision and Miscellaneous Verses*.

**1919–20** Mellstock Edition of novels and verse (37 volumes).

**1922** *Late Lyrics and Earlier with Many Other Verses*.

**1923** *The Famous Tragedy of the Queen of Cornwall* (drama).

**1924** Dramatized *Tess* performed at Dorchester. Hardy infatuated with the local woman, Gertrude Bugler, who played Tess.

**1925** *Human Shows, Far Phantasies, Songs and Trifles*.

**1928** Hardy died on 11 January. His heart was buried in Emma's grave at Stinsford, his ashes in Westminster Abbey. *Winter Words in Various Moods and Metres* published posthumously. Hardy's brother, Henry, died.

**1928–30** Hardy's autobiography published (on his instructions) under his second wife's name.

**1937** Florence Hardy (his second wife) died.

**1940** Hardy's last sibling, Kate, died.

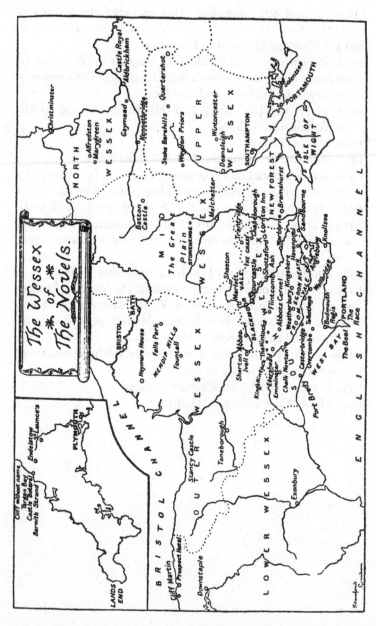

This map is from the Wessex Novels Edition, 1895–6

# Bibliographical Note

The following abbreviations are used for frequently cited sources:

*Biography*: Michael Millgate, *Thomas Hardy: A Biography* (Oxford: Oxford University Press, 1982)

Brady: Kristin Brady, *The Short Stories of Thomas Hardy: Tales of Past and Present* (Basingstoke: Macmillan, 1982)

*Collected Letters*: Thomas Hardy, *The Collected Letters of Thomas Hardy*, ed. Richard Little Purdy and Michael Millgate, 7 vols. (Oxford: Clarendon, 1978–88)

Gatrell: Simon Gatrell, *Hardy the Creator: A Textual Biography* (Oxford: Clarendon, 1988)

Hutchins: John Hutchins, *The History and Antiquities of the County of Dorset* (1774; 3rd ed., Westminster: J. B. Nichols, 1861–73)

Kay-Robinson: Denys Kay-Robinson, *The Landscape of Thomas Hardy* (Exeter: Webb & Bower, 1984)

Lea: Hermann Lea, *Thomas Hardy's Wessex* (1913; Basingstoke: Macmillan, 1977)

*Life*: Thomas Hardy, *The Life and Work of Thomas Hardy*, ed. Michael Millgate (Basingstoke: Macmillan, 1984)

*Literary Notebooks*: Thomas Hardy, *The Literary Notebooks of Thomas Hardy*, ed. Lennart A. Björk, 2 vols. (New York: New York University Press, 1985)

*Personal Notebooks*: Thomas Hardy, *The Personal Notebooks of Thomas Hardy*, ed. Richard H. Taylor (Basingstoke: Macmillan, 1979)

*Personal Writings*: Thomas Hardy, *Thomas Hardy's Personal*

*Writings: Prefaces, Literary Opinions, Reminiscences*, ed. Harold Orel (London: Macmillan, 1967)

*Poetical Works*: Thomas Hardy, *The Complete Poetical Works of Thomas Hardy*, ed. Samuel Hynes, 5 vols. (Oxford: Clarendon, 1982–95)

*Public Voice: Thomas Hardy's Public Voice: The Essays, Speeches, and Miscellaneous Prose*, ed. Michael Millgate (Oxford: Clarendon, 2001)

Purdy: Richard Little Purdy, *Thomas Hardy: A Bibliographical Study* (1954; Oxford: Clarendon, 1968)

Ray: Martin Ray, *Thomas Hardy: A Textual Study of the Short Stories* (Aldershot: Ashgate, 1997)

*Withered Arm*: Thomas Hardy, *The Withered Arm and Other Stories 1874–1888*, ed. Kristin Brady (Harmondsworth: Penguin, 1999)

The following abbreviations are used for particular printings of Hardy's stories:

1888 *UR*: 1888 printing of 'A Tragedy of Two Ambitions' in *Universal Review*

1889 *H*: 1889 printing of 'The First Countess of Wessex' in *Harper's New Monthly Magazine*

1890 *BT*: 1890 printing of 'The Melancholy Hussar' in *Bristol Times and Mirror*

1890 *G*: 1890 printing of 'Barbara (Daughter of Sir John Grebe)', published as part of *A Group of Noble Dames* in *Graphic*

1890 *HW*: 1890 printing of 'Barbara, Daughter of Sir John Grebe' published as part of *A Group of Noble Dames* in *Harper's Weekly*

1891 *EIM*: 1891 printing of 'On the Western Circuit' in *English Illustrated Magazine*

1891 *FR*: 1891 printing of 'For Conscience Sake' in *Fortnightly Review*

1891 *GND*: *A Group of Noble Dames* (London: Osgood, McIlvaine, 1891)

1891 *HW*: 1891 printing of 'On the Western Circuit' in *Harper's Weekly*

1891 *ILN*: 1891 printing of 'The Son's Veto' in *Illustrated London News*

1893 *SM*: 1893 printing of 'The Fiddler of the Reels' in *Scribner's Magazine*

1894 *LLI*: *Life's Little Ironies, A Set of Tales with Some Colloquial Sketches Entitled A Few Crusted Characters* (London: Osgood, McIlvaine, 1894)

1894 *PMM*: 1894 printing of 'An Imaginative Woman' in *Pall Mall Magazine*

1896 *GND*: *A Group of Noble Dames* (London: Osgood, McIlvaine, 1896)

1896 *LLI*: *Life's Little Ironies, A Set of Tales with Some Colloquial Sketches Entitled A Few Crusted Characters* (London: Osgood, McIlvaine, 1896)

1896 *WT*: *Wessex Tales: Strange, Lively, and Commonplace* (London: Osgood, McIlvaine, 1896)

1900 *C*: 1900 printing of 'A Changed Man' in *Cosmopolitan*

1900 *S*: 1900 printing of 'A Changed Man' in *Sphere*

1912 *WT*: *Wessex Tales: Strange, Lively, and Commonplace* (London: Macmillan, 1912)

1912 *GND*: *A Group of Noble Dames* (London: Macmillan, 1912)

1912 *LLI*: *Life's Little Ironies, A Set of Tales with Some Colloquial Sketches Entitled A Few Crusted Characters* (London: Macmillan, 1912)

1913 *CM*: *A Changed Man, The Waiting Supper, and Other Tales, Concluding With The Romantic Adventures of a Milkmaid* (London: Macmillan, 1913)

# Introduction

*New readers are advised that this Introduction makes the details of the plots explicit.*

In her Introduction to *The Withered Arm and Other Stories 1874–1888*, the first half of this two-volume selection of short stories by Thomas Hardy, Kristin Brady noted that she had 'attempted to draw together stories that are both engaging for readers and representative of different phases in Hardy's career as a writer of short narrative'.[1] This volume follows the same principle, focusing on stories that first appeared between late 1888 and 1900. Like its predecessor, it places the stories in the order in which they were first published, although 'The Melancholy Hussar of the German Legion' is moved from third to first place in order to indicate the point when most of it was written. This associates it more closely with the narratives of the recent regional past assembled for Hardy's first volume of short stories, *Wessex Tales* (1888).[2] Certainly it has marked differences from the types of story that characterize Hardy's second and third collections: *A Group of Noble Dames* (1891), a compilation of ten aristocratic historically based fantasies set primarily in the seventeenth and eighteenth centuries, and *Life's Little Ironies* (1894), a group of tragic or ironic dramas most of which are contemporary in setting. The variety of forms taken by Hardy's short stories in the last decade of the nineteenth century indicates something of their importance to him, both as works destined for volume publication (and hence for review in serious journals) and as testing grounds for ideas that would receive more sustained treatment in his most innovative and controversial novels, most notably *Tess of the D'Urbervilles* (1891) and *Jude the Obscure* (1896 [1895]). Ultimately, with the publication of *A Changed Man and Other Tales* (1913), all but seven of Hardy's short stories would receive in his lifetime the status implied by their collection between hard covers.[3]

On the last day of 1887, Hardy wrote in his journal that the year had been 'a fairly friendly one', enabling him 'to hold my own in fiction, whatever that may be worth, by the completion of "The Woodlanders"'.[4] This mood of relative optimism seems to have continued into the subsequent year. By the end of February, Hardy had sent off *Wessex Tales*, which was published in May, and by July he had almost completed a story that had been promised to a new journal, the *Universal Review*. He wrote to Harry Quilter, its editor,

> I am settling down to your story. It is of a picturesque kind – a tale of the camp of German Hussars on the hills near here, when Geo. III was King, & living at Weymouth. It has some foundation in truth. The scenery is of course of the period; York Hussars, a camp, downs, old stone manor-house inside a wall, sea in the distance, &c. Daughter of the house is the heroine. Then there is an escape by night, a boat, Weymouth harbour, &c.[5]

This description of 'The Melancholy Hussar' at a fairly advanced stage of its composition contains many trademarks of a standard 'Wessex Tale', with its local rural setting and early nineteenth-century historical framework. Hardy speculated, in the same letter, that Quilter may not have wanted 'a tale of that sort for your very modern review' and offered as a substitute

> a story of a different character – embodying present day aspirations – i.e., concerning the ambitions of two men, their struggles for education, a position in the Church, & so on, ending tragically. If you much prefer the latter sort of thing I will abandon the first – though that is the most advanced, & could be sent in a week or ten days. The other would take a little more time, as it exists at present only in the form of half a dozen notes.

Quilter obviously accepted Hardy's proposal for the second story, for the result, 'A Tragedy of Two Ambitions', appeared in the December 1888 issue of his journal, while 'The Melancholy

Hussar' was not completed until almost a year later for its January 1890 publication in the *Bristol Times and Mirror*.

'The Melancholy Hussar', the first story to be substantially written, though not completed, after the successful publication of *Wessex Tales*, has strong affinities with many of Hardy's earlier fictional works. Set in the Napoleonic era, it returns to the world of *The Trumpet-Major* (1880) and 'A Tradition of Eighteen Hundred and Four', a story first published in 1882. Begun soon after the completion of 'The Withered Arm', it also derives much of its power from Hardy's personal memories of oral sources and his sense that its painful events (both stories conclude with executions) were based on actual occurrences. He wrote in his Preface to the 1896 Wessex Novels edition of *Life's Little Ironies*,

> A story-teller's interest in his own stories is usually independent of any merits or demerits they may show as specimens of narrative art; turning on something behind the scenes, something real in their history, which may have no attraction for a reader even if known to him – a condition by no means likely. In the present collection 'The Melancholy Hussar of the German Legion' has just such a hold upon myself for the technically inadmissible reasons that the old people who gave me their recollections of its incidents did so in circumstances that linger pathetically in the memory; that she who, at the age of ninety, pointed out the unmarked resting-place of the two soldiers of the tale, was probably the last remaining eyewitness of their death and interment; that the extract from the register of burials is literal, to be read any day in the original by the curious who recognize the village.[6]

The story came to Hardy through a number of channels. He told George Meredith's nephew, Stewart Marsh Ellis, that it was related to him in 1855 by an old woman,[7] and an annotation in his personal copy of the 1912 *Wessex Tales* names sources he had already mentioned in a personal note of 1877:[8] 'The execution . . . was witnessed by James Bushrod of Broadmayne, who described the details to James Selby, a few years younger than himself. Selby in his old age told them to the writer.'[9]

During 1878–9, Hardy had also copied down in his 'Trumpet-Major Notebook' an account of the execution taken from the *Morning Chronicle* of 4 July 1801, details from which were used in the story's 1894 first volume printing in *Life's Little Ironies* (the copy-text for this edition). And at some point before the 1890 serialization, he had examined the Bincombe parish registers in order to quote them in the story's conclusion.[10]

Other aspects of 'The Melancholy Hussar' may have resulted from its compositional association with *Tess of the D'Urbervilles*, Hardy's most controversial novel to that point in his career and one which had provoked a series of rejections by publishers before it finally appeared, in bowdlerized form, in the *Graphic* in 1891. As Michael Millgate has noted, Hardy had first sent the early sections of the novel on 9 September 1889 to Tillotson & Son's Newspaper Fiction Bureau, which had already put them in proof form when its head reader discovered their potentially dangerous content and demanded changes. After Hardy refused to modify the text, Tillotson's agreed to cancel the contract and on 25 September, as an expression of its continuing goodwill, asked for a short story. Hardy then quickly completed 'The Melancholy Hussar' and sent it off on 22 October.[11] The story was an acceptably respectable substitute for Hardy's scandalous novel: unlike Tess Durbeyfield, Phyllis Grove is 'a pure woman' in a physical as well as a moral sense. But in both texts the female protagonist is presented as a victim and the narrator, who offers his own personal memories of Phyllis in old age, resolutely defends her against the 'injustice [inflicted] upon her memory' because 'such fragments of her story as got abroad at the time, and have been kept alive ever since, are precisely those which are most unfavourable to her character'. Though her situation may recall that of Eustacia Vye in *The Return of the Native* (1878) – she too is a middle-class woman from Budmouth who is forced by a self-absorbed father-figure to live in rural isolation – her nature could not be more different from the fickle and manipulative Eustacia's. Like Tess, she is a woman who, despite her capacity for emotional response, has all the virtues of instinctive respectability, reinforced by reciprocal qualities in the man with whom she agrees to elope: 'She always said that the one feature in his proposal which overcame her hesitation was the obvious purity and straightforwardness of his intentions. He showed himself to be so virtuous and kind; he treated her with a respect to which she had never before been accustomed.' And also like Tess, she becomes the victim of the very respectability she embodies, acting out of what Brady calls 'a naive sense of honour'[12] and in the process committing an act of socially sanctioned betrayal that costs her lover his life. The story's compassionate vindication of Phyllis from the 'injustice [inflicted] upon her memory' is thus twofold, its evocation of the complex poignancies of the tragedy implicitly refuting both the enduring rumours of sexual irregularity and the possible charge that her unfortunate lover paid an even higher price for her over-fastidious social conscience than did Phyllis herself.

The plot of 'The Melancholy Hussar' turns as much on cross-generational as on romantic relationship: memories of his lonely mother lie at the heart of Matthäus's homesickness, while the enclosed solipsism of Phyllis's father is the direct cause of her oppressive seclusion. The complexity of both parental and filial obligation, compounded further by the unyielding imperatives of class, also informs 'A Tragedy of Two Ambitions', which, like 'A Melancholy Hussar', has associations with *Tess* in its rendering of both familial havoc wrought by the alcoholism of a parent and the careerist opportunism of two brothers: in their self-reference and failures of charity, the Halborough brothers bear some resemblance to the more fortunately situated Cuthbert and Felix Clare. But the closer novelistic connection suggested by its bleak view of educational aspiration is with *Jude the Obscure*, which had itself been originally conceived of as a short story and had evolved, according to Hardy's Preface to its first edition, 'from notes made in 1887',[13] the year before he wrote 'A Tragedy of Two Ambitions'. Both story and novel foreground characters who consider, as Hardy himself once had, entering the ministry, and both works explore the anguish of the intelligent man of humble origins who seeks the education and status of a gentleman, initially through the autodidact's 'untutored reading of Greek and Latin'.[14]

The Halborough brothers are, however, unlike Jude Fawley in the moral question mark that hovers over their aspirations. The surviving manuscript indicates that Hardy originally considered 'The Shame of the Halboroughs' for the story's title, and although his final choice appropriately highlights the conjunction between ambition and a tragic fall, the earlier possibility draws attention to what might be seen as the narrative's two conflicting shames: the unavoidable social shame of the alcoholic father and the culpable moral shame of his sons' allowing him to drown, seemingly seen by Hardy himself as unquestionably a murder.[15] The ethical wrongness of the choice made by the two apparently devout brothers is emphasized by a detail added to the conclusion of the story for its first volume appearance in *Life's Little Ironies* (the copy-text for this edition). This episode, in which Joshua notices that his drowned father's walking-stick, hidden in the sedge by Joshua himself, has taken root and become a 'straight little silver-poplar', recalls most immediately a Dorset legend about an ash tree that grew from the whip of Heedless William, a drunken post-van driver who drowned.[16] But it also has resonant religious echoes, evoking not only the budding Aaron's rod in the Epistle to the Hebrews (9.4), the text that the brothers are translating at the beginning of the story, but also the flowering thorn supposedly derived from the pilgrim's staff planted by Joseph of Arimathaea at Glastonbury.[17] Thus the growing poplar, at which the two brothers 'could not bear to look', ironically underscores, in tacit contradistinction to the priestly authority of both Aaron and Joseph, the Halboroughs' priestly failures, failures occasioned by an overwhelming desire for mere social authority and the professional success that bestows it. That Joshua, the leader in the decision to leave their father to his fate, should bear the name of Moses' successor, the prophet who finally takes the Israelites into the Promised Land, compounds the irony.

The nub of this 'tragedy' of ambition is that understandable social aspiration should become, through the very act of parricide that seeks to assure its fulfilment, the occasion for a lifetime of guilt. But the story does not focus exclusively on the brothers' shared culpability. It evokes understandingly the meagre professional choices available to two impoverished young men, who are fired as much by a sense of responsibility for ensuring their sister's future as they are by their own ambitions. The caustic advice of Joshua to his younger brother is not mere rationalization but a convincing indictment of the systemic hypocrisies of an inflexibly classed society: 'To succeed in the Church, people must believe in you, first of all, as a gentleman, secondly as a man of means, thirdly as a scholar, fourthly as a preacher, fifthly, perhaps, as a Christian, – but always first as a gentleman, with all their heart and soul and strength.' This emphasis on the contribution made by class vulnerability to moral failing may well have been a source of the story's interest for so many of its original readers. Not only was it a favourite of Hardy and his second wife, Florence, but Edmund Gosse also singled it out for special commendation, Marcel Proust read it in a French translation, and Stanislaus Joyce suggested that even the hostile response to it by his brother, James, who 'animadverted almost petulantly on Hardy's "incredible woodenness"', constituted wilful blindness to a parallel situation in their own family.[18]

Hardy's engagement with class issues took protean forms throughout his writing life and at this period was not limited to the contemporary trials of socially ambitious youths, charged as this recurrent theme was for him by the still raw memory of his own earlier personal history as a gifted young man without the means to attend Oxford or Cambridge. Soon after completing 'A Tragedy of Two Ambitions' in August 1888, he began work on 'The First Countess of Wessex', a historic tale, set during the 1730s and 40s, whose prime focus, again one involving cross-generational conflict, is the potential destructiveness of arranged marriage. Its historicity is frequently asserted and validated in narratorial asides that emphasize the distance between past and present: Tupcombe is loyal to the Dornells 'in a degree which has no counterpart in these latter days', smallpox is 'a disease whose prevalence at that period was a terror of which we at present can hardly form a conception', Reynard has already dined when Dornell calls on him at four o'clock 'for people dined early then'. Surviving artifacts – Reynard's epitaph 'still extant in King's-Hintock church', Betty's 'little white frock ... carefully preserved among the relics at King's-Hintock Court' – testify as much to the passage of time as to the tale's authenticity. The distancing effect of these details is counter-balanced, however, by the story's immediacy, perhaps a reflection of Hardy's undeclared personal involvement with its historical context. For although he took some factual details from John Hutchins's massive *History and Antiquities of the County of Dorset*, a more direct link with its eighteenth-century originals, the first Earl and Countess of Ilchester, was his mother, Jemima Hardy (née Hand), who had been raised in poverty, but whose yeoman ancestors had once owned property later subsumed by the Ilchester estate (see Appendix II).

This connection with Hardy's mother points to an intriguing relationship between 'The First Countess of Wessex' and *Tess of the D'Urbervilles*, which Hardy began writing immediately after mailing off the story's periodical version in the autumn of 1888 and whose bowdlerized serialization he was correcting in proof as he prepared the second version of 'The First Countess of Wessex' for its inclusion in the 1891 volume edition of *A Group of Noble Dames* (the copy-text for this edition).[19] On the one hand, the two texts are complementary, for the novel dwells on precisely what is excluded from the short story: the history of those, like Jemima Hardy, whose formerly prosperous families have lost their property, wealth and social status. In other respects, however, there are significant parallels between the story and the novel, for both Betty Dornell and Tess Durbey-field become sexual chattels used by their parents to accomplish their own questionable ends. While the virginal Tess is delivered into the hands of the wealthy Alec D'Urberville by a destitute mother ambitious for her daughter's future, Betty Dornell, through the machinations of her heiress mother, is married when still a child to a man of thirty primarily because he has influence at court. Both Tess and Betty also have irresponsible fathers who fail their daughters at crucial junctures, and both have relationships with two men. Indeed, their radically differing fates have as much to do with luck as with their contrasting economic and social circumstances: the man forced upon

Betty by Susannah Dornell turns out to be a gallant lover and devoted husband, while the man to whom Joan Durbeyfield sends Tess is a feckless manipulator who makes her his mistress rather than his wife. In both stories, moreover, the measure of a husband's worth is gauged by his ability to accept the sexual history of his wife. A striking contrast to the idealistic Angel Clare, who rejects Tess on their honeymoon because of her past sexual history, the practical Stephen Reynard values future promise over past fact, displaying the intelligence and kindness of a 'contriving, sagacious, gentle-mannered man, a philosopher who saw that the only constant attribute of life is change'. But this is an outcome suggestive merely of Betty's good fortune and, more fundamentally, both works expose the powerlessness of women in the sexual marketplace of their respective periods. The happiness of Betty Dornell and the unhappiness of Tess Durbeyfield are both finally determined by the temperamental predispositions of their male partners.

The version of 'The First Countess of Wessex' in this volume is markedly different from its 1889 periodical publication in *Harper's New Monthly Magazine*, for this later incarnation – which includes several concluding paragraphs about a historian-narrator and his listeners (see A Note on the History of the Texts and Appendix II for other differences) – was adapted in 1891 for *A Group of Noble Dames*. The added paragraphs had been revised from the six-story version of *A Group of Noble Dames* that had appeared at the end of 1890 in the *Graphic*, and they establish for the group of narratives a mediating context. The collection overall had contained such potentially controversial content that the *Graphic* editors had demanded substantial changes. For the 1891 volume publication, into which Hardy incorporated revised versions of four other stories that had already been published separately, he basically restored the unbowdlerized versions of the six narratives that had appeared in the periodical.[20] Hardy had already described 'The First Countess of Wessex' to one editor as 'near ... in character'[21] to the other stories in *A Group of Noble Dames*, and he gave it a special prominence in the volume both by placing it at the very beginning and by moving the initial conversation among the men, which had appeared before the first story in the *Graphic*, to the conclusion of the narrative about Betty Dornell. This addition to and rearrangement of the material from the shorter collection accomplished two ends: it gave primacy to the originating aristocrats of 'Wessex', whose story happens also to have links with Hardy's personal past, and it partially distanced their tale of ultimate marital contentment, told now by a historian mentioned in the initial sentence, from the ironizing framework that introduces the remaining, mostly bleaker, stories. For although the historian is one of the several speakers of what Hardy was to call his 'Tale of Tales',[22] his story has its impact before the reader is told that it 'was made to do duty for the regulation papers on deformed butterflies, fossil ox-horns, prehistoric dung-mixens, and such like, that usually occupied the more serious attention' of the storm-bound Wessex Field and Antiquarian Club.

The speakers construct their narratives while surrounded by miscellaneous objects suggestive of an ancient and even prehistoric past: 'varnished skulls, urns, penates, tesserae, costumes, coats of mail, weapons ... missals ... fossilized ichthyosaurus and iguanodon ... stuffed birds'. The appropriateness to these historical stories of the museum setting (based on the Dorset County Museum) is further emphasized by the storytellers revealing in their confident male judgements on their aristocratic female subjects the same taxonomic impulses as those of the Victorian antiquarian and natural scientist. But while Hardy's treatment of the framing device thereby further ironizes the narrative points of view,[23] the stories have often been read without much attention being paid to their narratorial context. This has come about for a number of reasons: they are sometimes decontextualized for inclusion in selections and anthologies; the supposed circumstance of their relation is not developed in much detail after the descriptive paragraphs at the end of 'The First Countess of Wessex'; and the stories themselves, among them some of the most shocking in situation and descriptive detail in all of Hardy's work, tend to displace the reader's memory of the Wessex Field and Antiquarian Club.

Hardy to some degree used the device of the Antiquarian

Club in order to protect himself from exactly the sort of response the collection provoked, first from the cautious editors of the *Graphic*, then from reviewers. For he was quick to defend himself in print, after the *Pall Mall Gazette* accused him of 'a hideous and hateful fantasy', by arguing that 'the action is thrown back into a second plane or middle distance, being described by a character to characters, and not point-blank by author to reader'.[24] This defensive strategy may also have emerged, however, from the very confidence that led Hardy to work with such controversial content. For especially after the late 1880s, by which time he was on familiar terms with some of the leading thinkers and public figures of the period, he was pitching his work partly to a select professional audience familiar with current intellectual debates. In 1887, for example, he sent presentation copies of *The Woodlanders* – his first book to challenge so openly conventional ideas about marriage – to Algernon Swinburne, whom he had long admired but never met; to Sir Frederick Leighton, the President of the Royal Academy; and to the first Earl of Lytton, poet and former Viceroy of India. Lytton also received a first edition of *A Group of Noble Dames* in 1891, as did Edward Clodd, a new friend who helped to direct Hardy's reading towards science and anthropology, and Edmund Gosse, a writer well-read in post-Darwinian theory who would later, in his memoir *Father and Son* (1907), chart the agonies suffered by his father, the scientist Philip Gosse, in his unsuccessful attempts to reconcile scientific and scriptural authority.[25] Such sophisticated readers may well have been in Hardy's mind when he presented 'dear, delightful Wessex' as an intellectual hinterland 'whose statuesque dynasties are even now only just beginning to feel the shaking of the new and strange spirit without, like that which entered the lonely valley of Ezekiel's vision and made the dry bones move'. The framing device allowed Hardy to stand at once inside and outside two contrasting intellectual streams: the secluded backwater of his Wessex storytellers and the ideational mainstream of his distinguished London friends. He could play with applying new ideas to historically, socially and temperamentally various incarnations of womanhood, while protecting himself with the mask of his narrators' provincialism.

This doubleness is nowhere more apparent than in 'Barbara of the House of Grebe', the first narrative in the *Graphic* publication of *A Group of Noble Dames* and the one immediately following 'The First Countess of Wessex' in the 1891 volume printing (the copy-text for this edition). In both versions, it is also the story that immediately follows the introduction of the Antiquarian Club, a significant positioning which foregrounds Hardy's own dissociation from direct responsibility for narration of its shocking contents. Here he comes closer than anywhere else in his work to exploring the almost sadomasochistic eroticism that had interested him as a young man reading Swinburne.[26] Barbara's 'craze' for Edmond Willowes – which is shared by her mother even as she disapproves of the class difference – is presented as a physiological response governed seemingly by post-Darwinian assumptions about the imperatives of sexual selection. The same contemporary emphasis in this historical tale also explains both Barbara's inability to sustain her love for Willowes during his absence and her physical aversion to him after his injuries when, trying to overcome her repulsion and fear, she 'involuntarily looked aside and shuddered' at finding him 'metamorphosed to a specimen of another species'. And while Barbara's behaviour is continually labelled as 'natural', she displays responses that suggest both the regressiveness of infantilism and the nervous over-refinement of hysteria – as, for example, when she runs from her disfigured husband and crouches on a flower-stand in the greenhouse, with 'her skirts gathered up, in fear of the field-mice which sometimes came there'. The flight from sexuality suggested by this image anticipates the even more neurotically disorientated Sue Bridehead in *Jude the Obscure*, who sleeps in a closet, despite her fear of spiders, to escape her husband's bed. Barbara's subsequent reproductive career becomes both a tacit biological revenge on Uplandtowers and the inevitable outcome of her disturbed mental and physiological state. She gives birth to eleven children in eight years, evidence of her continuing submission to her manipulative husband's sexual will, 'but half of them came prematurely into the world, or died a few days old' and 'only one, a girl, attained to maturity'. Thus with the failure of her relationship with her natural partner, Edmond Willowes, she declines into years of submissive and attenuated sexuality that can produce no living male heir.

These suggestive psycho-sexual motifs in 'Barbara of the House of Grebe' are appropriate to the story's narration by a surgeon.[27] For although some of the later stories in A Group of Noble Dames are only superficially connected to the professions of their tellers, the clinical content and tone of this story depend on a speaker who claims expertise in matters both physiological and psychological. Thus the surgeon of the Antiquarian Club – 'the son of a surgeon' and 'a man who ha[s] seen much and heard more' – can pronounce confidently on Barbara's 'compound state of mind' and on the natural impulsiveness of a woman 'who has long been imposing upon herself a policy of reserve'. But when he elaborates on her overwrought devotions before the marmoreal image of her lost Apollonian first love – her words 'intermingled with sobs, and streaming tears, and dishevelled hair' – from which she returns to her current marital bed 'shaken by spent sobs and sighs', he surrenders clinical dispassion to the prurient relish of the voyeur, a rhetorical shift seemingly anticipated by the Antiquarian Club's crimson maltster, who in the introductory frame at the end of 'The First Countess of Wessex' winks at the Spark when the surgeon apologizes in advance for his tale 'as being perhaps a little too professional'. The suggestiveness of Betty's assignations with the statue, especially given their location – a 'tabernacle' in a 'deep recess' of her boudoir – is neither subtle nor clinical but rather, from the standpoint of the surgeon's audience, a flirtation with the pornographic, as was suggested by George Moore in his satirical account of the story.[28]

Thus the framing context, both temporal and narratorial, for A Group of Noble Dames in some degree freed Hardy to explore controversial aspects of female sexual response, a subject, as he was about to discover in the reactions to Tess of the D'Urbervilles and later to Jude the Obscure, not without risks when addressed in fictions placed within social settings at once more contemporary and less socially exalted. The stories collected for *Life's Little Ironies* (1894), the first edition of which provides the copy-text for the next four stories in this selection, show Hardy taking the risk of attempting to engage with what might broadly be conceived of as contemporary problems, primarily though not exclusively related to marital circumstance, as if in preparation for their more ambitious treatment in *Jude the Obscure*.

The situational skeleton of 'For Conscience' Sake' was provided for Hardy by an old country woman, a Mrs Cross, whom he met in December 1882. As Hardy recalled in the self-authored biography published under his wife's name, Mrs Cross told him of a girl 'betrayed and deserted by a lover' who 'kept her child by her own exertions, and lived bravely and throve'. When her poverty-stricken lover returned and wanted to marry her, she refused to be 'made respectable', and the lover ended in the workhouse: 'The eminently modern idea embodied in this example – of a woman's not becoming necessarily the chattel and slave of her seducer – impressed Hardy as being one of the first glimmers of woman's enfranchisement; and he made use of it in succeeding years in more than one case in his fiction and verse.'[29] He also made recurrent use of situations that explore the ambiguous morality of attempts to right past sexual wrongs, attempts often founded in the conventional but emotionally destructive assumption that primacy in sexual possession of a woman, whether inside or outside marriage, both grants rights to and imposes duties on the man who first has sexual knowledge of her. While the situation faced by Michael Henchard in *The Mayor of Casterbridge* (1886), the first novel written after Hardy's meeting with Mrs Cross, is complicated by his being the husband rather than the seducer of the woman he effectively sells at auction, there is no starker example in nineteenth-century fiction of a woman being treated as 'chattel and slave', and certainly Henchard's attempt, with his wife's complicity, retroactively to right this wrong proves disastrous. *Tess of the D'Urbervilles*, the novel that Hardy completed at about the time (late 1890) that he began working on 'For Conscience' Sake', has Tess's husband, Angel Clare, advance as the ultimate reason for his desertion of her upon discovery of her past sexual history the fact that her seducer still lives, and therefore has a prior claim to quasi-marital possession: 'How can we live together while that man lives?' (Chapter XXXVI). This view is shared by the seducer himself, Alec D'Urberville, who, like Millborne in 'For Conscience' Sake', attempts to assuage his own guilt, not only by saving Tess's soul but also by making an honest woman of her.[30] Emotional confusions wrought by an over-literal sense of the absolute duties and rights bestowed by primacy of sexual possession will also further complicate the tortured exchanges between Jude Fawley, Richard Phillotson and Sue Bridehead in *Jude the Obscure*. This almost obsessive motif, which places the disorderliness of emotional flux in the balance against false faith in structural absolutes (whether defined by the legal designation of spouse or mere rights of sexual precedence), was apparent from an early stage of Hardy's work, and responsible for the recurrent intermeshing triadic character patterns in nearly all his novels. But the psychological complexity with which such situations are explored becomes markedly more pronounced in Hardy's later novels, a development perhaps associable with his experiments with such situations in his shorter fictions.

The same might be said of another motif foregrounded in 'For Conscience' Sake'. The enduring power, both genetic and imaginative, of heredity had already been emphasized in *Tess of the D'Urbervilles*, manifested in family history in, for example, the suggestion that Tess's 'mailed ancestors rollicking home from a fray had dealt ... even more ruthlessly' with peasant girls than Alec has just dealt with Tess (Chapter XI), family legend (the D'Urberville coach) and the family face, which parodically echoes Tess's own features as it lours down at her on her ill-fated wedding night from the D'Urberville portraits on the wall of the ancestral manor (Chapter XXXIV). In late 1890, soon after revising *Tess* for serialization, Hardy read August Weismann's *Essays on Heredity*,[31] a work that may have influenced not only the central revelatory event of 'For Conscience' Sake' ('It was as if ... a mysterious veil had been lifted, temporarily revealing a strange pantomime of the past') but also the evolution of *The Pursuit of the Well-Beloved* (substantially written in 1891), a novel whose main plot pursues heredity across three generations. By the time Hardy was writing *Jude the Obscure*, he was more interested in the psychological than the physical imprint imposed by heredity, with the malign power of the Fawley heritage compounded in the union of the cousins Sue and Jude into 'a terrible intensification of unfitness – two bitters in one dish' (III. vi). While the gothic extravagances encompassing Jude's tragedy, culminating in the self-annihilating verses from the Book of Job he whispers to himself on his deathbed, far surpass in their horror the low-key self-effacement of Millborne, who is condemned merely to a self-sacrificial exile of 'harmless' pseudonymous solitude, the source of the personal failures is markedly similar in the two cases: the combined power of social convention and heredity.

Both forces tend to converge in the person of the child, often figured in Hardy's later fiction as both victim and victimizer, a conflation seen in its most extreme form in Little Father Time of *Jude the Obscure*. In 'For Conscience' Sake', Frances Frankland's vitriolic attack on her father ('Why were you so weak, mother, as to admit such an enemy to your house – one so obviously your evil genius') seems far in excess of what his selfishly muddled good intentions have warranted, especially given that the most enduring inheritance from his status as 'evil genius' to Leonora Frankland is Frances herself: the indictment of the father is tacitly the indictment of her own existence. The effect of Frances's attack is to redirect Millborne's conscience away from the need to re-implicate himself in the Frankland women's lives out of some spurious sense of honour and towards an act of self-effacement that leaves him in exiled isolation. Similarly, in 'The Son's Veto', Randolph Twycott's existence is premised upon his father's antecedent willingness to commit 'social suicide' by marrying beneath him. In condemning such social solecisms by forbidding his mother the same marital class descent perpetrated by his father, Randolph, like Frances Frankland, condemns the very forces that created him. As with Frances Frankland's ascent to the status of wife to a cleric, the price for Randolph's secure hold on priestly respectability is paid by a parent, a mother who declines into loveless solitude and an early death. And as in 'A Tragedy of Two Ambitions', the social marker that most separates parent from child is education, with Randolph's condescension to his mother increasing at every stage of his educational advance through public school, to university, to ordination.

While 'The Son's Veto' is unequivocal in its implicit judgement of Randolph's almost hysterical self-reference ('I am ashamed of you! It will ruin me! A miserable boor! a churl! a clown! It will degrade me in the eyes of all the gentlemen of England!'), preventing as it does his mother's return to marital fulfilment in the class from which she originates, cross-class alliances fail in Hardy's work for reasons beyond their disruption of the adamantine social barriers dear to the cruel rectitude of middle-class vicars, recurrent though clergymen are in Hardy's work as convenient agents to embody contemptible acts of snobbery. For Hardy the social convention that makes fleeting physical and emotional attraction a source of enduring misery is destructive because it translates a transient and impulsive truth into a permanent falsehood. Class difference may exacerbate the effects of such circumstances, locking together two people formed by different worlds who share nothing but a passing sexual *frisson*. But the more fundamental tragedy, that people change while contractual avowals and the social states they legitimate do not, is no respecter of class. When Hardy adopted 'the letter killeth'[32] as the epigraph to *Jude the Obscure*, he was foregrounding a metaphor whose truth had long been recurrently demonstrated in his fiction. The potential for a changed inner and private state to be misrepresented by an external emblem of that state (a love letter, a marriage licence, the indelible social designator of 'husband' or 'wife', or for that matter 'fallen woman') is for Hardy what inevitably ironizes, often tragically, the most complex of human emotions: sexual passion and the affectional impulses that accompany it. Examples from the major novels written in the same general period as the short stories in this collection are legion. In *The Woodlanders*, the marriage bond of Grace Melbury and Edred Fitzpiers proves imperviously resistant to the elusive freedom seemingly offered to Grace by new divorce laws. In *The Mayor of Casterbridge*, love letters, attesting to an intimacy that no longer reflects an emotional reality, bring about the disastrous skimmity-ride that ultimately kills both parties to the correspondence. In *Tess of the D'Urbervilles*, the question of who has the greater title to the designator 'husband' is tragically complicated by the non-delivery to the man Tess is about to marry of a wedding-eve confessional letter. And in *Jude the Obscure* a man whose job is to carve living language into dead stone sees both educational and domestic hopes destroyed when they pit themselves against the impregnable walls of social orthodoxy. In all these instances, emotional realities fall foul of inflexible or misleading structures of law, language and convention that maim those they entrap.

'On the Western Circuit' offers one of Hardy's most compelling explorations of the external artifact that treacherously misrepresents the inner state to which it apparently attests. The story may be founded in part in his boyhood memory of writing love letters for local illiterate girls,[33] and certainly the irrevocable blighting of Charles Raye's life is a function of the educational chasm between classes. Thus his realization that he has been 'ruined' comes not in response to the mere fact of marriage to a social inferior, which he has been prepared to risk in light of 'the unexpected mines of brightness and warmth that her letters had disclosed to be lurking in her sweet nature'. Only after his discovery that Anna is not the possessor of the sympathetic and delicate sensibility conveyed in the letters written on her behalf by Edith Harnham does Raye despair. When he observes to Edith 'Legally I have married her ... in soul and spirit I have married you,' he provides incontrovertible testimony to the capacity for an external cipher, both epistolary and marital, of an inner quality ironically to belie the truth it apparently affirms. He also underlines the subjectivist presuppositions informing Hardy's view of the relationship between the individual and the 'real' world. Shared imaginative sympathy has created the bond between Raye and a woman he has barely met, and the same imaginative responsiveness has the power, albeit temporarily, to remake the world, substituting an aesthetically mediated ideal for the coarser fleshly reality.

Hardy's experiments in many of his short stories with attempting to mediate romantic yearning through external artistic forms (sculpture in the case of 'Barbara of the House of Grebe', letters in 'On the Western Circuit', music in 'The Fiddler of the Reels', poetry in 'An Imaginative Woman') may again be related to the difficulties he was already experiencing in his longer fiction in addressing female sexual response in ways that carried psychological conviction without offending against contemporary norms of good taste and literary propriety. The use of states of aesthetic rapture to convey sexual arousal is seen in two of Hardy's most emotionally charged stories, 'The Fiddler of the Reels' and 'An Imaginative Woman', both of which, in very different ways, suggest an almost supernatural element in the imprinting of a man's imaginative power on a woman's consciousness. This is not to suggest that the mysterious impact of Mop Ollamoor's fiddle-playing or Robert Trewe's poems is merely an oblique literary convenience for rendering female sexuality more safely than, for example, the blunt description of Arabella Donn as 'a complete and substantial female animal' who lobs 'the characteristic part of a barrow-pig' at her intended lover (*Jude the Obscure*, I. vi). Both stories explore the essential part that imagination plays in sexual infatuation, most overwhelming for those who suspend actual circumstance, especially contexts of emotional deprivation, and enter states of quasi-enchantment that offer the promise of romantic fulfilment. This yearning for the unattainable as a route out of the unendurable characterizes a number of Hardy's later protagonists, invariably bringing them to disaster.

For the suggestive women of 'The Fiddler of the Reels' and 'An Imaginative Woman', that yearning has mysteriously physical repercussions that bridge the notional divide between imagination and reality. In the case of Car'line Aspent, who is not presented as innately one of nature's more sensitive souls, sexual response would seem superficially to have less to do with imaginative aspiration than with spasmodic reflex, analogous to convulsive 'galvanic shock'. But Mop Ollamoor's demonic musical power, which allied with a different character might have made of him 'a second Paganini', has an explicitly sexualized imaginative source, rooted in old country-dance tunes, entirely alien to his rival's plodding placidity. Ned Hipcroft, who 'had not the slightest ear for music', is by contrast a 'respectable mechanic' possessed of 'a nature not greatly dependent upon the ministrations of the other sex for its comforts'. The fact that Ned is working on construction of the Great Exhibition's modern architectural marvel, the Crystal Palace (a plot detail presumably suggested by the story's having been commissioned for a special Chicago World's Fair edition of *Scribner's Magazine* (13 May 1893)), defines him in relation to an urban technological world in 'an era of great hope and activity among the nations and industries', to which Car'line travels on another modern wonder, the 'excursion-train'. These contrasting states – figuring individuality, antiquity, aesthetic inspiration and demonic passion on the one hand, collectivity, modernity, industrialism and sexual placidity on the other – are mutually exclusive, the mythic Ollamoor disappearing with his daughter into a timeless realm of folk-history and rumour, leaving Ned, for all his centrality to the modern 'movement', to a childless existence with a peevish wife in contemporary London.

If Car'line Aspent's saltatory excesses are rooted in hysteria, as her father suspects, the *danses macabres* she performs as surviving vestiges of a dying rural culture are ominous in their neurotic intensity, suggesting divorce from rather than engagement with a genuine community. As Brady has observed,[34] it is significant that Ollamoor's 'date was a little later than that of the old Mellstock quire-band', whose members 'despised the new man's style' as being 'all fantastical' with 'no "plumness" in it – no bowing, no solidity'. While the Mellstock quire constitutes the collective musical voice, in both secular and sacred incarnations, of a village community, Ollamoor plays alone. Similarly, in her last encounter with Ollamoor, Car'line begins her dancing within a community of partners but ends by dancing alone, 'defiantly as she thought, but in truth slavishly and abjectly, subject to every wave of the melody, and probed by the gimlet-like gaze of her fascinator's open eye'. A musical art that is founded in the joyous celebration of group ritual has declined into quasi-onanistic self-projection in a sexual battle of wills that pits dancer against fiddler even as she submits to the hypnotic power of his music.[35]

A similar inwardness characterizes Ella Marchmill's infatuation with the image of Robert Trewe in 'An Imaginative Woman' (copy-text for this edition is its first book appearance in the 1896 reissue of *Wessex Tales*. It was subsequently (1912) moved to the opening position in *Life's Little Ironies*). While the dynamics of this infatuation seem at first glance very different from the volatility of Car'line Aspent's reaction to Ollamoor's playing, and certainly require no action on Trewe's part to generate Ella Marchmill's preoccupation with him, its effects are comparably overwhelming. They are again founded in the mediation of sexual response through an art form, not music this time but poetry, along with the more mundane artifacts – clothing, furniture, photograph, bedding – by which Trewe's physical rather than imaginative presence is defined. The main distinction from Car'line's situation in 'The Fiddler of the Reels' lies in Trewe's entirely passive role in the stimulation of Ella's imaginative obsession: 'all that moved her was the instinct to specialize a waiting emotion on the first fit thing that came to hand'. Yet despite Trewe's lack of direct responsibility for the effect that he has, there is again, as in 'The Fiddler of the Reels', a very active creative/destructive reciprocity in the woman's response to this sexualized medium of exchange. The work of Trewe that most vibrantly inflames Ella is, like Ollamoor's music, work in some sense still in performance:

Then she scanned again by the light of the candle the half-obliterated pencillings on the wall-paper beside her head. There they were – phrases, couplets, *bouts-rimés*, beginnings and middles of lines, ideas in the rough, like Shelley's scraps, and the least of them so intense, so sweet, so palpitating, that it seemed as if his very breath, warm and loving, fanned her cheeks from those walls, walls that had surrounded his head times and times as they surrounded her own now. He must often have put up his hand so – with the pencil in it. Yes, the writing was sideways, as it would be if executed by one who extended his arm thus.

Like Ollamoor's fiddling, these pencillings are works in process that embody the physical identity of their creator, inflame
sexually the woman they inspire aesthetically, and inhabit, as
incomplete but soon to *be* completed works, an ongoing creative
present in which Ella's body describes movements ('He must
often have put up his hand so', 'the writing was sideways, as it
would be if executed by one who extended his arm thus') elicited
by her fellow artist's own performative acts. And although in
this story Ella's last child (yet another victimized and victimizing
infant, this time one 'who had been the death of his mother'[36])
has, unlike Car'line Aspent's Carry, an unimpeachably respectable physical paternity, his features bear 'the dreamy and peculiar expression of the poet's face'. Thus just as Carry, Ollamoor's
actual daughter, disappears from her story into an unknown
future in the possession of her musical father, so Ella's child,
rejected by his actual blood father, would seem to face his
future possessed by 'the transmitted idea' of the features of his
imaginary poet-father.

It has long been recognized that this story of an 'imaginative
woman' never met by the melancholic poet with whom she is
infatuated (and who himself dies for lack of a desired 'imaginary
woman') owes much to the relationship of Hardy with Florence
Henniker, the 'charming, *intuitive* woman'[37] Hardy did meet,
about three months before beginning work on 'An Imaginative
Woman'. By the time he was working on his own short story,
he was already collaborating with Florence Henniker on another
story, 'The Spectre of the Real', the most palpable product of
a friendship, founded in considerable part on shared literary
interests, that lasted until Henniker's death in 1923. Hardy's
early relationship with Henniker (married not, like Ella
Marchmill, unhappily to an arms manufacturer but happily
to an army officer) effectively inverts that of 'An Imaginative
Woman', with Hardy figuring as the infatuated and Henniker
as the infatuee, until her early indication of the platonic terms on
which she wanted their friendship to proceed subdued Hardy's
romantic impulses.[38] This use of broadly autobiographical but
heavily disguised material, which we have seen occurring in a
number of the stories in this collection, distinguishes also 'A

Changed Man', the story that gave its name to the last collection of short fiction published in Hardy's lifetime (*A Changed Man and Other Tales* (1913)), but published here using as copy-text the serial version published in the *Sphere* (21 and 28 April 1900). Maumbry's noble, and ultimately fatal, selflessness in battling the cholera outbreak in his parish is based upon the comparable efforts of Henry Moule (vicar of St George's, Fordington, and father of Hardy's good friend Horace Moule) during the 1854 cholera epidemic. The association ends there – Henry Moule did not share Maumbry's colourful earlier career, troubled marital circumstances or tragic end – but may have been responsible for Hardy's feeling that the story was the best of those collected in the volume to which it gave its name.[39]

'A Changed Man' and 'Enter a Dragoon' (copy-text for which is also the serial version, *Harper's Monthly Magazine*, December 1900) are the last two stories written by Hardy. They both return to the regional military subject-matter, although of mid-century rather than the Napoleonic period, with which this volume of selected short stories opened. But perhaps as appropriate to their terminal position in both this selection and Hardy's career as a writer of fiction is their preoccupation with what had been, virtually from the outset of his writing life, the most recurrent motif in his fiction: the irony – by turns comic, pathetic and tragic – of sexual exchange in a world where intention and fulfilment are invariably at odds and changing emotional verities or social circumstances inevitably relativize the destructive absolutism of marital roles. Again Hardy resorts to the familiar device of triadic patterning. Laura Maumbry conceives of herself as the wife of a soldier. When his transformation into a parson requires her to remake herself as a parson's wife, she resists, redefining herself instead as lover to another, parodically named, soldier, Lieutenant Vannicock. When her husband sacrifices himself in the line of parsonical duty, thereby tacitly confirming his claim that 'a curate *is* a soldier – of the church militant', Laura loses interest in her lover, honours her dead husband's memory, and 'lived and died a widow'. A similar, if less poignant, irony informs Selina Paddock's situation in 'Enter a Dragoon', albeit an irony imposed as much by the perversity of circumstance as by her own emotional proclivities. Loyal to her soldier lover until she believes him to be dead, she then plans to marry to provide a secure home for her illegitimate child. When the 'dead' lover returns immediately before her marriage she reverts to him, only to see him die in reality on the evening of his return. She then stays true to the lover whose 'widow in the eyes of Heaven' she believes herself to be only to discover, after it is too late to marry his successor, that he had faithlessly married another woman before returning to her. Like Laura Maumbry, Selina, having faced the need to choose between two men and having chosen the one with most moral claim to the title of 'husband', is left with neither.

While 'A Changed Man' and 'Enter a Dragoon' were not collected for many years after their serial publication (appearing eventually in the final, and least thematically cohesive, of Hardy's volumes of short stories), had these two satires of marital circumstance been written a few years earlier, they would have seemed perfectly suited to inclusion in *Life's Little Ironies*. But their poignant evocation of temperamental and situational crossed purposes also seems an appropriate prelude to the very different, and much more ambitious, work that was already preoccupying Hardy as he ended his career as a writer of fiction. Three years after the serial publication of these stories the first volume of Hardy's great epic-drama, *The Dynasts* appeared. Its subject-matter, overtly the political and military history of Napoleonic Europe from just before Trafalgar to just after Waterloo, was ultimately more ambitious than even this daunting historical range would suggest, and more intimately connected with the recurrent concerns of the antecedent prose fictions. For *The Dynasts* was to offer Hardy's most elaborate, and philosophically informed, working out of the complex relationship between the unpredictability of a universe governed by little more than contingency and the temperamentally various modes of human response that attempt to make meaning out of that arbitrariness. In *The Dynasts*, that constitutional range is embodied as much in the 'phantom intelligences' (the Spirits of the Years, Pities, Sinister, Ironic and Rumour) who oversee the human action as in the historical protagonists themselves. The ironies and self-contradictions implicit in that most human of gifts and burdens, consciousness, were also to provide the predominant thematic ground for Hardy's shorter poems, the first volume of which had already appeared before his farewell to fiction. As this two-volume selection has demonstrated, Hardy's short stories in all their tonal variety occupy an important place in his lifelong exploration of the human tragicomedy, as experienced by a writer who remained convinced that 'If you look beneath the surface of any farce you see a tragedy; and, on the contrary, if you blind yourself to the deeper issues of a tragedy you see a farce.'[40]

# NOTES

1.  *Withered Arm*, xviii.
2.  Hardy himself underscored this connection during his preparation of the collected Wessex Edition of his works (1912) by transferring 'The Melancholy Hussar' (started in 1888, completed in 1889 and published in 1890) from its original location in *Life's Little Ironies* (1894) to *Wessex Tales*.
3.  The remainder were brought together, along with the two stories on which he collaborated with Florence Dugdale, his future second wife, and the one story on which he collaborated with Florence Henniker, in Thomas Hardy, *The Excluded and Collaborative Stories*, ed. Pamela Dalziel (Oxford: Clarendon, 1992).
4.  *Life*, 212.
5.  *Collected Letters*, I, 178.
6.  *Personal Writings*, 30–31.
7.  S. M. Ellis, 'Thomas Hardy: Some Personal Recollections', *Fortnightly Review*, NS 123 (1928), 398.
8.  For this earlier note see n. 19 to 'The Melancholy Hussar'.
9.  Quoted in Ray, 22–3. Selby, who worked for Hardy's father and 'had been a smuggler' (*Life*, 170), may be the original for the lively narrator of 'A Tradition of Eighteen Hundred and Four', whose name is Solomon Selby.
10. *Personal Notebooks*, 124–5; Carl J. Weber, *Hardy and the Lady from Madison Square* (Waterville, ME: Colby College Press, 1952), p. 93. In 1875, Hardy also wrote down a story he heard

from a British Waterloo veteran who had failed to keep a similar appointment with his French sweetheart (*Life*, 109).

11.  See *Biography*, 299–300; Purdy, 72–3; and *Collected Letters*, I, 201.

12.  Brady, 19.

13.  See *Personal Writings*, 32.

14.  For a discussion of the story's connections with *Jude the Obscure*, see Patricia Alden, 'A Short Story Prelude to *Jude the Obscure*: More Light on the Genesis of Hardy's Last Novel', *Colby Library Quarterly* 19 (1983), 45–52. Millgate notes that Hardy began thinking about the short-story plot for *Jude* in April 1888, 'at the time of a House of Commons debate on secondary education and "the ladder from the primary schools to the university"' (*Biography*, 346).

15.  In a letter to Edmund Gosse (1 August 1888), written during the composition of 'A Tragedy of Two Ambitions', Hardy refers to being 'at present up to the elbows in a cold blooded murder which I hope to get finished in a day or two' (*Collected Letters*, I, 179).

16.  See Kay-Robinson, 45.

17.  For a fuller account of the flowering of Aaron's rod as symbol of the house of Levi, the tribe chosen by God to assist the Jewish priests, see Numbers 17.3–10. In Exodus 7.8–12, the rod proves Aaron's priestly status by turning into a snake. The Glastonbury thorn, which flowers at Christmas, is also associated with Joseph of Arimathaea's hiding of the Holy Grail, and is therefore appropriately suggestive both of faith vindicated and quest only partially, and ambiguously, fulfilled.

18.  See *Letters of Emma and Florence Hardy*, ed. Michael Millgate (Oxford: Clarendon, 1996), p. 189; *Life*, 225; Peter J. Casagrande, *Hardy's Influence on the Modern Novel* (Totowa, NJ: Barnes & Noble, 1987), p. 116; and Stanislaus Joyce, *My Brother's Keeper*, ed. Richard Ellmann (London: Faber & Faber, 1958), p. 68.

19.  See *Collected Letters*, I, 180; and *Biography*, 293 and 310.

20.  As Ray (74) notes, the American *Harper's Weekly* 'issued the stories more or less as Hardy had originally written them and as they were to appear in the first book edition'. For the fullest account of Hardy's difficulties with the *Graphic* over *A Group of Noble Dames*, see Gatrell, 80–96.

21.  *Collected Letters*, VII, 113.

22.  Ibid.

23. On the framing device, see also Brady, 89–94; and J. Hillis Miller, 'Prosopopoeia in Hardy and Stevens', *Alternative Hardy*, ed. Lance St John Butler (New York: St Martin's, 1989), pp. 110–27.

24. Quoted in Michael Millgate, *Thomas Hardy: His Career as a Novelist* (1971; rev. edn. Basingstoke: Macmillan, 1994), p. 289.

25. See *Biography*, 284 and 315–16.

26. For Hardy's interest in Swinburne, see *Collected Letters*, II, 148; and his poem 'A Singer Asleep', *Poetical Works*, II, 31–3.

27. Even William Locker (son of Arthur Locker, the *Graphic*'s editor), who wrote to Hardy to explain that while the stories in *A Group of Noble Dames* would 'be very suitable and entirely harmless to the robust minds of a Club smoking-room' they were 'not at all suitable for the more delicate imaginations of young girls', could see the match between narrator and story: 'its main incident is very horrible – just the sort of story an old surgeon might be expected to tell, but none the less unpleasant for that' (quoted in Gatrell, 81–2).

28. See George Moore, *Conversations in Ebury Street* (New York: Boni and Liveright, 1924), pp. 127–43.

29. *Life*, 162–3.

30. Given these situational echoes between *Tess of the D'Urbervilles* and 'For Conscience' Sake', it is of passing interest that Millborne's confidant, Dr Bindon, who advises against Millborne's intrusive attempt to right past wrongs, bears the same name as Bindon Abbey, the original for the ruined abbey-church whose grounds contain the empty abbot's coffin in which the sleepwalking Angel Clare lays Tess in simulation of her death (Chapter XXXVII).

31. See *Life*, 240.

32. The derivation is the Second Epistle of Paul to the Corinthians 3.6: 'for the letter killeth, but the spirit giveth life'.

33. See *Biography*, 47. Manuscript deletions reveal that Hardy originally contemplated for this story titles that would immediately foreground the letter-writing motif, first 'The Amanuensis', subsequently 'The Writer of the Letters' (see Ray, 202).

34. Brady, 139.

35. In April 1892, about seven months before beginning work on 'The Fiddler of the Reels', Hardy had twice seen, and been impressed by, Lottie Collins's performance of her spectacular 'Ta-ra-ra-boom-de-ay' song and dance, a performance so frenetic that it is thought to have contributed to her early death (see

*Collected Letters*, VII, 121). This may well have had an influence on the core situation of 'The Fiddler of the Reels'.

36. Given the bleakness of the child's own ultimate situation, cruelly rejected by a misguided father whose physical paternity is in no doubt, the story is oddly caustic in its attribution of responsibility for his mother's death: 'she was lying in her room, pulseless and bloodless, with hardly strength enough left to follow up one feeble breath with another, the infant for whose unnecessary life she was slowly parting with her own being fat and well'.

37. See *Life*, 270. For the association between Florence Henniker and 'An Imaginative Woman', see Ray, 172–4. For Hardy's collaboration with Florence Henniker on the short story 'The Spectre of the Real', see Thomas Hardy, *The Excluded and Collaborative Stories*, ed. Pamela Dalziel, pp. 260–88. For the nature of the imaginative sympathy between Hardy and Florence Henniker and evidence of her possible influence on his own poetry, see Keith Wilson, 'Thomas Hardy and Florence Henniker: A Probable Source for Hardy's "Had You Wept"', *Thomas Hardy Year Book* 6 (1977), 62–6.

38. See *Biography*, 335–44.

39. See *Collected Letters*, IV, 297.

40. *Life*, 224.

# Further Reading

Three indispensable books are exclusively devoted to Hardy's short fiction: Kristin Brady, *The Short Stories of Thomas Hardy: Tales of Past and Present* (Basingstoke: Macmillan, 1982); Thomas Hardy, *The Excluded and Collaborative Stories*, ed. Pamela Dalziel (Oxford: Clarendon, 1992); and Martin Ray, *Thomas Hardy: A Textual Study of the Short Stories* (Aldershot: Ashgate, 1997). Equally valuable, although not exclusively concerned with the short stories, is Simon Gatrell, *Hardy the Creator: A Textual Biography* (Oxford: Clarendon, 1988). Michael Millgate, *Thomas Hardy: His Career as a Novelist* (London: Bodley Head, 1971; rev. ed. Basingstoke: Macmillan, 1994) remains the most useful single introduction to Hardy's fiction, and contains illuminating material on the short stories. Also recommended are Norman Page, 'Hardy's Short Stories: A Reconsideration', *Studies in Short Fiction* 11 (1974), 75–84; A. F. Cassis, 'A Note on the Structure of Hardy's Short Stories', *Colby Library Quarterly* 10 (1974), 287–96; Maire A. Quinn, 'Thomas Hardy and the Short Story' in *Budmouth Essays on Thomas Hardy: Papers Presented at the 1975 Summer School*, ed. F. B. Pinion (Dorchester: Thomas Hardy Society, 1976), pp. 74–85; J. B. Smith, 'Dialect in Hardy's Short Stories', *Thomas Hardy Annual* 3 (1985), 79–92; T. R. Wright, 'Diabolical Dames and Grotesque Desires: The Short Stories' in his *Hardy and the Erotic* (New York: St Martin's, 1989), pp. 89–105; Norman D. Prentiss, 'The Poetics of Interruption in Hardy's Poetry and Short Stories', *Victorian Poetry* 31 (1993), 41–60; and the web pages on Hardy's short stories maintained by Martin Ray at http://www.abdn.ac.uk/english/

thsna/stories.htm under the auspices of the Thomas Hardy Association (http://www.yale.edu/hardysoc).

Studies of specific stories from this edition include the following. On 'The Melancholy Hussar of the German Legion', see George Lanning, 'Hardy and the Hanoverian Hussars', *Thomas Hardy Journal* 6 (1990), 69–73. On 'A Tragedy of Two Ambitions', see Patricia Alden, 'A Short Story Prelude to *Jude the Obscure*: More Light on the Genesis of Hardy's Last Novel', *Colby Library Quarterly* 19 (1983), 45–52. On 'Barbara of the House of Grebe', see Francesco Marroni, 'The Negation of Eros in "Barbara of the House of Grebe"', *Thomas Hardy Journal* 10 (1994), 33–41. On 'On the Western Circuit', see Penelope Pether, 'Hardy and the Law', *Thomas Hardy Journal* 7 (1991), 28–41 (also on 'An Imaginative Woman'). On 'The Fiddler of the Reels', see Frank R. Giordano Jr, 'Characterization and Conflict in Hardy's "The Fiddler of the Reels"', *Texas Studies in Literature and Language* 17 (1975), 617–33; Michael Benazon, 'Dark and Fair: Character Contrast in Hardy's "Fiddler of the Reels"', *Ariel* 9 (1978), 75–82; Andrew Radford, 'Thomas Hardy's "The Fiddler of the Reels" and Musical Folklore', *Thomas Hardy Journal* 15 (1999), 72–81; and Rosemary Sumner, '"The Fiddler of the Reels": A Response to Andrew Radford's Article', *Thomas Hardy Journal* 15 (1999), 103–6. For the manuscript evolution of 'A Tragedy of Two Ambitions', 'For Conscience' Sake' and 'On the Western Circuit', see Alan Manford, '*Life's Little Ironies*: The Manchester Manuscripts', *Bulletin of the John Rylands University Library of Manchester* 72 (1990), 89–100.

Hardy's own comments on many of his short stories and allied matters can be found in *The Collected Letters of Thomas Hardy*, ed. Richard Little Purdy and Michael Millgate, 7 vols. (Oxford: Clarendon, 1978–88); *The Life and Work of Thomas Hardy*, ed. Michael Millgate (Basingstoke: Macmillan, 1984); *Thomas Hardy's Public Voice: The Essays, Speeches, and Miscellaneous Prose*, ed. Michael Millgate (Oxford: Clarendon, 2001); *The Literary Notebooks of Thomas Hardy*, ed. Lennart A. Björk, 2 vols. (New York: New York University Press, 1985); *The Personal Notebooks of Thomas Hardy*, ed. Richard H.

Taylor (Basingstoke: Macmillan, 1979); *Thomas Hardy's Personal Writings: Prefaces, Literary Opinions, Reminiscences*, ed. Harold Orel (London: Macmillan, 1967).

The standard, meticulously researched, biography is Michael Millgate, *Thomas Hardy: A Biography* (Oxford: Oxford University Press, 1982). The standard bibliography for editions of Hardy's own works is Richard Little Purdy, *Thomas Hardy: A Bibliographical Study* (1954; Oxford: Clarendon, 1968).

# A Note on the History of the Texts

*New readers are advised that this Note on the History of the Texts makes the details of the plots explicit.*

As Kristin Brady explained in her textual note to *The Withered Arm and Other Stories*, the companion volume to this one, choice of copy-text for Hardy's short stories is complicated by the fact that many of them were not collected for volume publication until some years after initial magazine appearance. Given the presiding principle of copy-text selection for this series, that it offers Hardy's texts 'as [his] readers first encountered them, in a form of which he in general approved, the version that his early critics reacted to' (General Editor's Preface), Brady elected to privilege the first versions for which Hardy invited the attention of reviewers by collecting them in book form. These are also the versions that allowed him to restore, as he saw fit, original intentions that the fastidiousness of magazine editors may have caused him to modify. The only exception to this rule, maintained in this volume, is that those stories that remained uncollected until the publication of *A Changed Man and Other Tales* (1913), some thirteen years after the last of them had actually been written, are printed in their serial versions to avoid compromising period integrity by the adoption of later changes contemporary with Hardy's revision of all his work for the 1912 Wessex Edition.[1]

The copy-text for 'The Melancholy Hussar of the German Legion' is the first English edition of *Life's Little Ironies*, published in 1894. The story had previously appeared in two instalments (4 and 11 January 1890), in the *Bristol Times and Mirror*. It was the last of four sold to Tillotson for syndication in provincial newspapers (see Purdy, 82 and 340–41), and was reprinted in *Three Notable Stories* (London: Spencer Blackett,

1890). For the Wessex Edition it was transferred to *Wessex Tales*, where Hardy felt it 'more naturally' belonged (see Author's Prefatory Note to 1912 *Life's Little Ironies*), at the same time reverting to its shorter serial title, 'The Melancholy Hussar'. The most significant revisions made for first volume publication relate to elaboration of the execution scene, with incorporation of the contemporary details drawn from the *Morning Chronicle* that Hardy had summarized many years earlier in the 'Trumpet-Major Notebook' (see *Personal Notebooks*, 124–5). A fair-copy manuscript of the story survives in the Huntington Library, and a fragment of an earlier draft in the Iowa State Historical Department (see Ray, 25–30).

'A Tragedy of Two Ambitions' was first published in the *Universal Review* (December 1888), accompanied by six illustrations by George Lambert. It was subsequently collected for 1894 *Life's Little Ironies*, the copy-text for this edition. For volume publication Hardy added one of the most evocative elements of the story, the episode of the discarded walking-stick growing into a poplar. As part of the general distribution in October 1911 of his manuscripts to museums and libraries that Hardy arranged through Sydney Cockerell, the fair-copy manuscript of the story was presented to the John Rylands Library at Manchester University.

'The First Countess of Wessex' appeared originally in *Harper's New Monthly Magazine* (December 1889), with four illustrations each by C. S. Reinhart and Alfred Parsons (see Appendix II). It was then collected for 1891 *A Group of Noble Dames*, the copy-text for this edition, where it became the opening story. Since the manuscript, sold in New York on 29 May 1906, subsequently disappeared (see Purdy, 65), it is impossible to know how accurately the collected version restored an original that had been bowdlerized for magazine publication, but certainly there are major differences between the two. In the serial version Betty does not deliberately contract smallpox, so her condition does not provide the occasion for the somewhat bizarre testing of Phelipson's and Reynard's devotion. Nor is there an elopement, Tupcombe having destabilized the ladder under the misapprehension that Reynard is with

Betty, thereby causing the death of Phelipson in a fall. This also means that Betty endures 'long slow months of listlessness' while mourning both father and lover, agreeing to receive Reynard only after her mother has advised him to approach her again; hence there is no pregnancy resulting from clandestine meetings between Betty and Reynard. The result is a story made appropriate to magazine publication by the sacrifice of much of its ironic point. Despite its greater forthrightness about sexual matters, the collected version may itself have included modifications designed to avoid offending the sensitivities of the Ilchester family (see Appendix II).

The serial version of 'Barbara of the House of Grebe' was also collected for 1891 *A Group of Noble Dames*, the copy-text for this edition, having formerly been published, in substantially bowdlerized form, under the title 'Barbara (Daughter of Sir John Grebe)' as one of the initial six stories collected as 'A Group of Noble Dames' in the *Graphic* Christmas Number (December 1890). As 'Barbara, Daughter of Sir John Grebe' it also appeared, with only minor excisions, in an American serialization, again as part of the six-story version of *A Group of Noble Dames* that ran in four issues of *Harper's Weekly* between 29 November and 20 December 1890. The removal of some of the more shocking details for the *Graphic* (most especially Uplandtowers' continued torture of Barbara by his placing of the mutilated statue in their bedroom for three nights to force her to declare her love for him and revulsion from Willowes) has the attendant effect of making Uplandtowers appear less grotesquely cruel. In all, the *Graphic* offers a less sado-masochistically charged story, with Barbara responding somewhat less hysterically to her disfigured first husband and being considerably less brutally treated by her second. The manuscript used for the *Graphic* version of *A Group of Noble Dames* (showing the material described above that was removed for the actual *Graphic* appearance) survives, and was presented by Hardy to the Library of Congress in October 1911.

'For Conscience' Sake' was published (its title lacking the apostrophe) in the *Fortnightly Review* for March 1891, and subsequently collected for 1894 *Life's Little Ironies*, the

copy-text for this edition. The sexual offence for which
Millborne seeks to atone having taken place in the distant past,
the story's subject-matter presented fewer problems for serial
publication, and distinctions between versions are therefore
relatively minor, showing Hardy's attention to textual detail
rather than attempts to satisfy editorial caution. The manuscript
was given to Manchester University Library in the October 1911
dispersal.

'The Son's Veto' – first published, accompanied by two illustrations by A. Forestier, in the Christmas Number of the *Illustrated London News* (1 December 1891), and collected for 1894
*Life's Little Ironies* (copy-text for this edition) – also shows
relatively minor distinctions between serial and book versions.
The most substantial changes made for the volume are more
elaborate descriptions of the Covent Garden-bound produce
carts and a slight heightening in the odiousness of Randolph,
most notably by the addition of the requirement that his mother
kneel before taking the oath that she will not marry Sam Hobson. A manuscript survives and is now at Geneva's Martin
Bodmer Foundation.

Serial publication of 'On the Western Circuit' presented
Hardy with somewhat greater difficulties again. In England it
appeared in the *English Illustrated Magazine* (December 1891),
with four illustrations by Walter Paget, and in America in
*Harper's Weekly* (28 November 1891), with one illustration by
W. T. Smedley, before being collected for 1894 *Life's Little
Ironies*, the copy-text for this edition. For the serials, Edith
Harnham becomes a widow living with her uncle, thereby
removing the taint of infidelity from her infatuation with Raye.
Nor does Anna become pregnant in the serials, a modification
that makes Edith's complicity in the deception that leads to the
marriage all the more questionable. 'On the Western Circuit' is
the third of the manuscripts presented to a Manchester institution, in this case the Manchester Central Public Library, in
the 1911 distribution.[2]

'The Fiddler of the Reels' was originally published in
*Scribner's Magazine* (May 1893), with an illustration by
W. Hatherell. Collected for 1894 *Life's Little Ironies*, the copy-

text for this edition, it underwent minor modifications that make Ned less malleable while Car'line becomes more manipulative before and more peevish after their marriage. There is no surviving manuscript.

'An Imaginative Woman' first appeared in *Pall Mall Magazine* (April 1894), with seven illustrations by Arthur Jule Goodman. Its first book publication, the copy-text for this edition, was in *Wessex Tales*, Volume XIII of the 1895–6 Osgood, McIlvaine Wessex Novels edition, being transferred in 1912 to *Life's Little Ironies*, as Volume VIII of the Wessex Edition. Many of the more significant revisions took place in manuscript, particularly in relation to what would have been the two most potentially controversial scenes: Ella Marchmill's taking of Trewe's photograph into her bed and her husband's closing fury at what he imagines to be the son's paternity. The manuscript of 'An Imaginative Woman' went to Aberdeen University Library in the 1911 distribution.

'A Changed Man' appeared originally in the *Sphere* in two instalments (21 and 28 April 1900), with an illustration by A. S. Hartrick accompanying each. This is the copy-text for this edition. It also appeared, unillustrated, in America in the *Cosmopolitan* (May 1900). It was not collected until 1913, when it became the title-story in *A Changed Man and Other Tales*. A manuscript survives in the New York Public Library (Berg Collection).

'Enter a Dragoon' first appeared in *Harper's Monthly Magazine* (December 1900), with one illustration by A. Hayman (this serial version is again the copy-text). It too was collected for *A Changed Man*. Both stories received Hardy's customary close attention at successive stages, but neither underwent major revision: the most interesting modifications involved the removal for book publication of a series of epigraphs that had appeared in the serial at the beginning of each section of 'Enter a Dragoon'. No manuscript survives for 'Enter a Dragoon'.

This edition follows exactly the chosen copy-texts, with minor exceptions. First, because the stories come from a variety of sources, I have standardized in the following instances: words with 'ise' and 'or' spellings have become 'ize' and 'our', respectively (e.g., 'recognize' and 'honour'); 'license' has become 'licence'; single quotation marks have been used, and punctuation at the end of a quotation has been moved outside the quotation marks, except in dialogue; M-dashes have become N-dashes, and 2M-dashes have become M-dashes; hyphens have been removed from such words and phrases as 'today', 'tomorrow', 'tonight', goodbye' (or 'goodby'), 'good morning', 'good afternoon', 'good evening' and 'good night'; in order to remove inconsistencies, hyphens have been added where necessary to 'turnpike-road', 'gravel-path', 'new-comer', 'trumpet-call', 'bugle-call', 'churchyard-gate', 'college-gate' and 'cathedral-choir', but removed from 'stepfather', 'stepmother' and 'churchyard'; hyphens are added where necessary to attributive phrases such as 'nine-days' wonder' and 'too-cold wife' in 'The First Countess of Wessex', and a hyphen has been added to 'semi-rural' in 'The Son's Veto'; there is no full stop after titles such as 'Mr'; punctuation appears in roman type after a word in italic, but remains in italic within a phrase or sentence in italic; ellipses have been standardized to three periods; and 'gray' has become 'grey'. I have also silently corrected typographical errors. While this edition does not have the scope of a variorum, it does include in its Notes all textual variants that significantly affect emphasis or contribute suggestively to our understanding of Hardy's compositional or editorial motivations.

## NOTES

1. For the most detailed and reliable analysis of the textual evolution of all stories in this selection, see Ray.
2. For the fullest description of the three Manchester manuscripts, see Alan Manford, '*Life's Little Ironies*: The Manchester Manuscripts', *Bulletin of the John Rylands University Library of Manchester* 72 (1990), 89–100.

# THE FIDDLER OF
# THE REELS AND
# OTHER STORIES
## 1888–1900

# THE MELANCHOLY HUSSAR
# OF THE GERMAN LEGION

## I

Here stretch the downs,[1] high and breezy and green, absolutely unchanged since those eventful days. A plough has never disturbed the turf, and the sod that was uppermost then is uppermost now. Here stood the camp; here are distinct traces of the banks thrown up for the horses of the cavalry, and spots where the midden-heaps lay are still to be observed. At night, when I walk across the lonely place, it is impossible to avoid hearing, amid the scourings of the wind over the grass-bents and thistles, the old trumpet- and bugle-calls, the rattle of the halters; to help seeing rows of spectral tents and the *impedimenta* of the soldiery. From within the canvases come guttural syllables of foreign tongues, and broken songs of the fatherland; for they were mainly regiments of the King's German Legion[2] that slept round the tent-poles hereabout at that time.

It was nearly ninety years ago. The British uniform of the period, with its immense epaulettes, queer cocked-hat, breeches, gaiters, ponderous cartridge-box, buckled shoes, and what not, would look strange and barbarous now. Ideas have changed; invention has followed invention. Soldiers were monumental objects then. A divinity still hedged kings[3] here and there; and war was considered a glorious thing.

Secluded old manor-houses and hamlets lie in the ravines and hollows among these hills, where a stranger had hardly ever been seen till the King chose to take the baths yearly at the sea-side watering-place a few miles to the south;[4] as a consequence of which battalions descended in a cloud upon the open country around. Is it necessary to add that the echoes of many characteristic tales, dating from that picturesque time, still linger about here in more or less fragmentary form, to be caught by the attentive ear? Some of them I have repeated; most of them I have forgotten; one I have never repeated, and assuredly can never forget.

Phyllis told me the story with her own lips. She was then an old lady of seventy-five, and her auditor a lad of fifteen. She enjoined silence as to her share in the incident, till she should be 'dead, buried, and forgotten'. Her life was prolonged twelve years after the day of her narration, and she has now been dead nearly twenty. The oblivion which in her modesty and humility she courted for herself has only partially fallen on her, with the unfortunate result of inflicting an injustice upon her memory; since such fragments of her story as got abroad at the time, and have been kept alive ever since, are precisely those which are most unfavourable to her character.

It all began with the arrival of the York Hussars, one of the foreign regiments above alluded to. Before that day scarcely a soul had been seen near her father's house for weeks. When a noise like the brushing skirt of a visitor was heard on the doorstep, it proved to be a scudding leaf; when a carriage seemed to be nearing the door, it was her father grinding his sickle on the stone in the garden for his favourite relaxation of trimming the box-tree borders[5] to the plots. A sound like luggage thrown down from the coach was a gun far away at sea; and what looked like a tall man by the gate at dusk was a yew bush cut into a quaint and attenuated shape. There is no such solitude in country places now as there was in those old days.

Yet all the while King George and his Court were at his favourite sea-side resort, not more than five miles off.

The daughter's seclusion was great, but beyond the seclusion of the girl lay the seclusion of the father. If her social condition was twilight, his was darkness. Yet he enjoyed his darkness, while her twilight oppressed her. Dr Grove had been a professional man whose taste for lonely meditation over metaphysical questions had diminished his practice till it no longer paid him to keep it going; after which he had relinquished it and hired at a nominal rent the small, dilapidated, half farm half manor-house of this obscure inland nook, to make a sufficiency of an income which in a town would have been inadequate for their maintenance. He stayed in his garden the greater part of the day, growing more and more irritable with the lapse of time, and the increasing perception that he had wasted his life in the pursuit of illusions. He saw his friends less and less frequently. Phyllis became so shy that if she met a stranger anywhere in her short rambles she felt ashamed at his gaze, walked awkwardly, and blushed to her shoulders.

Yet Phyllis was discovered even here by an admirer, and her hand most unexpectedly asked in marriage.

The King, as aforesaid, was at the neighbouring town, where he had taken up his abode at Gloucester Lodge; and his presence in the town naturally brought many county people thither. Among these idlers – many of whom professed to have connections and interests with the Court – was one Humphrey Gould, a bachelor; a personage neither young nor old; neither good-looking nor positively plain. Too steady-going to be 'a buck' (as fast and unmarried men were then called), he was an approximately fashionable man of a mild type. This bachelor of thirty found his way to the village on the down: beheld Phyllis; made her father's acquaintance[6] in order to make hers; and by some means or other she sufficiently inflamed his heart to lead him in that direction almost daily; till he became engaged to marry her.

As he was of an old local family, some of whose members were held in respect in the county, Phyllis, in bringing him to her feet, had accomplished what was considered a brilliant move for one in her constrained position. How she had done it was not quite known to Phyllis herself. In those days unequal marriages were regarded rather as a violation of the laws of nature than as a mere infringement of convention, the more modern view, and hence when Phyllis, of the watering-place *bourgeoisie*, was chosen by such a gentlemanly fellow, it was as if she were going to be taken to heaven, though perhaps the uninformed would have seen no great difference in the respective positions of the pair, the said Gould being as poor as a crow.

This pecuniary condition was his excuse – probably a true

one – for postponing their union, and as the winter drew nearer, and the King departed for the season, Mr Humphrey Gould set out for Bath, promising to return to Phyllis in a few weeks. The winter arrived, the date of his promise passed, yet Gould postponed his coming, on the ground that he could not very easily leave his father in the city of their sojourn, the elder having no other relative near him. Phyllis, though lonely in the extreme, was content. The man who had asked her in marriage was a desirable husband for her in many ways; her father highly approved of his suit; but this neglect of her was awkward, if not painful, for Phyllis. Love him in the true sense of the word she assured me she never did, but she had a genuine regard for him; admired a certain methodical and dogged way in which he sometimes took his pleasure; valued his knowledge of what the Court was doing, had done, or was about to do; and she was not without a feeling of pride that he had chosen her when he might have exercised a more ambitious choice.

But he did not come; and the spring developed. His letters were regular though formal; and it is not to be wondered that the uncertainty of her position, linked with the fact that there was not much passion in her thoughts of Humphrey, bred an indescribable dreariness in the heart of Phyllis Grove. The spring was soon summer, and the summer brought the King; but still no Humphrey Gould. All this while the engagement by letter was maintained intact.

At this point of time a golden radiance flashed in upon the lives of people here, and charged all youthful thought with emotional interest. This radiance was the aforesaid York Hussars.

## II

The present generation has probably but a very dim notion of the celebrated York Hussars of ninety years ago. They were one of the regiments of the King's German Legion, and (though they somewhat degenerated later on) their brilliant uniform, their splendid horses, and above all, their foreign air and mustachios (rare appendages then), drew crowds of admirers of both sexes wherever they went. These with other regiments had come to encamp on the downs and pastures, because of the presence of the King in the neighbouring town.

The spot was high and airy, and the view extensive, commanding the Isle of Portland in front, and reaching to St Aldhelm's Head eastward, and almost to the Start on the west.[7]

Phyllis, though not precisely a girl of the village, was as interested as any of them in this military investment. Her father's home stood somewhat apart, and on the highest point of ground to which the lane ascended, so that it was almost level with the top of the church tower in the lower part of the parish. Immediately from the outside of the garden-wall the grass spread away to a great distance, and it was crossed by a path which came close to the wall. Ever since her childhood it had been Phyllis's pleasure to clamber up this fence and sit on the top – a feat not so difficult as it may seem, the walls in this district being built of rubble, without mortar, so that there were plenty of crevices for small toes.

She was sitting up here one day, listlessly surveying the pasture without, when her attention was arrested by a solitary figure walking along the path. It was one of the renowned German Hussars, and he moved onward with his eyes on the ground, and with the manner of one who wished to escape company. His head would probably have been bent like his eyes but for his stiff neck-gear. On nearer view she perceived that his face was marked with deep sadness. Without observing her, he advanced by the footpath till it brought him almost immediately under the wall.

Phyllis was much surprised to see a fine, tall soldier in such a mood as this. Her theory of the military, and of the York Hussars in particular (derived entirely from hearsay, for she had never talked to a soldier in her life), was that their hearts were as gay as their accoutrements.

At this moment the Hussar lifted his eyes and noticed her on her perch, the white muslin neckerchief which covered her shoulders and neck where left bare by her low gown, and her white raiment in general, showing conspicuously in the bright sunlight of this summer day. He blushed a little at the suddenness of the encounter, and without halting a moment from his pace passed on.

All that day the foreigner's face haunted Phyllis; its aspect was so striking, so handsome, and his eyes were so blue, and sad, and abstracted. It was perhaps only natural that on some following day at the same hour she should look over that wall again, and wait till he had passed a second time. On this occasion he was reading a letter, and at the sight of her his manner was that of one who had half expected or hoped to discover her. He almost stopped, smiled, and made a courteous salute. The end of the meeting was that they exchanged a few words. She asked him what he was reading, and he readily informed her that he was re-perusing letters from his mother in Germany; he did not get them often, he said, and was forced to read the old ones a great many times. This was all that passed at the present interview, but others of the same kind followed.

Phyllis used to say that his English, though not good, was quite intelligible to her, so that their acquaintance was never hindered by difficulties of speech. Whenever the subject became too delicate, subtle, or tender, for such words of English as were at his command, the eyes no doubt helped out the tongue, and – though this was later on – the lips helped out the eyes. In short this acquaintance, unguardedly made, and rash enough on her part, developed and ripened. Like Desdemona,[8] she pitied him, and learnt his history.

His name was Matthäus Tina, and Saarbrück[9] his native town, where his mother was still living. His age was twenty-two, and he had already risen to the grade of corporal, though he had not long been in the army. Phyllis used to assert that no such refined or well-educated young man could have been found in the ranks of the purely English regiments, some of these foreign soldiers having rather the graceful manner and presence of our native officers than of our rank and file.

She by degrees learnt from her foreign friend a circumstance about himself and his comrades which Phyllis would least have expected of the York Hussars. So far from being as gay as its uniform, the regiment was pervaded by a dreadful melancholy, a chronic home-sickness, which depressed many of the men to such an extent that they could hardly attend to their drill. The worst sufferers were the younger soldiers who had not been over here long. They hated England and English life; they took no interest whatever in King George and his island kingdom, and they only wished to be out of it and never to see it any more. Their bodies were here, but their hearts and minds were always far away in their dear fatherland, of which – brave men and stoical as they were in many ways – they would speak with tears in their eyes. One of the worst of the sufferers from this home-woe, as he called it in his own tongue,[10] was Matthäus Tina, whose dreamy musing nature felt the gloom of exile still more intensely from the fact that he had left a lonely mother at home with nobody to cheer her.

Though Phyllis, touched by all this, and interested in his history, did not disdain her soldier's acquaintance, she declined (according to her own account, at least) to permit the young man to overstep the line of mere friendship for a long while – as long, indeed, as she considered herself likely to become the possession of another; though it is probable that she had lost her heart to Matthäus before she was herself aware. The stone wall of necessity made anything like intimacy difficult;[11] and he had never ventured to come, or to ask to come, inside the garden, so that all their conversation had been overtly conducted across this boundary.

## III

But news reached the village from a friend of Phyllis's father concerning Mr Humphrey Gould, her remarkably cool and patient betrothed. This gentleman had been heard to say in Bath that he considered his overtures to Miss Phyllis Grove to have reached only the stage of a half-understanding; and in view of his enforced absence on his father's account, who was too great an invalid now to attend to his affairs, he thought it best that there should be no definite promise as yet on either side. He was not sure, indeed, that he might not cast his eyes elsewhere.

This account – though only a piece of hearsay, and as such

entitled to no absolute credit – tallied so well with the
infrequency of his letters and their lack of warmth, that Phyllis
did not doubt its truth for one moment; and from that hour she
felt herself free to bestow her heart as she should choose. Not
so her father; he declared the whole story to be a fabrication.
He had known Mr Gould's family from his boyhood; and if
there was one proverb which expressed the matrimonial aspect
of that family well, it was 'Love me little, love me long.'[12]
Humphrey was an honourable man, who would not think of
treating his engagement so lightly. 'Do you wait in patience,' he
said; 'all will be right enough in time.'

From these words Phyllis at first imagined that her father was
in correspondence with Mr Gould; and her heart sank within
her; for in spite of her original intentions she had been relieved
to hear that her engagement had come to nothing. But she
presently learnt that her father had heard no more of Humphrey
Gould than she herself had done; while he would not write and
address her affianced directly on the subject, lest it should be
deemed an imputation on that bachelor's honour.

'You want an excuse for encouraging one or other of those
foreign fellows to flatter you with his unmeaning attentions,'
her father exclaimed, his mood having of late been a very unkind one towards her. 'I see more than I say. Don't you ever
set foot outside that garden-fence without my permission. If
you want to see the camp I'll take you myself some Sunday
afternoon.'

Phyllis had not the smallest intention of disobeying him in
her actions, but she assumed herself to be independent with
respect to her feelings. She no longer checked her fancy for the
Hussar, though she was far from regarding him as her lover in
the serious sense in which an Englishman might have been
regarded as such. The young foreign soldier was almost an ideal
being to her, with none of the appurtenances of an ordinary
house-dweller; one who had descended she knew not whence,
and would disappear she knew not whither; the subject of a
fascinating dream – no more.

They met continually now – mostly at dusk – during the brief
interval between the going down of the sun and the minute at

which the last trumpet-call summoned him to his tent. Perhaps her manner had become less restrained latterly; at any rate that of the Hussar was so; he had grown more tender every day, and at parting after these hurried interviews she reached down her hand from the top of the wall that he might press it. One evening he held it so long that she exclaimed, 'The wall is white, and somebody in the field may see your shape against it!'

He lingered so long that night that it was with the greatest difficulty that he could run across the intervening stretch of ground and enter the camp in time. On the next occasion of his awaiting her she did not appear in her usual place at the usual hour. His disappointment was unspeakably keen; he remained staring blankly at the spot, like a man in a trance. The trumpets and tattoo sounded, and still he did not go.

She had been delayed purely by an accident. When she arrived she was anxious because of the lateness of the hour, having heard as well as he the sounds denoting the closing of the camp. She implored him to leave immediately.

'No,' he said gloomily. 'I shall not go in yet – the moment you come – I have thought of your coming all day.'

'But you may be disgraced at being after time?'

'I don't mind that. I should have disappeared from the world some time ago if it had not been for two persons – my beloved, here, and my mother in Saarbrück. I hate the army. I care more for a minute of your company than for all the promotion in the world.'

Thus he stayed and talked to her, and told her interesting details of his native place, and incidents of his childhood, till she was in a simmer of distress at his recklessness in remaining. It was only because she insisted on bidding him good night and leaving the wall that he returned to his quarters.

The next time that she saw him he was without the stripes that had adorned his sleeve. He had been broken to the level of private for his lateness that night; and as Phyllis considered herself to be the cause of his disgrace her sorrow was great. But the position was now reversed; it was his turn to cheer her.

'Don't grieve, meine Liebliche!' he said. 'I have got a remedy for whatever comes. First, even supposing I regain my stripes, would your father allow you to marry a non-commissioned officer in the York Hussars?'

She flushed. This practical step had not been in her mind in relation to such an unrealistic person as he was; and a moment's reflection was enough for it. 'My father would not – certainly would not,' she answered unflinchingly. 'It cannot be thought of! My dear friend, please do forget me: I fear I am ruining you and your prospects!'

'Not at all!' said he. 'You are giving this country of yours just sufficient interest to me to make me care to keep alive in it. If my dear land were here also, and my old parent, with you, I could be happy as I am, and would do my best as a soldier. But it is not so. And now listen. This is my plan. That you go with me to my own country, and be my wife there, and live there with my mother and me. I am not a Hanoverian, as you know, though I entered the army as such; my country is by the Saar,[13] and is at peace with France, and if I were once in it I should be free.'

'But how get there?' she asked. Phyllis had been rather amazed than shocked at his proposition. Her position in her father's house was growing irksome and painful in the extreme; his parental affection seemed to be quite dried up. She was not a native of the village, like all the joyous girls around her; and in some way Matthäus Tina had infected her with his own passionate longing for his country, and mother, and home.[14]

'But how?' she repeated, finding that he did not answer. 'Will you buy your discharge?'

'Ah, no,' he said. 'That's impossible in these times. No; I came here against my will; why should I not escape? Now is the time, as we shall soon be striking camp, and I might see you no more. This is my scheme. I will ask you to meet me on the highway two miles off, on some calm night next week that may be appointed. There will be nothing unbecoming in it, or to cause you shame; you will not fly alone with me, for I will bring with me my devoted young friend Christoph, an Alsatian, who has lately joined the regiment, and who has agreed to assist in this enterprise. We shall have come from yonder harbour, where we shall have examined the boats, and found one suited to our purpose. Christoph has already a chart of the Channel, and we will then go to the harbour, and at midnight cut the boat from her moorings, and row away round the point out of sight; and by the next morning we are on the coast of France, near Cherbourg. The rest is easy, for I have saved money for the land journey, and can get a change of clothes. I will write to my mother, who will meet us on the way.'

He added details in reply to her inquiries, which left no doubt in Phyllis's mind of the feasibility of the undertaking. But its magnitude almost appalled her; and it is questionable if she would ever have gone further in the wild adventure if, on entering the house that night, her father had not accosted her in the most significant terms.

'How about the York Hussars?' he said.

'They are still at the camp; but they are soon going away, I believe.'

'It is useless for you to attempt to cloak your actions in that way. You have been meeting one of those fellows; you have been seen walking with him – foreign barbarians, not much better than the French themselves! I have made up my mind – don't speak a word till I have done, please! – I have made up my mind that you shall stay here no longer while they are on the spot. You shall go to your aunt's.'

It was useless for her to protest that she had never taken a walk with any soldier or man under the sun except himself. Her protestations were feeble, too, for though he was not literally correct in his assertion, he was virtually only half in error.

The house of her father's sister was a prison to Phyllis. She had quite recently undergone experience of its gloom; and when her father went on to direct her to pack what would be necessary for her to take, her heart died within her. In after years she never attempted to excuse her conduct during this week of agitation; but the result of her self-communing was that she decided to join in the scheme of her lover and his friend, and fly to the country which he had coloured with such lovely hues in her imagination. She always said that the one feature in his proposal which overcame her hesitation was the obvious purity and straightforwardness of his intentions. He showed himself to be so virtuous and kind; he treated her with a respect to which she had never before been accustomed; and she was braced to the obvious risks of the voyage by her confidence in him.

## IV

It was on a soft, dark evening of the following week that they engaged in the adventure. Tina was to meet her at a point in the highway at which the lane to the village branched off. Christoph was to go ahead of them to the harbour where the boat lay, row it round the Nothe[15] – or Look-out as it was called in those days – and pick them up on the other side of the promontory, which they were to reach by crossing the harbour-bridge on foot, and climbing over the Look-out hill.

As soon as her father had ascended to his room she left the house, and, bundle in hand, proceeded at a trot along the lane. At such an hour not a soul was afoot anywhere in the village, and she reached the junction of the lane with the highway unobserved. Here she took up her position in the obscurity formed by the angle of a fence, whence she could discern every one who approached along the turnpike-road, without being herself seen.

She had not remained thus waiting for her lover longer than a minute – though from the tension of her nerves the lapse of even that short time was trying – when, instead of the expected footsteps, the stage-coach could be heard descending the hill. She knew that Tina would not show himself till the road was clear, and waited impatiently for the coach to pass. Nearing the corner where she was it slackened speed, and, instead of going by as usual, drew up within a few yards of her. A passenger alighted, and she heard his voice. It was Humphrey Gould's.

He had brought a friend with him, and luggage. The luggage was deposited on the grass, and the coach went on its route to the royal watering-place.

'I wonder where that young man is with the horse and trap?' said her former admirer to his companion. 'I hope we shan't have to wait here long. I told him half-past nine o'clock precisely.'

'Have you got her present safe?'

'Phyllis's? O, yes. It is in this trunk. I hope it will please her.'

'Of course it will. What woman would not be pleased with such a handsome peace-offering?'

'Well – she deserves it. I've treated her rather badly. But she has been in my mind these last two days much more than I should care to confess to everybody. Ah, well; I'll say no more about that. It cannot be that she is so bad as they make out. I am quite sure that a girl of her good wit would know better than to get entangled with any of those Hanoverian soldiers. I won't believe it of her, and there's an end on't.'

More words in the same strain were casually dropped as the two men waited; words which revealed to her, as by a sudden illumination, the enormity of her conduct. The conversation was at length cut off by the arrival of the man with the vehicle. The luggage was placed in it, and they mounted, and were driven on in the direction from which she had just come.

Phyllis was so conscience-stricken that she was at first inclined to follow them; but a moment's reflection led her to feel that it would only be bare justice to Matthäus to wait till he arrived, and explain candidly that she had changed her mind – difficult as the struggle would be when she stood face to face with him. She bitterly reproached herself for having believed reports which represented Humphrey Gould as false to his engagement, when, from what she now heard from his own lips, she gathered that he had been living full of trust in her. But she knew well enough who had won her love. Without him her life seemed a dreary prospect, yet the more she looked at his proposal the more she feared to accept it – so wild as it was, so vague, so venturesome. She had promised Humphrey Gould, and it was only his assumed faithlessness which had led her to treat that promise as nought. His solicitude in bringing her these gifts touched her; her promise must be kept, and esteem must take the place of love. She would preserve her self-respect. She would stay at home, and marry him, and suffer.

Phyllis had thus braced herself to an exceptional fortitude when, a few minutes later, the outline of Matthäus Tina appeared behind a field-gate, over which he lightly leapt as she stepped forward. There was no evading it, he pressed her to his breast.

'It is the first and last time!' she wildly thought as she stood encircled by his arms.

How Phyllis got through the terrible ordeal of that night she could never clearly recollect. She always attributed her success in carrying out her resolve to her lover's honour, for as soon as she declared to him in feeble words that she had changed her mind, and felt that she could not, dared not, fly with him, he forbore to urge her, grieved as he was at her decision. Unscrupulous pressure on his part, seeing how romantically she had become attached to him, would no doubt have turned the balance in his favour. But he did nothing to tempt her unduly or unfairly.

On her side, fearing for his safety, she begged him to remain. This, he declared, could not be. 'I cannot break faith with my friend,' said he. Had he stood alone he would have abandoned his plan. But Christoph, with the boat and compass and chart, was waiting on the shore; the tide would soon turn; his mother had been warned of his coming; go he must.

Many precious minutes were lost while he tarried, unable to tear himself away. Phyllis held to her resolve, though it cost her many a bitter pang. At last they parted, and he went down the hill. Before his footsteps had quite died away she felt a desire to behold at least his outline once more, and running noiselessly after him regained view of his diminishing figure. For one moment she was sufficiently excited to be on the point of rushing forward and linking her fate with his. But she could not. The courage which at the critical instant failed Cleopatra of Egypt[16] could scarcely be expected of Phyllis Grove.

A dark shape, similar to his own, joined him in the highway. It was Christoph, his friend. She could see no more; they had hastened on in the direction of the town and harbour, four miles ahead. With a feeling akin to despair she turned and slowly pursued her way homeward.

Tattoo sounded in the camp; but there was no camp for her now. It was as dead as the camp of the Assyrians[17] after the passage of the Destroying Angel.

She noiselessly entered the house, seeing nobody, and went to bed. Grief, which kept her awake at first, ultimately wrapped her in a heavy sleep. The next morning her father met her at the foot of the stairs.

'Mr Gould is come!' he said triumphantly.

Humphrey was staying at the inn, and had already called to inquire for her. He had brought her a present of a very handsome looking-glass in a frame of *repoussé* silverwork, which her father held in his hand. He had promised to call again in the course of an hour to ask Phyllis to walk with him.

Pretty mirrors were rarer in country-houses at that day than they are now, and the one before her won Phyllis's admiration. She looked into it, saw how heavy her eyes were, and endeavoured to brighten them. She was in that wretched state of mind which leads a woman to move mechanically onward in what she conceives to be her allotted path. Mr Humphrey had, in his undemonstrative way, been adhering all along to the old understanding; it was for her to do the same, and to say not a word of her own lapse. She put on her bonnet and tippet, and when he arrived at the hour named she was at the door awaiting him.

## V

Phyllis thanked him for his beautiful gift; but the talking was soon entirely on Humphrey's side as they walked along. He told her of the latest movements of the world of fashion – a subject which she willingly discussed to the exclusion of anything more personal – and his measured language helped to still her disquieted heart and brain. Had not her own sadness been what it was she must have observed his embarrassment. At last he abruptly changed the subject.

'I am glad you are pleased with my little present,' he said. 'The truth is that I brought it to propitiate 'ee, and to get you to help me out of a mighty difficulty.'

It was inconceivable to Phyllis that this independent bachelor – whom she admired in some respects – could have a difficulty.

'Phyllis – I'll tell you my secret at once; for I have a monstrous secret to confide before I can ask your counsel. The case is, then, that I am married: yes, I have privately married a dear young belle; and if you knew her, and I hope you will, you would say everything in her praise. But she is not quite the one that my father would have chose for me – you know the paternal idea as well as I – and I have kept it secret. There will be a terrible noise, no doubt; but I think that with your help I may get over it. If you would only do me this good turn – when I have told my father, I mean – say that you never could have married me, you know, or something of that sort – 'pon my life it will help to smooth the way vastly. I am so anxious to win him round to my point of view, and not to cause any estrangement.'

What Phyllis replied she scarcely knew, or how she counselled him as to his unexpected situation. Yet the relief that his announcement brought her was perceptible. To have confided her trouble in return was what her aching heart longed to do; and had Humphrey been a woman she would instantly have poured out her tale. But to him she feared to confess; and there was a real reason for silence, till a sufficient time had elapsed to allow her lover and his comrade to get out of harm's way.

As soon as she reached home again she sought a solitary place, and spent the time in half regretting that she had not gone away, and in dreaming over the meetings with Matthäus Tina from their beginning to their end. In his own country, amongst his own countrywomen, he would possibly soon forget her, even to her very name.

Her listlessness was such that she did not go out of the house for several days. There came a morning which broke in fog and mist, behind which the down[18] could be discerned in greenish grey; and the outlines of the tents, and the rows of horses at the ropes. The smoke from the canteen fires drooped heavily.

The spot at the bottom of the garden where she had been accustomed to climb the wall to meet Matthäus, was the only inch of English ground in which she took any interest; and in spite of the disagreeable haze prevailing she walked out there till she reached the well-known corner. Every blade of grass was weighted with little liquid globes, and slugs and snails had crept out upon the plots. She could hear the usual faint noises from the camp, and in the other direction the trot of farmers on the road to the town, for it was market-day. She observed that her frequent visits to this corner had quite trodden down the grass in the angle of the wall, and left marks of garden soil on the stepping-stones by which she had mounted to look over the top. Seldom having gone there till dusk, she had not considered that her traces might be visible by day. Perhaps it was these which had revealed her trysts to her father.

While she paused in melancholy regard, she fancied that the customary sounds from the tents were changing their character. Indifferent as Phyllis was to camp doings now, she mounted by the steps to the old place. What she beheld at first awed and perplexed her; then she stood rigid, her fingers hooked to the wall, her eyes starting out of her head, and her face as if hardened to stone.

On the open green stretching before her all the regiments in the camp were drawn up in line, in the mid-front of which two empty coffins lay on the ground. The unwonted sounds which she had noticed came from an advancing procession. It consisted of the band of the York Hussars playing a dead march; next two soldiers of that regiment in a mourning coach, guarded on each side, and accompanied by two priests. Behind came a crowd of rustics who had been attracted by the event. The melancholy procession marched along the front of the line, returned to the centre, and halted beside the coffins, where the two condemned men were blindfolded, and each placed kneeling on his coffin; a few minutes' pause was now given, while they prayed.

A firing-party of twenty-four men stood ready with levelled carbines.[19] The commanding officer, who had his sword drawn, waved it through some cuts of the sword-exercise till he reached the downward stroke, whereat the firing-party discharged their volley. The two victims fell, one upon his face across his coffin, the other backwards.

As the volley resounded there arose a shriek from the wall of Dr Grove's garden, and some one fell down inside; but nobody among the spectators without noticed it at the time. The two executed Hussars were Matthäus Tina and his friend Christoph.

The soldiers on guard placed the bodies in the coffins almost instantly; but the colonel of the regiment, an Englishman, rode up and exclaimed in a stern voice: 'Turn them out – as an example to the men!'

The coffins were lifted endwise, and the dead Germans flung out upon their faces on the grass. Then all the regiments wheeled in sections, and marched past the spot in slow time. When the survey[20] was over the corpses were again coffined, and borne away.

Meanwhile Dr Grove, attracted by the noise of the volley, had rushed out into his garden, where he saw his wretched daughter lying motionless against the wall. She was taken indoors, but it was long before she recovered consciousness; and for weeks they despaired of her reason.

It transpired that the luckless deserters from the York Hussars had cut the boat from her moorings in the adjacent harbour, according to their plan, and, with two other comrades who were smarting under ill-treatment from their colonel, had sailed in safety across the Channel. But mistaking their bearings they steered into Jersey,[21] thinking that island the French coast. Here they were perceived to be deserters, and delivered up to the authorities. Matthäus and Christoph interceded for the other two at the court-martial, saying that it was entirely by the former's representations that these were induced to go. Their sentence was accordingly commuted to flogging, the death punishment being reserved for their leaders.

The visitor to the well-known old Georgian watering-place, who may care to ramble to the neighbouring village under the hills, and examine the register of burials, will there find two entries in these words:–

'*Matth: Tina (Corpl.) in His Majesty's Regmt. of York Hussars, and Shot for Desertion, was Buried June 30th, 1801, aged 22 years. Born in the town of Sarrbruk, Germany.*

'*Christoph Bless, belonging to His Majesty's Regmt. of York Hussars, who was Shot for Desertion, was Buried June 30th, 1801, aged 22 years. Born at Lothaargen, Alsatia.*'

Their graves were dug at the back of the little church, near the wall. There is no memorial to mark the spot, but Phyllis pointed it out to me. While she lived she used to keep their mounds neat; but now they are overgrown with nettles, and sunk nearly flat. The older villagers, however, who know of the episode from their parents, still recollect the place where the soldiers lie.[22] Phyllis lies near.

# A TRAGEDY OF TWO
# AMBITIONS

I

The shouts of the village-boys came in at the window, accompanied by broken laughter from loungers at the inn-door; but the brothers Halborough[1] worked on.

They were sitting in a bedroom of the master-millwright's house, engaged in the untutored reading of Greek and Latin. It was no tale of Homeric blows and knocks, Argonautic voyaging, or Theban family woe[2] that inflamed their imaginations and spurred them onward. They were plodding away at the Greek Testament, immersed in a chapter of the idiomatic and difficult Epistle to the Hebrews.

The Dog-day sun in its decline[3] reached the low ceiling with slanting sides, and the shadows of the great goat's-willow swayed and interchanged upon the walls like a spectral army manœuvring. The open casement which admitted the remoter sounds now brought the voice of some one close at hand. It was their sister, a pretty girl of fourteen, who stood in the court below.

'I can see the tops of your heads! What's the use of staying up there? I like you not to go out with the street-boys; but do come and play with me!'

They treated her as an inadequate interlocutor, and put her off with some slight word. She went away disappointed. Presently there was a dull noise of heavy footsteps at the side of the house, and one of the brothers sat up. 'I fancy I hear him coming,' he murmured, his eyes on the window.

A man in the light drab clothes of an old-fashioned country

tradesman[4] approached from round the corner, reeling as he came. The elder son flushed with anger, rose from his books, and descended the stairs. The younger sat on, till, after the lapse of a few minutes, his brother re-entered the room.

'Did Rosa see him?'

'No.'

'Nor anybody?'

'No.'

'What have you done with him?'

'He's in the straw-shed. I got him in with some trouble, and he has fallen asleep. I thought this would be the explanation of his absence! No stones dressed for Miller Kench, the great wheel of the saw-mills waiting for new float-boards, even the poor folk not able to get their waggons wheeled.'[5]

'What *is* the use of poring over this!' said the younger, shutting up Donnegan's *Lexicon*[6] with a slap. 'O if we had only been able to keep mother's nine hundred pounds,[7] what we could have done!'

'How well she had estimated the sum necessary! Four hundred and fifty each, she thought. And I have no doubt that we could have done it on that, with care.'

This loss of the nine hundred pounds was the sharp thorn of their crown. It was a sum which their mother had amassed with great exertion and self-denial, by adding to a chance legacy such other small amounts as she could lay hands on from time to time; and she had intended with the hoard to indulge the dear wish of her heart – that of sending her sons, Joshua and Cornelius, to one of the Universities, having been informed that from four hundred to four hundred and fifty each might carry them through their terms with such great economy as she knew she could trust them to practise. But she had died a year or two before this time, worn out by too keen a strain towards these ends; and the money, coming unreservedly into the hands of their father, had been nearly dissipated. With its exhaustion went all opportunity and hope of a university degree for the sons.

'It drives me mad when I think of it,' said Joshua, the elder. 'And here we work and work in our own bungling way, and the utmost we can hope for is a term of years as national schoolmasters, and possible admission to a theological college, and ordination as despised licentiates.'[8]

The anger of the elder was reflected as simple sadness in the face of the other. 'We can preach the Gospel as well without a hood on our surplices as with one,' he said with feeble consolation.

'Preach the Gospel – true,' said Joshua with a slight pursing of mouth. 'But we can't rise!'

'Let us make the best of it, and grind on.'

The other was silent, and they drearily bent over their books again.

The cause of all this gloom, the millwright Halborough, now snoring in the shed, had been a thriving master-machinist, notwithstanding his free and careless disposition, till a taste for a more than adequate quantity of strong liquor took hold of him; since when his habits had interfered with his business sadly. Already millers went elsewhere for their gear, and only one set of hands was now kept going, though there were formerly two. Already he found a difficulty in meeting his men at the week's end, and though they had been reduced in number there was barely enough work to do for those who remained.

The sun dropped lower and vanished, the shouts of the village children ceased to resound, darkness cloaked the students' bedroom, and all the scene outwardly breathed peace. None knew of the fevered youthful ambitions that throbbed in two breasts within the quiet creeper-covered walls of the millwright's house.

In a few months the brothers left the village of their birth to enter themselves as students in a training college for schoolmasters; first having placed their young sister Rosa under as efficient a tuition at a fashionable watering-place as the means at their disposal could command.

## II

A man in semi-clerical dress was walking along the road which led from the railway-station into a provincial town. As he walked he read persistently, only looking up once now and then to see that he was keeping on the foot-track and to avoid other passengers. At those moments, whoever had known the former students at the millwright's would have perceived that one of them, Joshua Halborough, was the peripatetic reader here.

What had been simple force in the youth's face was energized judgment in the man's. His character was gradually writing itself out in his countenance. That he was watching his own career with deeper and deeper interest, that he continually 'heard his days before him',[9] and cared to hear little else, might have been hazarded from what was seen there. His ambitions were, in truth, passionate, yet controlled; so that the germs of many more plans than ever blossomed to maturity had place in him; and forward visions were kept purposely in twilight, to avoid distraction.

Events so far had been encouraging. Shortly after assuming the mastership of his first school he had obtained an introduction to the Bishop of a diocese far from his native county, who had looked upon him as a promising young man and taken him in hand. He was now in the second year of his residence at the theological college of the cathedral-town, and would soon be presented for ordination.

He entered the town, turned into a back street, and then into a yard, keeping his book before him till he set foot under the arch of the latter place. Round the arch was written 'National School', and the stonework of the jambs was worn away as nothing but boys and the waves of ocean will wear it. He was soon amid the sing-song accents of the scholars.

His brother Cornelius, who was the schoolmaster here, laid down the pointer with which he was directing attention to the Capes of Europe, and came forward.

'That's his brother Jos!' whispered one of the sixth-standard boys. 'He's going to be a pa'son. He's now at college.'

'Corney is going to be one too, when he's saved enough money,' said another.

After greeting his brother, whom he had not seen for several months, the junior began to explain his system of teaching geography.

But Halborough the elder took no interest in the subject. 'How about your own studies?' he asked. 'Did you get the books I sent?'

Cornelius had received them, and he related what he was doing.

'Mind you work in the morning. What time do you get up?'

The younger replied: 'Half-past five.'

'Half-past four is not a minute too soon this time of the year. There is no time like the morning for construing. I don't know why, but when I feel even too dreary to read a novel I can translate – there is something mechanical about it I suppose. Now, Cornelius, you are rather behindhand, and have some heavy reading before you if you mean to get out of this next Christmas.'

'I am afraid I have.'

'We must soon sound the Bishop. I am sure you will get a title without difficulty when he has heard all. The sub-dean, the principal of my college, says that the best plan will be for you to come there when his lordship is present at an examination, and he'll get you a personal interview with him. Mind you make a good impression upon him. I found in my case that that was everything, and doctrine almost nothing. You'll do for a deacon, Corney, if not for a priest.'

The younger remained thoughtful. 'Have you heard from Rosa lately?' he asked; 'I had a letter this morning.'

'Yes. The little minx writes rather too often. She is homesick – though Brussels must be an attractive place enough. But she must make the most of her time over there. I thought a year would be enough for her, after that high-class school at Sand-bourne,[10] but I have decided to give her two, and make a good job of it, expensive as the establishment is.'

Their two rather harsh faces had softened directly they began to speak of their sister, whom they loved more ambitiously than they loved themselves.[11]

'But where is the money to come from, Joshua?'

'I have already got it.' He looked round, and finding that some boys were near withdrew a few steps. 'I have borrowed it at five per cent from the farmer who used to occupy the farm next our field. You remember him.'

'But about paying him?'

'I shall pay him by degrees out of my stipend. No, Cornelius, it was no use to do the thing by halves. She promises to be a most attractive, not to say beautiful, girl. I have seen that for years; and if her face is not her fortune, her face and her brains together will be, if I observe and contrive aright. That she should be, every inch of her, an accomplished and refined woman, was indispensable for the fulfilment of her destiny, and for moving onwards and upwards with us; and she'll do it, you will see. I'd half starve myself rather than take her away from that school now.'

They looked round the school they were in. To Cornelius it was natural and familiar enough, but to Joshua, with his limited human sympathies, who had just dropped in from a superior sort of place, the sight jarred unpleasantly, as being that of something he had left behind. 'I shall be glad when you are out of this,' he said, 'and in your pulpit, and well through your first sermon.'

'You may as well say inducted into my fat living, while you are about it.'

'Ah, well – don't think lightly of the Church. There's a fine work for any man of energy in the Church, as you'll find,' he said fervidly. 'Torrents of infidelity to be stemmed, new views of old subjects to be expounded, truths in spirit to be substituted for truths in the letter . . .' He lapsed into reverie with the vision of his career, persuading himself that it was ardour for Christianity which spurred him on, and not pride of place. He had shouldered a body of doctrine, and was prepared to defend it tooth and nail, solely for the honour and glory that warriors win.

'If the Church is elastic, and stretches to the shape of the time, she'll last, I suppose,' said Cornelius. 'If not—. Only think, I bought a copy of Paley's *Evidences*,[12] best edition, broad margins, excellent preservation, at a bookstall the other day for – ninepence; and I thought that at this rate Christianity must be in rather a bad way.'

'No, no!' said the other almost angrily. 'It only shows that such defences are no longer necessary. Men's eyes can see the truth without extraneous assistance. Besides, we are in for Christianity, and must stick to her whether or no. I am just now going right through Pusey's *Library of the Fathers*.'

'You'll be a bishop, Joshua, before you have done!'

'Ah!' said the other bitterly, shaking his head. 'Perhaps I might have been – I might have been! But where is my D.D. or LL.D.; and how be a bishop without that kind of appendage? Archbishop Tillotson was the son of a Sowerby clothier, but he was sent to Clare College.[13] To hail Oxford or Cambridge as *alma mater* is not for me – for us! My God! when I think of what we should have been – what fair promise has been blighted by that cursed, worthless—'

'Hush, hush! . . . But I feel it, too, as much as you. I have seen it more forcibly lately. You would have obtained your degree long before this time – possibly fellowship – and I should have been on my way to mine.'

'Don't talk of it,' said the other. 'We must do the best we can.'

They looked out of the window sadly, through the dusty panes, so high up that only the sky was visible. By degrees the haunting trouble loomed again, and Cornelius broke the silence with a whisper: 'He has called on me!'

The living pulses died on Joshua's face, which grew arid as a clinker. 'When was that?' he asked quickly.

'Last week.'

'How did he get here – so many miles?'

'Came by railway. He came to ask for money.'

'Ah!'

'He says he will call on you.'

Joshua replied resignedly. The theme of their conversation spoilt his buoyancy for that afternoon. He returned in the evening, Cornelius accompanying him to the station; but he did not read in the train which took him back to the Fountall Theological College, as he had done on the way out. That in-

eradicable trouble still remained as a squalid spot in the expanse
of his life. He sat with the other students in the cathedral-choir
next day; and the recollection of the trouble obscured the purple
splendour thrown by the panes upon the floor.

It was afternoon. All was as still in the Close as a cathedral-
green can be between the Sunday services, and the incessant
cawing of the rooks was the only sound. Joshua Halborough
had finished his ascetic lunch, and had gone into the library,
where he stood for a few moments looking out of the large
window facing the green. He saw walking slowly across it a
man in a fustian coat and a battered white hat with a much-
ruffled nap, having upon his arm a tall gipsy-woman wearing
long brass earrings. The man was staring quizzically at the west
front of the cathedral, and Halborough recognized in him the
form and features of his father. Who the woman was he knew
not. Almost as soon as Joshua became conscious of these things,
the sub-dean, who was also the principal of the college, and of
whom the young man stood in more awe than of the Bishop
himself, emerged from the gate and entered a path across the
Close. The pair met the dignitary, and to Joshua's horror his
father turned and addressed the sub-dean.

What passed between them he could not tell. But as he stood
in a cold sweat he saw his father place his hand familiarly on
the sub-dean's shoulder; the shrinking response of the latter,
and his quick withdrawal, told his feeling. The woman seemed
to say nothing, but when the sub-dean had passed by they came
on towards the college-gate.

Halborough flew along the corridor and out at a side door,
so as to intercept them before they could reach the front
entrance, for which they were making. He caught them behind
a clump of laurel.

'By Jerry, here's the very chap! Well, you're a fine fellow, Jos,
never to send your father as much as a twist o' baccy on such
an occasion, and to leave him to travel all these miles to find
ye out!'

'First, who is this?' said Joshua Halborough with pale dignity,
waving his hand towards the buxom woman with the great
earrings.

'Dammy, the mis'ess! Your stepmother! Didn't you know I'd married? She helped me home from market one night, and we came to terms, and struck the bargain. Didn't we, Selinar?'

'Oi, by the great Lord an' we did!' simpered the lady.

'Well, what sort of a place is this you are living in?' asked the millwright. 'A kind of house-of-correction, apparently?'

Joshua listened abstractedly, his features set to resignation. Sick at heart he was going to ask them if they were in want of any necessary, any meal, when his father cut him short by saying, 'Why, we've called to ask ye to come round and take pot-luck with us at the Cock-and-Bottle, where we've put up for the day, on our way to see mis'ess's friends at Binegar Fair,[14] where they'll be lying under canvas for a night or two. As for the victuals at the Cock I can't testify to 'em at all; but for the drink, they've the rarest drop of Old Tom that I've tasted for many a year.'

'Thanks; but I am a teetotaller; and I have lunched,' said Joshua, who could fully believe his father's testimony to the gin, from the odour of his breath. 'You see we have to observe regular habits here; and I couldn't be seen at the Cock-and-Bottle just now.'

'O dammy, then don't come, your reverence. Perhaps you won't mind standing treat for those who can be seen there?'

'Not a penny,' said the younger firmly. 'You've had enough already.'

'Thank you for nothing. By the bye, who was that spindle-legged, shoe-buckled parson feller we met by now? He seemed to think we should poison him!'

Joshua remarked coldly that it was the principal of his college, guardedly inquiring, 'Did you tell him whom you were come to see?'

His father did not reply. He and his strapping gipsy wife – if she were his wife – stayed no longer, and disappeared in the direction of the High Street. Joshua Halborough went back to the library. Determined as was his nature, he wept hot tears upon the books, and was immeasurably more wretched that afternoon than the unwelcome millwright. In the evening he sat down and wrote a letter to his brother, in which, after stating

what had happened, and expatiating upon this new disgrace in
the gipsy wife, he propounded a plan for raising money sufficient
to induce the couple to emigrate to Canada. 'It is our only
chance,' he said. 'The case as it stands is maddening. For a
successful painter, sculptor, musician, author, who takes society
by storm, it is no drawback, it is sometimes even a romantic
recommendation, to hail from outcasts and profligates. But for
a clergyman of the Church of England! Cornelius, it is fatal! To
succeed in the Church, people must believe in you, first of all,
as a gentleman, secondly as a man of means, thirdly as a scholar,
fourthly as a preacher, fifthly, perhaps, as a Christian, – but
always first as a gentleman, with all their heart and soul and
strength.[15] I would have faced the fact of being a small machin-
ist's son, and have taken my chance, if he'd been in any sense
respectable and decent. The essence of Christianity is humility,
and by the help of God I would have brazened it out. But this
terrible vagabondage and disreputable connection! If he does
not accept my terms and leave the country, it will extinguish us
and kill me. For how can we live, and relinquish our high aim,
and bring down our dear sister Rosa to the level of a gipsy's
stepdaughter?'

## III

There was excitement in the parish of Narrobourne[16] one day.
The congregation had just come out from morning service, and
the whole conversation was of the new curate, Mr Halborough,
who had officiated for the first time, in the absence of the rector.

Never before had the feeling of the villagers approached a
level which could be called excitement on such a matter as this.
The droning which had been the rule in that quiet old place for
a century seemed ended at last. They repeated the text to each
other as a refrain: 'O Lord, be thou my helper!'[17] Not within
living memory till today had the subject of the sermon formed
the topic of conversation from the church door to churchyard-
gate, to the exclusion of personal remarks on those who had
been present, and on the week's news in general.

The thrilling periods of the preacher hung about their minds all that day. The parish being steeped in indifferentism, it happened that when the youths and maidens, middle-aged and old people, who had attended church that morning, recurred as by a fascination to what Halborough had said, they did so more or less indirectly, and even with the subterfuge of a light laugh that was not real, so great was their shyness under the novelty of their sensations.

What was more curious than that these unconventional villagers should have been excited by a preacher of a new school after forty years of familiarity with the old hand who had had charge of their souls, was the effect of Halborough's address upon the occupants of the manor-house pew, including the owner of the estate. These thought they knew how to discount the mere sensational sermon, how to minimize flash oratory to its bare proportions; but they had yielded like the rest of the assembly to the charm of the new-comer.

Mr Fellmer, the landowner, was a young widower, whose mother, still in the prime of life, had returned to her old position in the family mansion since the death of her son's wife in the year after her marriage, at the birth of a fragile little girl. From the date of his loss to the present time, Fellmer had led an inactive existence in the seclusion of the parish; a lack of motive seemed to leave him listless. He had gladly reinstated his mother in the gloomy house, and his main occupation now lay in stewarding his estate, which was not large. Mrs Fellmer, who had sat beside him under Halborough this morning, was a cheerful, straightforward woman, who did her marketing and her alms-giving in person, was fond of old-fashioned flowers, and walked about the village on very wet days visiting the parishioners. These, the only two great ones of Narrobourne, were impressed by Joshua's eloquence as much as the cottagers.

Halborough had been briefly introduced to them on his arrival some days before, and, their interest being kindled, they waited a few moments till he came out of the vestry, to walk down the churchyard-path with him. Mrs Fellmer spoke warmly of the sermon, of the good fortune of the parish in his advent, and hoped he had found comfortable quarters.

Halborough, faintly flushing, said that he had obtained very fair lodgings in the roomy house of a farmer, whom he named.

She feared he would find it very lonely, especially in the evenings, and hoped they would see a good deal of him. When would he dine with them? Could he not come that day – it must be so dull for him the first Sunday evening in country lodgings?

Halborough replied that it would give him much pleasure, but that he feared he must decline. 'I am not altogether alone,' he said. 'My sister, who has just returned from Brussels, and who felt, as you do, that I should be rather dismal by myself, has accompanied me hither to stay a few days till she has put my rooms in order and set me going. She was too fatigued to come to church, and is waiting for me now at the farm.'

'Oh, but bring your sister – that will be still better! I shall be delighted to know her. How I wish I had been aware! Do tell her, please, that we had no idea of her presence.'

Halborough assured Mrs Fellmer that he would certainly bear the message; but as to her coming he was not so sure. The real truth was, however, that the matter would be decided by him, Rosa having an almost filial respect for his wishes. But he was uncertain as to the state of her wardrobe, and had determined that she should not enter the manor-house at a disadvantage that evening, when there would probably be plenty of opportunities in the future of her doing so becomingly.

He walked to the farm in long strides. This, then, was the outcome of his first morning's work as curate here. Things had gone fairly well with him. He had been ordained; he was in a comfortable parish, where he would exercise almost sole supervision, the rector being infirm. He had made a deep impression at starting, and the absence of a hood seemed to have done him no harm. Moreover, by considerable persuasion and payment, his father and the dark woman had been shipped off to Canada, where they were not likely to interfere greatly with his interests.

Rosa came out to meet him. 'Ah! you should have gone to church like a good girl,' he said.

'Yes – I wished I had afterwards. But I do so hate church as a

rule that even your preaching was underestimated in my mind.
It was too bad of me!'

The girl who spoke thus playfully was fair, tall, and sylph-like,
in a muslin dress, and with just the coquettish *désinvolture*
which an English girl brings home from abroad, and loses again
after a few months of native life. Joshua was the reverse of
playful; the world was too important a concern for him to
indulge in light moods. He told her in decided, practical phraseology of the invitation.

'Now, Rosa, we must go – that's settled – if you've a dress
that can be made fit to wear all on the hop like this. You
didn't, of course, think of bringing an evening dress to such an
out-of-the-way place?'

But Rosa had come from the wrong city to be caught napping
in those matters. 'Yes, I did,' said she. 'One never knows what
may turn up.'

'Well done! Then off we go at seven.'

The evening drew on, and at dusk they started on foot, Rosa
pulling up the edge of her skirt under her cloak out of the way
of the dews, so that it formed a great wind-bag all round her,
and carrying her satin shoes under her arm. Joshua would not
let her wait till she got indoors before changing them, as she
proposed, but insisted on her performing that operation under
a tree, so that they might enter as if they had not walked. He
was nervously formal about such trifles, while Rosa took the
whole proceeding – walk, dressing, dinner, and all – as a pastime.
To Joshua it was a serious step in life.

A more unexpected kind of person for a curate's sister was
never presented at a dinner. The surprise of Mrs Fellmer was
unconcealed. She had looked forward to a Dorcas, or Martha,
or Rhoda[18] at the outside, and a shade of misgiving crossed her
face. It was possible that, had the young lady accompanied
her brother to church, there would have been no dining at
Narrobourne House that day.

Not so with the young widower, her son. He resembled a
sleeper who had awaked in a summer noon expecting to find it
only dawn. He could scarcely help stretching his arms and
yawning in their faces, so strong was his sense of being suddenly

aroused to an unforeseen thing. When they had sat down to table he at first talked to Rosa somewhat with the air of a ruler in the land; but the woman lurking in the acquaintance soon brought him to his level, and the girl from Brussels saw him looking at her mouth, her hands, her contour, as if he could not quite comprehend how they got created: then he dropped into the more satisfactory stage which discerns no particulars.

He talked but little; she said much. The homeliness of the Fellmers, to her view, though they were regarded with such awe down here, quite disembarrassed her. The squire had become so unpractised, had dropped so far into the shade during the last year or so of his life, that he had almost forgotten what the world contained till this evening reminded him. His mother, after her first moments of doubt, appeared to think that he must be left to his own guidance, and gave her attention to Joshua.

With all his foresight and doggedness of aim, the result of that dinner exceeded Halborough's expectations. In weaving his ambitions he had viewed his sister Rosa as a slight, bright thing to be helped into notice by his abilities; but it now began to dawn upon him that the physical gifts of nature to her might do more for them both than nature's intellectual gifts to himself. While he was patiently boring the tunnel Rosa seemed about to fly over the mountain.

He wrote the next day to his brother, now occupying his own old rooms in the theological college, telling him exultingly of the unanticipated *début* of Rosa at the manor-house. The next post brought him a reply of congratulation, dashed with the counteracting intelligence that his father did not like Canada – that his wife had deserted him, which made him feel so dreary that he thought of returning home.

In his recent satisfaction at his own successes Joshua Halborough had well-nigh forgotten his chronic trouble – latterly screened by distance. But it now returned upon him; he saw more in this brief announcement than his brother seemed to see. It was the cloud no bigger than a man's hand.[19]

# IV

The following December, a day or two before Christmas, Mrs Fellmer and her son were walking up and down the broad gravel-path which bordered the east front of the house. Till within the last half-hour the morning had been a drizzling one, and they had just emerged for a short turn before luncheon.

'You see, dear mother,' the son was saying, 'it is the peculiarity of my position which makes her appear to me in such a desirable light. When you consider how I have been crippled at starting, how my life has been maimed; that I feel anything like publicity distasteful, that I have no political ambition, and that my chief aim and hope lie in the education of the little thing Annie has left me, you must see how desirable a wife like Miss Halborough would be, to prevent my becoming a mere vegetable.'

'If you adore her, I suppose you must have her!' replied his mother with dry indirectness. 'But you'll find that she will not be content to live on here as you do, giving her whole mind to a young child.'

'That's just where we differ. Her very disqualification, that of being a nobody, as you call it, is her recommendation in my eyes. Her lack of influential connections limits her ambition. From what I know of her, a life in this place is all that she would wish for. She would never care to go outside the park-gates if it were necessary to stay within.'

'Being in love with her, Albert, and meaning to marry her, you invent your practical reasons to make the case respectable. Well, do as you will; I have no authority over you, so why should you consult me? You mean to propose on this very occasion, no doubt. Don't you, now?'

'By no means. I am merely revolving the idea in my mind. If on further acquaintance she turns out to be as good as she has hitherto seemed – well, I shall see. Admit, now, that you like her.'

'I readily admit it. She is very captivating at first sight. But as a stepmother to your child! You seem mighty anxious, Albert, to get rid of me!'

'Not at all. And I am not so reckless as you think. I don't make up my mind in a hurry. But the thought having occurred to me, I mention it to you at once, mother. If you dislike it, say so.'

'I don't say anything. I will try to make the best of it if you are determined. When does she come?'

'Tomorrow.'

All this time there were great preparations in train at the curate's, who was now a householder. Rosa, whose two or three weeks' stay on two occasions earlier in the year had so affected the squire, was coming again, and at the same time her younger brother Cornelius, to make up a family party. Rosa, who journeyed from the Midlands, could not arrive till late in the evening, but Cornelius was to get there in the afternoon, Joshua going out to meet him in his walk across the fields from the railway.

Everything being ready in Joshua's modest abode he started on his way, his heart buoyant and thankful, if ever it was in his life. He was of such good report himself that his brother's path into holy orders promised to be unexpectedly easy; and he longed to compare experiences with him, even though there was on hand a more exciting matter still. From his youth he had held that, in old-fashioned country places, the Church conferred social prestige up to a certain point at a cheaper price than any other profession or pursuit; and events seemed to be proving him right.

He had walked about half-an-hour when he saw Cornelius coming along the path; and in a few minutes the two brothers met. The experiences of Cornelius had been less immediately interesting than those of Joshua, but his personal position was satisfactory, and there was nothing to account for the singularly subdued manner that he exhibited, which at first Joshua set down to the fatigue of over-study; and he proceeded to the subject of Rosa's arrival in the evening, and the probable consequences of this her third visit. 'Before next Easter she'll be his wife, my boy,' said Joshua with grave exultation.

Cornelius shook his head. 'She comes too late!' he returned.

'What do you mean?'

'Look here.' He produced the Fountall paper, and placed his

finger on a paragraph, which Joshua read. It appeared under the report of Petty Sessions, and was a commonplace case of disorderly conduct, in which a man was sent to prison for seven days for breaking windows in that town.

'Well?' said Joshua.

'It happened during an evening that I was in the street; and the offender is our father.'

'Not – how – I sent him more money on his promising to stay in Canada?'

'He is home, safe enough.' Cornelius in the same gloomy tone gave the remainder of his information. He had witnessed the scene, unobserved of his father, and had heard him say that he was on his way to see his daughter, who was going to marry a rich gentleman. The only good fortune attending the untoward incident was that the millwright's name had been printed as Joshua Alborough.

'Beaten! We are to be beaten on the eve of our expected victory!' said the elder brother. 'How did he guess that Rosa was likely to marry? Good Heaven! Cornelius, you seem doomed to bring bad news always, do you not!'

'I do,' said Cornelius. 'Poor Rosa!'

It was almost in tears, so great was their heart-sickness and shame, that the brothers walked the remainder of the way to Joshua's dwelling. In the evening they set out to meet Rosa, bringing her to the village in a fly; and when she had come into the house, and was sitting down with them, they almost forgot their secret anxiety in contemplating her, who knew nothing about it.

Next day the Fellmers came, and the two or three days after that were a lively time. That the squire was yielding to his impulses – making up his mind – there could be no doubt. On Sunday Cornelius read the lessons, and Joshua preached. Mrs Fellmer was quite maternal towards Rosa, and it appeared that she had decided to welcome the inevitable with a good grace. The pretty girl was to spend yet another afternoon with the elder lady, superintending some parish treat at the house in observance of Christmas, and afterwards to stay on to dinner, her brothers to fetch her in the evening. They were also invited to dine, but they could not accept owing to an engagement.

The engagement was of a sombre sort. They were going to meet their father, who would that day be released from Fountall Gaol, and try to persuade him to keep away from Narrobourne. Every exertion was to be made to get him back to Canada, to his old home in the Midlands – anywhere, so that he would not impinge disastrously upon their courses, and blast their sister's prospects of the auspicious marriage which was just then hanging in the balance.

As soon as Rosa had been fetched away by her friends at the manor-house her brothers started on their expedition, without waiting for dinner or tea. Cornelius, to whom the millwright always addressed his letters when he wrote any, drew from his pocket and re-read as he walked the curt note which had led to this journey being undertaken; it was despatched by their father the night before, immediately upon his liberation, and stated that he was setting out for Narrobourne at the moment of writing; that having no money he would be obliged to walk all the way; that he calculated on passing through the intervening town of Ivell[20] about six on the following day, where he should sup at the Castle Inn, and where he hoped they would meet him with a carriage-and-pair, or some other such conveyance, that he might not disgrace them by arriving like a tramp.

'That sounds as if he gave a thought to our position,' said Cornelius.

Joshua knew the satire that lurked in the paternal words, and said nothing. Silence prevailed during the greater part of their journey. The lamps were lighted in Ivell when they entered the streets, and Cornelius, who was quite unknown in this neighbourhood, and who, moreover, was not in clerical attire, decided that he should be the one to call at the Castle Inn. Here, in answer to his inquiry under the darkness of the archway, they told him that such a man as he had described left the house about a quarter of an hour earlier, after making a meal in the kitchen-settle. He was rather the worse for liquor.

'Then,' said Joshua, when Cornelius joined him outside with

this intelligence, 'we must have met and passed him! And now that I think of it, we did meet some one who was unsteady in his gait, under the trees on the other side of Hendford Hill, where it was too dark to see him.'

They rapidly retraced their steps; but for a long stretch of the way home could discern nobody. When, however, they had gone about three-quarters of the distance, they became conscious of an irregular footfall in front of them, and could see a whitish figure in the gloom. They followed dubiously. The figure met another wayfarer – the single one that had been encountered upon this lonely road – and they distinctly heard him ask the way to Narrobourne. The stranger replied – what was quite true – that the nearest way was by turning in at the stile by the next bridge, and following the footpath which branched thence across the meadows.

When the brothers reached the stile they also entered the path, but did not overtake the subject of their worry till they had crossed two or three meads, and the lights from Narrobourne manor-house were visible before them through the trees. Their father was no longer walking; he was seated against the wet bank of an adjoining hedge. Observing their forms he shouted, 'I'm going to Narrobourne; who may you be?'

They went up to him, and revealed themselves, reminding him of the plan which he had himself proposed in his note, that they should meet him at Ivell.

'By Jerry, I'd forgot it!' he said. 'Well, what do you want me to do?' His tone was distinctly quarrelsome.

A long conversation followed, which became embittered at the first hint from them that he should not come to the village. The millwright drew a quart bottle from his pocket, and challenged them to drink if they meant friendly and called themselves men. Neither of the two had touched alcohol for years, but for once they thought it best to accept, so as not to needlessly provoke him.

'What's in it?' said Joshua.

'A drop of weak gin-and-water. It won't hurt ye. Drink from the bottle.' Joshua did so, and his father pushed up the bottom of the vessel so as to make him swallow a good deal in spite of himself. It went down into his stomach like molten lead.

'Ha, ha, that's right!' said old Halborough. 'But 'twas raw spirit – ha, ha!'

'Why should you take me in so!' said Joshua, losing his self-command, try as he would to keep calm.

'Because you took me in, my lad, in banishing me to that cursed country under pretence that it was for my good. You were a pair of hypocrites to say so. It was done to get rid of me – no more nor less. But, by Jerry, I'm a match for ye now! I'll spoil your souls for preaching. My daughter is going to be married to the squire here. I've heard the news – I saw it in a paper!'

'It is premature—'

'I know it is true; and I'm her father, and I shall give her away, or there'll be a hell of a row, I can assure ye! Is that where the gennleman lives?'

Joshua Halborough writhed in impotent despair. Fellmer had not yet positively declared himself, his mother was hardly won round; a scene with their father in the parish would demolish as fair a palace of hopes as was ever builded. The millwright rose. 'If that's where the squire lives I'm going to call. Just arrived from Canady with her fortune – ha, ha! I wish no harm to the gennleman, and the gennleman will wish no harm to me. But I like to take my place in the family, and stand upon my rights, and lower people's pride!'

'You've succeeded already! Where's that woman you took with you—'

'Woman! She was my wife as lawful as the Constitution – a sight more lawful than your mother was till some time after you were born!'

Joshua had for many years before heard whispers that his father had cajoled his mother in their early acquaintance, and had made somewhat tardy amends; but never from his father's lips till now. It was the last stroke, and he could not bear it. He sank back against the hedge. 'It is over!' he said. 'He ruins us all!'

The millwright moved on, waving his stick triumphantly, and the two brothers stood still. They could see his drab figure stalking along the path, and over his head the lights from the conservatory of Narrobourne House, inside which Albert Fellmer might possibly be sitting with Rosa at that moment, holding her hand, and asking her to share his home with him.

The staggering whitey-brown form, advancing to put a blot on all this, had been diminishing in the shade; and now suddenly disappeared beside a weir. There was the noise of a flounce in the water.

'He has fallen in!'[21] said Cornelius, starting forward to run for the place at which his father had vanished.

Joshua, awaking from the stupefied reverie into which he had sunk, rushed to the other's side before he had taken ten steps. 'Stop, stop, what are you thinking of?' he whispered hoarsely, grasping Cornelius's arm.

'Pulling him out!'

'Yes, yes – so am I. But – wait a moment—'

'But, Joshua!'

'Her life and happiness, you know – Cornelius – and your reputation and mine – and our chance of rising together, all three—'

He clutched his brother's arm to the bone; and as they stood breathless the splashing and floundering in the weir continued; over it they saw the hopeful lights from the manor-house conservatory winking through the trees as their bare branches waved to and fro.[22]

The floundering and splashing grew weaker, and they could hear gurgling words: 'Help – I'm drownded! Rosie – Rosie!'

'We'll go – we *must* save him. O Joshua!'

'Yes, yes! we must!'

Still they did not move, but waited, holding each other, each thinking the same thought. Weights of lead seemed to be affixed to their feet, which would no longer obey their wills. The mead became silent. Over it they fancied they could see figures moving in the conservatory. The air up there seemed to emit gentle kisses.

Cornelius started forward at last, and Joshua almost simultaneously. Two or three minutes brought them to the brink of the stream. At first they could see nothing in the water, though it was not so deep nor the night so dark but that their father's light kerseymere coat would have been visible if he had lain at the bottom. Joshua looked this way and that.

'He has drifted into the culvert,' he said.

Below the foot-bridge of the weir the stream suddenly narrowed to half its width, to pass under a barrel arch or culvert constructed for waggons to cross into the middle of the mead in haymaking time. It being at present the season of high water the arch was full to the crown, against which the ripples clucked every now and then. At this point he had just caught sight of a pale object slipping under. In a moment it was gone.

They went to the lower end, but nothing emerged. For a long time they tried at both ends to effect some communication with the interior, but to no purpose.

'We ought to have come sooner!' said the conscience-stricken Cornelius, when they were quite exhausted, and dripping wet.

'I suppose we ought,' replied Joshua heavily. He perceived his father's walking-stick on the bank; hastily picking it up he stuck it into the mud among the sedge. Then they went on.

'Shall we – say anything about this accident?' whispered Cornelius as they approached the door of Joshua's house.

'What's the use? It can do no good. We must wait until he is found.'

They went indoors and changed their clothes; after which they started for the manor-house, reaching it about ten o'clock. Besides their sister there were only three guests; an adjoining landowner and his wife, and the infirm old rector.

Rosa, although she had parted from them so recently, grasped their hands in an ecstatic, brimming, joyful manner, as if she had not seen them for years. 'You look pale,' she said.

The brothers answered that they had had a long walk, and were somewhat tired. Everybody in the room seemed charged full with some sort of interesting knowledge: the squire's neighbour and his wife looked wisely around; and Fellmer himself played the part of host with a preoccupied bearing which approached fervour. They left at eleven, not accepting the carriage offered, the distance being so short and the roads dry. The squire came rather farther into the dark with them than he need have done, and wished Rosa good night in a mysterious manner, slightly apart from the rest.

When they were walking along Joshua said, with a desperate attempt at joviality, 'Rosa, what's going on?'

'O, I—' she began between a gasp and a bound. 'He—'

'Never mind – if it disturbs you.'

She was so excited that she could not speak connectedly at first, the practised air which she had brought home with her having disappeared. Calming herself she added, 'I am not disturbed, and nothing has happened. Only he said he wanted to ask me *something*, some day; and I said never mind that now. He hasn't asked yet, and is coming to speak to you about it. He would have done so tonight, only I asked him not to be in a hurry. But he will come tomorrow, I am sure!'

## V

It was summer-time, six months later, and mowers and haymakers were at work in the meads. The manor-house, being opposite them, frequently formed a peg for conversation during these operations; and the doings of the squire, and the squire's young wife, the curate's sister – who was at present the admired of most of them, and the interest of all – met with their due amount of criticism.

Rosa was happy, if ever woman could be said to be so. She had not learnt the fate of her father, and sometimes wondered – perhaps with a sense of relief – why he did not write to her from his supposed home in Canada. Her brother Joshua had been presented to a living in a small town, shortly after her marriage, and Cornelius had thereupon succeeded to the vacant curacy of Narrobourne.

These two had awaited in deep suspense the discovery of their father's body; and yet the discovery had not been made. Every day they expected a man or a boy to run up from the meads with the intelligence; but he had never come. Days had accumulated to weeks and months; the wedding had come and gone: Joshua had tolled and read himself in at his new parish:[23] and never a shout of amazement over the millwright's remains.

But now, in June, when they were mowing the meads, the hatches had to be drawn and the water let out of its channels for the convenience of the mowers. It was thus that the discovery was made. A man, stooping low with his scythe, caught a view of the culvert lengthwise, and saw something entangled in the recently bared weeds of its bed. A day or two after there was an inquest; but the body was unrecognizable. Fish and flood had been busy with the millwright; he had no watch or marked article which could be identified; and a verdict of the accidental drowning of a person unknown settled the matter.

As the body was found in Narrobourne parish, there it had to be buried. Cornelius wrote to Joshua, begging him to come and read the service, or to send some one; he himself could not do it. Rather than let in a stranger Joshua came, and silently scanned the coroner's order handed him by the undertaker:–

'I, Henry Giles, Coroner for the Mid-Division of Outer Wessex, do hereby order the Burial of the Body now shown to the Inquest Jury as the Body of an Adult Male Person Unknown . . .,' etc.

Joshua Halborough got through the service in some way, and rejoined his brother Cornelius at his house. Neither accepted an invitation to lunch at their sister's; they wished to discuss parish matters together. In the afternoon she came down, though they had already called on her, and had not expected to see her again. Her bright eyes, brown hair, flowery bonnet, lemon-coloured gloves, and flush beauty, were like an irradiation into the apartment, which they in their gloom could hardly bear.

'I forgot to tell you,' she said, 'of a curious thing which happened to me a month or two before my marriage – something which I have thought may have had a connection with the accident to the poor man you have buried today. It was on that evening I was at the manor-house waiting for you to fetch me; I was in the winter-garden with Albert, and we were sitting silent together, when we fancied we heard a cry. We opened the door, and while Albert ran to fetch his hat, leaving me standing there, the cry was repeated, and my excited senses made me think I heard my own name. When Albert came back all was silent, and we decided that it was only a drunken shout, and not a cry for help. We both forgot the incident, and it never has occurred to me till since the funeral today that it might have been this stranger's cry. The name of course was only fancy, or he might have had a wife or child with a name something like mine, poor man!'

When she was gone the brothers were silent till Cornelius said, 'Now mark this, Joshua. Sooner or later she'll know.'

'How?'

'From one of us. Do you think human hearts are iron-cased safes, that you suppose we can keep this secret for ever?'

'Yes, I think they are, sometimes,' said Joshua.

'No. It will out. We shall tell.'

'What, and ruin her – kill her? Disgrace her children, and pull down the whole auspicious house of Fellmer about our ears? No! May I – drown where he was drowned before I do it! Never, never. Surely you can say the same, Cornelius!'

Cornelius seemed fortified, and no more was said. For a long time after that day he did not see Joshua, and before the next year was out a son and heir was born to the Fellmers. The villagers rang the three bells every evening for a week and more, and were made merry by Mr Fellmer's ale; and when the christening came on Joshua paid Narrobourne another visit.

Among all the people who assembled on that day the brother clergymen were the least interested. Their minds were haunted by a spirit in kerseymere. In the evening they walked together in the fields.

'She's all right,' said Joshua. 'But here are you doing journey-work, Cornelius, and likely to continue at it till the end of the day, as far as I can see. I, too, with my petty living – what am I after all? . . . To tell the truth, the Church[24] is a poor forlorn hope for people without influence, particularly when their enthusiasm begins to flag. A social regenerator has a better chance outside, where he is unhampered by dogma and tradition. As for me, I would rather have gone on mending mills, with my crust of bread and liberty.'

Almost automatically they had bent their steps along the margin of the river; they now paused. They were standing on the brink of the well-known weir. There were the hatches, there was the culvert; they could see the pebbly bed of the stream through the pellucid water. The notes of the church-bells were audible, still jangled by the enthusiastic villagers.

'Why see – it was there I hid his walking-stick!' said Joshua, looking towards the sedge. The next moment, during a passing breeze, something flashed white on the spot to which the attention of Cornelius was drawn.

From the sedge rose a straight little silver-poplar, and it was the leaves of this sapling which caused the flicker of whiteness.

'His walking-stick has grown!' Joshua added. 'It was a rough one – cut from the hedge, I remember.'

At every puff of wind the tree turned white, till they could not bear to look at it; and they walked away.[25]

'I see him every night,' Cornelius murmured ... 'Ah, we read our *Hebrews* to little account, Jos! '*Τπέμεινε σταυρὸν, αἰσκύνης καταφρονήσας.*[26] To have *endured* the cross, *despising* the shame – there lay greatness! But now I often feel that I should like to put an end to trouble here in this self-same spot.'

'I have thought of it myself,' said Joshua.

'Perhaps we shall, some day,' murmured his brother.

'Perhaps,' said Joshua moodily.

With that contingency to consider in the silence of their nights and days they bent their steps homewards.

# THE FIRST COUNTESS
# OF WESSEX

By the Local Historian.[1]

King's-Hintock Court[2] (said the narrator, turning over his memoranda for reference) – King's-Hintock Court is, as we know, one of the most imposing of the mansions that overlook our beautiful Blackmoor or Blakemore Vale.[3] On the particular occasion of which I have to speak this building stood, as it had often stood before, in the perfect silence of a calm clear night, lighted only by the cold shine of the stars. The season was winter, in days long ago, the last century[4] having run but little more than a third of its length. North, south, and west, not a casement was unfastened, not a curtain undrawn; eastward, one window on the upper floor was open, and a girl of twelve or thirteen[5] was leaning over the sill. That she had not taken up the position for purposes of observation was apparent at a glance, for she kept her eyes covered with her hands.

The room occupied by the girl was an inner one of a suite, to be reached only by passing through a large bed-chamber adjoining. From this apartment voices in altercation were audible, everything else in the building being so still. It was to avoid listening to these voices that the girl had left her little cot, thrown a cloak round her head and shoulders, and stretched into the night air.

But she could not escape the conversation, try as she would. The words reached her in all their painfulness, one sentence in masculine tones, those of her father, being repeated many times.

'I tell 'ee there shall be no such betrothal! I tell 'ee there sha'n't! A child like her!'

Headpiece.

She knew the subject of dispute to be herself. A cool feminine voice, her mother's, replied:

'Have done with you, and be wise. He is willing to wait a good five or six years before the marriage takes place, and there's not a man in the county to compare with him.'

'It shall not be! He is over thirty. It is wickedness.'

'He is just thirty, and the best and finest man alive – a perfect match for her.'

'He is poor!'

'But his father and elder brothers are made much of at Court[6] – none so constantly at the palace as they; and with her fortune, who knows? He may be able to get a barony.'

'I believe you are in love with en yourself!'

'How can you insult me so, Thomas! And is it not monstrous[7] for you to talk of my wickedness when you have a like scheme in your own head? You know you have. Some bumpkin of your own choosing – some petty gentleman who lives down at that outlandish place of yours, Falls-Park[8] – one of your pot-companions' sons—'

There was an outburst of imprecation on the part of her husband in lieu of further argument. As soon as he could utter a connected sentence he said: 'You crow and you domineer, mistress, because you are heiress-general here. You are in your own house; you are on your own land. But let me tell 'ee that if I did come here to you instead of taking you to me, it was done at the dictates of convenience merely. H—! I'm no beggar! Ha'n't I a place of my own? Ha'n't I an avenue as long as thine? Ha'n't I beeches that will more than match thy oaks? I should have lived in my own quiet house and land, contented, if you had not called me off with your airs and graces. Faith, I'll go back there; I'll not stay with thee longer! If it had not been for our Betty I should have gone long ago!'

After this there were no more words; but presently, hearing the sound of a door opening and shutting below, the girl again looked from the window. Footsteps crunched on the gravel-walk, and a shape in a drab greatcoat, easily distinguishable as her father, withdrew from the house. He moved to the left, and she watched him diminish down the long east front till he had turned the corner and vanished. He must have gone round to the stables.

She closed the window and shrank into bed, where she cried herself to sleep. This child, their only one, Betty, beloved ambitiously by her mother, and with uncalculating passionateness by her father, was frequently made wretched by such episodes as this; though she was too young to care very deeply, for her own sake, whether her mother betrothed her to the gentleman discussed or not.

The Squire had often gone out of the house in this manner, declaring that he would never return, but he had always reappeared in the morning. The present occasion, however, was different in the issue: next day she was told that her father had ridden to his estate at Falls-Park early in the morning on business with his agent, and might not come back for some days.

Falls-Park was over twenty miles from King's-Hintock Court, and was altogether a more modest centre-piece to a more modest possession than the latter. But as Squire Dornell came in view of it that February morning, he thought that he had been a fool ever to leave it, though it was for the sake of the greatest heiress in Wessex. Its classic front, of the period of the second Charles,[9] derived from its regular features a dignity which the great, battlemented, heterogeneous mansion of his wife could not eclipse.[10] Altogether he was sick at heart, and the gloom which the densely-timbered park threw over the scene did not tend to remove the depression of this rubicund man of eight-and-forty, who sat so heavily upon his gelding.[11] The child, his darling Betty: there lay the root of his trouble. He was unhappy when near his wife, he was unhappy when away from his little girl; and from this dilemma there was no practicable escape. As a consequence he indulged rather freely in the pleasures of the table, became what was called a three-bottle man, and, in his wife's estimation, less and less presentable to her polite friends from town.

He was received by the two or three old servants who were in charge of the lonely place, where a few rooms only were kept habitable for his use or that of his friends when hunting; and

Falls-Park.

during the morning he was made more comfortable by the arrival of his faithful servant Tupcombe from King's-Hintock. But after a day or two spent here in solitude he began to feel that he had made a mistake in coming. By leaving King's-Hintock in his anger he had thrown away his best opportunity of counteracting his wife's preposterous notion of promising his poor little Betty's hand to a man she had hardly seen. To protect her from such a repugnant bargain he should have remained on the spot. He felt it almost as a misfortune that the child would inherit so much wealth. She would be a mark for all the adventurers in the kingdom. Had she been only the heiress to his own unassuming little place at Falls, how much better would have been her chances of happiness!

His wife had divined truly when she insinuated that he himself had a lover in view for this pet child. The son of a dear deceased friend[12] of his, who lived not two miles from where the Squire now was, a lad a couple of years his daughter's senior, seemed in her father's opinion the one person in the world likely to make her happy. But as to breathing such a scheme to either of the young people with the indecent haste that his wife had shown, he would not dream of it; years hence would be soon enough for that. They had already seen each other, and the Squire fancied that he noticed a tenderness on the youth's part which promised well. He was strongly tempted to profit by his wife's example, and forestall her match-making by throwing the two young people together there at Falls. The girl, though marriageable in the views of those days, was too young to be in love, but the lad was fifteen, and already felt an interest in her.

Still better than keeping watch over her at King's-Hintock, where she was necessarily much under her mother's influence, would it be to get the child to stay with him at Falls for a time, under his exclusive control. But how accomplish this without using main force? The only possible chance was that his wife might, for appearance' sake, as she had done before, consent to Betty paying him a day's visit, when he might find means of detaining her till Reynard, the suitor whom his wife favoured, had gone abroad, which he was expected to do the following week. Squire Dornell determined to return to King's-Hintock and attempt the enterprise. If he were refused, it was almost in him to pick up Betty bodily and carry her off.

The journey back, vague and Quixotic[13] as were his intentions, was performed with a far lighter heart than his setting forth. He would see Betty, and talk to her, come what might of his plan.

So he rode along the dead level which stretches between the hills skirting Falls-Park and those bounding the town of Ivell,[14] trotted through that borough, and out by the King's-Hintock highway, till, passing the village, he entered the mile-long drive through the park to the Court. The drive being open, without an avenue, the Squire could discern the north front and door of the Court a long way off, and was himself visible from the windows on that side; for which reason he hoped that Betty might perceive him coming, as she sometimes did on his return from an outing, and run to the door or wave her handkerchief.

But there was no sign. He inquired for his wife as soon as he set foot to earth.

'Mistress is away. She was called to London, sir.'

'And Mistress Betty?' said the Squire blankly.

'Gone likewise, sir, for a little change. Mistress has left a letter for you.'

The note explained nothing, merely stating that she had posted to London on her own affairs, and had taken the child to give her a holiday. On the fly-leaf were some words from Betty herself to the same effect, evidently written in a state of high jubilation at the idea of her jaunt. Squire Dornell murmured a few expletives, and submitted to his disappointment. How long his wife meant to stay in town she did not say; but on investigation he found that the carriage had been packed with sufficient luggage for a sojourn of two or three weeks.

King's-Hintock Court was in consequence as gloomy as Falls-Park had been. He had lost all zest for hunting of late, and had hardly attended a meet that season. Dornell read and re-read Betty's scrawl, and hunted up some other such notes of hers to look over, this seeming to be the only pleasure there was left for him. That they were really in London he learnt in a few days by another letter from Mrs Dornell, in which she explained that they hoped to be home in about a week, and that she had had no idea he was coming back to King's-Hintock so soon, or she would not have gone away without telling him.

Squire Dornell wondered if, in going or returning, it had been her plan to call at the Reynards' place near Melchester, through which city their journey lay. It was possible that she might do this in furtherance of her project, and the sense that his own might become the losing game was harassing.

He did not know how to dispose of himself, till it occurred to him that, to get rid of his intolerable heaviness, he would invite some friends to dinner and drown his cares in grog and wine. No sooner was the carouse decided upon[15] than he put it in hand; those invited being mostly neighbouring landholders, all smaller men than himself, members of the hunt; also the doctor from Evershead, and the like – some of them rollicking blades whose presence his wife would not have countenanced had she been at home. 'When the cat's away —!' said the Squire.

They arrived, and there were indications in their manner that they meant to make a night of it. Baxby of Sherton Castle[16] was late, and they waited a quarter of an hour for him, he being one of the liveliest of Dornell's friends; without whose presence no such dinner as this would be considered complete, and, it may be added, with whose presence no dinner which included both sexes could be conducted with strict propriety. He had just returned from London, and the Squire was anxious to talk to him – for no definite reason; but he had lately breathed the atmosphere in which Betty was.

At length they heard Baxby driving up to the door, whereupon the host and the rest of his guests crossed over to the dining-room. In a moment Baxby came hastily in at their heels, apologizing for his lateness.

'I only came back last night, you know,' he said; 'and the truth o't is, I had as much as I could carry.' He turned to the Squire. 'Well, Dornell – so cunning Reynard[17] has stolen your little ewe lamb? Ha, ha!'

'What?' said Squire Dornell vacantly, across the dining-table, round which they were all standing, the cold March sunlight streaming in upon his full, clean-shaven face.

'Surely th'st know what all the town knows? – you've had a letter by this time? – that Stephen Reynard has married your Betty? Yes, as I'm a living man. It was a carefully-arranged thing: they parted at once, and are not to meet for five or six years. But, Lord, you must know!'

A thud on the floor was the only reply of the Squire. They quickly turned. He had fallen down like a log behind the table, and lay motionless on the oak boards.

Those at hand hastily bent over him, and the whole group were in confusion. They found him to be quite unconscious, though puffing and panting like a blacksmith's bellows. His face was livid, his veins swollen, and beads of perspiration stood upon his brow.

'What's happened to him?' said several.

'An apoplectic fit,' said the doctor from Evershead, gravely.

He was only called in at the Court for small ailments, as a rule, and felt the importance of the situation. He lifted the Squire's head, loosened his cravat and clothing, and rang for the servants, who took the Squire upstairs.

There he lay as if in a drugged sleep. The surgeon drew a basin-full of blood[18] from him, but it was nearly six o'clock before he came to himself. The dinner was completely disorganized, and some had gone home long ago; but two or three remained.

'Bless my soul,' Baxby kept repeating, 'I didn't know things had come to this pass between Dornell and his lady! I thought the feast he was spreading today was in honour of the event, though privately kept for the present! His little maid married without his knowledge!'

As soon as the Squire recovered consciousness he gasped: ''Tis abduction! 'Tis a capital felony! He can be hung! Where is Baxby? I am very well now. What items[19] have ye heard, Baxby?'

The bearer of the untoward news was extremely unwilling to agitate Dornell further, and would say little more at first. But an hour after, when the Squire had partially recovered and was sitting up, Baxby told as much as he knew, the most important particular being that Betty's mother was present at the marriage, and showed every mark of approval. 'Everything appeared to have been done so regularly that I, of course, thought you knew all about it,' he said.

'I knew no more than the underground dead that such a step was in the wind! A child not yet thirteen![20] How Sue hath outwitted me! Did Reynard go up to Lon'on with 'em, d'ye know?'

'I can't say. All I know is that your lady and daughter were walking along the street, with the footman behind 'em; that they entered a jeweller's shop, where Reynard was standing; and that there, in the presence o' the shopkeeper and your man, who was called in on purpose, your Betty said to Reynard – so the story goes: 'pon my soul I don't vouch for the truth of it – she said, "Will you marry me?" or, "I want to marry you: will you have me – now or never?" she said.'

'What she said means nothing,' murmured the Squire, with wet eyes. 'Her mother put the words into her mouth to avoid the serious consequences that would attach to any suspicion of force. The words be not the child's – she didn't dream of marriage – how should she, poor little maid! Go on.'

'Well, be that as it will, they were all agreed apparently. They bought the ring on the spot, and the marriage took place at the nearest church within half-an-hour.'[21]

A day or two later there came a letter from Mrs Dornell to her husband, written before she knew of his stroke. She related the circumstances of the marriage in the gentlest manner, and gave cogent reasons and excuses for consenting to the premature union, which was now an accomplished fact indeed. She had no idea, till sudden pressure was put upon her, that the contract was expected to be carried out so soon, but being taken half unawares, she had consented, having learned that Stephen Reynard, now their son-in-law, was becoming a great favourite at Court, and that he would in all likelihood have a title[22] granted him before long. No harm could come to their dear daughter by this early marriage-contract, seeing that her life would be continued under their own eyes, exactly as before, for some years. In fine, she had felt that no other such fair opportunity for a good marriage with a shrewd courtier and wise man of the world, who was at the same time noted for his excellent personal qualities, was within the range of probability, owing to the rusticated lives they led at King's-Hintock. Hence she had yielded to Stephen's solicitation, and hoped her husband would forgive her. She wrote, in short, like a woman who, having had her way as to the deed, is prepared to make any concession as to words and subsequent behaviour.

All this Dornell took at its true value, or rather, perhaps, at less than its true value. As his life depended upon his not getting into a passion, he controlled his perturbed emotions as well as he was able, going about the house sadly and utterly unlike his former self. He took every precaution to prevent his wife knowing of the incidents of his sudden illness, from a sense of shame at having a heart so tender; a ridiculous quality, no doubt, in her eyes, now that she had become so imbued with town ideas. But rumours of his seizure somehow reached her, and she let him know that she was about to return to nurse him. He thereupon packed up and went off to his own place at Falls-Park.

Here he lived the life of a recluse for some time. He was still too unwell to entertain company, or to ride to hounds or elsewhither; but more than this, his aversion to the faces of strangers and acquaintances, who knew by that time of the trick his wife had played him, operated to hold him aloof.

Nothing could influence him to censure Betty for her share in the exploit. He never once believed that she had acted voluntarily. Anxious to know how she was getting on, he despatched the trusty servant Tupcombe to Evershead village, close to King's-Hintock, timing his journey so that he should reach the place under cover of dark. The emissary arrived without notice, being out of livery, and took a seat in the chimney-corner of the Sow-and-Acorn.[23]

The conversation of the droppers-in was always of the nine-days' wonder – the recent marriage. The smoking listener learnt that Mrs Dornell and the girl had returned to King's-Hintock for a day or two, that Reynard had set out for the Continent, and that Betty had since been packed off to school. She did not

At the Sow-and-Acorn.

realize her position as Reynard's child-wife – so the story went – and though somewhat awe-stricken at first by the ceremony, she had soon recovered her spirits on finding that her freedom was in no way to be interfered with.

After that, formal messages began to pass between Dornell and his wife, the latter being now as persistently conciliating as she was formerly masterful. But her rustic, simple, blustering husband still held personally aloof. Her wish to be reconciled – to win his forgiveness for her stratagem – moreover, a genuine tenderness and desire to soothe his sorrow, which welled up in her at times, brought her at last to his door at Falls-Park one day.

They had not met since that night of altercation, before her departure for London and his subsequent illness. She was shocked at the change in him. His face had become expressionless, as blank as that of a puppet, and what troubled her still more was that she found him living in one room, and indulging freely in stimulants, in absolute disobedience to the physician's order. The fact was obvious that he could no longer be allowed to live thus uncouthly.

So she sympathized, and begged his pardon, and coaxed. But though after this date there was no longer such a complete estrangement as before, they only occasionally saw each other, Dornell for the most part making Falls his headquarters still.

Three or four years passed thus. Then she came one day, with more animation in her manner, and at once moved him by the simple statement that Betty's schooling had ended; she had returned, and was grieved because he was away. She had sent a message to him in these words: 'Ask father to come home to his dear Betty.'

'Ah! Then she is very unhappy!' said Squire Dornell.

His wife was silent.

' 'Tis that accursed marriage!' continued the Squire.

Still his wife would not dispute with him. 'She is outside in the carriage,' said Mrs Dornell gently.

'What – Betty?'

'Yes.'

'Why didn't you tell me?' Dornell rushed out, and there was

the girl awaiting his forgiveness, for she supposed herself, no less than her mother, to be under his displeasure.

Yes, Betty had left school, and had returned to King's-Hintock. She was nearly seventeen, and had developed to quite a young woman. She looked not less a member of the household for her early marriage-contract, which she seemed, indeed, to have almost forgotten. It was like a dream to her; that clear cold March day, the London church, with its gorgeous pews, and green-baize linings, and the great organ in the west gallery – so different from their own little church in the shrubbery of King's-Hintock Court – the man of thirty, to whose face she had looked up with so much awe, and with a sense that he was rather ugly and formidable; the man whom, though they corresponded politely, she had never seen since; one to whose existence she was now so indifferent that if informed of his death, and that she would never see him more, she would merely have replied, 'Indeed!' Betty's passions as yet still slept.

'Hast heard from thy husband lately?' said Squire Dornell, when they were indoors, with an ironical laugh of fondness which demanded no answer.

The girl winced, and he noticed that his wife looked appealingly at him. As the conversation went on, and there were signs that Dornell would express sentiments that might do harm to a position which they could not alter, Mrs Dornell suggested that Betty should leave the room till her father and herself had finished their private conversation; and this Betty obediently did.

Dornell renewed his animadversions freely. 'Did you see how the sound of his name frightened her?' he presently added. 'If you didn't, I did. Zounds! what a future is in store for that poor little unfortunate wench o' mine! I tell 'ee, Sue, 'twas not a marriage at all, in morality, and if I were a woman in such a position, I shouldn't feel it as one. She might, without a sign of sin, love a man of her choice as well now as if she were chained up to no other at all. There, that's my mind, and I can't help it. Ah, Sue, my man was best! He'd ha' suited her.'

'I don't believe it,' she replied incredulously.

'You should see him; then you would. He's growing up a fine fellow, I can tell 'ee.'

'Hush! not so loud!' she answered, rising from her seat and going to the door of the next room, whither her daughter had betaken herself. To Mrs Dornell's alarm, there sat Betty in a reverie, her round eyes fixed on vacancy, musing so deeply that she did not perceive her mother's entrance. She had heard every word, and was digesting the new knowledge.

Her mother felt that Falls-Park was dangerous ground for a young girl of the susceptible age, and in Betty's peculiar position, while Dornell talked and reasoned thus. She called Betty to her, and they took leave. The Squire would not clearly promise to return and make King's-Hintock Court his permanent abode; but Betty's presence there, as at former times, was sufficient to make him agree to pay them a visit soon.

All the way home Betty remained preoccupied and silent. It was too plain to her anxious mother that Squire Dornell's free views had been a sort of awakening to the girl.

The interval before Dornell redeemed his pledge to come and see them was unexpectedly short. He arrived one morning about twelve o'clock, driving his own pair of black-bays in the curricle-phaeton with yellow panels and red wheels, just as he had used to do, and his faithful old Tupcombe on horseback behind. A young man sat beside the Squire in the carriage, and Mrs Dornell's consternation could scarcely be concealed when, abruptly entering with his companion, the Squire announced him as his friend Phelipson of Elm-Cranlynch.[24]

Dornell passed on to Betty in the background and tenderly kissed her. 'Sting your mother's conscience, my maid!' he whispered. 'Sting her conscience by pretending you are struck with Phelipson, and would ha' loved him, as your old father's choice, much more than him she has forced upon 'ee.'

The simple-souled speaker fondly imagined that it was entirely in obedience to this direction that Betty's eyes stole interested glances at the frank and impulsive Phelipson that day at dinner, and he laughed grimly within himself to see how this joke of his, as he imagined it to be, was disturbing the peace of mind of the lady of the house. 'Now Sue sees what a mistake she has made!' said he.

Mrs Dornell was verily greatly alarmed, and as soon as she

could speak a word with him alone she upbraided him. 'You ought not to have brought him here. Oh Thomas, how could you be so thoughtless! Lord, don't you see, dear, that what is done cannot be undone, and how all this foolery jeopardizes her happiness with her husband? Until you interfered, and spoke in her hearing about this Phelipson, she was as patient and as willing as a lamb, and looked forward to Mr Reynard's return with real pleasure. Since her visit to Falls-Park she has been monstrous close-mouthed and busy with her own thoughts. What mischief will you do? How will it end?'

'Own, then, that my man was best suited to her. I only brought him to convince you.'

'Yes, yes; I do admit it. But oh! do take him back again at once! Don't keep him here! I fear she is even attracted by him already.'

'Nonsense, Sue. 'Tis only a little trick to tease 'ee!'

Nevertheless her motherly eye was not so likely to be deceived as his, and if Betty were really only playing at being love-struck that day, she played at it with the perfection of a Rosalind,[25] and would have deceived the best professors into a belief that it was no counterfeit. The Squire, having obtained his victory, was quite ready to take back the too attractive youth, and early in the afternoon they set out on their return journey.

A silent figure who rode behind them was as interested as Dornell in that day's experiment. It was the staunch Tupcombe, who, with his eyes on the Squire's and young Phelipson's backs, thought how well the latter would have suited Betty, and how greatly the former had changed for the worse during these last two or three years. He cursed his mistress as the cause of the change.

After this memorable visit to prove his point, the lives of the Dornell couple flowed on quietly enough for the space of a twelvemonth, the Squire for the most part remaining at Falls, and Betty passing and repassing between them now and then, once or twice alarming her mother by not driving home from her father's house till midnight.

The repose of King's-Hintock was broken by the arrival of a special messenger. Squire Dornell had had an access of gout so violent as to be serious. He wished to see Betty again: why had she not come for so long?

Mrs Dornell was extremely reluctant to take Betty in that direction too frequently; but the girl was so anxious to go, her interests latterly seeming to be so entirely bound up in Falls-Park and its neighbourhood, that there was nothing to be done but to let her set out and accompany her.

Squire Dornell had been impatiently awaiting her arrival. They found him very ill and irritable. It had been his habit to take powerful medicines to drive away his enemy, and they had failed in their effect on this occasion.

The presence of his daughter, as usual, calmed him much, even while, as usual too, it saddened him; for he could never forget that she had disposed of herself for life in opposition to his wishes, though she had secretly assured him that she would never have consented had she been as old as she was now.

As on a former occasion, his wife wished to speak to him alone about the girl's future, the time now drawing nigh at which Reynard was expected to come and claim her. He would have done so already, but he had been put off by the earnest request of the young woman herself, which accorded with that of her parents, on the score of her youth. Reynard had deferentially submitted to their wishes in this respect, the understanding between them having been that he would not visit her before she was eighteen, except by the mutual consent of all parties. But this could not go on much longer, and there was no doubt, from the tenor of his last letter, that he would soon take possession of her whether or no.

To be out of the sound of this delicate discussion Betty was accordingly sent downstairs, and they soon saw her walking away into the shrubberies, looking very pretty in her sweeping green gown, and flapping broad-brimmed hat overhung with a feather.

On returning to the subject, Mrs Dornell found her husband's reluctance to reply in the affirmative to Reynard's letter to be as great as ever.

'She is three months short of eighteen!' he exclaimed. ''Tis too soon. I won't hear of it! If I have to keep him off sword in hand, he shall not have her yet.'

'But, my dear Thomas,' she expostulated, 'consider if anything should happen to you or to me, how much better it would be that she should be settled in her home with him!'

'I say it is too soon!' he argued, the veins of his forehead beginning to swell. 'If he gets her this side o' Candlemas[26] I'll challenge en – I'll take my oath on't! I'll be back to King's-Hintock in two or three days, and I'll not lose sight of her day or night!'

She feared to agitate him further, and gave way, assuring him, in obedience to his demand, that if Reynard should write again before he got back, to fix a time for joining Betty, she would put the letter in her husband's hands, and he should do as he chose. This was all that required discussion privately, and Mrs Dornell went to call in Betty, hoping that she had not heard her father's loud tones.

She had certainly not done so this time. Mrs Dornell followed the path along which she had seen Betty wandering, but went a considerable distance without perceiving anything of her. The Squire's wife then turned round to proceed to the other side of the house by a short cut across the grass, when, to her surprise and consternation, she beheld the object of her search sitting on the horizontal bough of a cedar, beside her being a young man, whose arm was round her waist. He moved a little, and she recognized him as young Phelipson.

Alas, then, she was right. The so-called counterfeit love was real. What Mrs Dornell called her husband at that moment, for his folly in originally throwing the young people together, it is not necessary to mention. She decided in a moment not to let the lovers know that she had seen them. She accordingly retreated, reached the front of the house by another route, and called at the top of her voice from a window, 'Betty!'

For the first time since her strategic marriage of the child, Susan Dornell doubted the wisdom of that step. Her husband had, as it were, been assisted by destiny to make his objection, originally trivial, a valid one. She saw the outlines of trouble in

'She beheld the object of her search sitting on the horizontal bough of a cedar.'

the future. Why had Dornell interfered? Why had he insisted upon producing his man? This, then, accounted for Betty's pleading for postponement whenever the subject of her husband's return was broached; this accounted for her attachment to Falls-Park. Possibly this very meeting that she had witnessed had been arranged by letter.

Perhaps the girl's thoughts would never have strayed for a moment if her father had not filled her head with ideas of repugnance to her early union, on the ground that she had been coerced into it before she knew her own mind; and she might have rushed to meet her husband with open arms on the appointed day.

Betty at length appeared in the distance in answer to the call, and came up pale, but looking innocent of having seen a living soul. Mrs Dornell groaned in spirit at such duplicity in the child of her bosom. This was the simple creature for whose development into womanhood they had all been so tenderly waiting – a forward minx, old enough not only to have a lover, but to conceal his existence as adroitly as any woman of the world! Bitterly did the Squire's lady regret that Stephen Reynard had not been allowed to come to claim her at the time he first proposed.

The two sat beside each other almost in silence on their journey back to King's-Hintock. Such words as were spoken came mainly from Betty, and their formality indicated how much her mind and heart were occupied with other things.

Mrs Dornell was far too astute a mother to openly attack Betty on the matter. That would be only fanning flame. The indispensable course seemed to her to be that of keeping the treacherous girl under lock and key till her husband came to take her off her mother's hands. That he would disregard Dornell's opposition, and come soon, was her devout wish.

It seemed, therefore, a fortunate coincidence that on her arrival at King's-Hintock a letter from Reynard was put into Mrs Dornell's hands. It was addressed to both her and her husband, and courteously informed them that the writer had landed at Bristol, and proposed to come on to King's-Hintock in a few days, at last to meet and carry off his darling Betty, if she and her parents saw no objection.

Betty had also received a letter of the same tenor. Her mother had only to look at her face to see how the girl received the information. She was as pale as a sheet.

'You must do your best to welcome him this time, my dear Betty,' her mother said gently.

'But – but – I—'

'You are a woman now,' added her mother severely, 'and these postponements must come to an end.'

'But my father – oh, I am sure he will not allow this! I am not ready. If he could only wait a year longer – if he could only wait a few months longer! Oh, I wish – I wish my dear father were here! I will send to him instantly.' She broke off abruptly, and falling upon her mother's neck, burst into tears, saying, 'O my mother, have mercy upon me – I do not love this man, my husband!'

The agonized appeal went too straight to Mrs Dornell's heart for her to hear it unmoved. Yet, things having come to this pass, what could she do? She was distracted, and for a moment was on Betty's side. Her original thought had been to write an affirmative reply to Reynard, allow him to come on to King's-Hintock, and keep her husband in ignorance of the whole proceeding till he should arrive from Falls on some fine day after his recovery, and find everything settled, and Reynard and Betty living together in harmony. But the events of the day, and her daughter's sudden outburst of feeling, had overthrown this intention. Betty was sure to do as she had threatened, and communicate instantly with her father, possibly attempt to fly to him. Moreover, Reynard's letter was addressed to Mr Dornell and herself conjointly, and she could not in conscience keep it from her husband.

'I will send the letter on to your father instantly,' she replied soothingly. 'He shall act entirely as he chooses, and you know that will not be in opposition to your wishes. He would ruin you rather than thwart you. I only hope he may be well enough to bear the agitation of this news. Do you agree to this?'

Poor Betty agreed, on condition that she should actually

witness the despatch of the letter. Her mother had no objection to offer to this; but as soon as the horseman had cantered down the drive toward the highway, Mrs Dornell's sympathy with Betty's recalcitration began to die out. The girl's secret affection for young Phelipson could not possibly be condoned. Betty might communicate with him, might even try to reach him. Ruin lay that way. Stephen Reynard must be speedily installed in his proper place by Betty's side.

She sat down and penned a private letter to Reynard, which threw light upon her plan.

'It is Necessary[27] that I should now tell you,' she said, 'what I have never Mentioned before – indeed I may have signified the Contrary – that her Father's Objection to your joining her has not as yet been overcome. As I personally Wish to delay you no longer – am indeed as anxious for your Arrival as you can be yourself, having the good of my Daughter at Heart – no course is left open to me but to assist your Cause without my Husband's Knowledge. He, I am sorry to say, is at present ill at Falls-Park, but I felt it my Duty to forward him your Letter. He will therefore be like to reply with a peremptory Command to you to go back again, for some Months, whence you came, till the Time he originally stipulated has expir'd. My Advice is, if you get such a Letter, to take no Notice of it, but to come on hither as you had proposed, letting me know the Day and Hour (after dark, if possible) at which we may expect you. Dear Betty is with me, and I warrant ye that she shall be in the House when you arrive.'

Mrs Dornell, having sent away this epistle unsuspected of anybody, next took steps to prevent her daughter leaving the Court, avoiding if possible to excite the girl's suspicions that she was under restraint. But, as if by divination, Betty had seemed to read the husband's approach in the aspect of her mother's face.

'He is coming!' exclaimed the maiden.

'Not for a week,' her mother assured her.

'He is then – for certain?'

'Well, yes.'[28]

Betty hastily retired to her room, and would not be seen.

To lock her up,[29] and hand over the key to Reynard when he should appear in the hall, was a plan charming in its simplicity, till her mother found, on trying the door of the girl's chamber softly, that Betty had already locked and bolted it on the inside, and had given directions to have her meals served where she was, by leaving them on a dumb-waiter outside the door.

Thereupon Mrs Dornell noiselessly sat down in her boudoir, which, as well as her bed-chamber, was a passage-room to the girl's apartment, and she resolved not to vacate her post night or day till her daughter's husband should appear, to which end she too arranged to breakfast, dine, and sup on the spot. It was impossible now that Betty should escape without her knowledge, even if she had wished, there being no other door to the chamber, except one admitting to a small inner dressing-room inaccessible by any second way.

But it was plain that the young girl had no thought of escape. Her ideas ran rather in the direction of intrenchment: she was prepared to stand a siege, but scorned flight. This, at any rate, rendered her secure. As to how Reynard would contrive a meeting with her coy daughter while in such a defensive humour, that, thought her mother, must be left to his own ingenuity to discover.

Betty had looked so wild and pale at the announcement of her husband's approaching visit, that Mrs Dornell, somewhat uneasy, could not leave her to herself. She peeped through the keyhole an hour later. Betty lay on the sofa, staring listlessly at the ceiling.

'You are looking ill, child,' cried her mother. 'You've not taken the air lately. Come with me for a drive.'

Betty made no objection. Soon they drove through the park towards the village, the daughter still in the strained, strung-up silence that had fallen upon her. They left the park to return by another route, and on the open road passed a cottage.

Betty's eye fell upon the cottage-window. Within it she saw a young girl about her own age, whom she knew by sight, sitting in a chair and propped by a pillow. The girl's face was covered with scales, which glistened in the sun. She was a convalescent from smallpox – a disease whose prevalence at that period was a terror of which we at present can hardly form a conception.

An idea suddenly energized Betty's apathetic features. She glanced at her mother; Mrs Dornell had been looking in the opposite direction. Betty said that she wished to go back to the cottage for a moment to speak to a girl in whom she took an interest. Mrs Dornell appeared suspicious, but observing that the cottage had no back-door, and that Betty could not escape without being seen, she allowed the carriage to be stopped. Betty ran back and entered the cottage, emerging again in about a minute, and resuming her seat in the carriage. As they drove on she fixed her eyes upon her mother and said, 'There, I have done it now!' Her pale face was stormy, and her eyes full of waiting tears.

'What have you done?' said Mrs Dornell.

'Nanny Priddle[30] is sick of the smallpox, and I saw her at the window, and I went in and kissed her, so that I might take it; and now I shall have it, and *he* won't be able to come near me!'

'Wicked girl!' cries her mother. 'Oh, what am I to do! What – bring a distemper on yourself, and usurp the sacred prerogative of God, because you can't palate the man you've wedded!'

The alarmed woman gave orders to drive home as rapidly as possible, and on arriving, Betty, who was by this time also somewhat frightened at her own enormity, was put into a bath, and fumigated, and treated in every way that could be thought of to ward off the dreadful malady that in a rash moment she had tried to acquire.

There was now a double reason for isolating the rebellious daughter and wife in her own chamber, and there she accordingly remained for the rest of the day and the days that followed; till no ill results seemed likely to arise from her wilfulness.[31]

Meanwhile the first letter from Reynard, announcing to Mrs Dornell and her husband jointly that he was coming in a few days, had sped on its way to Falls-Park. It was directed under cover to Tupcombe, the confidential servant, with instructions not to put it into his master's hands till he had been refreshed by a good long sleep. Tupcombe much regretted his commission, letters sent in this way always disturbing the Squire; but guessing that it would be infinitely worse in the end to withhold the news than to reveal it, he chose his time, which was early the next morning, and delivered the missive.

The utmost effect that Mrs Dornell had anticipated from the message was a peremptory order from her husband to Reynard to hold aloof a few months longer. What the Squire really did was to declare that he would go himself and confront Reynard at Bristol, and have it out with him there by word of mouth.

'But, master,' said Tupcombe, 'you can't. You cannot get out of bed.'

'You leave the room, Tupcombe, and don't say "can't" before me! Have Jerry saddled in an hour.'

The long-tried Tupcombe thought his employer demented, so utterly helpless was his appearance just then, and he went out reluctantly. No sooner was he gone than the Squire, with great difficulty, stretched himself over to a cabinet by the bedside, unlocked it, and took out a small bottle. It contained a gout specific, against whose use he had been repeatedly warned by his regular physician, but whose warning he now cast to the winds.

He took a double dose, and waited half an hour. It seemed to produce no effect. He then poured out a treble dose, swallowed it, leant back upon his pillow, and waited. The miracle he anticipated had been worked at last. It seemed as though the second draught had not only operated with its own strength, but had kindled into power the latent forces of the first. He put away the bottle, and rang up Tupcombe.

Less than an hour later one of the housemaids, who of course was quite aware that the Squire's illness was serious, was surprised to hear a bold and decided step descending the stairs from the direction of Mr Dornell's room, accompanied by the humming of a tune. She knew that the doctor had not paid a visit that morning, and that it was too heavy to be the valet or any other man-servant. Looking up, she saw Squire Dornell fully dressed, descending toward her in his drab caped riding-coat and boots, with the swinging easy movement of his prime. Her face expressed her amazement.

'What the devil beest looking at?' said the Squire. 'Did you never see a man walk out of his house before, wench?'[32]

Resuming his humming – which was of a defiant sort – he proceeded to the library, rang the bell, asked if the horses were ready, and directed them to be brought round. Ten minutes later he rode away in the direction of Bristol, Tupcombe behind him, trembling at what these movements might portend.

They rode on through the pleasant woodlands and the monotonous straight lanes at an equal pace. The distance traversed might have been about fifteen miles when Tupcombe could perceive that the Squire was getting tired – as weary as he would have been after riding three times the distance ten years before. However, they reached Bristol without any mishap, and put up at the Squire's accustomed inn. Dornell almost immediately proceeded on foot to the inn which Reynard had given as his address, it being now about four o'clock.

Reynard had already dined – for people dined early then – and he was staying indoors. He had already received Mrs Dornell's reply to his letter; but before acting upon her advice and starting for King's-Hintock he made up his mind to wait another day, that Betty's father might at least have time to write to him if so minded. The returned traveller much desired to obtain the Squire's assent, as well as his wife's, to the proposed visit to his bride, that nothing might seem harsh or forced in his method of taking his position as one of the family. But though he anticipated some sort of objection from his father-in-law, in consequence of Mrs Dornell's warning, he was surprised at the announcement of the Squire in person.

Stephen Reynard formed the completest of possible contrasts to Dornell as they stood confronting each other in the best parlour of the Bristol tavern. The Squire, hot-tempered, gouty, impulsive, generous, reckless; the younger man, pale, tall, sedate, self-possessed – a man of the world, fully bearing out at least one couplet in his epitaph, still extant in King's-Hintock church,[33] which places in the inventory of his good qualities

'He rode away in the direction of Bristol.'

> 'Engaging Manners, cultivated Mind,
> Adorn'd by Letters, and in Courts refin'd.'

He was at this time about five-and-thirty, though careful living and an even, unemotional temperament caused him to look much younger than his years.

Squire Dornell plunged into his errand without much ceremony or preface.

'I am your humble servant, sir,' he said. 'I have read your letter writ to my wife and myself, and considered that the best way to answer it would be to do so in person.'

'I am vastly honoured by your visit, sir,' said Mr Stephen Reynard, bowing.

'Well, what's done can't be undone,' said Dornell, 'though it was mighty early, and was no doing of mine. She's your wife; and there's an end on't. But in brief, sir, she's too young for you to claim yet; we mustn't reckon by years; we must reckon by nature. She's still a girl; 'tis onpolite of 'ee to come yet; next year will be full soon enough for you to take her to you.'

Now, courteous as Reynard could be, he was a little obstinate when his resolution had once been formed. She had been promised him by her eighteenth birthday at latest – sooner if she were in robust health. Her mother had fixed the time on her own judgment, without a word of interference on his part. He had been hanging about foreign courts till he was weary. Betty was now a woman, if she would ever be one, and there was not, in his mind, the shadow of an excuse for putting him off longer. Therefore, fortified as he was by the support of her mother, he blandly but firmly told the Squire that he had been willing to waive his rights, out of deference to her parents, to any reasonable extent, but must now, in justice to himself and her insist on maintaining them. He therefore, since she had not come to meet him, should proceed to King's-Hintock in a few days to fetch her.

This announcement, in spite of the urbanity with which it was delivered, set Dornell in a passion.

'Oh dammy, sir; you talk about rights, you do, after stealing her away, a mere child, against my will and knowledge! If we'd begged and prayed 'ee to take her, you could say no more.'

'Upon my honour, your charge is quite baseless, sir,' said his son-in-law. 'You must know by this time – or if you do not, it has been a monstrous cruel injustice to me that I should have been allowed to remain in your mind with such a stain upon my character – you must know that I used no seductiveness or temptation of any kind. Her mother assented; she assented. I took them at their word. That you was really opposed to the marriage was not known to me till afterwards.'

Dornell professed to believe not a word of it. 'You sha'n't have her till she's dree sixes full – no maid ought to be married till she's dree sixes! – and my daughter sha'n't be treated out of nater!' So he stormed on till Tupcombe, who had been alarmedly listening in the next room, entered suddenly, declaring to Reynard that his master's life was in danger if the interview were prolonged, he being subject to apoplectic strokes at these crises. Reynard immediately said that he would be the last to wish to injure Squire Dornell, and left the room, and as soon as the Squire had recovered breath and equanimity, he went out of the inn, leaning on the arm of Tupcombe.

Tupcombe was for sleeping in Bristol that night, but Dornell, whose energy seemed as invincible as it was sudden, insisted upon mounting and getting back as far as Falls-Park, to continue the journey to King's-Hintock on the following day. At five they started, and took the southern road toward the Mendip Hills.[34] The evening was dry and windy, and, excepting that the sun did not shine, strongly reminded Tupcombe of the evening of that March month, nearly five years earlier, when news had been brought to King's-Hintock Court of the child Betty's[35] marriage in London – news which had produced upon Dornell such a marked effect for the worse ever since, and indirectly upon the household of which he was the head. Before that time the winters were lively at Falls-Park, as well as at King's-Hintock, although the Squire had ceased to make it his regular residence. Hunting-guests and shooting-guests came and went, and open house was kept. Tupcombe disliked the clever courtier who had put a stop

'So he stormed on till Tupcombe entered suddenly.'

to this by taking away from the Squire the only treasure he valued.

It grew darker with their progress along the lanes, and Tupcombe discovered from Mr Dornell's manner of riding that his strength was giving way; and spurring his own horse close alongside, he asked him how he felt.

'Oh, bad; damn bad, Tupcombe! I can hardly keep my seat. I shall never be any better, I fear! Have we passed Three-Man-Gibbet yet?'

'Not yet by a long ways, sir.'

'I wish we had. I can hardly hold on.' The Squire could not repress a groan now and then, and Tupcombe knew he was in great pain. 'I wish I was underground – that's the place for such fools as I! I'd gladly be there if it were not for Mistress Betty. He's coming on to King's-Hintock tomorrow – he won't put it off any longer; he'll set out and reach there tomorrow night, without stopping at Falls; and he'll take her unawares, and I want to be there before him.'

'I hope you may be well enough to do it, sir. But really—'

'I *must*, Tupcombe! You don't know what my trouble is; it is not so much that she is married to this man without my agreeing – for, after all, there's nothing to say against him, so far as I know; but that she don't take to him at all, seems to fear him – in fact, cares nothing about him; and if he comes forcing himself into the house upon her, why, 'twill be rank cruelty. Would to the Lord something would happen to prevent him!'

How they reached home that night Tupcombe hardly knew. The Squire was in such pain that he was obliged to recline upon his horse, and Tupcombe was afraid every moment lest he would fall into the road. But they did reach home at last, and Mr Dornell was instantly assisted to bed.

Next morning it was obvious that he could not possibly go to King's-Hintock for several days at least, and there on the bed he lay, cursing his inability to proceed on an errand so personal and so delicate that no emissary could perform it. What he wished to do was to ascertain from Betty's own lips if her aversion to Reynard was so strong that his presence would be

The Drive – King's-Hintock park.

positively distasteful to her. Were that the case, he would have borne her away bodily on the saddle behind him.

But all that was hindered now, and he repeated a hundred times in Tupcombe's hearing, and in that of the nurse and other servants, 'I wish to God something would happen to him!'

This sentiment, reiterated by the Squire as he tossed in the agony induced by the powerful drugs of the day before, entered sharply into the soul of Tupcombe and of all who were attached to the house of Dornell, as distinct from the house of his wife at King's-Hintock. Tupcombe, who was an excitable man, was hardly less disquieted by the thought of Reynard's return than the Squire himself was. As the week drew on, and the afternoon advanced at which Reynard would in all probability be passing near Falls on his way to the Court, the Squire's feelings became acuter, and the responsive Tupcombe could hardly bear to come near him. Having left him in the hands of the doctor, the former went out upon the lawn, for he could hardly breathe in the contagion of excitement caught from the employer who had virtually made him his confidant. He had lived with the Dornells from his boyhood, had been born under the shadow of their walls; his whole life was annexed and welded to the life of the family in a degree which has no counterpart in these latter days.

He was summoned indoors, and learnt that it had been decided to send for Mrs Dornell: her husband was in great danger. There were two or three who could have acted as messenger, but Dornell wished Tupcombe to go, the reason showing itself when, Tupcombe being ready to start, Squire Dornell summoned him to his chamber and leaned down so that he could whisper in his ear:

'Put Peggy along smart, Tupcombe, and get there before him, you know – before him. This is the day he fixed. He has not passed Falls cross-roads yet. If you can do that you will be able to get Betty to come – d'ye see? – after her mother has started; she'll have a reason for not waiting for him.[36] Bring her by the lower road – he'll go by the upper. Your business is to make 'em miss each other – d'ye see? – but that's a thing I couldn't write down.'

Five minutes after, Tupcombe was astride the horse and on

his way – the way he had followed so many times since his master, a florid young countryman, had first gone wooing to King's-Hintock Court. As soon as he had crossed the hills in the immediate neighbourhood of the manor, the road lay over a plain, where it ran in long straight stretches for several miles. In the best of times, when all had been gay in the united houses, that part of the road had seemed tedious. It was gloomy in the extreme now that he pursued it, at night and alone, on such an errand.

He rode and brooded. If the Squire were to die, he, Tupcombe, would be alone in the world and friendless, for he was no favourite with Mrs Dornell; and to find himself baffled, after all, in what he had set his mind on, would probably kill the Squire.[37] Thinking thus, Tupcombe stopped his horse every now and then, and listened for the coming husband. The time was drawing on to the moment when Reynard might be expected to pass along this very route. He had watched the road well during the afternoon, and had inquired of the tavern-keepers as he came up to each, and he was convinced that the premature descent of the stranger-husband upon his young mistress had not been made by this highway as yet.

Besides the girl's mother, Tupcombe was the only member of the household who suspected Betty's tender feelings towards young Phelipson, so unhappily generated on her return from school; and he could therefore imagine, even better than her fond father, what would be her emotions on the sudden announcement of Reynard's advent that evening at King's-Hintock Court.

So he rode and rode, desponding and hopeful by turns. He felt assured that, unless in the unfortunate event of the almost immediate arrival of her son-in-law at his own heels, Mrs Dornell would not be able to hinder Betty's departure for her father's bedside.

It was about nine o'clock that, having put twenty miles of country behind him, he turned in at the lodge-gate nearest to Ivell and King's-Hintock village, and pursued the long north drive – itself much like a turnpike-road – which led thence through the park to the Court. Though there were so many trees in King's-Hintock park, few bordered the carriage roadway; he could see it stretching ahead in the pale night light like an unrolled deal shaving. Presently the irregular frontage of the house came in view, of great extent, but low, except where it rose into the outlines of a broad square tower.

As Tupcombe approached he rode aside upon the grass, to make sure, if possible, that he was the first comer, before letting his presence be known. The Court was dark and sleepy, in no respect as if a bridegroom were about to arrive.

While pausing he distinctly heard the tread of a horse upon the track behind him, and for a moment despaired of arriving in time: here, surely, was Reynard! Pulling up closer to the densest tree at hand he waited, and found he had retreated nothing too soon, for the second rider avoided the gravel also, and passed quite close to him. In the profile he recognized young Phelipson.[38]

Before Tupcombe could think what to do, Phelipson had gone on; but not to the door of the house. Swerving to the left, he passed round to the east angle, where, as Tupcombe knew, were situated Betty's apartments. Dismounting, he left the horse tethered to a hanging bough, and walked on to the house.

Suddenly his eye caught sight of an object which explained the position immediately. It was a ladder stretching from beneath the trees, which there came pretty close to the house, up to a first-floor window – one which lighted Miss Betty's rooms. Yes, it was Betty's chamber; he knew every room in the house well.

The young horseman who had passed him, having evidently left his steed somewhere under the trees also, was perceptible at the top of the ladder, immediately outside Betty's window. While Tupcombe watched, a cloaked female figure stepped timidly over the sill, and the two cautiously descended, one before the other, the young man's arms enclosing the young woman between his grasp of the ladder, so that she could not fall. As soon as they reached the bottom, young Phelipson quickly removed the ladder and hid it under the bushes. The pair disappeared; till, in a few minutes, Tupcombe could discern a horse emerging from a remoter part of the umbrage. The horse carried double, the girl being on a pillion behind her lover.

'Betty lay upon the floor.'

[This illustration of an episode deleted when the story was collected for book publication shows Betty after she has fainted at the sight of the accident that has killed Phelipson (see A Note on the History of the Texts).]

Tupcombe hardly knew what to do or think; yet, though this was not exactly the kind of flight that had been intended, she had certainly escaped. He went back to his own animal, and rode round to the servants' door, where he delivered the letter for Mrs Dornell. To leave a verbal message for Betty was now impossible.

The Court servants desired him to stay over the night, but he would not do so, desiring to get back to the Squire as soon as possible and tell what he had seen. Whether he ought not to have intercepted the young people, and carried off Betty himself to her father, he did not know. However, it was too late to think of that now, and without wetting his lips or swallowing a crumb, Tupcombe turned his back upon King's-Hintock Court.

It was not till he had advanced a considerable distance on his way homeward that, halting under the lantern of a roadside-inn while the horse was watered, there came a traveller from the opposite direction in a hired coach; the lantern lit the stranger's face as he passed along and dropped into the shade. Tupcombe exulted for the moment, though he could hardly have justified his exultation. The belated traveller was Reynard; and another had stepped in before him.

You may now be willing to know of the fortunes of Miss Betty. Left much to herself through the intervening days, she had ample time to brood over her desperate attempt at the stratagem of infection – thwarted, apparently, by her mother's promptitude. In what other way to gain time she could not think. Thus drew on the day and the hour of the evening on which her husband was expected to announce himself.

At some period after dark, when she could not tell, a tap at the window, twice and thrice repeated, became audible. It caused her to start up, for the only visitant in her mind was the one whose advances she had so feared as to risk health and life to repel them. She crept to the window, and heard a whisper without.

'It is I – Charley,' said the voice.

Betty's face fired with excitement. She had latterly begun to doubt her admirer's staunchness, fancying his love to be going off in mere attentions which neither committed him nor herself very deeply. She opened the window, saying in a joyous whisper, 'Oh Charley; I thought you had deserted me quite!'

He assured her he had not done that, and that he had a horse in waiting, if she would ride off with him. 'You must come quickly,' he said; 'for Reynard's on the way!'

To throw a cloak round herself was the work of a moment, and assuring herself that her door was locked against a surprise, she climbed over the window-sill and descended with him as we have seen.

Her mother meanwhile, having received Tupcombe's note, found the news of her husband's illness so serious, as to displace her thoughts of the coming son-in-law, and she hastened to tell her daughter of the Squire's dangerous condition, thinking it might be desirable to take her to her father's bedside. On trying the door of the girl's room, she found it still locked. Mrs Dornell called, but there was no answer. Full of misgivings, she privately fetched the old house-steward and bade him burst open the door – an order by no means easy to execute, the joinery of the Court being massively constructed. However, the lock sprang open at last, and she entered Betty's chamber only to find the window unfastened and the bird flown.

For a moment Mrs Dornell was staggered. Then it occurred to her that Betty might have privately obtained from Tupcombe the news of her father's serious illness, and, fearing she might be kept back to meet her husband, have gone off with that obstinate and biassed servitor to Falls-Park. The more she thought it over the more probable did the supposition appear; and binding her own head-man to secrecy as to Betty's movements, whether as she conjectured, or otherwise, Mrs Dornell herself prepared to set out.

She had no suspicion how seriously her husband's malady had been aggravated by his ride to Bristol, and thought more of Betty's affairs than of her own. That Betty's husband should arrive by some other road tonight, and find neither wife nor mother-in-law to receive him, and no explanation of their absence, was possible; but never forgetting chances, Mrs Dornell as she journeyed kept her eyes fixed upon the highway on the off-side, where, before she had reached the town of Ivell, the hired coach containing Stephen Reynard flashed into the lamp-light of her own carriage.

Mrs Dornell's coachman pulled up, in obedience to a direction she had given him at starting; the other coach was hailed, a few words passed, and Reynard alighted and came to Mrs Dornell's carriage-window.

'Come inside,' says she. 'I want to speak privately to you. Why are you so late?'

'One hindrance and another,' says he. 'I meant to be at the Court by eight at latest. My gratitude for your letter. I hope —'

'You must not try to see Betty yet,' said she. 'There be far other and newer reasons against your seeing her now than there were when I wrote.'

The circumstances were such that Mrs Dornell could not possibly conceal them entirely; nothing short of knowing some of the facts would prevent his blindly acting in a manner which might be fatal to the future. Moreover, there are times when deeper intriguers than Mrs Dornell feel that they must let out a few truths, if only in self-indulgence. So she told so much of recent surprises as that Betty's heart had been attracted by another image than his, and that his insisting on visiting her now might drive the girl to desperation. 'Betty has, in fact, rushed off to her father to avoid you,' she said. 'But if you wait she will soon forget this young man, and you will have nothing to fear.'

As a woman and a mother she could go no further, and Betty's desperate attempt to infect herself the week before as a means of repelling him, together with the alarming possibility that, after all, she had not gone to her father but to her lover, was not revealed.

'Well,' sighed the diplomatist, in a tone unexpectedly quiet, 'such things have been known before. After all, she may prefer me to him some day, when she reflects how very differently I might have acted than I am going to act towards her. But I'll say no more about that now. I can have a bed at your house for tonight?'

'Tonight, certainly. And you leave tomorrow morning early?' She spoke anxiously, for on no account did she wish him to make further discoveries. 'My husband is so seriously ill,' she continued, 'that my absence and Betty's on your arrival is naturally accounted for.'

He promised to leave early, and to write to her soon. 'And when I think the time is ripe,' he said, 'I'll write to her. I may have something to tell her that will bring her to graciousness.'

It was about one o'clock in the morning when Mrs Dornell reached Falls-Park. A double blow awaited her there. Betty had not arrived; her flight had been elsewhither; and her stricken mother divined with whom. She ascended to the bedside of her husband, where to her concern she found that the physician had given up all hope. The Squire was sinking, and his extreme weakness had almost changed his character, except in the particular that his old obstinacy sustained him in a refusal to see a clergyman. He shed tears at the least word, and sobbed at the sight of his wife. He asked for Betty, and it was with a heavy heart that Mrs Dornell told him that the girl had not accompanied her.

'He is not keeping her away?'

'No, no. He is going back – he is not coming to her for some time.'

'Then what is detaining her – cruel, neglectful maid!'

'No, no, Thomas; she is — She could not come.'

'How's that?'

Somehow the solemnity of these last moments of his gave him inquisitorial power, and the too-cold wife could not conceal from him the flight which had taken place from King's-Hintock that night.

To her amazement, the effect upon him was electrical.

'What – Betty – a trump after all? Hurrah! She's her father's own maid! She's game! She knew he was her father's own choice! She vowed that my man should win! Well done, Bet! – haw! haw! Hurrah!'

He had raised himself in bed by starts as he spoke, and now fell back exhausted. He never uttered another word, and died before the dawn. People said there had not been such an ungenteel death[39] in a good county family for years.

*

Now I will go back to the time of Betty's riding off on the pillion behind her lover. They left the park by an obscure gate to the east, and presently found themselves in the lonely and solitary length of the old Roman road now called Long-Ash Lane.[40]

By this time they were rather alarmed at their own performance, for they were both young and inexperienced. Hence they proceeded almost in silence till they came to a mean roadside inn which was not yet closed; when Betty, who had held on to him with much misgiving all this while, felt dreadfully unwell, and said she thought she would like to get down.

They accordingly dismounted from the jaded animal that had brought them, and were shown into a small dark parlour, where they stood side by side awkwardly, like the fugitives they were. A light was brought, and when they were left alone Betty threw off the cloak which had enveloped her. No sooner did young Phelipson see her face than he uttered an alarmed exclamation.

'Why, Lord, Lord, you are sickening for the smallpox!' he cried.

'Oh – I forgot!' faltered Betty. And then she informed him that, on hearing of her husband's approach the week before, in a desperate attempt to keep him from her side, she had tried to imbibe the infection – an act which till this moment she had supposed to have been ineffectual, imagining her feverishness to be the result of her excitement.

The effect of this discovery upon young Phelipson was overwhelming. Better-seasoned men than he would not have been proof against it, and he was only a little over her own age. 'And you've been holding on to me!' he said. 'And suppose you get worse, and we both have it, what shall we do? Won't you be a fright in a month or two, poor, poor Betty!'

In his horror he attempted to laugh, but the laugh ended in a weakly giggle. She was more woman than girl by this time, and realized his feeling.

'What – in trying to keep off him, I keep off you?' she said miserably. 'Do you hate me because I am going to be ugly and ill?'

'Oh – no, no!' he said soothingly. 'But I – I am thinking if it is quite right for us to do this. You see, dear Betty, if you was

not married it would be different. You are not in honour married
to him we've often said; still you are his by law, and you can't
be mine whilst he's alive.[41] And with this terrible sickness coming
on, perhaps you had better let me take you back, and – climb in
at the window again.'

'Is *this* your love?' said Betty reproachfully. 'Oh, if you was
sickening for the plague itself, and going to be as ugly as the
Ooser in the church-vestry, I wouldn't—'

'No, no, you mistake, upon my soul!'

But Betty with a swollen heart had rewrapped herself and
gone out of the door. The horse was still standing there. She
mounted by the help of the upping-stock, and when he had
followed her she said, 'Do not come near me, Charley; but
please lead the horse, so that if you've not caught anything
already you'll not catch it going back. After all, what keeps off
you may keep off him. Now onward.'

He did not resist her command, and back they went by the
way they had come, Betty shedding bitter tears at the retribution
she had already brought upon herself; for though she had
reproached Phelipson, she was staunch enough not to blame
him in her secret heart for showing that his love was only
skin-deep. The horse was stopped in the plantation, and they
walked silently to the lawn, reaching the bushes wherein the
ladder still lay.

'Will you put it up for me?' she asked mournfully.

He re-erected the ladder without a word; but when she
approached to ascend he said, 'Goodbye, Betty!'

'Goodbye!' said she; and involuntarily turned her face
towards his. He hung back from imprinting the expected kiss:
at which Betty started as if she had received a poignant wound.
She moved away so suddenly that he hardly had time to follow
her up the ladder to prevent her falling.

'Tell your mother to get the doctor at once!' he said anxiously.

She stepped in without looking behind; he descended, withdrew the ladder, and went away.

Alone in her chamber, Betty flung herself upon her face on
the bed, and burst into shaking sobs. Yet she would not admit
to herself that her lover's conduct was unreasonable; only that

her rash act of the previous week had been wrong. No one had heard her enter, and she was too worn out, in body and mind, to think or care about medical aid. In an hour or so she felt yet more unwell, positively ill; and nobody coming to her at the usual bedtime, she looked towards the door. Marks of the lock having been forced were visible, and this made her chary of summoning a servant. She opened the door cautiously and sallied forth downstairs.

In the dining-parlour, as it was called, the now sick and sorry Betty was startled to see at that late hour not her mother, but a man sitting, calmly finishing his supper. There was no servant in the room. He turned, and she recognized her husband.

'Where's my mamma?' she demanded without preface.

'Gone to your father's. Is that —' He stopped, aghast.

'Yes, sir. This spotted object is your wife! I've done it because I don't want you to come near me!'

He was sixteen years her senior; old enough to be compassion-ate. 'My poor child, you must get to bed directly! Don't be afraid of me – I'll carry you upstairs, and send for a doctor instantly.'

'Ah, you don't know what I am!' she cried. 'I had a lover once; but now he's gone! 'Twasn't I who deserted him. He has deserted me; because I am ill he wouldn't kiss me, though I wanted him to!'

'Wouldn't he? Then he was a very poor slack-twisted sort of fellow. Betty, *I've* never kissed you since you stood beside me as my little wife, twelve years and a half old! May I kiss you now?'

Though Betty by no means desired his kisses, she had enough of the spirit of Cunigonde in Schiller's ballad[42] to test his daring. 'If you have courage to venture, yes sir!' said she. 'But you may die for it, mind!'

He came up to her and imprinted a deliberate kiss full upon her mouth, saying, 'May many others follow!'

She shook her head, and hastily withdrew, though secretly pleased at his hardihood. The excitement had supported her for the few minutes she had passed in his presence, and she could hardly drag herself back to her room. Her husband summoned the servants, and, sending them to her assistance, went off himself for a doctor.

The next morning Reynard waited at the Court till he had learnt from the medical man that Betty's attack promised to be a very light one – or, as it was expressed, 'very fine'; and in taking his leave sent up a note to her:

'Now I must be Gone. I promised your Mother I would not see You yet, and she may be anger'd if she finds me here. Promise to see me as Soon as you are well?'

He was of all men then living one of the best able to cope with such an untimely situation as this. A contriving, sagacious, gentle-mannered man, a philosopher who saw that the only constant attribute of life is change,[43] he held that, as long as she lives, there is nothing finite[44] in the most impassioned attitude a woman may take up. In twelve months his girl-wife's recent infatuation might be as distasteful to her mind as it was now to his own. In a few years her very flesh would change – so said the scientific; – her spirit, so much more ephemeral, was capable of changing in one. Betty was his, and it became a mere question of means how to effect that change.

During the day Mrs Dornell, having closed her husband's eyes, returned to the Court. She was truly relieved to find Betty there, even though on a bed of sickness. The disease ran its course, and in due time Betty became convalescent, without having suffered deeply for her rashness, one little speck[45] beneath her ear, and one beneath her chin, being all the marks she retained.

The Squire's body was not brought back to King's-Hintock. Where he was born, and where he had lived before wedding his Sue, there he had wished to be buried. No sooner had she lost him than Mrs Dornell, like certain other wives, though she had never shown any great affection for him while he lived, awoke suddenly to his many virtues, and zealously embraced his opinion about delaying Betty's union with her husband, which she had formerly combated strenuously.[46] 'Poor man! how right he was, and how wrong was I!' Eighteen was certainly the lowest age at which Mr Reynard should claim her child – nay, it was too low! Far too low!

So desirous was she of honouring her lamented husband's sentiments in this respect, that she wrote to her son-in-law suggesting that, partly on account of Betty's sorrow for her father's loss, and out of consideration for his known wishes for delay, Betty should not be taken from her till her nineteenth birthday.

However much or little Stephen Reynard might have been to blame in his marriage, the patient man now almost deserved to be pitied. First Betty's skittishness; now her mother's remorseful *volte-face*: it was enough to exasperate anybody; and he wrote to the widow in a tone which led to a little coolness between those hitherto firm friends. However, knowing that he had a wife not to claim but to win, and that young Phelipson had been packed off to sea by his parents,[47] Stephen was complaisant to a degree, returning to London, and holding quite aloof from Betty and her mother, who remained for the present in the country. In town he had a mild visitation of the distemper he had taken from Betty, and in writing to her he took care not to dwell upon its mildness. It was now that Betty began to pity him for what she had inflicted upon him by the kiss, and her correspondence acquired a distinct flavour of kindness thenceforward.

Owing to his rebuffs, Reynard had grown to be truly in love with Betty in his mild, placid, durable way – in that way which perhaps, upon the whole, tends most generally to the woman's comfort under the institution of marriage, if not particularly to her ecstasy. Mrs Dornell's exaggeration of her husband's wish for delay in their living together was inconvenient, but he would not openly infringe it. He wrote tenderly to Betty, and soon announced that he had a little surprise in store for her. The secret was that the King had been graciously pleased to inform him privately, through a relation, that His Majesty was about to offer him a Barony. Would she like the title to be Ivell? Moreover, he had reason for knowing that in a few years the dignity would be raised to that of an Earl, for which creation he thought the title of Wessex would be eminently suitable, considering the position of much of their property. As Lady

Ivell, therefore, and future Countess of Wessex, he should beg leave to offer her his heart a third time.

He did not add, as he might have added, how greatly the consideration of the enormous estates at King's-Hintock and elsewhere which Betty would inherit, and her children after her, had conduced to this desirable honour.

Whether the impending titles had really any effect upon Betty's regard for him I cannot state,[48] for she was one of those close characters who never let their minds be known upon anything. That such honour was absolutely unexpected by her from such a quarter is, however, certain; and she could not deny that Stephen had shown her kindness, forbearance, even magnanimity; had forgiven her for an errant passion which he might with some reason have denounced, notwithstanding her cruel position as a child entrapped into marriage ere able to understand its bearings.[49]

Her mother, in her grief and remorse for the loveless life she had led with her rough, though open-hearted, husband, made now a creed of his merest whim; and continued to insist that, out of respect to his known desire, her son-in-law should not reside with Betty till the girl's father had been dead a year at least, at which time the girl would still be under nineteen. Letters must suffice for Stephen till then.

'It is rather long for him to wait,' Betty hesitatingly said one day.

'What!' said her mother. 'From *you*? not to respect your dear father—'

'Of course it is quite proper,' said Betty hastily. 'I don't gainsay it. I was but thinking that – that—'

In the long slow months of the stipulated interval her mother tended and trained Betty carefully for her duties. Fully awake now to the many virtues of her dear departed one, she, among other acts of pious devotion to his memory, rebuilt the church of King's-Hintock village, and established valuable charities in all the villages of that name, as far as to Little-Hintock, several miles eastward.

In superintending these works, particularly that of the church-

building, her daughter Betty was her constant companion, and
the incidents of their execution were doubtless not without a
soothing effect upon the young creature's heart. She had sprung
from girl to woman by a sudden bound, and few would have
recognized in the thoughtful face of Betty now the same person
who, the year before, had seemed to have absolutely no idea
whatever of responsibility, moral or other. Time passed thus till
the Squire had been nearly a year in his vault; and Mrs Dornell
was duly asked by letter by the patient Reynard if she were
willing for him to come soon.[50] He did not wish to take Betty
away if her mother's sense of loneliness would be too great, but
would willingly live at King's-Hintock awhile with them.

Before the widow had replied to this communication, she one
day happened to observe Betty walking on the south terrace in
the full sunlight, without hat or mantle, and was struck by
her child's figure.[51] Mrs Dornell called her in, and said suddenly:
'Have you seen your husband since the time of your poor
father's death?'

'Well – yes, mamma,' says Betty, colouring.

'What – against my wishes and those of your dear father! I
am shocked at your disobedience!'

'But my father said eighteen, ma'am, and you made it much
longer—'

'Why, of course – out of consideration for you! When have
ye seen him?'

'Well,' stammered Betty, 'in the course of his letters to me he
said that I belonged to him, and if nobody knew that we met it
would make no difference. And that I need not hurt your feelings
by telling you.'

'Well?'

'So I went to Casterbridge[52] that time you went to London
about five months ago—'

'And met him there? When did you come back?'

'Dear, mamma, it grew very late, and he said it was safer not
to go back till next day, as the roads were bad; and as you were
away from home—'

'I don't want to hear any more! This is your respect for your father's memory,' groaned the widow. 'When did you meet him again?'

'Oh – not for more than a fortnight.'

'A fortnight! How many times have ye seen him altogether?'

'I'm sure, mamma, I've not seen him altogether a dozen times.'[53]

'A dozen! And eighteen and a half years old barely!'

'Twice we met by accident,' pleaded Betty. 'Once at Abbot's-Cernel, and another time at the Red Lion, Melchester.'

'O thou deceitful girl!' cried Mrs Dornell. 'An accident took you to the Red Lion whilst I was staying at the White Hart! I remember – you came in at twelve o'clock at night and said you'd been to see the cathedral by the light o' the moon!'

'My ever-honoured mamma, so I had! I only went to the Red Lion with him afterwards.'

'Oh Betty, Betty! That my child should have deceived me even in my widowed days!'

'But, my dearest mamma, you made me marry him!' says Betty with spirit, 'and of course I've to obey him more than you now!'

Mrs Dornell sighed. 'All I have to say is, that you'd better get your husband to join you as soon as possible,' she remarked. 'To go on playing the maiden like this – I'm ashamed to see you!'

She wrote instantly to Stephen Reynard: 'I wash my hands of the whole matter as between you two; though I should advise you to *openly* join each other as soon as you can – if you wish to avoid scandal.'

He came, though not till the promised title had been granted, and he could call Betty archly 'My Lady.'

People said in after years that she and her husband were very happy. However that may be, they had a numerous family; and she became in due course first Countess of Wessex, as he had foretold.

The little white frock in which she had been married to him at the tender age of twelve was carefully preserved among the relics at King's-Hintock Court, where it may still be seen by the curious – a yellowing, pathetic testimony to the small count taken of the happiness of an innocent child in the social strategy of those days, which might have led, but providentially did not lead, to great unhappiness.[54]

When the Earl died Betty wrote him an epitaph, in which she described him as the best of husbands, fathers, and friends, and called herself his disconsolate widow.

Such is woman; or rather (not to give offence by so sweeping an assertion), such was Betty Dornell.

It was at a meeting of one of the Wessex Field and Antiquarian Clubs[55] that the foregoing story, partly told, partly read from a manuscript, was made to do duty for the regulation papers on deformed butterflies, fossil ox-horns, prehistoric dung-mixens, and such like, that usually occupied the more serious attention of the members.

This Club was of an inclusive and intersocial character; to a degree, indeed, remarkable for the part of England in which it had its being – dear, delightful Wessex, whose statuesque dynasties are even now only just beginning to feel the shaking of the new and strange spirit without, like that which entered the lonely valley of Ezekiel's vision and made the dry bones move:[56] where the honest squires, tradesmen, parsons, clerks, and people still praise the Lord with one voice for His best of all possible worlds.[57]

The present meeting, which was to extend over two days, had opened its proceedings at the museum of the town whose buildings and environs were to be visited by the members. Lunch had ended, and the afternoon excursion had been about to be undertaken, when the rain came down in an obstinate spatter, which revealed no sign of cessation. As the members waited they grew chilly, although it was only autumn, and a fire was lighted, which threw a cheerful shine upon the varnished skulls, urns, penates, tesseræ, costumes, coats of mail, weapons, and missals, animated the fossilized ichthyosaurus and iguanodon; while the dead eyes of the stuffed birds – those never-absent familiars in such collections, though murdered to extinction out of doors – flashed as they had flashed to the rising sun above

the neighbouring moors on the fatal morning when the trigger
was pulled which ended their little flight. It was then that the
historian produced his manuscript, which he had prepared, he
said, with a view to publication. His delivery of the story having
concluded as aforesaid, the speaker expressed his hope that the
constraint of the weather, and the paucity of more scientific
papers, would excuse any inappropriateness in his subject.

Several members observed that a storm-bound club could not
presume to be selective, and they were all very much obliged to
him for such a curious chapter from the domestic histories of
the county.

The President looked gloomily from the window at the
descending rain, and broke a short silence by saying that though
the Club had met, there seemed little probability of its being
able to visit the objects of interest set down among the *agenda*.

The Treasurer observed that they had at least a roof over their
heads; and they had also a second day before them.

A sentimental member, leaning back in his chair, declared
that he was in no hurry to go out, and that nothing would
please him so much as another county story, with or without
manuscript.

The Colonel added that the subject should be a lady, like
the former, to which a gentleman known as the Spark said
'Hear, hear!'

Though these had spoken in jest, a rural dean who was present
observed blandly that there was no lack of materials. Many,
indeed, were the legends and traditions of gentle and noble
dames, renowned in times past in that part of England, whose
actions and passions were now, but for men's memories, buried
under the brief inscription on a tomb or an entry of dates in a
dry pedigree.

Another member, an old surgeon, a somewhat grim though
sociable personage, was quite of the speaker's opinion, and
felt quite sure that the memory of the reverend gentleman
must abound with such curious tales of fair dames, of their loves
and hates, their joys and their misfortunes, their beauty and
their fate.

The parson, a trifle confused, retorted that their friend the surgeon, the son of a surgeon, seemed to him, as a man who had seen much and heard more during the long course of his own and his father's practice, the member of all others most likely to be acquainted with such lore.

The bookworm, the Colonel, the historian, the Vice-president, the churchwarden, the two curates, the gentleman-tradesman, the sentimental member, the crimson maltster, the quiet gentleman, the man of family, the Spark, and several others, quite agreed, and begged that he would recall something of the kind. The old surgeon said that, though a meeting of the Mid-Wessex Field and Antiquarian Club was the last place at which he should have expected to be called upon in this way, he had no objection; and the parson said he would come next. The surgeon then reflected, and decided to relate the history of a lady named Barbara, who lived towards the end of the last century, apologizing for his tale as being perhaps a little too professional. The crimson maltster winked to the Spark at hearing the nature of the apology, and the surgeon began.

# BARBARA OF THE
# HOUSE OF GREBE

By the Old Surgeon.

It was apparently an idea, rather than a passion, that inspired
Lord Uplandtowers'[1] resolve to win her. Nobody ever knew
when he formed it, or whence he got his assurance of success in
the face of her manifest dislike of him. Possibly not until after
that first important act of her life which I shall presently mention. His matured and cynical doggedness at the age of nineteen,
when impulse mostly rules calculation, was remarkable, and
might have owed its existence as much to his succession to the
earldom and its accompanying local honours in childhood, as
to the family character; an elevation which jerked him into
maturity, so to speak, without his having known adolescence.
He had only reached his twelfth year when his father, the fourth
Earl, died, after a course of the Bath waters.

Nevertheless, the family character had a great deal to do
with it. Determination was hereditary in the bearers of that
escutcheon; sometimes for good, sometimes for evil.

The seats of the two families were about ten miles apart,
the way between them lying along the now old, then new,
turnpike-road connecting Havenpool and Warborne with the
city of Melchester:[2] a road which, though only a branch from
what was known as the Great Western Highway, is probably,
even at present, as it has been for the last hundred years, one of
the finest examples of a macadamized turnpike-track that can
be found in England.

The mansion of the Earl, as well as that of his neighbour,
Barbara's father, stood back about a mile from the highway,

with which each was connected by an ordinary drive and lodge. It was along this particular highway that the young Earl drove on a certain evening at Christmastide some twenty years before the end of the last century, to attend a ball at Chene Manor,[3] the home of Barbara, and her parents Sir John and Lady Grebe. Sir John's was a baronetcy created a few years before the breaking out of the Civil War, and his lands were even more extensive than those of Lord Uplandtowers himself, comprising this Manor of Chene, another on the coast near, half the Hundred of Cockdene,[4] and well-enclosed lands in several other parishes, notably Warborne and those contiguous. At this time Barbara was barely seventeen, and the ball is the first occasion on which we have any tradition of Lord Uplandtowers attempting tender relations with her; it was early enough, God knows.

An intimate friend – one of the Drenkhards[5] – is said to have dined with him that day, and Lord Uplandtowers had, for a wonder, communicated to his guest the secret design of his heart.

'You'll never get her – sure; you'll never get her!' this friend had said at parting. 'She's not drawn to your lordship by love: and as for thought of a good match, why, there's no more calculation in her than in a bird.'

'We'll see,' said Lord Uplandtowers impassively.

He no doubt thought of his friend's forecast as he travelled along the highway in his chariot; but the sculptural repose of his profile against the vanishing daylight on his right hand would have shown his friend that the Earl's equanimity was undisturbed. He reached the solitary wayside tavern called Lornton Inn[6] – the rendezvous of many a daring poacher for operations in the adjoining forest; and he might have observed, if he had taken the trouble, a strange post-chaise standing in the halting-space before the inn. He duly sped past it, and half-an-hour after through the little town of Warborne. Onward, a mile farther, was the house of his entertainer.

At this date it was an imposing edifice – or, rather, congeries of edifices – as extensive as the residence of the Earl himself, though far less regular. One wing showed extreme antiquity, having huge chimneys, whose substructures projected from the external walls like towers; and a kitchen of vast dimensions, in which (it was said) breakfasts had been cooked for John of Gaunt. Whilst he was yet in the forecourt he could hear the rhythm of French horns and clarionets, the favourite instruments of those days at such entertainments.[7]

Entering the long parlour, in which the dance had just been opened by Lady Grebe with a minuet – it being now seven o'clock, according to the tradition – he was received with a welcome befitting his rank, and looked round for Barbara. She was not dancing, and seemed to be preoccupied – almost, indeed, as though she had been waiting for him. Barbara at this time was a good and pretty girl, who never spoke ill of any one, and hated other pretty women the very least possible. She did not refuse him for the country-dance which followed, and soon after was his partner in a second.

The evening wore on, and the horns and clarionets tootled merrily. Barbara evinced towards her lover neither distinct preference nor aversion; but old eyes would have seen that she pondered something. However, after supper she pleaded a headache, and disappeared. To pass the time of her absence, Lord Uplandtowers went into a little room adjoining the long gallery, where some elderly ones were sitting by the fire – for he had a phlegmatic dislike of dancing for its own sake, – and, lifting the window-curtains, he looked out of the window into the park and wood, dark now as a cavern. Some of the guests appeared to be leaving even so soon as this, two lights showing themselves as turning away from the door and sinking to nothing in the distance.

His hostess put her head into the room to look for partners for the ladies, and Lord Uplandtowers came out. Lady Grebe informed him that Barbara had not returned to the ball-room: she had gone to bed in sheer necessity.

'She has been so excited over the ball all day,' her mother continued, 'that I feared she would be worn out early ... But sure, Lord Uplandtowers, you won't be leaving yet?'

He said that it was near twelve o'clock, and that some had already left.

'I protest nobody has gone yet,' said Lady Grebe.

To humour her he stayed till midnight, and then set out. He had made no progress in his suit; but he had assured himself that Barbara gave no other guest the preference, and nearly everybody in the neighbourhood was there.

''Tis only a matter of time,' said the calm young philosopher.

The next morning he lay till near ten o'clock, and he had only just come out upon the head of the staircase when he heard hoofs upon the gravel without; in a few moments the door had been opened, and Sir John Grebe met him in the hall, as he set foot on the lowest stair.

'My lord – where's Barbara – my daughter?'

Even the Earl of Uplandtowers could not repress amazement. 'What's the matter, my dear Sir John,' says he.

The news was startling, indeed. From the Baronet's disjointed explanation Lord Uplandtowers gathered that after his own and the other guests' departure Sir John and Lady Grebe had gone to rest without seeing any more of Barbara; it being understood by them that she had retired to bed when she sent word to say that she could not join the dancers again. Before then she had told her maid that she would dispense with her services for this night; and there was evidence to show that the young lady had never lain down at all, the bed remaining unpressed. Circumstances seemed to prove that the deceitful girl had feigned indisposition to get an excuse for leaving the ball-room, and that she had left the house within ten minutes, presumably during the first dance after supper.

'I saw her go,' said Lord Uplandtowers.

'The devil[8] you did!' says Sir John.

'Yes.' And he mentioned the retreating carriage-lights, and how he was assured by Lady Grebe that no guest had departed.

'Surely that was it!' said the father. 'But she's not gone alone, d'ye know!'

'Ah – who is the young man?'

'I can on'y guess. My worst fear is my most likely guess. I'll say no more. I thought – yet I would not believe – it possible that you was the sinner. Would that you had been! But 'tis t'other, 'tis t'other, by G—! I must e'en up, and after 'em!'

'Whom do you suspect?'

Sir John would not give a name, and, stultified rather than agitated, Lord Uplandtowers accompanied him back to Chene. He again asked upon whom were the Baronet's suspicions directed; and the impulsive Sir John was no match for the insistence of Uplandtowers.

He said at length, 'I fear 'tis Edmond Willowes.'

'Who's he?'

'A young fellow of Shottsford-Forum⁹ – a widow-woman's son,' the other told him, and explained that Willowes's father, or grandfather, was the last of the old glass-painters in that place, where (as you may know) the art lingered on when it had died out in every other part of England.

'By G— that's bad – mighty bad!' said Lord Uplandtowers, throwing himself back in the chaise in frigid despair.

They despatched emissaries in all directions; one by the Melchester Road, another by Shottsford-Forum, another coastwards.

But the lovers had a ten-hours' start; and it was apparent that sound judgment had been exercised in choosing as their time of flight the particular night when the movements of a strange carriage would not be noticed, either in the park or on the neighbouring highway, owing to the general press of vehicles. The chaise which had been seen waiting at Lornton Inn was, no doubt, the one they had escaped in; and the pair of heads which had planned so cleverly thus far had probably contrived marriage ere now.

The fears of her parents were realized. A letter sent by special messenger from Barbara, on the evening of that day, briefly informed them that her lover and herself were on the way to London, and before this communication reached her home they would be united as husband and wife. She had taken this extreme step because she loved her dear Edmond as she could love no other man, and because she had seen closing round her the doom of marriage with Lord Uplandtowers, unless she put that threatened fate out of possibility by doing as she had done. She had well considered the step beforehand, and was prepared to live like any other country-townsman's wife if her father repudiated her for her action.

'D— her!' said Lord Uplandtowers, as he drove homeward that night. 'D— her for a fool!' – which shows the kind of love he bore her.

Well; Sir John had already started in pursuit of them as a matter of duty, driving like a wild man to Melchester, and thence by the direct highway to the capital. But he soon saw that he was acting to no purpose; and by and by, discovering that the marriage had actually taken place, he forebore all attempts to unearth them in the City, and returned and sat down with his lady to digest the event as best they could.

To proceed against this Willowes for the abduction of our heiress was, possibly, in their power; yet, when they considered the now unalterable facts, they refrained from violent retribution. Some six weeks[10] passed, during which time Barbara's parents, though they keenly felt her loss, held no communication with the truant, either for reproach or condonation. They continued to think of the disgrace she had brought upon herself; for, though the young man was an honest fellow, and the son of an honest father, the latter had died so early, and his widow had had such struggles to maintain herself, that the son was very imperfectly educated. Moreover, his blood was, as far as they knew, of no distinction whatever, whilst hers, through her mother, was compounded of the best juices of ancient baronial distillation, containing tinctures of Maundeville, and Mohun, and Syward, and Peverell, and Culliford, and Talbot, and Plantagenet, and York, and Lancaster,[11] and God knows what besides, which it was a thousand pities to throw away.

The father and mother sat by the fireplace that was spanned by the four-centred arch bearing the family shields on its haunches, and groaned aloud – the lady more than Sir John.

'To think this should have come upon us in our old age!' said he.

'Speak for yourself!' she snapped through her sobs. 'I am only one-and-forty! . . . Why didn't ye ride faster and overtake 'em!'

In the meantime the young married lovers, caring no more about their blood than about ditch-water, were intensely happy – happy, that is, in the descending scale which, as we all know, Heaven in its wisdom has ordained for such rash cases; that is to say, the first week they were in the seventh heaven, the second in the sixth, the third week temperate, the fourth reflective, and so on; a lover's heart after possession being comparable to the earth in its geologic stages, as described to us sometimes by our worthy President; first a hot coal, then a warm one, then a cooling cinder, then chilly – the simile shall be pursued no further. The long and the short of it was that one day a letter, sealed with their daughter's own little seal, came into Sir John and Lady Grebe's hands; and, on opening it, they found it to contain an appeal from the young couple to Sir John to forgive them for what they had done, and they would fall on their naked knees and be most dutiful children for evermore.

Then Sir John and his lady sat down again by the fireplace with the four-centred arch, and consulted, and re-read the letter. Sir John Grebe, if the truth must be told, loved his daughter's happiness far more, poor man, than he loved his name and lineage; he recalled to his mind all her little ways, gave vent to a sigh; and, by this time acclimatized to the idea of the marriage, said that what was done could not be undone, and that he supposed they must not be too harsh with her. Perhaps Barbara and her husband were in actual need; and how could they let their only child starve?

A slight consolation had come to them in an unexpected manner. They had been credibly informed that an ancestor of plebeian Willowes was once honoured with intermarriage with a scion of the aristocracy who had gone to the dogs. In short, such is the foolishness of distinguished parents, and sometimes of others also, that they wrote that very day to the address Barbara had given them, informing her that she might return home and bring her husband with her; they would not object to see him, would not reproach her, and would endeavour to welcome both, and to discuss with them what could best be arranged for their future.

In three or four days a rather shabby post-chaise drew up at the door of Chene Manor-house, at sound of which the tender-hearted baronet and his wife ran out as if to welcome a prince and princess of the blood. They were overjoyed to see their spoilt child return safe and sound – though she was only

Mrs Willowes, wife of Edmond Willowes of nowhere. Barbara burst into penitential tears, and both husband and wife were contrite enough, as well they might be, considering that they had not a guinea to call their own.

When the four had calmed themselves, and not a word of chiding had been uttered to the pair, they discussed the position soberly, young Willowes sitting in the background with great modesty till invited forward by Lady Grebe in no frigid tone.

'How handsome he is!' she said to herself. 'I don't wonder at Barbara's craze for him.'

He was, indeed, one of the handsomest men who ever set his lips on a maid's. A blue coat, murrey waistcoat, and breeches of drab set off a figure that could scarcely be surpassed. He had large dark eyes, anxious now, as they glanced from Barbara to her parents and tenderly back again to her; observing whom, even now in her trepidation, one could see why the *sang froid* of Lord Uplandtowers had been raised to more than luke-warmness. Her fair young face (according to the tale handed down by old women) looked out from under a grey conical hat, trimmed with white ostrich-feathers, and her little toes peeped from a buff petticoat worn under a puce gown.[12] Her features were not regular: they were almost infantine, as you may see from miniatures in possession of the family, her mouth showing much sensitiveness, and one could be sure that her faults would not lie on the side of bad temper unless for urgent reasons.

Well, they discussed their state as became them, and the desire of the young couple to gain the goodwill of those upon whom they were literally dependent for everything induced them to agree to any temporizing measure that was not too irksome. Therefore, having been nearly two months united, they did not oppose Sir John's proposal that he should furnish Edmond Willowes with funds sufficient for him to travel a year on the Continent in the company of a tutor, the young man undertaking to lend himself with the utmost diligence to the tutor's instructions, till he became polished outwardly and inwardly to the degree required in the husband of such a lady as Barbara. He was to apply himself to the study of languages, manners, history, society, ruins, and everything else that came under his eyes, till he should return to take his place without blushing by Barbara's side.

'And by that time,' said worthy Sir John, 'I'll get my little place out at Yewsholt[13] ready for you and Barbara to occupy on your return. The house is small and out of the way; but it will do for a young couple for a while.'

'If 'twere no bigger than a summer-house it would do!' says Barbara.

'If 'twere no bigger than a sedan-chair!'[14] says Willowes. 'And the more lonely the better.'

'We can put up with the loneliness,' said Barbara, with less zest. 'Some friends will come, no doubt.'

All this being laid down, a travelled tutor was called in – a man of many gifts and great experience, – and on a fine morning away tutor and pupil went. A great reason urged against Barbara accompanying her youthful husband was that his attentions to her would naturally be such as to prevent his zealously applying every hour of his time to learning and seeing – an argument of wise prescience, and unanswerable. Regular days for letter-writing were fixed, Barbara and her Edmond exchanged their last kisses at the door, and the chaise swept under the archway into the drive.

He wrote to her from Le Havre, as soon as he reached that port, which was not for seven days, on account of adverse winds; he wrote from Rouen, and from Paris; described to her his sight of the King and Court at Versailles, and the wonderful marble-work and mirrors in that palace; wrote next from Lyons; then, after a comparatively long interval, from Turin, narrating his fearful adventures in crossing Mont Cenis on mules, and how he was overtaken with a terrific snowstorm, which had well-nigh been the end of him, and his tutor, and his guides. Then he wrote glowingly of Italy; and Barbara could see the development of her husband's mind reflected in his letters month by month; and she much admired the forethought of her father in suggesting this education for Edmond. Yet she sighed some-times – her husband being no longer in evidence to fortify her in her choice of him – and timidly dreaded what mortifications might be in store for her by reason of this *mésalliance*. She went out very little; for on the one or two occasions on which she had shown herself to former friends she noticed a distinct difference in their manner, as though they should say, 'Ah, my happy swain's wife; you're caught!'

Edmond's letters were as affectionate as ever; even more affectionate, after a while, than hers were to him. Barbara observed this growing coolness in herself; and like a good and honest lady was horrified and grieved, since her only wish was to act faithfully and uprightly. It troubled her so much that she prayed for a warmer heart, and at last wrote to her husband to beg him, now that he was in the land of Art, to send her his portrait, ever so small, that she might look at it all day and every day, and never for a moment forget his features.

Willowes was nothing loth, and replied that he would do more than she wished: he had made friends with a sculptor in Pisa,[15] who was much interested in him and his history; and he had commissioned this artist to make a bust of himself in marble, which when finished he would send her. What Barbara had wanted was something immediate; but she expressed no objection to the delay; and in his next communication Edmond told her that the sculptor, of his own choice, had decided to increase the bust to a full-length statue, so anxious was he to get a specimen of his skill introduced to the notice of the English aristocracy. It was progressing well, and rapidly.

Meanwhile, Barbara's attention began to be occupied at home with Yewsholt Lodge, the house that her kind-hearted father was preparing for her residence when her husband returned. It was a small place on the plan of a large one – a cottage built in the form of a mansion, having a central hall with a wooden gallery running round it, and rooms no bigger than closets to follow this introduction. It stood on a slope so solitary, and surrounded by trees so dense, that the birds who inhabited the boughs sang at strange hours, as if they hardly could distinguish night from day.

During the progress of repairs at this bower Barbara frequently visited it. Though so secluded by the dense growth, it was near the high road, and one day while looking over the fence she saw Lord Uplandtowers riding past. He saluted her courteously, yet with mechanical stiffness, and did not halt. Barbara went home, and continued to pray that she might never cease to love her husband. After that she sickened, and did not come out of doors again for a long time.

The year of education had extended to fourteen months, and the house was in order for Edmond's return to take up his abode there with Barbara, when, instead of the accustomed letter for her, came one to Sir John Grebe in the handwriting of the said tutor, informing him of a terrible catastrophe that had occurred to them at Venice. Mr Willowes and himself had attended the theatre one night during the Carnival[16] of the preceding week, to witness the Italian comedy,[17] when, owing to the carelessness of one of the candle-snuffers, the theatre had caught fire, and been burnt to the ground. Few persons had lost their lives, owing to the superhuman exertions of some of the audience in getting out the senseless sufferers; and, among them all, he who had risked his own life the most heroically was Mr Willowes. In re-entering for the fifth time to save his fellow-creatures some fiery beams had fallen upon him, and he had been given up for lost. He was, however, by the blessing of Providence, recovered, with the life still in him, though he was fearfully burnt; and by almost a miracle he seemed likely to survive, his constitution being wondrously sound. He was, of course, unable to write, but he was receiving the attention of several skilful surgeons. Further report would be made by the next mail or by private hand.

The tutor said nothing in detail of poor Willowes's sufferings, but as soon as the news was broken to Barbara she realized how intense they must have been, and her immediate instinct was to rush to his side, though, on consideration, the journey seemed impossible to her. Her health was by no means what it had been, and to post across Europe at that season of the year, or to traverse the Bay of Biscay in a sailing-craft, was an undertaking that would hardly be justified by the result. But she was anxious to go till, on reading to the end of the letter, her husband's tutor was found to hint very strongly against such a step if it should be contemplated, this being also the opinion of the surgeons. And though Willowes's comrade refrained from giving his reasons, they disclosed themselves plainly enough in the sequel.

The truth was that the worst of the wounds resulting from the fire had occurred to his head and face – that handsome face which had won her heart from her, – and both the tutor and the surgeons knew that for a sensitive young woman to see him before his wounds had healed would cause more misery to her by the shock than happiness to him by her ministrations.

Lady Grebe blurted out what Sir John and Barbara had thought, but had had too much delicacy to express.

'Sure, 'tis mighty hard for you, poor Barbara, that the one little gift he had to justify your rash choice of him – his wonderful good looks – should be taken away like this, to leave 'ee no excuse at all for your conduct in the world's eyes ... Well, I wish you'd married t'other – that do I!' And the lady sighed.

'He'll soon get right again,' said her father soothingly.

Such remarks as the above were not often made; but they were frequent enough to cause Barbara an uneasy sense of self-stultification. She determined to hear them no longer; and the house at Yewsholt being ready and furnished, she withdrew thither with her maids, where for the first time she could feel mistress of a home that would be hers and her husband's exclusively, when he came.

After long weeks[18] Willowes had recovered sufficiently to be able to write himself, and slowly and tenderly he enlightened her upon the full extent of his injuries. It was a mercy, he said, that he had not lost his sight entirely; but he was thankful to say that he still retained full vision in one eye, though the other was dark for ever. The sparing manner in which he meted out particulars of his condition told Barbara how appalling had been his experience. He was grateful for her assurance that nothing could change her; but feared she did not fully realize that he was so sadly disfigured as to make it doubtful if she would recognize him. However, in spite of all, his heart was as true to her as it ever had been.

Barbara saw from his anxiety how much lay behind. She replied that she submitted to the decrees of Fate, and would welcome him in any shape as soon as he could come. She told him of the pretty retreat in which she had taken up her abode, pending their joint occupation of it, and did not reveal how much she had sighed over the information that all his good looks were gone. Still less did she say that she felt a certain strangeness in awaiting him, the weeks they had lived together having been so short by comparison with the length of his absence.

Slowly drew on the time when Willowes found himself well enough to come home. He landed at Southampton, and posted thence towards Yewsholt. Barbara arranged to go out to meet him as far as Lornton Inn – the spot between the Forest and the Chase at which he had waited for night on the evening of their elopement. Thither she drove at the appointed hour in a little pony-chaise, presented her by her father on her birthday for her especial use in her new house; which vehicle she sent back on arriving at the inn, the plan agreed upon being that she should perform the return journey with her husband in his hired coach.

There was not much accommodation for a lady at this wayside tavern; but, as it was a fine evening in early summer, she did not mind – walking about outside, and straining her eyes along the highway for the expected one. But each cloud of dust that enlarged in the distance and drew near was found to disclose a conveyance other than his post-chaise. Barbara remained till the appointment was two hours passed, and then began to fear that owing to some adverse wind in the Channel he was not coming that night.

While waiting she was conscious of a curious trepidation that was not entirely solicitude, and did not amount to dread; her tense state of incertitude bordered both on disappointment and on relief. She had lived six or seven weeks with an imperfectly educated yet handsome husband whom now she had not seen for seventeen months, and who was so changed physically by an accident that she was assured she would hardly know him. Can we wonder at her compound state of mind?

But her immediate difficulty was to get away from Lornton Inn, for her situation was becoming embarrassing. Like too many of Barbara's actions, this drive had been undertaken without much reflection. Expecting to wait no more than a few minutes for her husband in his post-chaise, and to enter it with him, she had not hesitated to isolate herself by sending back her own little vehicle. She now found that, being so well known in this neighbourhood, her excursion to meet her long-absent husband was exciting great interest. She was conscious that more eyes were watching her from the inn-windows than met her own gaze. Barbara had decided to get home by hiring whatever kind of conveyance the tavern afforded, when, straining her eyes for the last time over the now darkening highway, she perceived yet another dust-cloud drawing near. She paused; a chariot ascended to the inn, and would have passed had not its occupant caught sight of her standing expectantly. The horses were checked on the instant.

'You here – and alone, my dear Mrs Willowes?' said Lord Uplandtowers, whose carriage it was.

She explained what had brought her into this lonely situation; and, as he was going in the direction of her own home, she accepted his offer of a seat beside him. Their conversation was embarrassed and fragmentary at first; but when they had driven a mile or two she was surprised to find herself talking earnestly and warmly to him: her impulsiveness was in truth but the natural consequence of her late existence – a somewhat desolate one by reason of the strange marriage she had made; and there is no more indiscreet mood than that of a woman surprised into talk who has long been imposing upon herself a policy of reserve. Therefore her ingenuous heart rose with a bound into her throat when, in response to his leading questions, or rather hints, she allowed her troubles to leak out of her. Lord Uplandtowers took her quite to her own door, although he had driven three miles out of his way to do so; and in handing her down she heard from him a whisper of stern reproach: 'It need not have been thus if you had listened to me!'

She made no reply, and went indoors. There, as the evening wore away, she regretted more and more that she had been so friendly with Lord Uplandtowers. But he had launched himself upon her so unexpectedly: if she had only foreseen the meeting with him, what a careful line of conduct she would have marked out! Barbara broke into a perspiration of disquiet when she thought of her unreserve, and, in self-chastisement, resolved to sit up till midnight on the bare chance of Edmond's return; directing that supper should be laid for him, improbable as his arrival till the morrow was.

The hours went past, and there was dead silence in and round about Yewsholt Lodge, except for the soughing of the trees; till, when it was near upon midnight, she heard the noise of hoofs and wheels approaching the door. Knowing that it could only be her husband, Barbara instantly went into the hall to meet him. Yet she stood there not without a sensation of faintness, so many were the changes since their parting! And, owing to her casual encounter with Lord Uplandtowers, his voice and image still remained with her, excluding Edmond, her husband, from the inner circle of her impressions.

But she went to the door, and the next moment a figure stepped inside, of which she knew the outline, but little besides. Her husband was attired in a flapping black cloak and slouched hat, appearing altogether as a foreigner, and not as the young English burgess who had left her side. When he came forward into the light of the lamp, she perceived with surprise, and almost with fright, that he wore a mask. At first she had not noticed this – there being nothing in its colour which would lead a casual observer to think he was looking on anything but a real countenance.

He must have seen her start of dismay at the unexpectedness of his appearance, for he said hastily: 'I did not mean to come in to you like this – I thought you would have been in bed. How good you are, dear Barbara!' He put his arm round her, but he did not attempt to kiss her.

'O Edmond – it *is* you? – it must be?' she said, with clasped hands, for though his figure and movement were almost enough to prove it, and the tones were not unlike the old tones, the enunciation was so altered as to seem that of a stranger.

'I am covered like this to hide myself from the curious eyes of the inn-servants and others,' he said, in a low voice. 'I will send back the carriage and join you in a moment.'

'You are quite alone?'

'Quite. My companion stopped at Southampton.'

The wheels of the post-chaise rolled away as she entered the dining-room, where the supper was spread; and presently he rejoined her there. He had removed his cloak and hat, but the mask was still retained; and she could now see that it was of special make, of some flexible material like silk, coloured so as to represent flesh; it joined naturally to the front hair, and was otherwise cleverly executed.

'Barbara – you look ill,' he said, removing his glove, and taking her hand.

'Yes – I have been ill,' said she.

'Is this pretty little house ours?'

'O – yes.' She was hardly conscious of her words, for the hand he had ungloved in order to take hers was contorted, and had one or two of its fingers missing; while through the mask she discerned the twinkle of one eye only.

'I would give anything to kiss you, dearest, now, at this moment!' he continued, with mournful passionateness. 'But I cannot – in this guise. The servants are abed, I suppose?'

'Yes,' said she. 'But I can call them? You will have some supper?'

He said he would have some, but that it was not necessary to call anybody at that hour. Thereupon they approached the table, and sat down, facing each other.

Despite Barbara's scared state of mind, it was forced upon her notice that her husband trembled, as if he feared the impression he was producing, or was about to produce, as much as, or more than, she. He drew nearer, and took her hand again.

'I had this mask made at Venice,' he began, in evident embarrassment. 'My darling Barbara – my dearest wife – do you think you – will mind when I take it off? You will not dislike me – will you?'

'O Edmond, of course I shall not mind,' said she. 'What has happened to you is our misfortune; but I am prepared for it.'

'Are you sure you are prepared?'

'O yes! You are my husband.'

'You really feel quite confident that nothing external can affect you?' he said again, in a voice rendered uncertain by his agitation.

'I think I am – quite,' she answered faintly.

He bent his head. 'I hope, I hope you are,' he whispered.

In the pause which followed, the ticking of the clock in the hall seemed to grow loud; and he turned a little aside to remove the mask. She breathlessly awaited the operation, which was one of some tediousness, watching him one moment, averting her face the next; and when it was done she shut her eyes at the hideous spectacle that was revealed. A quick spasm of horror had passed through her; but though she quailed she forced herself to regard him anew, repressing the cry that would naturally have escaped from her ashy lips. Unable to look at him longer, Barbara sank down on the floor beside her chair, covering her eyes.

'You cannot look at me!' he groaned in a hopeless way. 'I am too terrible an object even for you to bear! I knew it; yet I hoped against it. Oh, this is a bitter fate – curse the skill of those Venetian surgeons who saved me alive! ... Look up, Barbara,' he continued beseechingly; 'view me completely; say you loathe me, if you do loathe me, and settle the case between us for ever!'

His unhappy wife pulled herself together for a desperate strain. He was her Edmond; he had done her no wrong; he had suffered. A momentary devotion to him helped her, and lifting her eyes as bidden she regarded this human remnant, this écorché, a second time. But the sight was too much. She again involuntarily looked aside and shuddered.[19]

'Do you think you can get used to this?' he said. 'Yes or no! Can you bear such a thing of the charnel-house near you? Judge for yourself, Barbara. Your Adonis,[20] your matchless man, has come to this!'

The poor lady stood beside him motionless, save for the restlessness of her eyes. All her natural sentiments of affection and pity were driven clean out of her by a sort of panic; she had just the same sense of dismay and fearfulness that she would have had in the presence of an apparition. She could nohow fancy this to be her chosen one – the man she had loved; he was metamorphosed to a specimen of another species. 'I do not loathe[21] you,' she said with trembling. 'But I am so horrified – so overcome! Let me recover myself. Will you sup now? And while you do so may I go to my room to – regain my old feeling for you? I will try, if I may leave you awhile? Yes, I will try!'

Without waiting for an answer from him, and keeping her gaze carefully averted, the frightened woman crept to the door and out of the room. She heard him sit down to the table, as if to begin supper; though, Heaven knows, his appetite was slight enough after a reception which had confirmed his worst surmises. When Barbara had ascended the stairs and arrived in her chamber she sank down, and buried her face in the coverlet of the bed.

Thus she remained for some time. The bed-chamber was over the dining-room, and presently as she knelt Barbara heard Willowes thrust back his chair, and rise to go into the hall. In five minutes that figure would probably come up the stairs and confront her again; it, – this new and terrible form,[22] that was not her husband's. In the loneliness of this night, with neither maid nor friend beside her, she lost all self-control, and at the first sound of his footstep on the stairs, without so much as flinging a cloak round her, she flew from the room, ran along the gallery to the back staircase, which she descended, and, unlocking the back door, let herself out. She scarcely was aware what she had done till she found herself in the greenhouse, crouching on a flower-stand.

Here she remained, her great timid eyes strained through the glass upon the garden without, and her skirts gathered up, in fear of the field-mice which sometimes came there. Every moment she dreaded to hear footsteps which she ought by law to have longed for, and a voice that should have been as music to her soul. But Edmond Willowes came not that way. The nights were getting short at this season, and soon the dawn appeared, and the first rays of the sun. By daylight she had less fear than in the dark. She thought she could meet him, and accustom herself to the spectacle.

So the much-tried young woman unfastened the door of the hot-house, and went back by the way she had emerged a few hours ago. Her poor husband[23] was probably in bed and asleep, his journey having been long; and she made as little noise as possible in her entry. The house was just as she had left it, and she looked about in the hall for his cloak and hat, but she could not see them; nor did she perceive the small trunk which had been all that he brought with him, his heavier baggage having been left at Southampton for the road-waggon. She summoned courage to mount the stairs; the bedroom-door was open as she had left it. She fearfully peeped round; the bed had not been pressed. Perhaps he had lain down on the dining-room sofa. She descended and entered; he was not there. On the table beside his unsoiled plate lay a note, hastily written on the leaf of a pocket-book. It was something like this:[24]

'MY EVER-BELOVED WIFE – The effect that my forbidding[25] appearance has produced upon you was one which I foresaw as quite possible. I hoped against it, but foolishly so. I was aware that no *human* love could survive such a catastrophe. I confess I thought yours *divine*; but, after so long an absence, there could not be left sufficient warmth to overcome the too natural first aversion. It was an experiment, and it has failed. I do not blame you; perhaps, even, it is better so. Goodbye. I leave England for one year. You will see me again[26] at the expiration of that time, if I live. Then I will ascertain your true feeling; and, if it be against me, go away for ever.

E. W.'

On recovering from her surprise, Barbara's remorse was such that she felt herself absolutely unforgiveable. She should have regarded him as an afflicted being, and not have been this slave to mere eyesight, like a child. To follow him and entreat him to return was her first thought. But on making inquiries she found that nobody had seen him: he had silently disappeared.

More than this, to undo the scene of last night was impossible. Her terror had been too plain, and he was a man unlikely to be coaxed back by her efforts to do her duty. She went and confessed to her parents all that had occurred; which, indeed, soon became known to more persons than those of her own family.

The year passed, and he did not return; and it was doubted[27] if he were alive. Barbara's contrition for her unconquerable repugnance was now such that she longed to build a church-aisle, or erect a monument, and devote herself to deeds of charity for the remainder of her days. To that end she made inquiry of the excellent parson under whom she sat on Sundays, at a vertical distance of twenty feet. But he could only adjust his wig and tap his snuff-box; for such was the lukewarm state of religion in those days, that not an aisle, steeple, porch, east window, Ten-Commandment board, lion-and-unicorn, or brass candlestick, was required anywhere at all in the neighbourhood as a votive offering from a distracted soul – the last century contrasting greatly in this respect with the happy times in which we live, when urgent appeals for contributions to such objects pour in by every morning's post, and nearly all churches have been made to look like new pennies.[28] As the poor lady could not ease her conscience this way, she determined at least to be charitable, and soon had the satisfaction of finding her porch thronged every morning by the raggedest, idlest, most drunken, hypocritical, and worthless tramps in Christendom.

But human hearts are as prone to change as the leaves of the creeper on the wall, and in the course of time, hearing nothing of her husband, Barbara could sit unmoved whilst her mother and friends said in her hearing, 'Well, what has happened is for the best.' She began to think so herself, for even now she could not summon up that lopped and mutilated form[29] without a shiver, though whenever her mind flew back to her early wedded days, and the man who had stood beside her then, a thrill of tenderness moved her, which if quickened by his living presence might have become strong. She was young and inexperienced, and had hardly on his late return grown out of the capricious fancies of girlhood.

But he did not come again, and when she thought of his word that he would return once more, if living, and how unlikely he was to break his word, she gave him up for dead. So did her parents; so also did another person – that man of silence, of irresistible incisiveness, of still countenance, who was as awake as seven sentinels[30] when he seemed to be as sound asleep as the figures on his family monument. Lord Uplandtowers, though not yet thirty, had chuckled like a caustic fogey of threescore when he heard of Barbara's terror and flight at her husband's return, and of the latter's prompt departure. He felt pretty sure, however, that Willowes, despite his hurt feelings, would have reappeared to claim his bright-eyed property if he had been alive at the end of the twelve months.

As there was no husband to live with her, Barbara had relinquished the house prepared for them by her father, and taken up her abode anew at Chene Manor, as in the days of her girlhood. By degrees the episode with Edmond Willowes seemed but a fevered dream, and as the months grew to years Lord Uplandtowers' friendship with the people at Chene – which had somewhat cooled after Barbara's elopement – revived considerably, and he again became a frequent visitor there. He could not make the most trivial alteration or improvement at Knollingwood Hall,[31] where he lived, without riding off to consult with his friend Sir John at Chene; and thus putting himself frequently under her eyes, Barbara grew accustomed to him, and talked to him as freely as to a brother. She even began to look up to him as a person of authority, judgment, and prudence; and though his severity on the bench towards poachers, smugglers, and turnip-stealers was matter of common notoriety, she trusted that much of what was said might be misrepresentation.

Thus they lived on till her husband's absence had stretched to years, and there could be no longer any doubt of his death. A passionless manner of renewing his addresses seemed no longer out of place in Lord Uplandtowers. Barbara did not love him, but hers was essentially one of those sweet-pea or with-wind natures which require a twig of stouter fibre than its own to hang upon and bloom.[32] Now, too, she was older, and admitted to herself that a man whose ancestor had run scores of Saracens through and through in fighting for the site of the Holy Sepulchre was a more desirable husband, socially[33] considered, than one who could only claim with certainty to know that his father and grandfather were respectable burgesses.

Sir John took occasion to inform her that she might legally consider herself a widow; and, in brief, Lord Uplandtowers carried his point with her, and she married him, though he could never get her to own that she loved him as she had loved Willowes. In my childhood I knew an old lady whose mother saw the wedding, and she said that when Lord and Lady Uplandtowers drove away from her father's house in the evening it was in a coach-and-four, and that my lady was dressed in green and silver, and wore the gayest hat and feather that ever were seen; though whether it was that the green did not suit her complexion, or otherwise, the Countess looked pale, and the reverse of blooming. After their marriage her husband took her to London, and she saw the gaieties of a season there; then they returned to Knollingwood Hall, and thus a year passed away.

Before their marriage her husband had seemed to care but little about her inability to love him passionately. 'Only let me win you,' he had said, 'and I will submit to all that.' But now her lack of warmth seemed to irritate him, and he conducted himself towards her with a resentfulness which led to her passing many hours with him in painful silence. The heir-presumptive to the title was a remote relative, whom Lord Uplandtowers did not exclude from the dislike he entertained towards many persons and things besides, and he had set his mind upon a lineal successor. He blamed her much that there was no promise of this,[34] and asked her what she was good for.

On a particular day in her gloomy life a letter, addressed to her as Mrs Willowes, reached Lady Uplandtowers from an unexpected quarter. A sculptor in Pisa, knowing nothing of her second marriage, informed her that the long-delayed life-size statue of Mr Willowes which, when her husband left that city, he had been directed to retain till it was sent for, was still in his studio. As his commission had not wholly been paid, and the statue was taking up room he could ill spare, he should be glad to have the debt cleared off, and directions where to forward the figure. Arriving at a time when the Countess was beginning to have little secrets (of a harmless kind, it is true) from her husband, by reason of their growing estrangement, she replied to this letter without saying a word to Lord Uplandtowers, sending off the balance that was owing to the sculptor, and telling him to despatch the statue to her without delay.

It was some weeks before it arrived at Knollingwood Hall,

and, by a singular coincidence, during the interval she received the first absolutely conclusive tidings of her Edmond's death. It had taken place years before, in a foreign land, about six months after their parting, and had been induced by the sufferings he had already undergone, coupled with much depression of spirit, which had caused him to succumb to a slight ailment. The news was sent her in a brief and formal letter from some relative of Willowes's in another part of England.

Her grief took the form of passionate[35] pity for his misfortunes, and of reproach to herself for never having been able to conquer her aversion to his latter image by recollection of what Nature had originally made him. The sad spectacle that had gone from earth had never been her Edmond at all to her. O that she could have met him as he was at first! Thus Barbara thought. It was only a few days later that a waggon with two horses, containing an immense packing-case, was seen at breakfast-time both by Barbara and her husband to drive round to the back of the house, and by and by they were informed that a case labelled 'Sculpture' had arrived for her ladyship.

'What can that be?' said Lord Uplandtowers.

'It is the statue of poor Edmond, which belongs to me, but has never been sent till now,' she answered.

'Where are you going to put it?' asked he.

'I have not decided,' said the Countess. 'Anywhere, so that it will not annoy you.'

'Oh, it won't annoy me,' says he.

When it had been unpacked in a back room of the house, they went to examine it. The statue was a full-length figure, in the purest Carrara marble, representing Edmond Willowes in all his original beauty, as he had stood at parting from her when about to set out on his travels; a specimen of manhood almost perfect in every line and contour. The work had been carried out with absolute fidelity.

'Phœbus-Apollo, sure,' said the Earl of Uplandtowers, who had never seen Willowes, real or represented, till now.

Barbara did not hear him. She was standing in a sort of trance before the first husband, as if she had no consciousness of the other husband at her side. The mutilated features of Willowes had disappeared from her mind's eye; this perfect being was really the man she had loved, and not that later pitiable figure; in whom love[36] and truth should have seen this image always, but had not done so.

It was not till Lord Uplandtowers said roughly, 'Are you going to stay here all the morning worshipping him?' that she roused herself.

Her husband had not till now the least suspicion that Edmond Willowes originally looked thus, and he thought how deep would have been his jealousy years ago if Willowes had been known to him. Returning to the Hall in the afternoon he found his wife in the gallery, whither the statue had been brought.

She was lost in reverie before it, just as in the morning.

'What are you doing?' he asked.

She started and turned. 'I am looking at my husb— my statue, to see if it is well done,' she stammered.[37] 'Why should I not?'

'There's no reason why,' he said. 'What are you going to do with the monstrous thing? It can't stand here for ever.'

'I don't wish it,' she said. 'I'll find a place.'

In her boudoir there was a deep recess, and while the Earl was absent from home for a few days in the following week, she hired joiners from the village, who under her directions enclosed the recess with a panelled door. Into the tabernacle thus formed she had the statue placed, fastening the door with a lock, the key of which she kept in her pocket.

When her husband returned he missed the statue from the gallery, and, concluding that it had been put away out of deference to his feelings, made no remark. Yet at moments he noticed something on his lady's face which he had never noticed there before. He could not construe it; it was a sort of silent ecstasy, a reserved beatification. What had become of the statue he could not divine, and growing more and more curious, looked about here and there for it till, thinking of her private room, he went towards that spot. After knocking he heard the shutting of a door, and the click of a key; but when he entered his wife was sitting at work, on what was in those days called knotting. Lord Uplandtowers' eye fell upon the newly-painted door where the recess had formerly been.

'You have been carpentering in my absence then, Barbara,' he said carelessly.

'Yes, Uplandtowers.'

'Why did you go putting up such a tasteless enclosure as that – spoiling the handsome arch of the alcove?'

'I wanted more closet-room; and I thought that as this was my own apartment—'

'Of course,' he returned. Lord Uplandtowers knew now where the statue of young Willowes was.

One night, or rather in the smallest hours of the morning, he missed the Countess from his side. Not being a man of nervous imaginings he fell asleep again before he had much considered the matter, and the next morning had forgotten the incident. But a few nights later the same circumstances occurred. This time he fully roused himself; but before he had moved to search for her, she entered the chamber in her dressing-gown, carrying a candle, which she extinguished as she approached, deeming him asleep. He could discover from her breathing that she was strangely moved; but not on this occasion either did he reveal that he had seen her. Presently, when she had lain down, affecting to wake, he asked her some trivial questions. 'Yes, *Edmond*,' she replied absently.

Lord Uplandtowers became convinced that she was in the habit of leaving the chamber in this queer way more frequently than he had observed, and he determined to watch. The next midnight he feigned deep sleep, and shortly after perceived her stealthily rise and let herself out of the room in the dark. He slipped on some clothing and followed. At the farther end of the corridor, where the clash of flint and steel would be out of the hearing of one in the bed-chamber, she struck a light. He stepped aside into an empty room till she had lit a taper and had passed on to her boudoir. In a minute or two he followed. Arrived at the door of the boudoir, he beheld the door of the private recess open, and Barbara within it, standing with her arms clasped tightly round the neck of her Edmond, and her mouth[38] on his. The shawl which she had thrown round her nightclothes had slipped from her shoulders, and her long white robe and pale face lent her the blanched appearance of a second statue embracing the first. Between her kisses, she apostrophized it in a low murmur of infantine tenderness:

'My only love – how could I be so cruel to you, my perfect one – so good and true – I am ever faithful to you, despite my seeming infidelity![39] I always think of you – dream of you – during the long hours of the day, and in the night-watches! O Edmond, I am always yours!' Such words as these, intermingled with sobs, and streaming tears, and dishevelled hair, testified to an intensity of feeling in his wife which Lord Uplandtowers had not dreamed of her possessing.

'Ha, ha!' says he to himself. 'This is where we evaporate – this is where my hopes of a successor in the title dissolve – ha, ha![40] This must be seen to, verily!'

Lord Uplandtowers was a subtle man when once he set himself to strategy; though in the present instance he never thought of the simple stratagem of constant tenderness. Nor did he enter the room and surprise his wife as a blunderer would have done, but went back to his chamber as silently as he had left it. When the Countess returned thither, shaken by spent sobs and sighs, he appeared to be soundly sleeping as usual. The next day he began his countermoves by making inquiries as to the whereabouts of the tutor who had travelled with his wife's first husband; this gentleman, he found, was now master of a grammar-school at no great distance from Knollingwood. At the first convenient moment Lord Uplandtowers went thither and obtained an interview with the said gentleman. The schoolmaster was much gratified by a visit from such an influential neighbour, and was ready to communicate anything that his lordship desired to know.

After some general conversation on the school and its progress, the visitor observed that he believed the schoolmaster had once travelled a good deal with the unfortunate Mr Willowes, and had been with him on the occasion of his accident. He, Lord Uplandtowers, was interested in knowing what had really happened at that time, and had often thought of inquiring. And then the Earl not only heard by word of mouth as much as he wished to know, but, their chat becoming more intimate, the schoolmaster drew upon paper a sketch of the disfigured head,[41] explaining with bated breath various details in the representation.

'It was very strange and terrible!' said Lord Uplandtowers, taking the sketch in his hand. 'Neither nose nor ears!'

A poor man in the town nearest to Knollingwood Hall, who combined the art of sign-painting with ingenious mechanical occupations, was sent for by Lord Uplandtowers to come to the Hall on a day in that week when the Countess had gone on a short visit to her parents. His employer made the man understand that the business in which his assistance was demanded was to be considered private, and money insured the observance of this request. The lock of the cupboard was picked, and the ingenious mechanic and painter, assisted by the schoolmaster's sketch, which Lord Uplandtowers had put in his pocket, set to work upon the god-like countenance of the statue under my lord's direction. What the fire had maimed in the original the chisel maimed in the copy. It was a fiendish disfigurement, ruthlessly carried out, and was rendered still more shocking by being tinted to the hues of life, as life had been after the wreck.[42]

Six hours after, when the workman was gone, Lord Uplandtowers looked upon the result, and smiled grimly, and said:

'A statue should represent a man as he appeared in life, and that's as he appeared. Ha! ha! But 'tis done to good purpose, and not idly.'

He locked the door of the closet with a skeleton key, and went his way to fetch the Countess home.

That night she slept, but he kept awake. According to the tale, she murmured soft words in her dream; and he knew that the tender converse of her imaginings was held with one whom he had supplanted but in name. At the end of her dream the Countess of Uplandtowers awoke and arose, and then the enactment of former nights was repeated. Her husband remained still and listened. Two strokes sounded from the clock in the pediment without, when, leaving the chamber-door ajar, she passed along the corridor to the other end, where, as usual, she obtained a light. So deep was the silence that he could even from his bed hear her softly blowing the tinder to a glow after striking the steel. She moved on into the boudoir, and he heard, or fancied he heard, the turning of the key in the closet-door. The next moment there came from that direction a loud and prolonged shriek, which resounded to the farthest corners of the house. It was repeated, and there was the noise of a heavy fall.

Lord Uplandtowers sprang out of bed. He hastened along the dark corridor to the door of the boudoir, which stood ajar, and, by the light of the candle within, saw his poor young Countess lying in a heap in her nightdress on the floor of the closet. When he reached her side he found that she had fainted, much to the relief of his fears that matters were worse. He quickly shut up and locked in the hated image which had done the mischief, and lifted his wife in his arms, where in a few instants she opened her eyes. Pressing her face to his without saying a word, he carried her back to her room, endeavouring as he went to disperse her terrors by a laugh in her ear, oddly compounded of causticity, predilection,[43] and brutality.

'Ho – ho – ho!' says he. 'Frightened, dear one, hey? What a baby 'tis! Only a joke, sure, Barbara – a splendid joke! But a baby should not go to closets at midnight to look for the ghost of the dear departed! If it do it must expect to be terrified at his aspect – ho – ho – ho!'

When she was in her bed-chamber,[44] and had quite come to herself, though her nerves were still much shaken, he spoke to her more sternly. 'Now, my lady, answer me: do you love him – eh?'

'No – no!' she faltered, shuddering, with her expanded eyes fixed on her husband. 'He is too terrible – no, no!'

'You are sure?'

'Quite sure!' replied the poor broken-spirited Countess.

But her natural elasticity asserted itself. Next morning he again inquired of her: 'Do you love him now?' She quailed under his gaze, but did not reply.

'That means that you do still, by G—!' he continued.

'It means that I will not tell an untruth, and do not wish to incense my lord,' she answered, with dignity.

'Then suppose we go and have another look at him?' As he

spoke, he suddenly took her by the wrist, and turned as if to lead her towards the ghastly closet.

'No – no! Oh – no!' she cried, and her desperate wriggle out of his hand revealed that the fright of the night had left more impression upon her delicate soul than superficially appeared.

'Another dose or two, and she will be cured,' he said to himself.

It was now so generally known that the Earl and Countess were not in accord, that he took no great trouble to disguise his deeds in relation to this matter. During the day he ordered four men with ropes and rollers to attend him in the boudoir. When they arrived, the closet was open, and the upper part of the statue tied up in canvas. He had it taken to the sleeping-chamber. What followed is more or less matter of conjecture. The story, as told to me, goes on to say that, when Lady Uplandtowers retired with him that night, she saw near the foot of the heavy oak four-poster, a tall dark wardrobe, which had not stood there before; but she did not ask what its presence meant.

'I have had a little whim,' he explained when they were in the dark.[45]

'Have you?' says she.

'To erect a little shrine, as it may be called.'

'A little shrine?'

'Yes; to one whom we both equally adore – eh? I'll show you what it contains.'

He pulled a cord which hung covered by the bed-curtains, and the doors of the wardrobe slowly opened, disclosing that the shelves within had been removed throughout, and the interior adapted to receive the ghastly figure, which stood there as it had stood in the boudoir, but with a wax-candle burning on each side of it to throw the cropped and distorted[46] features into relief. She clutched him, uttered a low scream, and buried her head in the bedclothes. 'Oh, take it away – please take it away!' she implored.

'All in good time; namely, when you love me best,' he returned calmly. 'You don't quite yet – eh?'

'I don't know – I think – O Uplandtowers, have mercy – I cannot bear it – O, in pity, take it away!'

'Nonsense; one gets accustomed to anything. Take another gaze.'

In short, he allowed the doors to remain unclosed at the foot of the bed, and the wax-tapers burning; and such was the strange fascination of the grisly exhibition that a morbid curiosity took possession of the Countess as she lay, and, at his repeated request, she did again look out from the coverlet, shuddered, hid her eyes, and looked again, all the while begging him to take it away, or it would drive her out of her senses. But he would not do so as yet, and the wardrobe was not locked till dawn.

The scene was repeated the next night. Firm in enforcing his ferocious correctives, he continued the treatment till the nerves of the poor lady were quivering in agony under the virtuous tortures inflicted[47] by her lord, to bring her truant heart back to faithfulness.

The third night, when the scene had opened as usual, and she lay staring with immense wild eyes at the horrid fascination, on a sudden she gave an unnatural laugh; she laughed more and more, staring at the image, till she literally shrieked with laughter: then there was silence, and[48] he found her to have become insensible. He thought she had fainted, but soon saw that the event was worse: she was in an epileptic fit. He started up, dismayed by the sense that, like many other subtle personages, he had been too exacting for his own interests. Such love as he was capable of, though rather a selfish gloating than a cherishing solicitude, was fanned into life on the instant. He closed the wardrobe with the pulley, clasped her in his arms, took her gently to the window, and did all he could to restore her.

It was a long time before the Countess came to herself, and when she did so, a considerable change seemed to have taken place in her emotions.[49] She flung her arms around him, and with gasps of fear abjectly kissed him many times, at last bursting into tears. She had never wept in this scene before.

'You'll take it away, dearest – you will!' she begged[50] plaintively.

'If you love me.'

'I do – oh, I do!'

'And hate him, and his memory?'

'Yes – yes!'

'Thoroughly?'

'I cannot endure recollection of him!' cried the poor Countess slavishly.[51] 'It fills me with shame – how could I ever be so depraved! I'll never behave badly again, Uplandtowers; and you will never put the hated statue again before my eyes?'

He felt that he could promise with perfect safety. 'Never,' said he.

'And then I'll love you,' she returned eagerly, as if dreading lest the scourge should be applied anew. 'And I'll never, never dream of thinking a single thought that seems like faithlessness to my marriage vow.'

The strange thing now was that this fictitious love wrung from her by terror took on, through mere habit of enactment, a certain quality of reality. A servile mood of attachment to the Earl became distinctly visible in her contemporaneously with an actual dislike for her late husband's memory. The mood of attachment grew and continued when the statue was removed. A permanent revulsion was operant in her, which intensified as time wore on. How fright could have effected such a change of idiosyncrasy learned physicians alone can say; but I believe such cases of reactionary instinct are not unknown.

The upshot was that the cure became so permanent as to be itself a new disease. She clung to him so tightly, that she would not willingly be out of his sight for a moment. She would have no sitting-room apart from his, though she could not help starting when he entered suddenly to her. Her eyes were well-nigh always fixed upon him. If he drove out, she wished to go with him; his slightest civilities to other women made her frantically jealous; till at length her very fidelity became a burden to him, absorbing his time, and curtailing his liberty, and causing him to curse and swear. If he ever spoke sharply to her now, she did not revenge herself by flying off to a mental world of her own; all that affection for another, which had provided her with a resource, was now a cold black cinder.

From that time the life of this scared and enervated[52] lady – whose existence might have been developed to so much higher purpose but for the ignoble ambition of her parents and the conventions of the time – was one of obsequious amativeness towards a perverse and cruel man. Little personal events came to her in quick succession – half a dozen, eight, nine, ten such events, – in brief, she bore him no less than eleven children in the eight following years,[53] but half of them came prematurely into the world, or died a few days old; only one, a girl, attained to maturity; she in after years became the wife of the Honourable Mr Beltonleigh, who was created Lord D'Almaine,[54] as may be remembered.

There was no living son and heir. At length, completely worn out in mind and body, Lady Uplandtowers was taken abroad by her husband, to try the effect of a more genial climate upon her wasted frame. But nothing availed to strengthen her, and she died at Florence, a few months after her arrival in Italy.

Contrary to expectation, the Earl of Uplandtowers did not marry again. Such affection as existed in him – strange, hard, brutal[55] as it was – seemed untransferable, and the title, as is known, passed at his death to his nephew. Perhaps it may not be so generally known that, during the enlargement of the Hall for the sixth Earl, while digging in the grounds for the new foundations, the broken fragments of a marble statue were unearthed. They were submitted to various antiquaries, who said that, so far as the damaged pieces would allow them to form an opinion, the statue seemed to be that of a mutilated Roman satyr; or if not, an allegorical figure of Death. Only one or two old inhabitants guessed whose statue those fragments had composed.

I should have added that, shortly after the death of the Countess, an excellent sermon was preached by the Dean of Melchester, the subject of which, though names were not mentioned, was unquestionably suggested by the aforesaid events. He dwelt upon the folly of indulgence in sensuous love for a handsome form[56] merely; and showed that the only rational and virtuous growths of that affection were those based upon intrinsic worth. In the case of the tender but somewhat shallow lady whose life I have related, there is no doubt that an infatuation for the person of young Willowes was the chief feeling that induced her to marry him; which was the more deplorable

in that his beauty, by all tradition, was the least of his recommen-
dations, every report bearing out the inference that he must
have been a man of steadfast nature, bright intelligence, and
promising life.

The company thanked[57] the old surgeon for his story, which the
rural dean declared to be a far more striking one than anything
he could hope to tell. An elderly member of the Club, who
was mostly called the Bookworm, said that a woman's natural
instinct of fidelity would, indeed, send back her heart to a man
after his death in a truly wonderful manner sometimes – if
anything occurred to put before her forcibly the original affection between them, and his original aspect in her eyes, – whatever his inferiority may have been, social or otherwise; and then
a general conversation ensued upon the power that a woman
has of seeing the actual in the representation, the reality in the
dream – a power which (according to the sentimental member)
men have no faculty of equalling.

The rural dean thought that such cases as that related by the
surgeon were rather an illustration of passion electrified back
to life than of a latent, true affection.[58] The story had suggested
that he should try to recount to them one which he had used to
hear in his youth, and which afforded an instance of the latter
and better kind of feeling, his heroine being also a lady who had
married beneath her, though he feared his narrative would be
of a much slighter kind than the surgeon's. The Club begged
him to proceed, and the parson began.

# FOR CONSCIENCE' SAKE

## I

Whether the utilitarian or the intuitive theory of the moral sense[1] be upheld, it is beyond question that there are a few subtle-souled persons with whom the absolute gratuitousness of an act of reparation is an inducement to perform it; while exhortation as to its necessity would breed excuses for leaving it undone. The case of Mr Millborne and Mrs Frankland particularly illustrated this, and perhaps something more.

There were few figures better known to the local crossing-sweeper than Mr Millborne's, in his daily comings and goings along a familiar and quiet London street,[2] where he lived inside the door marked eleven, though not as householder. In age he was fifty at least, and his habits were as regular as those of a person can be who has no occupation but the study of how to keep himself employed. He turned almost always to the right on getting to the end of his street, then he went onward down Bond Street to his club, whence he returned by precisely the same course about six o'clock, on foot; or, if he went to dine, later on in a cab. He was known to be a man of some means, though apparently not wealthy. Being a bachelor he seemed to prefer his present mode of living as a lodger in Mrs Towney's best rooms, with the use of furniture which he had bought ten times over in rent during his tenancy, to having a house of his own.

None among his acquaintance tried to know him well, for his manner and moods did not excite curiosity or deep friendship. He was not a man who seemed to have anything on his mind, anything to conceal, anything to impart. From his casual remarks it was generally understood that he was country-born, a native of some place in Wessex; that he had come to London as a young man in a banking-house, and had risen to a post of responsibility; when, by the death of his father, who had been fortunate in his investments, the son succeeded to an income which led him to retire from a business life somewhat early.

One evening, when he had been unwell for several days, Doctor Bindon[3] came in, after dinner, from the adjoining medical quarter, and smoked with him over the fire. The patient's ailment was not such as to require much thought, and they talked together on indifferent subjects.

'I am a lonely man, Bindon – a lonely man,' Millborne took occasion to say, shaking his head gloomily. 'You don't know such loneliness as mine ... And the older I get the more I am dissatisfied with myself. And today I have been, through an accident, more than usually haunted by what, above all other events of my life, causes that dissatisfaction – the recollection of an unfulfilled promise made twenty years ago. In ordinary affairs I have always been considered a man of my word; and perhaps it is on that account that a particular vow I once made, and did not keep, comes back to me with a magnitude out of all proportion (I daresay) to its real gravity,[4] especially at this time of day. You know the discomfort caused at night by the half-sleeping sense that a door or window has been left unfastened, or in the day by the remembrance of unanswered letters. So does that promise haunt me from time to time, and has done today particularly.'

There was a pause, and they smoked on. Millborne's eyes, though fixed on the fire, were really regarding attentively a town in the West of England.

'Yes,' he continued, 'I have never quite forgotten it, though during the busy years of my life it was shelved and buried under the pressure of my pursuits. And, as I say, today in particular, an incident in the law-report of a somewhat similar kind has brought it back again vividly. However, what it was I can tell you in a few words, though no doubt you, as a man of the world, will smile at the thinness of my skin when you hear it ...

I came up to town at one-and-twenty, from Toneborough,[5] in Outer Wessex, where I was born, and where, before I left, I had won the heart of a young woman of my own age. I promised her marriage, took advantage of my promise, and – am a bachelor.'

'The old story.'

The other nodded.

'I left the place, and thought at the time I had done a very clever thing in getting so easily out of an entanglement. But I have lived long enough for that promise to return to bother me – to be honest, not altogether as a pricking of the conscience, but as a dissatisfaction with myself as a specimen of the heap of flesh called humanity.[6] If I were to ask you to lend me fifty pounds, which I would repay you next midsummer, and I did not repay you, I should consider myself a shabby sort of fellow, especially if you wanted the money badly. Yet I promised that girl just as distinctly; and then coolly broke my word, as if doing so were rather smart conduct than a mean action, for which the poor victim herself, encumbered with a child, and not I, had really to pay the penalty, in spite of certain pecuniary aid that was given ... There, that's the retrospective trouble that I am always unearthing; and you may hardly believe that though so many years have elapsed, and it is all gone by and done with, and she must be getting on for an old woman now, as I am for an old man, it really often destroys my sense of self-respect still.'

'O, I can understand it. All depends upon the temperament. Thousands of men would have forgotten all about it; so would you, perhaps, if you had married and had a family. Did she ever marry?'

'I don't think so. O no – she never did. She left Toneborough, and later on appeared under another name at Exonbury, in the next county, where she was not known. It is very seldom that I go down into that part of the country, but in passing through Exonbury, on one occasion, I learnt that she was quite a settled resident there, as a teacher of music, or something of the kind. That much I casually heard when I was there two or three years ago. But I have never set eyes on her since our original acquaintance, and should not know her if I met her.'

'Did the child live?' asked the doctor.

'For several years, certainly,' replied his friend. 'I cannot say if she is living now. It was a little girl. She might be married by this time as far as years go.'

'And the mother – was she a decent, worthy young woman?'

'O yes; a sensible, quiet girl, neither attractive nor unattractive to the ordinary observer; simply commonplace. Her position at the time of our acquaintance was not so good as mine. My father was a solicitor, as I think I have told you. She was a young girl in a music-shop; and it was represented to me that it would be beneath my position to marry her. Hence the result.'

'Well, all I can say is that after twenty years it is probably too late to think of mending such a matter. It has doubtless by this time mended itself. You had better dismiss it from your mind as an evil past your control. Of course, if mother and daughter are alive, or either, you might settle something upon them, if you were inclined, and had it to spare.'

'Well, I haven't much to spare; and I have relations in narrow circumstances – perhaps narrower than theirs. But that is not the point. Were I ever so rich I feel I could not rectify the past by money. I did not promise to enrich her. On the contrary, I told her it would probably be dire poverty for both of us. But I did promise to make her my wife.'

'Then find her and do it,' said the doctor jocularly as he rose to leave.

'Ah, Bindon. That, of course, is the obvious jest. But I haven't the slightest desire for marriage; I am quite content to live as I have lived. I am a bachelor by nature, and instinct, and habit, and everything. Besides, though I respect her still (for she was not an atom to blame), I haven't any shadow of love for her. In my mind she exists as one of those women you think well of, but find uninteresting. It would be purely with the idea of putting wrong right that I should hunt her up, and propose to do it off-hand.'

'You don't think of it seriously?' said his surprised friend.

'I sometimes think that I would, if it were practicable; simply, as I say, to recover my sense of being a man of honour.'

'I wish you luck in the enterprise,' said Doctor Bindon. 'You'll soon be out of that chair, and then you can put your impulse to the test. But – after twenty years of silence – I should say, don't!'

## II

The doctor's advice remained counterpoised, in Millborne's mind, by the aforesaid mood of seriousness and sense of principle, approximating often to religious sentiment, which had been evolving itself in his breast for months, and even years.

The feeling, however, had no immediate effect upon Mr Millborne's actions. He soon got over his trifling illness, and was vexed with himself for having, in a moment of impulse, confided such a case of conscience to anybody.

But the force which had prompted it, though latent, remained with him and ultimately grew stronger. The upshot was that about four months after the date of his illness and disclosure, Millborne found himself on a mild spring morning at Paddington Station, in a train that was starting for the west. His many intermittent thoughts on his broken promise from time to time, in those hours when loneliness brought him face to face with his own personality, had at last resulted in this course.

The decisive stimulus had been given when, a day or two earlier, on looking into a Post-Office Directory, he learnt that the woman he had not met for twenty years was still living on at Exonbury under the name she had assumed when, a year or two after her disappearance from her native town and his, she had returned from abroad as a young widow with a child, and taken up her residence at the former city. Her condition was apparently but little changed, and her daughter seemed to be with her, their names standing in the Directory as 'Mrs Leonora Frankland and Miss Frankland, Teachers of Music and Dancing.'

Mr Millborne reached Exonbury in the afternoon, and his first business, before even taking his luggage into the town, was to find the house occupied by the teachers. Standing in a central and open place it was not difficult to discover, a well-burnished brass doorplate bearing their names prominently. He hesitated to enter without further knowledge, and ultimately took lodgings over a toyshop opposite, securing a sitting-room which faced a similar drawing- or sitting-room at the Franklands', where the dancing lessons were given. Installed here he was enabled to make indirectly, and without suspicion, inquiries and observations on the character of the ladies over the way, which he did with much deliberateness.

He learnt that the widow, Mrs Frankland, with her one daughter, Frances, was of cheerful and excellent repute, energetic and painstaking with her pupils, of whom she had a good many, and in whose tuition her daughter assisted her. She was quite a recognized townswoman, and though the dancing branch of her profession was perhaps a trifle worldly, she was really a serious-minded lady who, being obliged to live by what she knew how to teach, balanced matters by lending a hand at charitable bazaars, assisting at sacred concerts, and giving musical recitations in aid of funds for bewildering happy savages, and other such enthusiasms of this enlightened country.[7] Her daughter was one of the foremost of the bevy of young women who decorated the churches at Easter and Christmas, was organist in one of those edifices, and had subscribed to the testimonial of a silver broth-basin that was presented to the Reverend Mr Walker as a token of gratitude for his faithful and arduous intonations of six months as sub-precentor in the Cathedral.[8] Altogether mother and daughter appeared to be a typical and innocent pair among the genteel citizens of Exonbury.

As a natural and simple way of advertising their profession they allowed the windows of the music-room to be a little open, so that you had the pleasure of hearing all along the street at any hour between sunrise and sunset[9] fragmentary gems of classical music as interpreted by the young people of twelve or fourteen who took lessons there. But it was said that Mrs Frankland made most of her income by letting out pianos on hire, and by selling them as agent for the makers.

The report pleased Millborne; it was highly creditable, and far better than he had hoped. He was curious to get a view of the two women who led such blameless lives.

He had not long to wait to gain a glimpse of Leonora. It

was when she was standing on her own doorstep, opening her parasol, on the morning after his arrival. She was thin, though not gaunt; and a good, well-wearing, thoughtful face had taken the place of the one which had temporarily attracted him in the days of his nonage. She wore black, and it became her in her character of widow. The daughter next appeared; she was a smoothed and rounded copy of her mother, with the same decision in her mien that Leonora had, and a bounding gait in which he traced a faint resemblance to his own at her age.

For the first time he absolutely made up his mind to call on them. But his antecedent step was to send Leonora a note the next morning, stating his proposal to visit her, and suggesting the evening as the time, because she seemed to be so greatly occupied in her professional capacity during the day. He purposely worded his note in such a form as not to require an answer from her which would be possibly awkward to write.

No answer came. Naturally he should not have been surprised at this; and yet he felt a little checked, even though she had only refrained from volunteering a reply that was not demanded.

At eight, the hour fixed by himself, he crossed over and was passively[10] admitted by the servant. Mrs Frankland, as she called herself, received him in the large music-and-dancing room on the first-floor front, and not in any private little parlour as he had expected. This cast a distressingly business-like colour over their first meeting after so many years of severance. The woman he had wronged stood before him, well-dressed, even to his metropolitan eyes, and her manner as she came up to him was dignified even to hardness. She certainly was not glad to see him. But what could he expect after a neglect of twenty years!

'How do you do, Mr Millborne?' she said cheerfully, as to any chance caller. 'I am obliged to receive you here because my daughter has a friend downstairs.'

'Your daughter – and mine.'

'Ah – yes, yes,' she replied hastily, as if the addition had escaped her memory. 'But perhaps the less said about that the better, in fairness to me. You will consider me a widow, please.'

'Certainly, Leonora . . .' He could not get on, her manner was so cold and indifferent. The expected scene of sad reproach, subdued to delicacy by the run of years, was absent altogether. He was obliged to come to the point without preamble.

'You are quite free, Leonora – I mean as to marriage? There is nobody who has your promise, or—'

'O yes; quite free, Mr Millborne,' she said, somewhat surprised.

'Then I will tell you why I have come. Twenty years ago I promised to make you my wife; and I am here to fulfil that promise. Heaven forgive my tardiness!'

Her surprise was increased, but she was not agitated. She seemed to become gloomy, disapproving. 'I could not entertain such an idea at this time of life,' she said after a moment or two. 'It would complicate matters too greatly. I have a very fair income, and require no help of any sort. I have no wish to marry[11] ... What could have induced you to come on such an errand now? It seems quite extraordinary, if I may say so!'

'It must – I daresay it does,' Millborne replied vaguely; 'and I must tell you that impulse – I mean in the sense of passion – has little to do with it. I wish to marry you, Leonora; I much desire to marry you. But it is an affair of conscience, a case of fulfilment. I promised you, and it was dishonourable of me to go away. I want to remove that sense of dishonour before I die. No doubt we might get to love each other as warmly as we did in old times?'

She dubiously shook her head. 'I appreciate your motives, Mr Millborne; but you must consider my position; and you will see that, short of the personal wish to marry, which I don't feel, there is no reason why I should change my state, even though by so doing I should ease your conscience. My position in this town is a respected one; I have built it up by my own hard labours, and, in short, I don't wish to alter it. My daughter, too, is just on the verge of an engagement to be married, to a young man who will make her an excellent husband. It will be in every way a desirable match for her. He is downstairs now.'

'Does she know – anything about me?'

'O no, no; God forbid! Her father is dead and buried to her. So that, you see, things are going on smoothly, and I don't want to disturb their progress.'

He nodded. 'Very well,' he said, and rose to go. At the door, however, he came back again.

'Still, Leonora,' he urged, 'I have come on purpose; and I don't see what disturbance would be caused. You would simply marry an old friend. Won't you reconsider? It is no more than right that we should be united, remembering the girl.'

She shook her head, and patted with her foot nervously.

'Well, I won't detain you,' he added. 'I shall not be leaving Exonbury yet. You will allow me to see you again?'

'Yes; I don't mind,' she said reluctantly.

The obstacles he had encountered, though they did not re-animate his dead passion for Leonora, did certainly make it appear indispensable to his peace of mind to overcome her coldness. He called frequently. The first meeting with the daughter was a trying ordeal, though he did not feel drawn towards her as he had expected to be; she did not excite his sympathies. Her mother confided to Frances the errand of 'her old friend', which was viewed by the daughter with strong disfavour. His desire being thus uncongenial to both, for a long time Millborne made not the least impression upon Mrs Frankland. His attentions pestered her rather than pleased her. He was surprised at her firmness, and it was only when he hinted at moral reasons for their union that she was ever shaken. 'Strictly speaking,' he would say, 'we ought, as honest persons, to marry; and that's the truth of it, Leonora.'

'I have looked at it in that light,' she said quickly. 'It struck me at the very first. But I don't see the force of the argument. I totally deny that after this interval of time I am bound to marry you for honour's sake. I would have married you, as you know well enough, at the proper time. But what is the use of remedies now?'

They were standing at the window. A scantly-whiskered[12] young man, in clerical attire, called at the door below. Leonora flushed with interest.

'Who is he?' said Mr Millborne.

'My Frances's lover. I am so sorry – she is not at home! Ah! they have told him where she is, and he has gone to find her . . . I hope that suit will prosper, at any rate!'

'Why shouldn't it?'

'Well, he cannot marry yet; and Frances sees but little of him now he has left Exonbury. He was formerly doing duty here, but now he is curate of St John's, Ivell,[13] fifty miles up the line. There is a tacit agreement between them, but – there have been friends of his who object, because of our vocation. However, he sees the absurdity of such an objection as that, and is not influenced by it.'

'Your marriage with me would help the match, instead of hindering it, as you have said.'

'Do you think it would?'

'It certainly would, by taking you out of this business altogether.'

By chance he had found the way to move her somewhat, and he followed it up. This view was imparted to Mrs Frankland's daughter, and it led her to soften her opposition. Millborne, who had given up his lodging in Exonbury, journeyed to and fro regularly, till at last he overcame her negations, and she expressed a reluctant assent.

They were married at the nearest church; and the goodwill – whatever that was – of the music-and-dancing connection was sold to a successor only too ready to jump into the place, the Millbornes having decided to live in London.

### III

Millborne was a householder in his old district, though not in his old street, and Mrs Millborne and their daughter had turned themselves into Londoners. Frances was well reconciled to the removal by her lover's satisfaction at the change. It suited him better to travel from Ivell a hundred miles to see her in London, where he frequently had other engagements, than fifty in the opposite direction where nothing but herself required his presence. So here they were, furnished up to the attics, in one of the small but popular streets of the West district, in a house whose front, till lately of the complexion of a chimney-sweep, had been scraped to show to the surprised wayfarer the bright yellow and red brick that had lain lurking beneath the soot of fifty years.

The social lift that the two women had derived from the alliance was considerable; but when the exhilaration which accompanies a first residence in London, the sensation of standing on a pivot of the world, had passed, their lives promised to be somewhat duller than when, at despised Exonbury, they had enjoyed a nodding acquaintance with three-fourths of the town. Mr Millborne did not criticize his wife; he could not. Whatever defects of hardness and acidity his original treatment and the lapse of years might have developed in her, his sense of a realized idea, of a re-established self-satisfaction, was always thrown into the scale on her side, and out-weighed all objections.

It was about a month after their settlement in town that the household decided to spend a week at a watering-place in the Isle of Wight, and while there the Reverend Percival Cope[14] (the young curate aforesaid) came to see them, Frances in particular. No formal engagement of the young pair had been announced as yet, but it was clear that their mutual understanding could not end in anything but marriage without grievous disappointment to one of the parties at least. Not that Frances was sentimental. She was rather of the imperious sort, indeed; and, to say all, the young girl had not fulfilled her father's expectations of her. But he hoped and worked for her welfare as sincerely as any father could do.

Mr Cope was introduced to the new head of the family, and stayed with them in the Island two or three days. On the last day of his visit they decided to venture on a two hours' sail in one of the small yachts which lay there for hire. The trip had not progressed far before all, except the curate, found that sailing in a breeze did not quite agree with them; but as he seemed to enjoy the experience, the other three bore their condition as well as they could without grimace or complaint, till the young man, observing their discomfort, gave immediate directions to tack about. On the way back to port they sat silent, facing each other.

Nausea in such circumstances, like midnight watching, fatigue, trouble, fright, has this marked effect upon the countenance, that it often brings out strongly the divergences of the individual from the norm of his race, accentuating superficial

peculiarities to radical distinctions.[15] Unexpected physi-
ognomies will uncover themselves at these times in well-known
faces; the aspect becomes invested with the spectral presence of
entombed and forgotten ancestors; and family lineaments of
special or exclusive cast, which in ordinary moments are masked
by a stereotyped expression and mien,[16] start up with crude
insistence to the view.

Frances, sitting beside her mother's husband, with Mr Cope
opposite, was naturally enough much regarded by the curate
during the tedious sail home; at first with sympathetic smiles.
Then, as the middle-aged father and his child[17] grew each grey-
faced, as the pretty blush of Frances disintegrated into spotty
stains, and the soft rotundities of her features diverged from
their familiar and reposeful beauty into elemental lines, Cope
was gradually struck with the resemblance between a pair in
their discomfort who in their ease presented nothing to the eye
in common. Mr Millborne and Frances in their indisposition
were strangely, startlingly alike.

The inexplicable fact absorbed Cope's attention quite. He
forgot to smile at Frances, to hold her hand; and when they
touched the shore he remained sitting for some moments like a
man in a trance.

As they went homeward, and recovered their complexions
and contours, the similarities one by one disappeared, and
Frances and Mr Millborne were again masked by the commonplace differences of sex and age. It was as if, during the voyage,
a mysterious veil had been lifted, temporarily revealing a strange
pantomime of the past.

During the evening he said to her casually: 'Is your stepfather
a cousin of your mother, dear Frances?'

'Oh, no,' said she. 'There is no relationship. He was only an
old friend of hers. Why did you suppose such a thing?'

He did not explain, and the next morning started to resume
his duties at Ivell.

Cope was an honest young fellow, and shrewd withal. At
home in his quiet rooms in St Peter's Street, Ivell, he pondered
long and unpleasantly on the revelations of the cruise. The tale
it told was distinct enough, and for the first time his position

was an uncomfortable one. He had met the Franklands at Exonbury as parishioners, had been attracted by Frances, and had floated thus far into an engagement which was indefinite only because of his inability to marry just yet. The Franklands' past had apparently contained mysteries, and it did not coincide with his judgment to marry into a family whose mystery was of the sort suggested. So he sat and sighed, between his reluctance to lose Frances and his natural dislike of forming a connection with people whose antecedents would not bear the strictest investigation.

A passionate lover of the old-fashioned sort might possibly never have halted to weigh these doubts; but though he was in the church Cope's affections were fastidious[18] – distinctly tempered with the alloys of the century's decadence. He delayed writing to Frances for some while, simply because he could not tune himself up to enthusiasm when worried by suspicions of such a kind.

Meanwhile the Millbornes had returned to London, and Frances was growing anxious. In talking to her mother of Cope she had innocently alluded to his curious inquiry if her mother and her stepfather were connected by any tie of cousinship. Mrs Millborne made her repeat the words. Frances did so, and watched with inquisitive eyes their effect upon her elder.

'What is there so startling in his inquiry then?' she asked. 'Can it have anything to do with his not writing to me?'

Her mother flinched, but did not inform her, and Frances also was now drawn within the atmosphere of suspicion. That night when standing by chance outside the chamber of her parents she heard for the first time their voices engaged in a sharp altercation.

The apple of discord[19] had, indeed, been dropped into the house of the Millbornes. The scene within the chamber-door was Mrs Millborne standing before her dressing-table, looking across to her husband in the dressing-room adjoining, where he was sitting down, his eyes fixed on the floor.

'Why did you come and disturb my life a second time?' she harshly asked. 'Why did you pester me with your conscience, till I was driven to accept you to get rid of your importunity?

Frances and I were doing well: the one desire of my life was that she should marry that good young man. And now the match is broken off by your cruel interference! Why did you show yourself in my world again, and raise this scandal upon my hard-won respectability – won by such weary years of labour as none will ever know!' She bent her face upon the table and wept passionately.

There was no reply from Mr Millborne. Frances lay awake nearly all that night, and when at breakfast-time the next morning still no letter appeared from Mr Cope, she entreated her mother to go to Ivell and see if the young man were ill.

Mrs Millborne went, returning the same day. Frances, anxious and haggard, met her at the station.

Was all well? Her mother could not say it was; though he was not ill.

One thing she had found out, that it was a mistake to hunt up a man when his inclinations were to hold aloof. Returning with her mother in the cab Frances insisted upon knowing what the mystery was which plainly had alienated her lover. The precise words which had been spoken at the interview with him that day at Ivell Mrs Millborne could not be induced to repeat; but thus far she admitted, that the estrangement was fundamentally owing to Mr Millborne having sought her out and married her.

'And why did he seek you out – and why were you obliged to marry him?' asked the distressed girl. Then the evidences pieced themselves together in her acute mind, and, her colour gradually rising, she asked her mother if what they pointed to was indeed the fact. Her mother admitted that it was.

A flush of mortification succeeded to the flush of shame upon the young woman's face. How could a scrupulously correct clergyman and lover like Mr Cope ask her to be his wife after this discovery of her irregular birth?[20] She covered her eyes with her hands in a silent despair.

In the presence of Mr Millborne they at first suppressed their anguish. But by and by their feelings got the better of them, and when he was asleep in his chair after dinner Mrs Millborne's irritation broke out. The embittered Frances joined her in reproaching the man who had come as the spectre to their intended feast of Hymen,[21] and turned its promise to ghastly failure.

'Why were you so weak, mother, as to admit such an enemy to your house – one so obviously your evil genius – much less accept him as a husband, after so long? If you had only told me all, I could have advised you better! But I suppose I have no right to reproach him, bitter as I feel, and even though he has blighted my life for ever!'

'Frances, I did hold out; I saw it was a mistake to have any more to say to a man who had been such an unmitigated curse to me! But he would not listen; he kept on about his conscience[22] and mine, till I was bewildered, and said Yes! . . . Bringing us away from a quiet town where we were known and respected – what an ill-considered thing it was! O the content of those days! We had society there, people in our own position, who did not expect more of us than we expected of them. Here, where there is so much, there is nothing! He said London society was so bright and brilliant that it would be like a new world. It may be to those who are in it; but what is that to us two lonely women; we only see it flashing past! . . . O the fool, the fool that I was!'

Now Millborne was not so soundly asleep as to prevent his hearing these animadversions that were almost execrations, and many more of the same sort. As there was no peace for him at home, he went again to his club, where, since his reunion with Leonora, he had seldom if ever been seen. But the shadow of the troubles in his household interfered with his comfort here also; he could not, as formerly, settle down into his favourite chair with the evening paper, reposeful in the celibate's[23] sense that where he was his world's centre had its fixture. His world was now an ellipse, with a dual centrality, of which his own was not the major.

The young curate of Ivell still held aloof, tantalizing Frances by his elusiveness. Plainly he was waiting upon events. Millborne bore the reproaches of his wife and daughter almost in silence; but by degrees he grew meditative, as if revolving a new idea. The bitter cry about[24] blighting their existence at length became so impassioned that one day Millborne calmly proposed to return again to the country; not necessarily to Exonbury, but, if they were willing, to a little old manor-house which he had found was to be let, standing a mile from Mr Cope's town of Ivell.

They were surprised, and, despite their view of him as the bringer of ill, were disposed to accede. 'Though I suppose,' said Mrs Millborne to him, 'it will end in Mr Cope's asking you flatly about the past, and your being compelled to tell him; which may dash all my hopes for Frances. She gets more and more like you every day, particularly when she is in a bad temper. People will see you together, and notice it;[25] and I don't know what may come of it!'

'I don't think they will see us together,' he said; but he entered into no argument when she insisted otherwise. The removal was eventually resolved on; the town-house was disposed of; and again came the invasion by furniture-men and vans, till all the movables and servants were whisked away. He sent his wife and daughter to an hotel while this was going on, taking two or three journeys himself to Ivell to superintend the refixing, and the improvement of the grounds. When all was done he returned to them in town.

The house was ready for their reception, he told them, and there only remained the journey. He accompanied them and their personal luggage to the station only, having, he said, to remain in town a short time on business with his lawyer. They went, dubious and discontented; for the much-loved Cope had made no sign.

'If we were going down to live here alone,' said Mrs Millborne to her daughter in the train; 'and there was no intrusive tell-tale presence! . . . But let it be!'

The house was a lovely little place in a grove of elms, and they liked it much. The first person to call upon them as new residents was Mr Cope. He was delighted to find that they had come so near, and (though he did not say this) meant to live in such excellent style. He had not, however, resumed the manner of a lover.

'Your father spoils all!' murmured Mrs Millborne.

But three days later she received a letter from her husband, which caused her no small degree of astonishment. It was written from Boulogne.

It began with a long explanation of settlements of his property, in which he had been engaged since their departure. The chief feature in the business was that Mrs Millborne found herself the absolute owner of a comfortable sum in personal estate, and Frances of a life-interest in a larger sum, the principal to be afterwards divided amongst her children if she had any. The remainder of his letter ran as hereunder: –

'I have learnt that there are some derelictions of duty which cannot be blotted out by tardy accomplishment. Our evil actions do not remain isolated in the past, waiting only to be reversed: like locomotive plants they spread and re-root, till to destroy the original stem has no material effect in killing them. I made a mistake in searching you out; I admit it; whatever the remedy may be in such cases it is not marriage, and the best thing for you and me is that you do not see me more. You had better not seek me, for you will not be likely to find me: you are well provided for, and we may do ourselves more harm than good by meeting again.

                                                                                    F. M.'

Millborne, in short, disappeared from that day forward. But a searching inquiry would have revealed that, soon after the Millbornes went to Ivell, an Englishman, who did not give the name of Millborne, took up his residence in Brussels; a man who might have been recognized by Mrs Millborne if she had met him. One afternoon in the ensuing summer, when this gentleman was looking over the English papers, he saw the announcement of Miss Frances Frankland's marriage. She had become the Reverend Mrs Cope.

'Thank God!' said the gentleman.

But his momentary satisfaction was far from being happiness. As he formerly had been weighted with a bad conscience, so now was he burdened with the heavy thought which oppressed Antigone, that by honourable observance of a rite he had obtained for himself the reward of dishonourable laxity.[26]

Occasionally he had to be helped to his lodgings by his servant from the *Cercle* he frequented, through having imbibed a little too much liquor to be able to take care of himself. But he was harmless, and even when he had been drinking said little.

# THE SON'S VETO

## I

To the eyes of a man viewing it from behind, the nut-brown hair was a wonder and a mystery. Under the black beaver hat, surmounted by its tuft of black feathers, the long locks, braided and twisted and coiled like the rushes of a basket, composed a rare, if somewhat barbaric,[1] example of ingenious art. One could understand such weavings and coilings being wrought to last intact for a year, or even a calendar month; but that they should be all demolished regularly at bedtime, after a single day of permanence, seemed a reckless waste of successful fabrication.

And she had done it all herself, poor thing. She had no maid, and it was almost the only accomplishment she could boast of. Hence the unstinted pains.

She was a young invalid lady – not so very much of an invalid – sitting in a wheeled chair, which had been pulled up in the front part of a green enclosure, close to a bandstand, where a concert was going on, during a warm June afternoon. It had place in one of the minor parks or private gardens that are to be found in the suburbs of London, and was the effort of a local association to raise money for some charity. There are worlds within worlds in the great city, and though nobody outside the immediate district had ever heard of the charity, or the band, or the garden, the enclosure was filled with an interested audience sufficiently informed on all these.

As the strains proceeded many of the listeners observed the chaired lady, whose back hair, by reason of her prominent

position, so challenged inspection. Her face was not easily discernible, but the aforesaid cunning tress-weavings, the white ear
and poll, and the curve of a cheek which was neither flaccid nor
sallow, were signals that led to the expectation of good beauty
in front. Such expectations are not infrequently disappointed as
soon as the disclosure comes; and in the present case, when the
lady, by a turn of the head, at length revealed herself, she was
not so handsome as the people behind her had supposed, and
even hoped – they did not know why.

For one thing (alas! the commonness of this complaint), she
was less young than they had fancied her to be. Yet attractive
her face unquestionably was, and not at all sickly. The revelation
of its details came each time she turned to talk to a boy of twelve
or thirteen who stood beside her, and the shape of whose hat
and jacket implied that he belonged to a well-known public
school.[2] The immediate bystanders could hear that he called
her 'Mother'.

When the end of the recital was reached, and the audience
withdrew, many chose to find their way out by passing at her
elbow. Almost all turned their heads to take a full and near look
at the interesting woman, who remained stationary in the chair
till the way should be clear enough for her to be wheeled out
without obstruction. As if she expected their glances, and did
not mind gratifying their curiosity, she met the eyes of several
of her observers by lifting her own, showing these to be soft,
brown, and affectionate orbs, a little plaintive in their regard.

She was conducted out of the gardens, and passed along the
pavement till she disappeared from view, the schoolboy walking
beside her. To inquiries made by some persons who watched
her away, the answer came that she was the second wife of the
incumbent of a neighbouring parish, and that she was lame. She
was generally believed to be a woman with a story – an innocent
one, but a story of some sort or other.

In conversing with her on their way home the boy who walked
at her elbow said that he hoped his father had not missed them.

'He have been so comfortable these last few hours that I am
sure he cannot have missed us,' she replied.

'*Has*, dear mother – not *have*!'[3] exclaimed the public-school boy, with an impatient fastidiousness that was almost harsh. 'Surely you know that by this time!'

His mother hastily adopted the correction, and did not resent his making it, or retaliate, as she might well have done, by bidding him to wipe that crumby mouth of his, whose condition had been caused by surreptitious attempts to eat a piece of cake without taking it out of the pocket wherein it lay concealed. After this the pretty woman and the boy went onward in silence.

That question of grammar bore upon her history, and she fell into reverie, of a somewhat sad kind to all appearance. It might have been assumed that she was wondering if she had done wisely in shaping her life as she had shaped it, to bring out such a result as this.

In a remote nook in North Wessex, forty miles from London, near the thriving county-town of Aldbrickham,[4] there stood a pretty village with its church and parsonage, which she knew well enough, but her son had never seen. It was her native village, Gaymead, and the first event bearing upon her present situation had occurred at that place when she was only a girl of nineteen.

How well she remembered it, that first act in her little tragi-comedy, the death of her reverend[5] husband's first wife. It happened on a spring evening, and she who now and for many years had filled that first wife's place was then parlour-maid in the parson's house.

When everything had been done that could be done,[6] and the death was announced, she had gone out in the dusk to visit her parents, who were living in the same village, to tell them the sad news. As she opened the white swing-gate and looked towards the trees which rose westward, shutting out the pale light of the evening sky, she discerned, without much surprise, the figure of a man standing in the hedge, though she roguishly exclaimed as a matter of form, 'Oh, Sam,[7] how you frightened me!'

He was a young gardener of her acquaintance. She told him the particulars of the late event, and they stood silent, these two young people, in that elevated, calmly philosophic mind which is engendered when a tragedy has happened close at hand, and has not happened to the philosophers themselves. But it had its bearing upon their relations.

'And will you stay on now at the Vicarage, just the same?' asked he.

She had hardly thought of that. 'Oh, yes – I suppose!' she said. 'Everything will be just as usual, I imagine?'

He walked beside her towards her mother's. Presently his arm stole round her waist. She gently removed it; but he placed it there again, and she yielded the point. 'You see, dear Sophy, you don't know that you'll stay on; you may want a home; and I shall be ready to offer one some day, though I may not be ready just yet.'

'Why, Sam, how can you be so fast! I've never even said I liked 'ee; and it is all your own doing, coming after me!'

'Still, it is nonsense to say I am not to have a try at you like the rest.' He stooped to kiss her a farewell, for they had reached her mother's door.

'No, Sam; you sha'n't!' she cried, putting her hand over his mouth. 'You ought to be more serious on such a night as this.' And she bade him adieu without allowing him to kiss her or to come indoors.

The vicar just left a widower was at this time a man about forty years of age, of good family, and childless. He had led a secluded existence in this college living,[8] partly because there were no resident landowners; and his loss now intensified his habit of withdrawal from outward observation. He was still less seen than heretofore, kept himself still less in time with the rhythm and racket of the movements called progress in the world without. For many months after his wife's decease the economy of his household remained as before; the cook, the house-maid, the parlour-maid, and the man out-of-doors performed their duties or left them undone, just as Nature prompted them – the vicar knew not which. It was then represented to him that his servants seemed to have nothing to do in his small family of one. He was struck with the truth of this representation, and decided to cut down his establishment. But he was forestalled by Sophy, the parlour-maid, who said one evening that she wished to leave him.

'And why?' said the parson.

'Sam Hobson has asked me to marry him, sir.'

'Well – do you want to marry?'

'Not much. But it would be a home for me. And we have heard that one of us will have to leave.'

A day or two after she said: 'I don't want to leave just yet, sir, if you don't wish it. Sam and I have quarrelled.'

He looked up at her. He had hardly ever observed her before, though he had been frequently conscious of her soft presence in the room. What a kitten-like, flexuous, tender creature she was! She was the only one of the servants with whom he came into immediate and continuous[9] relation. What should he do if Sophy were gone?

Sophy did not go, but one of the others did, and things went on quietly again.

When Mr Twycott, the vicar, was ill, Sophy brought up his meals to him, and she had no sooner left the room one day than he heard a noise on the stairs. She had slipped down with the tray, and so twisted her foot that she could not stand. The village surgeon was called in; the vicar got better, but Sophy was incapacitated for a long time; and she was informed that she must never again walk much or engage in any occupation which required her to stand long on her feet. As soon as she was comparatively well she spoke to him alone. Since she was forbidden to walk and bustle about, and, indeed, could not do so, it became her duty to leave. She could very well work at something sitting down, and she had an aunt a seamstress.

The parson had been very greatly moved by what she had suffered on his account, and he exclaimed, 'No, Sophy; lame or not lame, I cannot let you go. You must never leave me again!'

He came close to her, and, though she could never exactly tell how it happened, she became conscious of his lips upon her cheek.[10] He then asked her to marry him. Sophy did not exactly love him, but she had a respect for him which almost amounted to veneration. Even if she had wished to get away from him she hardly dared refuse a personage so reverend and august in her eyes, and she assented forthwith to be his wife.

Thus it happened that one fine morning, when the doors of

the church were naturally open for ventilation, and the singing birds fluttered in and alighted on the tie-beams of the roof, there was a marriage-service at the communion-rails, which hardly a soul knew of. The parson and a neighbouring curate had entered at one door, and Sophy at another, followed by two necessary persons, whereupon in a short time there emerged a newly-made husband and wife.

Mr Twycott knew perfectly well that he had committed social suicide by this step, despite Sophy's spotless character, and he had taken his measures accordingly. An exchange of livings had been arranged with an acquaintance who was incumbent of a church in the south of London, and as soon as possible the couple removed thither, abandoning their pretty country home, with trees and shrubs and glebe, for a narrow, dusty house in a long, straight street, and their fine peal of bells for the wretchedest one-tongued clangour that ever tortured mortal ears. It was all on her account. They were, however, away from every one who had known her former position; and also under less observation from without than they would have had to put up with in any country parish.

Sophy the woman was as charming a partner as a man could possess, though Sophy the lady had her deficiencies. She showed a natural aptitude for little domestic refinements, so far as related to things and manners; but in what is called culture she was less intuitive. She had now been married more than fourteen years, and her husband had taken much trouble with her education; but she still held confused ideas on the use of 'was' and 'were', which did not beget a respect for her among the few acquaintances she made. Her great grief in this relation was that her only child, on whose education no expense had been and would be spared, was now old enough to perceive these deficiencies in his mother, and not only to see them but to feel irritated at their existence.

Thus she lived on in the city, and wasted hours in braiding her beautiful hair, till her once apple cheeks waned to pink of the very faintest.[11] Her foot had never regained its natural strength after the accident, and she was mostly obliged to avoid walking altogether. Her husband had grown to like London for its freedom and its domestic privacy; but he was twenty years his Sophy's senior, and had latterly been seized with a serious illness. On this day, however, he had seemed to be well enough to justify her accompanying her son Randolph[12] to the concert.

## II

The next time we get a glimpse of her is when she appears in the mournful attire of a widow.

Mr Twycott had never rallied, and now lay in a well-packed cemetery to the south of the great city,[13] where, if all the dead it contained had stood erect and alive, not one would have known him or recognized his name. The boy had dutifully followed him to the grave, and was now again at school.

Throughout these changes Sophy had been treated like the child she was in nature though not in years. She was left with no control over anything that had been her husband's beyond her modest personal income. In his anxiety lest her inexperience should be over-reached he had safeguarded with trustees all he possibly could. The completion of the boy's course at the public school, to be followed in due time by Oxford and ordination, had been all previsioned and arranged, and she really had nothing to occupy her in the world but to eat and drink, and make a business of indolence, and go on weaving and coiling the nut-brown hair, merely keeping a home open for the son whenever he came to her during vacations.

Foreseeing his probable decease long years before her, her husband in his lifetime had purchased for her use a semi-detached villa in the same long, straight road whereon the church and parsonage faced, which was to be hers as long as she chose to live in it. Here she now resided, looking out upon the fragment of lawn in front, and through the railings at the ever-flowing traffic; or, bending forward over the window-sill on the first floor, stretching her eyes far up and down the vista of sooty trees, hazy air, and drab[14] house-façades, along which echoed the noises common to a suburban main thoroughfare.

Somehow, her boy, with his aristocratic school-knowledge,

his grammars, and his aversions, was losing those wide infantine sympathies, extending as far as to the sun and moon themselves, with which he, like other children, had been born, and which his mother, a child of nature herself,[15] had loved in him; he was reducing their compass to a population of a few thousand wealthy and titled people, the mere veneer of a thousand million or so of others who did not interest him at all. He drifted further and further away from her. Sophy's *milieu* being a suburb of minor tradesmen and under-clerks, and her almost only companions the two servants of her own house, it was not surprising that after her husband's death she soon lost the little artificial tastes she had acquired from him, and became – in her son's eyes – a mother whose mistakes and origin it was his painful lot as a gentleman to blush for. As yet he was far from being man enough – if he ever would be – to rate these sins of hers at their true infinitesimal value beside the yearning fondness that welled up and remained penned in her heart till it should be more fully accepted by him, or by some other person or thing. If he had lived at home with her he would have had all of it; but he seemed to require so very little in present circumstances, and it remained stored.

Her life became insupportably dreary; she could not take walks, and had no interest in going for drives, or, indeed, in travelling anywhere. Nearly two years passed without an event, and still she looked on that suburban road, thinking of the village in which she had been born, and whither she would have gone back – O how gladly! – even to work in the fields.

Taking no exercise, she often could not sleep, and would rise in the night or early morning and look out upon the then vacant thoroughfare, where the lamps stood like sentinels waiting for some procession to go by. An approximation to such a procession was indeed made every early morning about one o'clock, when the country vehicles passed up with loads of vegetables for Covent Garden market. She often saw them creeping along at this silent and dusky hour – waggon after waggon, bearing green bastions of cabbages nodding to their fall, yet never falling, walls of baskets enclosing masses of beans and peas, pyramids of snow-white turnips, swaying howdahs of mixed produce

– creeping along behind aged night-horses, who seemed ever patiently wondering between their hollow coughs why they had always to work at that still hour when all other sentient creatures were privileged to rest.[16] Wrapped in a cloak, it was soothing to watch and sympathize with them when depression and nervousness hindered sleep, and to see how the fresh green-stuff brightened to life as it came opposite the lamp, and how the sweating animals steamed and shone with their miles of travel.

They had an interest, almost a charm, for Sophy, these semi-rural people and vehicles moving in an urban atmosphere,[17] leading a life quite distinct from that of the daytime toilers on the same road. One morning a man who accompanied a waggon-load of potatoes gazed rather hard at the house-fronts as he passed, and with a curious emotion she thought his form was familiar to her. She looked out for him again. His being an old-fashioned conveyance, with a yellow front, it was easily recognizable, and on the third night after she saw it a second time. The man alongside was, as she had fancied, Sam Hobson, formerly gardener at Gaymead, who would at one time have married her.

She had occasionally thought of him, and wondered if life in a cottage with him would not have been a happier lot than the life she had accepted. She had not thought of him passionately, but her now dismal situation lent an interest to his resurrection – a tender interest which it is impossible to exaggerate. She went back to bed, and began thinking. When did these market-gardeners, who travelled up to town so regularly at one or two in the morning, come back? She dimly recollected seeing their empty waggons, hardly noticeable amid the ordinary day-traffic, passing down at some hour before noon.

It was only April, but that morning, after breakfast, she had the window opened, and sat looking out, the feeble sun shining full upon her. She affected to sew, but her eyes never left the street. Between ten and eleven the desired waggon, now unladen, reappeared on its return journey. But Sam was not looking round him then, and drove on in a reverie.

'Sam!' cried she.

Turning with a start, his face lighted up. He called to him a little boy to hold the horse, alighted, and came and stood under her window.

'I can't come down easily, Sam, or I would!' she said. 'Did you know I lived here?'

'Well, Mrs Twycott, I knew you lived along here somewhere. I have often looked out for 'ee.'

He briefly explained his own presence on the scene. He had long since given up his gardening in the village near Aldbrickham, and was now manager at a market-gardener's on the south side of London, it being part of his duty to go up to Covent Garden with waggon-loads of produce two or three times a week. In answer to her curious inquiry, he admitted that he had come to this particular district because he had seen in the Aldbrickham paper, a year or two before, the announcement of the death in South London[18] of the aforetime vicar of Gaymead, which had revived an interest in her dwelling-place that he could not extinguish, leading him to hover about the locality till his present post had been secured.

They spoke of their native village in dear old North Wessex, the spots in which they had played together as children. She tried to feel that she was a dignified personage now, that she must not be too confidential with Sam. But she could not keep it up, and the tears hanging in her eyes were indicated in her voice.

'You are not happy, Mrs Twycott, I'm afraid?' he said.

'O, of course not! I lost my husband only the year before last.'

'Ah! I meant in another way. You'd like to be home again?'

'This is my home – for life. The house belongs to me. But I understand—' She let it out then. 'Yes, Sam. I long for home – *our* home! I *should* like to be there, and never leave it, and die there.' But she remembered herself. 'That's only a momentary feeling. I have a son, you know, a dear boy. He's at school now.'

'Somewhere handy, I suppose? I see there's lots on 'em along this road.'

'O no! Not in one of these wretched holes![19] At a public school – one of the most distinguished in England.'

'Chok' it all! of course! I forget, ma'am, that you've been a lady for so many years.'

'No, I am not a lady,' she said sadly. 'I never shall be. But he's a gentleman, and that – makes it – O how difficult for me!'

## III

The acquaintance thus oddly reopened proceeded apace. She often looked out to get a few words with him, by night or by day. Her sorrow was that she could not accompany her one old friend on foot a little way, and talk more freely than she could do while he paused before the house. One night, at the beginning of June, when she was again on the watch after an absence of some days from the window, he entered the gate and said softly, 'Now, wouldn't some air do you good? I've only half a load this morning. Why not ride up to Covent Garden with me? There's a nice seat on the cabbages, where I've spread a sack. You can be home again in a cab before anybody is up.'

She refused at first, and then, trembling with excitement, hastily finished her dressing, and wrapped herself up in cloak and veil, afterwards sidling[20] downstairs by the aid of the hand-rail, in a way she could adopt on an emergency. When she had opened the door she found Sam on the step, and he lifted her bodily on his strong arm across the little forecourt into his vehicle. Not a soul was visible or audible in the infinite length of the straight, flat highway, with its ever-waiting lamps converging to points in each direction. The air was fresh as country air at this hour, and the stars shone, except to the north-eastward, where there was a whitish light – the dawn. Sam carefully placed her in the seat, and drove on.

They talked as they had talked in old days, Sam pulling himself up now and then, when he thought himself too familiar. More than once she said with misgiving that she wondered if she ought to have indulged in the freak. 'But I am so lonely in my house,' she added, 'and this makes me so happy!'

'You must come again, dear Mrs Twycott. There is no time o' day for taking the air like this.'

It grew lighter and lighter. The sparrows became busy in the streets, and the city waxed denser around them. When they approached the river it was day, and on the bridge they beheld the full blaze of morning sunlight in the direction of St Paul's, the river glistening towards it, and not a craft stirring.

Near Covent Garden he put her into a cab, and they parted, looking into each other's faces like the very old friends they were. She reached home without adventure, limped to the door, and let herself in with her latch-key unseen.

The air and Sam's presence had revived her: her cheeks were quite pink – almost beautiful. She had something to live for in addition to her son. A woman of pure instincts, she knew there had been nothing really wrong in the journey, but supposed it conventionally to be very wrong indeed.

Soon, however, she gave way to the temptation of going with him again, and on this occasion their conversation was distinctly tender, and Sam said he never should forget her, notwithstanding that she had served him rather badly at one time.[21] After much hesitation he told her of a plan it was in his power to carry out, and one he should like to take in hand, since he did not care for London work: it was to set up as a master-greengrocer down at Aldbrickham, the county-town of their native place. He knew of an opening – a shop kept by aged people who wished to retire.

'And why don't you do it, then, Sam?' she asked with a slight heartsinking.

'Because I'm not sure if – you'd join me. I know you wouldn't – couldn't! Such a lady as ye've been so long, you couldn't be a wife to a man like me.'

'I hardly suppose I could!' she assented, also frightened at the idea.

'If you could,' he said eagerly, 'you'd on'y have to sit in the back parlour and look through the glass partition when I was away sometimes – just to keep an eye on things. The lameness wouldn't hinder that . . . I'd keep you as genteel as ever I could, dear Sophy – if I might think of it!' he pleaded.

'Sam, I'll be frank,' she said, putting her hand on his. 'If it were only myself I would do it, and gladly, though everything I possess would be lost to me by marrying again.'[22]

'I don't mind that! It's more independent.'

'That's good of you, dear, dear Sam. But there's something else. I have a son ... I almost fancy when I am miserable sometimes that he is not really mine, but one I hold in trust for my late husband. He seems to belong so little to me personally, so entirely to his dead father. He is so much educated and I so little that I do not feel dignified enough to be his mother ... Well, he would have to be told.'

'Yes. Unquestionably.' Sam saw her thought and her fear. 'Still, you can do as you like, Sophy – Mrs Twycott,' he added. 'It is not you who are the child, but he.'

'Ah, you don't know! Sam, if I could, I would marry you, some day. But you must wait a while, and let me think.'

It was enough for him, and he was blithe at their parting. Not so she. To tell Randolph seemed impossible. She could wait till he had gone up to Oxford, when what she did would affect his life but little. But would he ever tolerate the idea? And if not, could she defy him?

She had not told him a word when the yearly cricket-match came on at Lord's between the public schools,[23] though Sam had already gone back to Aldbrickham. Mrs Twycott felt stronger than usual: she went to the match with Randolph, and was able to leave her chair and walk about occasionally. The bright idea occurred to her that she could casually broach the subject while moving round among the spectators, when the boy's spirits were high with interest in the game, and he would weigh domestic matters as feathers in the scale beside the day's victory. They promenaded under the lurid July sun, this pair, so wide apart, yet so near, and Sophy saw the large proportion of boys like her own, in their broad white collars and dwarf hats, and all around the rows of great coaches under which was jumbled the *débris* of luxurious luncheons; bones, pie-crusts, champagne-bottles, glasses, plates, napkins, and the family silver; while on the coaches sat the proud fathers and mothers; but never a poor mother like her.[24] If Randolph had not appertained to these, had not centred all his interests in them, had not cared exclusively for the class they belonged to, how happy would things have been! A great huzza at some small performance with the bat burst from the multitude of relatives, and Randolph jumped wildly into the air to see what had happened. Sophy fetched up the sentence that had been already shaped; but she could not get it out. The occasion was, perhaps, an inopportune one. The contrast between her story and the display of fashion to which Randolph had grown to regard himself as akin would be fatal. She awaited a better time.

It was on an evening when they were alone in their plain suburban residence, where life was not blue but brown, that she ultimately broke silence, qualifying her announcement of a probable second marriage by assuring him that it would not take place for a long time to come, when he would be living quite independently of her.

The boy thought the idea a very reasonable one, and asked if she had chosen anybody? She hesitated; and he seemed to have a misgiving. He hoped his stepfather would be a gentleman? he said.

'Not what you call a gentleman,' she answered timidly.[25] 'He'll be much as I was before I knew your father;' and by degrees she acquainted him with the whole. The youth's face remained fixed for a moment; then he flushed, leant on the table, and burst into passionate tears.

His mother went up to him, kissed all of his face that she could get at, and patted his back as if he were still the baby he once had been, crying herself the while. When he had somewhat recovered from his paroxysm he went hastily to his own room and fastened the door.

Parleyings were attempted through the keyhole, outside which she waited and listened. It was long before he would reply, and when he did it was to say sternly at her from within: 'I am ashamed of you! It will ruin me! A miserable boor! a churl! a clown! It will degrade me in the eyes of all the gentlemen of England!'

'Say no more – perhaps I am wrong! I will struggle against it!' she cried miserably.

Before Randolph left her that summer a letter arrived from Sam to inform her that he had been unexpectedly fortunate in obtaining the shop. He was in possession; it was the largest in the town, combining fruit with vegetables, and he thought it would form a home worthy even of her some day. Might he not run up to town to see her?

She met him by stealth, and said he must still wait for her final answer. The autumn dragged on, and when Randolph was home at Christmas for the holidays she broached the matter again. But the young gentleman was inexorable.

It was dropped for months; renewed again; abandoned under his repugnance; again attempted; and thus the gentle creature reasoned and pleaded till four or five long years had passed. Then the faithful Sam revived his suit with some peremptoriness.[26] Sophy's son, now an undergraduate, was down from Oxford one Easter, when she again opened the subject. As soon as he was ordained, she argued, he would have a home of his own, wherein she, with her bad grammar and her ignorance, would be an encumbrance to him. Better obliterate her as much as possible.

He showed a more manly anger now, but would not agree. She on her side was more persistent, and he had doubts whether she could be trusted in his absence. But by indignation and contempt for her taste he completely maintained his ascendency; and finally taking her before a little cross and altar that he had erected in his bedroom for his private devotions, there bade her kneel, and swear[27] that she would not wed Samuel Hobson without his consent. 'I owe this to my father!' he said.

The poor woman swore, thinking he would soften as soon as he was ordained and in full swing of clerical work. But he did not. His education had by this time sufficiently ousted his humanity to keep him quite firm; though his mother might have led an idyllic life with her faithful fruiterer and greengrocer, and nobody have been anything the worse in the world.

Her lameness became more confirmed as time went on, and she seldom or never left the house in the long southern thoroughfare, where she seemed to be pining her heart away. 'Why mayn't I say to Sam that I'll marry him? Why mayn't I?' she would murmur plaintively to herself when nobody was near.

Some four years after this date a middle-aged man was standing at the door of the largest fruiterer's shop in Aldbrickham. He was the proprietor, but today, instead of his usual business attire, he wore a neat suit of black; and his window was partly shuttered. From the railway-station a funeral procession was seen approaching: it passed his door and went out of the town towards the village of Gaymead. The man, whose eyes were wet,[28] held his hat in his hand as the vehicles moved by; while from the mourning coach a young smooth-shaven priest in a high waistcoat looked black as a cloud at the shop-keeper standing there.

# ON THE WESTERN CIRCUIT[1]

## I

The man who played the disturbing part in the two quiet lives hereafter depicted – no great man, in any sense, by the way – first had knowledge of them on an October evening, in the city of Melchester.[2] He had been standing in the Close, vainly endeavouring to gain amid the darkness a glimpse of the most homogeneous pile of mediæval architecture in England, which towered and tapered from the damp and level sward in front of him. While he stood the presence of the Cathedral walls was revealed rather by the ear than by the eyes; he could not see them, but they reflected sharply a roar of sound which entered the Close by a street leading from the city square, and, falling upon the building, was flung back upon him.

He postponed till the morrow his attempt to examine the deserted edifice, and turned his attention to the noise. It was compounded of steam barrel-organs, the clanging of gongs, the ringing of hand-bells, the clack of rattles, and the undistinguishable shouts of men. A lurid light hung in the air in the direction of the tumult. Thitherward he went, passing under the arched gateway, along a straight street, and into the square.

He might have searched Europe over for a greater contrast between juxtaposed scenes. The spectacle was that of the eighth chasm of the Inferno as to colour and flame, and, as to mirth, a development of the Homeric heaven.[3] A smoky glare, of the complexion of brass-filings, ascended from the fiery tongues of innumerable naphtha lamps affixed to booths, stalls, and other temporary erections which crowded the spacious market-square. In front of this irradiation scores of human figures, more or less in profile, were darting athwart and across, up, down, and around, like gnats against a sunset.

Their motions were so rhythmical that they seemed to be moved by machinery. And it presently appeared that they were moved by machinery indeed; the figures being those of the patrons of swings, see-saws, flying-leaps, above all of the three steam roundabouts which occupied the centre of the position. It was from the latter that the din of steam-organs came.

Throbbing humanity in full light was, on second thoughts, better than architecture[4] in the dark. The young man, lighting a short pipe, and putting his hat on one side and one hand in his pocket, to throw himself into harmony with his new environment, drew near to the largest and most patronized of the steam circuses, as the roundabouts were called by their owners. This was one of brilliant finish, and it was now in full revolution. The musical instrument around which and to whose tones the riders revolved, directed its trumpet-mouths of brass upon the young man, and the long plate-glass mirrors set at angles, which revolved with the machine, flashed the gyrating personages and hobby-horses kaleidoscopically into his eyes.

It could now be seen that he was unlike the majority of the crowd. A gentlemanly young fellow, one of the species found in large towns only, and London particularly, built on delicate lines, well, though not fashionably dressed, he appeared to belong to the professional class; he had nothing square or practical about his look, much that was curvilinear and sensuous. Indeed, some would have called him a man not altogether typical of the middle-class male of a century wherein sordid ambition is the master-passion that seems to be taking the time-honoured place of love.

The revolving figures passed before his eyes with an unexpected and quiet grace in a throng whose natural movements did not suggest gracefulness or quietude as a rule. By some contrivance there was imparted to each of the hobby-horses a motion which was really the triumph and perfection of roundabout inventiveness – a galloping rise and fall, so timed that, of each pair of steeds, one was on the spring while the other was on the pitch. The riders were quite fascinated by these equine undulations in this most delightful holiday-game[5] of our times. There were riders as young as six, and as old as sixty years, with every age between. At first it was difficult to catch a personality, but by and by the observer's eyes centred on the prettiest girl out of the several pretty ones revolving.

It was not that one with the light frock and light hat whom he had been at first attracted by; no, it was the one with the black cape, grey skirt, light gloves and – no, not even she, but the one behind her; she with the crimson skirt, dark jacket, brown hat and brown gloves.[6] Unmistakably that was the prettiest girl.

Having finally selected her, this idle spectator studied her as well as he was able during each of her brief transits across his visual field. She was absolutely unconscious of everything save the act of riding: her features were rapt in an ecstatic dreaminess; for the moment she did not know her age or her history or her lineaments, much less her troubles. He himself was full of vague latter-day glooms and popular melancholies, and it was a refreshing sensation to behold this young thing then and there, absolutely as happy as if she were in a Paradise.

Dreading the moment when the inexorable stoker, grimily lurking behind the glittering rococo-work, should decide that this set of riders had had their pennyworth, and bring the whole concern of steam-engine, horses, mirrors, trumpets, drums, cymbals, and such-like to pause and silence,[7] he waited for her every reappearance, glancing indifferently over the intervening forms, including the two plainer girls, the old woman and child, the two youngsters, the newly-married couple, the old man with a clay pipe, the sparkish youth with a ring, the young ladies in the chariot, the pair of journeyman-carpenters, and others, till his select country beauty followed on again in her place. He had never seen a fairer product of nature, and at each round she made a deeper mark in his sentiments. The stoppage then came, and the sighs of the riders were audible.

He moved round to the place at which he reckoned she would alight; but she retained her seat. The empty saddles began to refill, and she plainly was deciding to have another turn. The young man drew up to the side of her steed, and pleasantly asked her if she had enjoyed her ride.

'O yes!' she said, with dancing eyes. 'It has been quite unlike anything I have ever felt in my life before!'

It was not difficult to fall into conversation with her. Unreserved – too unreserved – by nature, she was not experienced enough to be reserved by art, and after a little coaxing she answered his remarks readily. She had come to live in Melchester from a village on the Great Plain,[8] and this was the first time that she had ever seen a steam-circus; she could not understand how such wonderful machines were made. She had come to the city on the invitation of Mrs Harnham, who had taken her into her household to train her as a servant, if she showed any aptitude. Mrs Harnham was a young lady[9] who before she married had been Miss Edith White, living in the country near the speaker's cottage; she was now very kind to her through knowing her in childhood so well. She was even taking the trouble to educate her. Mrs Harnham was the only friend she had in the world, and being without children had wished to have her near her in preference to anybody else, though she had only lately come; allowed her to do almost as she liked, and to have a holiday whenever she asked for it. The husband of this kind young lady was a rich wine-merchant of the town, but Mrs Harnham did not care much about him. In the daytime you could see the house from where they were talking. She, the speaker, liked Melchester better than the lonely country, and she was going to have a new hat for next Sunday that was to cost fifteen and ninepence.

Then she inquired of her acquaintance where he lived, and he told her in London, that ancient and smoky city, where everybody lived who lived at all, and died because they could not live there. He came into Wessex two or three times a year for professional reasons; he had arrived from Wintoncester[10] yesterday, and was going on into the next county in a day or two. For one thing he did like the country better than the town, and it was because it contained such girls as herself.

Then the pleasure-machine started again, and, to the light-hearted girl, the figure of the handsome young man, the market-square with its lights and crowd, the houses beyond, and the world at large, began moving round as before, countermoving in the revolving mirrors on her right hand, she being as it were the fixed point in an undulating, dazzling, lurid universe, in which loomed forward most prominently of all the form of her late interlocutor. Each time that she approached the half of her orbit that lay nearest him they gazed at each other with smiles, and with that unmistakable expression which means so little at the moment, yet so often leads up to passion,[11] heart-ache, union, disunion, devotion, overpopulation, drudgery, content, resignation, despair.

When the horses slowed anew he stepped to her side and proposed another heat. 'Hang the expense for once,' he said. 'I'll pay!'

She laughed till the tears came.

'Why do you laugh, dear?' said he.

'Because – you are so genteel that you must have plenty of money, and only say that for fun!' she returned.

'Ha-ha!' laughed the young man in unison, and gallantly producing his money she was enabled to whirl on again.

As he stood smiling there in the motley crowd, with his pipe in his hand, and clad in the rough pea-jacket and wideawake that he had put on for his stroll, who would have supposed him to be Charles Bradford Raye, Esquire, stuff-gownsman, educated at Wintoncester, called to the Bar at Lincoln's-Inn,[12] now going the Western Circuit, merely detained in Melchester by a small arbitration after his brethren had moved on to the next county-town?

## II

The square was overlooked from its remoter corner by the house of which the young girl had spoken, a dignified residence of considerable size, having several windows on each floor. Inside one of these, on the first floor, the apartment being a large drawing-room, sat a lady, in appearance from twenty-eight to thirty years of age. The blinds were still undrawn, and the lady was absently surveying the weird scene without, her cheek resting on her hand. The room was unlit from within, but enough of the glare from the market-place entered it to reveal the lady's face. She was what is called an interesting creature rather than a handsome woman; dark-eyed, thoughtful, and with sensitive lips.[13]

A man sauntered into the room from behind and came forward.

'O, Edith, I didn't see you,' he said. 'Why are you sitting here in the dark?'

'I am looking at the fair,' replied the lady in a languid voice.

'Oh? Horrid nuisance every year! I wish it could be put a stop to.'

'I like it.'

'H'm. There's no accounting for taste.'

For a moment he gazed from the window with her, for politeness sake, and then went out again.

In a few minutes she rang.

'Hasn't Anna come in?' asked Mrs Harnham.

'No m'm.'

'She ought to be in by this time. I meant her to go for ten minutes only.'

'Shall I go and look for her, m'm?' said the house-maid alertly.

'No. It is not necessary: she is a good girl and will come soon.'

However, when the servant had gone Mrs Harnham arose, went up to her room, cloaked and bonneted herself, and proceeded downstairs, where she found her husband.

'I want to see the fair,' she said; 'and I am going to look for Anna. I have made myself responsible for her, and must see she comes to no harm. She ought to be indoors. Will you come with me?'

'Oh, she's all right. I saw her on one of those whirligig things, talking to her young man as I came in. But I'll go if you wish, though I'd rather go a hundred miles the other way.'

'Then please do so. I shall come to no harm alone.'

She left the house and entered the crowd which thronged the market-place, where she soon discovered Anna, seated on the revolving horse. As soon as it stopped Mrs Harnham advanced and said severely, 'Anna, how can you be such a wild girl? You were only to be out for ten minutes.'

Anna looked blank, and the young man, who had dropped into the background, came to her assistance.

'Please don't blame her,' he said politely. 'It is my fault that she has stayed. She looked so graceful on the horse that I induced her to go round again. I assure you that she has been quite safe.'

'In that case I'll leave her in your hands,' said Mrs Harnham, turning to retrace her steps.

But this for the moment it was not so easy to do. Something had attracted the crowd to a spot in their rear, and the wine-merchant's wife, caught by its sway, found herself pressed against Anna's acquaintance without power to move away. Their faces were within a few inches of each other, his breath fanned her cheek as well as Anna's. They could do no other than smile at the accident; but neither spoke, and each waited passively. Mrs Harnham then felt a man's hand clasping her fingers, and from the look of consciousness on the young fellow's face she knew the hand to be his: she also knew that from the position of the girl he had no other thought than that the imprisoned hand was Anna's. What prompted her to refrain from undeceiving him she could hardly tell. Not content with holding the hand, he playfully slipped two of his fingers inside her glove, against her palm. Thus matters continued till the pressure lessened; but several minutes passed before the crowd thinned sufficiently to allow Mrs Harnham to withdraw.

'How did they get to know each other, I wonder?' she mused as she retreated. 'Anna is really very forward – and he very wicked and nice.'[14]

She was so gently stirred with the stranger's manner and voice, with the tenderness of his idle touch, that instead of re-entering the house she turned back again and observed the pair from a screened nook. Really she argued (being little less impulsive than Anna herself) it was very excusable in Anna to encourage him, however she might have contrived to make his acquaintance; he was so gentlemanly, so fascinating, had such beautiful eyes. The thought that he was several years her junior produced a reasonless sigh.

At length the couple turned from the roundabout towards the door of Mrs Harnham's house, and the young man could be heard saying that he would accompany her home. Anna, then, had found a lover, apparently a very devoted one. Mrs Harnham was quite interested in him. When they drew near the door of the wine-merchant's house, a comparatively deserted spot by this time, they stood invisible for a little while in the shadow of a wall, where they separated, Anna going on to the entrance, and her acquaintance returning across the square.

'Anna,' said Mrs Harnham, coming up. 'I've been looking at you! That young man kissed you at parting, I am almost sure.'

'Well,' stammered Anna; 'he said, if I didn't mind – it would do me no harm, and, and, him a great deal of good!'

'Ah, I thought so! And he was a stranger till tonight?'

'Yes ma'am.'

'Yet I warrant you told him your name and everything about yourself?'

'He asked me.'

'But he didn't tell you his?'

'Yes ma'am, he did!' cried Anna victoriously. 'It is Charles Bradford, of London.'

'Well, if he's respectable, of course I've nothing to say against your knowing him,' remarked her mistress, prepossessed, in spite of general principles, in the young man's favour. 'But I must reconsider all that, if he attempts to renew your acquaintance. A country-bred girl like you, who has never lived in Melchester till this month, who had hardly ever seen a black-coated man till you came here, to be so sharp as to capture a young Londoner like him!'

'I didn't capture him. I didn't do anything,' said Anna, in confusion.

When she was indoors and alone Mrs Harnham thought what a well-bred[15] and chivalrous young man Anna's companion had seemed. There had been a magic in his wooing touch of her hand; and she wondered how he had come to be attracted by the girl.

The next morning the emotional Edith Harnham went to the usual week-day service in Melchester cathedral. In crossing the Close through the fog she again perceived him who had interested her the previous evening, gazing up thoughtfully at the high-piled architecture of the nave: and as soon as she had taken her seat he entered and sat down in a stall opposite hers.

He did not particularly heed her; but Mrs Harnham was continually occupying her eyes with[16] him, and wondered more than ever what had attracted him in her unfledged maid-servant. The mistress was almost as unaccustomed as the maiden herself to the end-of-the-age young man, or she might have wondered less. Raye, having looked about him awhile, left abruptly, without regard to the service that was proceeding; and Mrs Harnham – lonely, impressionable creature that she was – took no further interest in praising the Lord. She wished she had married a London man who knew the subtleties of love-making as they were evidently known to him who had mistakenly caressed her hand.

## III

The calendar at Melchester had been light, occupying the court only a few hours; and the assizes at Casterbridge, the next county-town on the Western Circuit, having no business[17] for Raye, he had not gone thither. At the next town after that they did not open till the following Monday, trials to begin on Tuesday morning. In the natural order of things Raye would have arrived at the latter place on Monday afternoon; but it was not till the middle of Wednesday that his gown and grey wig, curled in tiers, in the best fashion of Assyrian bas-reliefs,[18] were seen blowing and bobbing behind him as he hastily walked up the High Street from his lodgings. But though he entered the assize building there was nothing for him to do, and sitting at the blue baize table in the well of the court, he mended pens with a mind far away from the case in progress. Thoughts of unpremeditated conduct, of which a week earlier he would not have believed himself capable, threw him into a mood of dissatisfied depression.[19]

He had contrived to see again the pretty rural maiden Anna,

the day after the fair, had walked out of the city with her to the earthworks of Old Melchester, and feeling a violent fancy for her, had remained in Melchester all Sunday, Monday, and Tuesday; by persuasion obtaining walks and meetings with the girl six or seven times during the interval; had in brief won her, body and soul.[20]

He supposed it must have been owing to the seclusion in which he had lived of late in town that he had given way so unrestrainedly to a passion for an artless creature whose inexperience had, from the first, led her to place herself unreservedly in his hands.[21] Much he deplored trifling with her feelings for the sake of a passing desire; and he could only hope that she might not live to suffer on his account.

She had begged him to come to her again; entreated him; wept. He had promised that he would do so, and he meant to carry out that promise. He could not desert her now.[22] Awkward as such unintentional connections were, the interspace of a hundred miles – which to a girl of her limited capabilities was like a thousand – would effectually hinder this summer fancy from greatly encumbering his life; while thought of her simple love might do him the negative good of keeping him from idle pleasures in town when he wished to work hard. His circuit journeys would take him to Melchester three or four times a year; and then he could always see her.

The pseudonym, or rather partial name, that he had given her as his before knowing how far the acquaintance was going to carry him, had been spoken on the spur of the moment, without any ulterior intention whatever. He had not afterwards disturbed Anna's error, but on leaving her he had felt bound to give her an address at a stationer's not far from his chambers, at which she might write to him under the initials 'C. B.'

In due time Raye returned to his London abode, having called at Melchester on his way and spent a few additional hours with his fascinating child of nature. In town he lived monotonously every day. Often he and his rooms were enclosed by a tawny fog from all the world besides, and when he lighted the gas to read or write by, his situation seemed so unnatural that he would look into the fire and think of that trusting[23] girl at

Melchester again and again. Often, oppressed by absurd fondness for her, he would enter the dim religious nave of the Law Courts by the north door, elbow other juniors habited like himself, and like him unretained; edge himself into this or that crowded court where a sensational case was going on, just as if he were in it, though the police officers at the door knew as well as he knew himself that he had no more concern with the business in hand than the patient idlers at the gallery-door outside, who had waited to enter since eight in the morning because, like him, they belonged to the classes that live on expectation.[24] But he would do these things to no purpose, and think how greatly the characters in such scenes contrasted with the pink and breezy Anna.

An unexpected feature in that peasant maiden's conduct was that she had not as yet written to him, though he had told her she might do so if she wished. Surely a young creature had never before been so reticent in such circumstances. At length he sent her a brief line, positively requesting her to write. There was no answer by the return post, but the day after a letter in a neat feminine hand, and bearing the Melchester post-mark, was handed to him by the stationer.

The fact alone of its arrival was sufficient to satisfy his imaginative sentiment. He was not anxious to open the epistle, and in truth did not begin to read it[25] for nearly half-an-hour, anticipating readily its terms of passionate retrospect and tender adjuration. When at last he turned his feet to the fireplace and unfolded the sheet, he was surprised and pleased to find that neither extravagance nor vulgarity was there. It was the most charming little missive he had ever received from woman. To be sure the language was simple and the ideas were slight; but it was so self-possessed; so purely that of a young girl who felt her womanhood to be enough for her dignity that he read it through twice. Four sides were filled, and a few lines written across,[26] after the fashion of former days; the paper, too, was common, and not of the latest shade and surface. But what of those things? He had received letters from women who were fairly called ladies, but never so sensible, so human a letter as this. He could not single out any one sentence and say it was at all remarkable or clever; the *ensemble* of the letter it was which won him; and beyond the one request that he would write[27] or come to her again soon there was nothing to show her sense of a claim upon him.

To write again and develop a correspondence was the last thing Raye would have preconceived as his conduct in such a situation; yet he did send a short, encouraging line or two, signed with his pseudonym, in which he asked for another letter, and cheeringly promised that he would try to see her again on some near day, and would never forget how much they had been to each other during their short acquaintance.

## IV

To return now to the moment at which Anna, at Melchester, had received Raye's letter.

It had been put into her own hand by the postman on his morning rounds. She flushed down to her neck on receipt of it, and turned it over and over. 'It is mine?' she said.

'Why, yes, can't you see it is?' said the postman, smiling as he guessed the nature of the document and the cause of the confusion.

'O yes, of course!' replied Anna, looking at the letter, forcedly tittering, and blushing still more.

Her look of embarrassment did not leave her with the postman's departure. She opened the envelope, kissed its contents, put away the letter in her pocket, and remained musing till her eyes filled with tears.

A few minutes later she carried up a cup of tea to Mrs Harnham in her bed-chamber. Anna's mistress looked at her, and said: 'How dismal you seem this morning, Anna. What's the matter?'

'I'm not dismal, I'm glad; only I—' She stopped to stifle a sob.

'Well?'

'I've got a letter – and what good is it to me, if I can't read a word in it!'

'Why, I'll read it, child, if necessary.'

'But this is from somebody – I don't want anybody to read it but myself!' Anna murmured.

'I shall not tell anybody. Is it from that young man?'

'I think so.' Anna slowly produced the letter, saying: 'Then will you read it to me, ma'am?'

This was the secret of Anna's embarrassment and flutterings. She could neither read nor write. She had grown up under the care of an aunt by marriage, at one of the lonely hamlets on the Great Mid-Wessex Plain where, even in days of national education,[28] there had been no school within a distance of two miles. Her aunt was an ignorant woman; there had been nobody to investigate Anna's circumstances, nobody to care about her learning the rudiments; though, as often in such cases, she had been well fed and clothed and not unkindly treated. Since she had come to live at Melchester with Mrs Harnham, the latter, who took a kindly interest in the girl, had taught her to speak correctly, in which accomplishment Anna showed considerable readiness, as is not unusual with the illiterate; and soon became quite fluent in the use of her mistress's phraseology. Mrs Harnham also insisted upon her getting a spelling and copy book, and beginning to practise in these. Anna was slower in this branch of her education, and meanwhile here was the letter.

Edith Harnham's large dark eyes expressed some interest in the contents, though, in her character of mere interpreter, she threw into her tone as much as she could of mechanical passiveness. She read the short epistle on to its concluding sentence, which idly requested Anna to send him a tender answer.

'Now – you'll do it for me, won't you, dear mistress?' said Anna eagerly. 'And you'll do it as well as ever you can, please? Because I couldn't bear him to think I am not able to do it myself. I should sink into the earth with shame if he knew that!'

From some words in the letter Mrs Harnham was led to ask questions, and the answers she received confirmed her suspicions.[29] Deep concern filled Edith's heart at perceiving how the girl had committed her happiness to the issue of this new-sprung attachment. She blamed herself for not interfering in a flirtation which had resulted so seriously for the poor little creature in her charge; though at the time of seeing the pair together she had a feeling that it was hardly within her province to nip young affection in the bud. However, what was done could not be undone, and it behoved her now, as Anna's only protector, to help her as much as she could. To Anna's eager request that she, Mrs Harnham, should compose and write the answer to this young London man's letter, she felt bound to accede, to keep alive his attachment to the girl if possible; though in other circumstances she might have suggested the cook as an amanuensis.

A tender reply was thereupon concocted, and set down in Edith Harnham's hand. This letter it had been which Raye had received and delighted in. Written in the presence of Anna it certainly was, and on Anna's humble note-paper, and in a measure indited by the young girl; but the life, the spirit, the individuality, were Edith Harnham's.

'Won't you at least put your name yourself?' she said. 'You can manage to write that by this time?'

'No, no,' said Anna, shrinking back. 'I should do it so bad. He'd be ashamed of me, and never see me again!'

The note, so prettily requesting another from him, had, as we have seen, power enough in its pages to bring one. He declared it to be such a pleasure to hear from her that she must write every week. The same process of manufacture was accordingly repeated by Anna and her mistress, and continued for several weeks in succession; each letter being penned and suggested by Edith, the girl standing by; the answer read and commented on by Edith, Anna standing by and listening again.

Late on a winter evening, after the dispatch of the sixth letter, Mrs Harnham was sitting alone by the remains of her fire. Her husband had retired to bed, and she had fallen into that fixity of musing which takes no count of hour or temperature. The state of mind had been brought about in Edith by a strange thing which she had done that day. For the first time since Raye's visit Anna had gone to stay over a night or two with her cottage friends on the Plain, and in her absence had arrived, out of its time, a letter from Raye. To this Edith had replied on her own responsibility, from the depths of her own heart, without waiting for her maid's collaboration. The luxury of writing to him what would be known to no consciousness but his was great, and she had indulged herself therein.

Why was it a luxury?

Edith Harnham led a lonely life. Influenced by the belief of the British parent that a bad marriage with its aversions is better than free womanhood with its interests, dignity, and leisure, she had consented to marry the elderly wine-merchant as a *pis aller*, at the age of seven-and-twenty – some three years before this date – to find afterwards that she had made a mistake. That contract had left her still a woman whose deeper nature had never been stirred.

She was now clearly realizing that she had become possessed to the bottom of her soul with the image of a man to whom she was hardly so much as a name. From the first he had attracted her by his looks and voice; by his tender touch; and, with these as generators, the writing of letter after letter and the reading of their soft answers had insensibly developed on her side an emotion which fanned his; till there had resulted a magnetic reciprocity between the correspondents, notwithstanding that one of them wrote in a character not her own. That he had been able to seduce another woman in two days was his crowning though unrecognized fascination for her as the she-animal.[30]

They were her own impassioned and pent-up ideas – lowered to monosyllabic phraseology in order to keep up the disguise – that Edith put into letters signed with another name, much to the shallow Anna's delight, who, unassisted, could not for the world have conceived such pretty fancies for winning him, even had she been able to write them. Edith found that it was these, her own foisted-in sentiments, to which the young barrister mainly responded. The few sentences occasionally added from Anna's own lips made apparently no impression upon him.

The letter-writing in her absence Anna never discovered; but on her return the next morning she declared she wished to see her lover about something at once, and begged Mrs Harnham to ask him to come.

There was a strange anxiety in her manner which did not escape Mrs Harnham, and ultimately resolved itself into a flood of tears. Sinking down at Edith's knees, she made confession that the result of her relations with her lover it would soon become necessary to disclose.

Edith Harnham was generous enough to be very far from inclined to cast Anna adrift at this conjuncture. No true woman ever is so inclined from her own personal point of view, however prompt she may be in taking such steps to safeguard those dear to her. Although she had written to Raye so short a time previously, she instantly penned another Anna-note hinting clearly though delicately the state of affairs.[31]

Raye replied by a hasty line to say how much he was affected by her news: he felt that he must run down to see her almost immediately.

But a week later the girl came to her mistress's room with another note, which on being read informed her that after all he could not find time for the journey. Anna was broken with grief; but by Mrs Harnham's counsel strictly refrained from hurling at him the reproaches and bitterness customary from young women so situated. One thing was imperative: to keep the young man's romantic interest in her alive. Rather therefore did Edith, in the name of her *protégée*, request him on no account to be distressed about the looming event, and not to inconvenience himself to hasten down. She desired above everything to be no weight upon him in his career, no clog upon his high activities. She had wished him to know what had befallen: he was to dismiss it again from his mind. Only he must write tenderly as ever, and when he should come again on the spring circuit it would be soon enough to discuss what had better be done.

It may well be supposed that Anna's own feelings had not been quite in accord with these generous expressions; but the mistress's judgment had ruled, and Anna had acquiesced. 'All I want is that *niceness* you can so well put into your letters, my dear, dear mistress, and that I can't for the life o' me make up out of my own head; though I mean the same thing and feel it exactly when you've written it down!'

When the letter had been sent off, and Edith Harnham was left alone, she bowed herself on the back of her chair and wept.

'I wish it was mine – I wish it was!'[32] she murmured. 'Yet how can I say such a wicked thing!'

## V

The letter moved Raye considerably when it reached him. The intelligence itself had affected him less than her unexpected manner of treating him in relation to it. The absence of any word of reproach, the devotion to his interests, the self-sacrifice apparent in every line, all made up a nobility of character that he had never dreamt of finding in womankind.

'God forgive me!' he said tremulously. 'I have been a wicked wretch. I did not know she was such a treasure as this!'

He reassured her instantly; declaring that he would not of course desert her, that he would provide a home for her somewhere. Meanwhile she was to stay where she was as long as her mistress would allow her.

But a misfortune supervened in this direction. Whether an inkling of Anna's circumstances reached the knowledge of Mrs Harnham's husband or not cannot be said, but the girl was compelled, in spite of Edith's entreaties, to leave the house. By her own choice she decided to go back for a while to the cottage on the Plain.[33] This arrangement led to a consultation as to how the correspondence should be carried on; and in the girl's inability to continue personally what had been begun in her name, and in the difficulty of their acting in concert as heretofore, she requested Mrs Harnham – the only well-to-do friend she had in the world – to receive the letters and reply to them off-hand, sending them on afterwards to herself on the Plain, where she might at least get some neighbour to read them to her, if a trustworthy one could be met with. Anna and her box then departed for the Plain.

Thus it befel that Edith Harnham found herself in the strange position of having to correspond, under no supervision by the real woman, with a man not her husband, in terms which were virtually those of a wife, concerning a condition that was not Edith's at all; the man being one for whom, mainly through the sympathies involved in playing this part, she secretly cherished a predilection, subtle and imaginative truly, but strong and absorbing. She opened each letter, read it as if intended for herself, and replied from the promptings of her own heart and no other.

Throughout this correspondence, carried on in the girl's absence, the high-strung Edith Harnham lived in the ecstasy of fancy; the vicarious intimacy engendered such a flow of passionateness as was never exceeded. For conscience' sake Edith at first sent on each of his letters to Anna, and even rough copies of her replies; but later on these so-called copies were much abridged, and many letters on both sides were not sent on at all.

Though selfish, and, superficially at least, infested with the self-indulgent vices of artificial society, there was a substratum of honesty and fairness in Raye's character. He had really a tender regard for the country girl, and it grew more tender than ever when he found her apparently capable of expressing the deepest sensibilities in the simplest words. He meditated, he wavered; and finally resolved to consult his sister, a maiden lady much older than himself, of lively sympathies and good intent. In making this confidence he showed her some of the letters.

'She seems fairly educated,' Miss Raye observed. 'And bright in ideas. She expresses herself with a taste that must be innate.'

'Yes. She writes very prettily, doesn't she, thanks to these elementary schools?'[34]

'One is drawn out towards her, in spite of one's self, poor thing.'

The upshot of the discussion was that though he had not been directly advised to do it, Raye wrote, in his real name, what he would never have decided to write on his own responsibility; namely that he could not live without her, and would come down in the spring and shelve her looming difficulty by marrying her.

This bold acceptance of the situation was made known to Anna by Mrs Harnham driving out immediately to the cottage on the Plain. Anna jumped for joy like a little child. And poor, crude directions for answering appropriately were given to Edith

Harnham, who on her return to the city carried them out with warm intensifications.

'O!' she groaned, as she threw down the pen. 'Anna – poor good little fool – hasn't intelligence enough to appreciate him! How should she? While I – don't bear his child!'[35]

It was now February. The correspondence had continued altogether for four months; and the next letter from Raye contained incidentally a statement of his position and prospects. He said that in offering to wed her he had, at first, contemplated the step of retiring from a profession which hitherto had brought him very slight emolument, and which, to speak plainly, he had thought might be difficult of practice after his union with her. But the unexpected mines of brightness and warmth that her letters had disclosed to be lurking in her sweet nature had led him to abandon that somewhat sad prospect. He felt sure that, with her powers of development, after a little private training in the social forms of London under his supervision, and a little help from a governess if necessary, she would make as good a professional man's wife as could be desired, even if he should rise to the woolsack.[36] Many a Lord Chancellor's wife had been less intuitively a lady than she had shown herself to be in her lines to him.

'O – poor fellow, poor fellow!' mourned Edith Harnham.

Her distress now raged as high as her infatuation. It was she who had wrought him to this pitch – to a marriage which meant his ruin; yet she could not, in mercy to her maid, do anything to hinder his plan. Anna was coming to Melchester that week, but she could hardly show the girl this last reply from the young man; it told too much of the second individuality that had usurped the place of the first.

Anna came, and her mistress took her into her own room for privacy. Anna began by saying with some anxiety that she was glad the wedding was so near.

'O Anna!' replied Mrs Harnham. 'I think we must tell him all – that I have been doing your writing for you? – lest he should not know it till after you become his wife, and it might lead to dissension and recriminations—'

'O mis'ess, dear mis'ess – please don't tell him now!' cried

Anna in distress. 'If you were to do it, perhaps he would not marry me; and what should I do then? It would be terrible what would come to me! And I am getting on with my writing, too. I have brought with me the copy-book you were so good as to give me, and I practise every day, and though it is so, so hard, I shall do it well at last, I believe, if I keep on trying.'

Edith looked at the copy-book. The copies had been set by herself, and such progress as the girl had made was in the way of grotesque facsimile of her mistress's hand. But even if Edith's flowing calligraphy were reproduced the inspiration would be another thing.

'You do it so beautifully,' continued Anna, 'and say all that I want to say so much better than I could say it, that I do hope you won't leave me in the lurch just now!'

'Very well,' replied the other. 'But I – but I thought I ought not to go on!'

'Why?'

Her strong desire to confide her sentiments led Edith to answer truly:

'Because of its effect upon me.'

'But it *can't* have any!'

'Why, child?'

'Because you are married already!'[37] said Anna with lucid simplicity.

'Of course it can't,' said her mistress hastily; yet glad, despite her conscience, that two or three outpourings still remained to her. 'But you must concentrate your attention on writing your name as I write it here.'


## VI


Soon Raye wrote about the wedding. Having decided to make the best of what he feared was a piece of romantic folly, he had acquired more zest for the grand experiment. He wished the ceremony to be in London, for greater privacy. Edith Harnham would have preferred it at Melchester; Anna was passive. His reasoning prevailed, and Mrs Harnham threw herself with mournful zeal into the preparations for Anna's departure. In a last desperate feeling that she must at every hazard be in at the death of her dream, and see once again the man who by a species of telepathy had exercised such an influence on her, she offered to go up with Anna and be with her through the ceremony – 'to see the end of her', as her mistress put it with forced gaiety; an offer which the girl gratefully accepted; for she had no other friend capable of playing the part of companion and witness, in the presence of a gentlemanly bridegroom, in such a way as not to hasten an opinion that he had made an irremediable social blunder.

It was a muddy morning in March when Raye alighted from a four-wheel cab at the door of a registry-office in the S.W. district of London, and carefully handed down Anna and her companion Mrs Harnham. Anna looked attractive in the somewhat fashionable clothes which Mrs Harnham had helped her to buy, though not quite so attractive as, an innocent child, she had appeared in her country gown on the back of the wooden horse at Melchester Fair.

Mrs Harnham had come up this morning by an early train, and a young man – a friend of Raye's – having met them at the door, all four entered the registry-office together. Till an hour before this time Raye had never known the wine-merchant's wife, except at that first casual encounter, and in the flutter of the performance before them he had little opportunity for more than a brief acquaintance. The contract of marriage at a registry is soon got through; but somehow, during its progress, Raye discovered a strange and secret gravitation between himself and Anna's friend.

The formalities of the wedding – or rather ratification of a previous union[38] – being concluded, the four went in one cab to Raye's lodgings, newly taken in a new suburb in preference to a house, the rent of which he could ill afford just then. Here Anna cut the little cake which Raye had bought at a pastrycook's on his way home from Lincoln's Inn the night before. But she did not do much besides. Raye's friend was obliged to depart almost immediately, and when he had left the only ones virtually present were Edith and Raye, who exchanged ideas with much animation. The conversation was indeed theirs only, Anna being as a domestic animal who humbly heard but understood not. Raye seemed startled in awakening to this fact, and began to feel dissatisfied with her inadequacy.

At last, more disappointed than he cared to own, he said, 'Mrs Harnham, my darling is so flurried that she doesn't know what she is doing or saying. I see that after this event a little quietude will be necessary before she gives tongue to that tender philosophy which she used to treat me to in her letters.'

They had planned to start early that afternoon for Knollsea,[39] to spend the few opening days of their married life there, and as the hour for departure was drawing near Raye asked his wife if she would go to the writing-desk in the next room and scribble a little note to his sister, who had been unable to attend through indisposition, informing her that the ceremony was over, thanking her for her little present, and hoping to know her well now that she was the writer's sister as well as Charles's.

'Say it in the pretty poetical way you know so well how to adopt,' he added, 'for I want you particularly to win her, and both of you to be dear friends.'

Anna looked uneasy, but departed to her task, Raye remaining to talk to their guest. Anna was a long while absent, and her husband suddenly rose and went to her.

He found her still bending over the writing-table, with tears brimming up in her eyes; and he looked down upon the sheet of note-paper with some interest, to discover with what tact she had expressed her goodwill in the delicate circumstances. To his surprise she had progressed but a few lines, in the characters and spelling of a child of eight, and with the ideas of a goose.[40]

'Anna,' he said, staring; 'what's this?'

'It only means – that I can't do it any better!' she answered, through her tears.

'Eh? Nonsense!'

'I can't!' she insisted, with miserable, sobbing hardihood. 'I – I – didn't write those letters, Charles! I only told *her* what to write! And not always that! But I am learning, O so fast, my dear, dear husband! And you'll forgive me, won't you, for not telling you before?' She slid to her knees, abjectly[41] clasped his waist and laid her face against him.

He stood a few moments, raised her, abruptly turned, and shut the door upon her, rejoining Edith in the drawing-room. She saw that something untoward had been discovered, and their eyes remained fixed on each other.

'Do I guess rightly?' he asked, with wan[42] quietude. '*You* were her scribe through all this?'

'It was necessary,' said Edith.

'Did she dictate every word you ever wrote to me?'

'Not every word.'

'In fact, very little?'

'Very little.'

'You wrote a great part of those pages every week from your own conceptions, though in her name!'

'Yes.'

'Perhaps you wrote many of the letters when you were alone, without communication with her?'

'I did.'

He turned to the bookcase, and leant with his hand over his face; and Edith, seeing his distress, became white as a sheet.

'You have deceived me – ruined me!' he murmured.

'O, don't say it!' she cried in her anguish,[43] jumping up and putting her hand on his shoulder. 'I can't bear that!'

'Delighting me deceptively! Why did you do it – *why* did you!'

'I began doing it in kindness to her! How could I do otherwise than try to save such a simple girl from misery? But I admit that I continued it for pleasure to myself.'

Raye looked up. 'Why did it give you pleasure?' he asked.

'I must not tell,' said she.

He continued to regard her, and saw that her lips suddenly began to quiver under his scrutiny, and her eyes to fill and droop. She started aside, and said that she must go to the station to catch the return train: could a cab be called immediately?

But Raye went up to her, and took her unresisting hand. 'Well, to think of such a thing as this!' he said. 'Why, you and I are friends – lovers – devoted lovers – by correspondence!'

'Yes; I suppose.'

'More.'

'More?'

'Plainly more. It is no use blinking that. Legally I have married her – God help us both! – in soul and spirit I have married you, and no other woman in the world!'

'Hush!'

'But I will not hush! Why should you try to disguise the full truth, when you have already owned half of it? Yes, it is between you and me that the bond is – not between me and her! Now I'll say no more. But, O my cruel one, I think I have one claim upon you!'

She did not say what, and he drew her towards him, and bent over her. 'If it was all pure invention in those letters,' he said emphatically, 'give me your cheek only. If you meant what you said, let it be lips. It is for the first and last time, remember!'

She put up her mouth, and he kissed her long. 'You forgive me?' she said crying.

'Yes.'

'But you are ruined!'

'What matter!' he said shrugging his shoulders. 'It serves me right!'

She withdrew, wiped her eyes, entered and bade goodbye to Anna, who had not expected her to go so soon, and was still wrestling with the letter. Raye followed Edith downstairs, and in three minutes she was in a hansom driving to the Waterloo station.

He went back to his wife. 'Never mind the letter, Anna, today,' he said gently. 'Put on your things. We, too, must be off shortly.'

The simple girl, upheld by the sense that she was indeed married, showed her delight at finding that he was as kind as ever after the disclosure. She did not know that before his eyes he beheld as it were a galley, in which he, the fastidious urban, was chained to work for the remainder of his life, with her, the unlettered peasant, chained to his side.

Edith travelled back to Melchester that day with a face that showed the very stupor of grief, her lips still tingling from the desperate pressure of his kiss. The end of her impassioned dream had come.[44] When at dusk she reached the Melchester station her husband was there to meet her, but in his perfunctoriness and her preoccupation they did not see each other, and she went out of the station alone.

She walked mechanically homewards without calling a fly. Entering, she could not bear the silence of the house, and went up in the dark to where Anna had slept, where she remained thinking awhile. She then returned to the drawing-room, and not knowing what she did, crouched down upon the floor.

'I have ruined him!' she kept repeating. 'I have ruined him; because I would not deal treacherously towards her!'

In the course of half-an-hour a figure opened the door of the apartment.

'Ah – who's that?' she said, starting up, for it was dark.

'Your husband – who should it be?' said the worthy merchant.

'Ah – my husband! – I forgot I had a husband!' she whispered to herself.

'I missed you at the station,' he continued. 'Did you see Anna safely tied up? I hope so, for 'twas time.'

'Yes – Anna is married.'[45]

Simultaneously with Edith's journey home Anna and her husband were sitting at the opposite windows of a second-class carriage which sped along to Knollsea. In his hand was a pocket-book full of creased sheets closely written over. Unfolding them one after another he read them in silence, and sighed.

'What are you doing, dear Charles?' she said timidly from the other window, and drew nearer to him as if he were a god.

'Reading over all those sweet letters to me signed "Anna",' he replied with dreary[46] resignation.

# THE FIDDLER OF
# THE REELS

'Talking of Exhibitions, World's Fairs, and what not,' said the old gentleman, 'I would not go round the corner to see a dozen of them nowadays. The only exhibition that ever made, or ever will make, any impression upon my imagination was the first of the series, the parent of them all, and now a thing of old times – the Great Exhibition of 1851,[1] in Hyde Park, London. None of the younger generation can realize the sense of novelty it produced in us who were then in our prime. A noun substantive went so far as to become an adjective in honour of the occasion. It was "exhibition" hat, "exhibition" razor-strop, "exhibition" watch; nay, even "exhibition" weather, "exhibition" spirits, sweethearts, babies, wives – for the time.

'For South Wessex, the year formed in many ways an extraordinary chronological frontier or transit-line, at which there occurred what one might call a precipice in Time. As in a geological "fault", we had presented to us a sudden bringing of ancient and modern into absolute contact, such as probably in no other single year since the Conquest[2] was ever witnessed in this part of the country.'

These observations led us onward to talk[3] of the different personages, gentle and simple, who lived and moved within our narrow and peaceful horizon at that time; and of three people in particular, whose queer little history was oddly touched at points by the Exhibition, more concerned with it than that of anybody else who dwelt in those outlying shades of the world, Stickleford, Mellstock, and Egdon.[4] First in prominence among these three came Wat Ollamoor – if that were his real name – whom the seniors in our party had known well.[5]

He was a woman's man, they said, – supremely so – externally little else. To men he was not attractive; perhaps a little repulsive at times.[6] Musician, dandy, and company-man in practice; veterinary surgeon in theory, he lodged awhile in Mellstock village, coming from nobody knew where; though some said his first appearance in this neighbourhood had been as fiddle-player in a show at Greenhill Fair.[7]

Many a worthy villager envied him his power over unsophisticated maidenhood – a power which seemed sometimes to have a touch of the weird and wizardly in it. Personally he was not ill-favoured, though rather un-English, his complexion being a rich olive, his rank hair dark and rather clammy – made still clammier by secret ointments, which, when he came fresh to a party, caused him to smell like 'boys'-love' (southernwood) steeped in lamp-oil. On occasion he wore curls – a double row – running almost horizontally around his head. But as these were sometimes noticeably absent, it was concluded that they were not altogether of Nature's making. By girls whose love for him had turned to hatred he had been nicknamed 'Mop', from this abundance of hair, which was long enough to rest upon his shoulders; as time passed the name more and more prevailed.

His fiddling possibly had the most to do with the fascination he exercised, for, to speak fairly, it could claim for itself a most peculiar and personal quality, like that in a moving preacher. There were tones in it which bred the immediate conviction that indolence and averseness to systematic application were all that lay between 'Mop' and the career of a second Paganini.[8]

While playing he invariably closed his eyes; using no notes, and, as it were, allowing the violin to wander on at will into the most plaintive passages ever heard by rustic man. There was a certain lingual character in the supplicatory expressions he produced, which would well-nigh have drawn an ache from the heart of a gate-post. He could make any child in the parish, who was at all sensitive to music, burst into tears in a few minutes by simply fiddling one of the old dance-tunes he almost entirely affected – country jigs, reels, and 'Favourite Quick Steps' of the last century – some mutilated remains of which even now reappear as nameless phantoms in new quadrilles and gallops,[9] where they are recognized only by the curious, or by such old-fashioned and far-between people as have been thrown with men like Wat Ollamoor in their early life.

His date was a little later than that of the old Mellstock quire-band which comprised the Dewys, Mail, and the rest – in fact, he did not rise above the horizon thereabout till those well-known musicians were disbanded as ecclesiastical functionaries.[10] In their honest love of thoroughness they despised the new man's style. Theophilus Dewy (Reuben the tranter's younger brother) used to say there was no 'plumness' in it – no bowing, no solidity – it was all fantastical. And probably this was true. Anyhow, Mop had, very obviously, never bowed a note of church-music from his birth; he never once sat in the gallery of Mellstock church where the others had tuned their venerable psalmody so many hundreds of times; had never, in all likelihood, entered a church at all. All were devil's tunes in his repertory. 'He could no more play the Wold Hundredth[11] to his true time than he could play the brazen serpent,' the tranter would say. (The brazen serpent was supposed in Mellstock to be a musical instrument particularly hard to blow.)

Occasionally Mop could produce the aforesaid moving effect upon the souls of grown-up persons, especially young women of fragile and responsive organization. Such an one was Car'line Aspent.[12] Though she was already engaged to be married before she met him, Car'line, of them all, was the most influenced by Mop Ollamoor's heart-stealing melodies, to her discomfort, nay, positive pain and ultimate injury. She was a pretty, invocating, weak-mouthed girl, whose chief defect as a companion with her sex was a tendency to peevishness now and then. At this time she was not a resident in Mellstock parish where Mop lodged, but lived some miles off at Stickleford, farther down the river.

How and where she first made acquaintance with him and his fiddling is not truly known, but the story was that it either began or was developed on one spring evening, when, in passing through Lower Mellstock, she chanced to pause on the bridge near his house to rest herself, and languidly leaned over the parapet. Mop was standing on his door-step, as was his custom, spinning the insidious thread of semi- and demi-semi-quavers from the E string of his fiddle for the benefit of passers-by, and laughing as the tears rolled down the cheeks of the little children hanging around him. Car'line pretended to be engrossed with the rippling of the stream under the arches, but in reality she was listening, as he knew. Presently the aching of the heart seized her simultaneously with a wild desire to glide airily in the mazes of an infinite dance. To shake off the fascination she resolved to go on, although it would be necessary to pass him as he played. On stealthily glancing ahead at the performer, she found to her relief that his eyes were closed in abandonment to instrumentation,[13] and she strode on boldly. But when closer her step grew timid, her tread convulsed itself more and more accordantly with the time of the melody, till she very nearly danced along. Gaining another glance at him when immediately opposite, she saw that *one* of his eyes was open, quizzing her as he smiled at her emotional state. Her gait could not divest itself of its compelled capers till she had gone a long way past the house; and Car'line was unable to shake off the strange infatuation for hours.

After that day, whenever there was to be in the neighbourhood a dance to which she could get an invitation, and where Mop Ollamoor was to be the musician, Car'line contrived to be present, though it sometimes involved a walk of several miles; for he did not play so often in Stickleford as elsewhere.

The next evidences of his influence over her were singular enough, and it would require a neurologist to fully explain them. She would be sitting quietly, any evening after dark, in the house of her father, the parish clerk, which stood in the middle of Stickleford village street, this being the highroad between Lower Mellstock and Moreford,[14] five miles eastward. Here, without a moment's warning, and in the midst of a general conversation between her father, sister, and the young man before alluded to, who devotedly wooed her in ignorance of her infatuation, she would start from her seat in the chimney-corner as if she had received a galvanic shock, and spring convulsively towards the ceiling;[15] then she would burst into tears, and it was not till some half-hour had passed that she grew calm as usual. Her

father, knowing her hysterical tendencies, was always excess-
ively anxious about this trait in his youngest girl, and feared
the attack to be a species of epileptic fit. Not so her sister Julia.
Julia had found out what was the cause. At the moment before
the jumping, only an exceptionally sensitive ear situated in the
chimney-nook could have caught from down the flue the beat
of a man's footstep along the highway without. But it was in
that footfall, for which she had been waiting, that the origin of
Car'line's involuntary springing lay. The pedestrian was Mop
Ollamoor, as the girl well knew; but his business that way was
not to visit her; he sought another woman whom he spoke of as
his Intended, and who lived at Moreford, two miles farther on.
On one, and only one, occasion did it happen that Car'line
could not control her utterance; it was when her sister alone
chanced to be present. 'Oh – oh – oh—!' she cried. 'He's going
to *her*, and not coming to *me*!'

To do the fiddler justice he had not at first thought greatly of,
or spoken much to, this girl of impressionable mould. But he
had soon found out her secret, and could not resist a little
by-play with her too easily hurt heart, as an interlude between
his more serious performances at Moreford. The two became
well acquainted, though only by stealth, hardly a soul in Stickleford except her sister, and her lover Ned Hipcroft, being aware
of the attachment. Her father disapproved of her coldness to
Ned; her sister, too, hoped she might get over this nervous
passion for a man of whom so little was known. The ultimate
result was that Car'line's manly and simple wooer Edward found
his suit becoming practically hopeless. He was a respectable
mechanic, in a far sounder position than Mop the nominal
horse-doctor; but when, before leaving her, Ned put his flat and
final question, would she marry him, then and there, now or
never, it was with little expectation of obtaining more than the
negative she gave him. Though her father supported him and
her sister supported him, he could not play the fiddle so as to
draw your soul out of your body like a spider's thread, as Mop
did, till you felt as limp as withy-wind and yearned for something
to cling to. Indeed, Hipcroft had not the slightest ear for music;
could not sing two notes in tune, much less play them.

The No he had expected and got from her, in spite of a preliminary encouragement, gave Ned a new start in life. It had been uttered in such a tone of sad entreaty that he resolved to persecute her no more; she should not even be distressed by a sight of his form in the distant perspective of the street and lane. He left the place, and his natural course was to London.

The railway to South Wessex was in process of construction,[16] but it was not as yet opened for traffic; and Hipcroft reached the capital by a six days' trudge on foot, as many a better man had done before him. He was one of the last of the artisan class who used that now extinct method of travel to the great centres of labour, so customary then from time immemorial.

In London he lived and worked regularly at his trade. More fortunate than many, his disinterested willingness recommended him from the first. During the ensuing four years he was never out of employment. He neither advanced nor receded in the modern sense; he improved as a workman, but he did not shift one jot in social position. About his love for Car'line he maintained a rigid silence. No doubt he often thought of her; but being always occupied, and having no relations at Stickleford, he held no communication with that part of the country, and showed no desire to return. In his quiet lodging in Lambeth he moved about after working-hours with the facility of a woman, doing his own cooking, attending to his stocking-heels, and shaping himself by degrees to a life-long bachelorhood. For this conduct one is bound to advance the canonical reason that time could not efface from his heart the image of little Car'line Aspent – and it may be in part true; but there was also the inference that his was a nature not greatly dependent upon the ministrations of the other sex for its comforts.

The fourth year of his residence as a mechanic in London was the year of the Hyde Park Exhibition already mentioned, and at the construction of this huge glasshouse,[17] then unexampled in the world's history, he worked daily. It was an era of great hope and activity among the nations and industries. Though Hipcroft was, in his small way, a central man in the movement, he plodded on with his usual outward placidity. Yet for him, too, the year was destined to have its surprises, for when the bustle of getting the building ready for the opening day was past, the ceremonies had been witnessed, and people were flocking thither from all parts of the globe, he received a letter from Car'line. Till that day the silence of four years between himself and Stickleford had never been broken.

She informed her old lover, in an uncertain penmanship which suggested a trembling hand, of the trouble she had been put to in ascertaining his address, and then broached the subject which had prompted her to write. Four years ago, she said with the greatest delicacy of which she was capable, she had been so foolish as to refuse him. Her wilful wrong-headedness had since been a grief to her many times, and of late particularly. As for Mr Ollamoor, he had been absent almost as long as Ned – she did not know where. She would gladly marry Ned now if he were to ask her again, and be a tender little[18] wife to him till her life's end.

A tide of warm feeling must have surged through Ned Hip-croft's frame on receipt of this news, if we may judge by the issue. Unquestionably he loved her still, even if not to the exclusion of every other happiness. This from his Car'line, she who had been dead to him these many years, alive to him again as of old, was in itself a pleasant, gratifying thing. Ned had grown so resigned to, or satisfied with, his lonely lot, that he probably would not have shown much jubilation at anything. Still, a certain ardour of preoccupation, after his first surprise, revealed how deeply her confession of faith in him had stirred him. Measured and methodical in his ways, he did not answer the letter that day, nor the next, nor the next. He was having 'a good think'. When he did answer it, there was a great deal of sound reasoning mixed in with the unmistakable tenderness of his reply; but the tenderness itself was sufficient to reveal that he was pleased with her straightforward frankness; that the anchorage she had once obtained in his heart was renewable, if it had not been continuously firm.

He told her – and as he wrote his lips twitched humorously over the few gentle words of raillery he indited among the rest of his sentences – that it was all very well for her to come round at this time of day. Why wouldn't she have him when he wanted her? She had no doubt learned that he was not married, but suppose his affections had since been fixed on another? She ought to beg his pardon. Still, he was not the man to forget her. But considering how he had been used, and what he had suffered, she could not quite expect him to go down to Stickleford and fetch her. But if she would come to him, and say she was sorry, as was only fair; why, yes, he would marry her, knowing what a good little woman she was at the core.[19] He added that the request for her to come to him was a less one to make than it would have been when he first left Stickleford, or even a few months ago; for the new railway into South Wessex was now open, and there had just begun to be run wonderfully contrived special trains, called excursion-trains,[20] on account of the Great Exhibition; so that she could come up easily alone.

She said in her reply how good it was of him to treat her so generously, after her hot and cold treatment of him; that though she felt frightened at the magnitude of the journey, and was never as yet in a railway-train, having only seen one pass at a distance, she embraced his offer with all her heart; and would, indeed, own to him how sorry she was, and beg his pardon, and try to be a good wife always, and make up for lost time.

The remaining details of when and where were soon settled, Car'line informing him, for her ready identification in the crowd, that she would be wearing 'my new sprigged-laylock cotton gown', and Ned gaily responding that, having married her the morning after her arrival, he would make a day of it by taking her to the Exhibition. One early summer afternoon, accordingly, he came from his place of work, and hastened towards Waterloo Station to meet her. It was as wet and chilly as an English June day can occasionally be, but as he waited on the platform in the drizzle he glowed inwardly, and seemed to have something to live for again.

The 'excursion-train' – an absolutely new departure in the history of travel – was still a novelty on the Wessex line, and probably everywhere. Crowds of people had flocked to all the stations on the way up to witness the unwonted sight of so long a train's passage, even where they did not take advantage of the opportunity it offered. The seats for the humbler class of travellers in these early experiments in steam-locomotion, were open trucks, without any protection whatever from the wind and rain; and damp weather having set in with the afternoon, the unfortunate occupants of these vehicles were, on the train drawing up at the London terminus, found to be in a pitiable condition from their long journey; blue-faced, stiff-necked, sneezing, rain-beaten, chilled to the marrow, many of the men being hatless; in fact, they resembled people who had been out all night in an open boat on a rough sea, rather than inland excursionists for pleasure. The women had in some degree protected themselves by turning up the skirts of their gowns over their heads, but as by this arrangement they were additionally exposed about the hips, they were all more or less in a sorry plight.

In the bustle and crush of alighting forms of both sexes which followed the entry of the huge concatenation into the station, Ned Hipcroft soon discerned the slim little figure his eye was in search of, in the sprigged lilac, as described. She came up to him with a frightened smile – still pretty, though so damp, weather-beaten, and shivering from long exposure to the wind.

'O Ned!' she sputtered, 'I – I—' He clasped her in his arms and kissed her, whereupon she burst into a flood of tears.

'You are wet, my poor dear! I hope you'll not get cold,' he said. And surveying her and her multifarious surrounding packages, he noticed that by the hand she led a toddling child – a little girl of three or so – whose hood was as clammy and tender face[21] as blue as those of the other travellers.

'Who is this – somebody you know?' asked Ned curiously.

'Yes, Ned. She's mine.'

'Yours?'

'Yes – my own!'

'Your own child?'

'Yes!'

'Well – as God's in—'[22]

'Ned, I didn't name it in my letter, because, you see, it would have been so hard to explain! I thought that when we met I could tell you how she happened to be born, so much better than in writing! I hope you'll excuse it this once, dear Ned, and not scold me, now I've come so many, many miles!'[23]

'This means Mr Mop Ollamoor, I reckon!' said Hipcroft, gazing palely at them from the distance of the yard or two to which he had withdrawn with a start.

Car'line gasped. 'But he's been gone away for years!' she supplicated. 'And I never had a young man before! And I was so onlucky to be catched the first time,[24] though some of the girls down there go on like anything!'

Ned remained in silence, pondering.

'You'll forgive me, dear Ned?' she added, beginning to sob outright. 'I haven't taken 'ee in after all, because – because you can pack us back again, if you want to; though 'tis hundreds o' miles, and so wet, and night a-coming on, and I with no money!'

'What the devil can I do!' Hipcroft groaned.

A more pitiable picture than the pair of helpless creatures presented was never seen on a rainy day, as they stood on the great, gaunt, puddled platform, a whiff of drizzle blowing under the roof upon them now and then; the pretty attire in which they had started from Stickleford in the early morning be-muddled and sodden, weariness on their faces, and fear of him in their eyes; for the child began to look as if she thought she too had done some wrong, remaining in an appalled silence till the tears rolled down her chubby cheeks.

'What's the matter, my little maid?' said Ned mechanically.

'I do want to go home!' she let out, in tones that told of a bursting heart. 'And my totties be cold, an' I shan't have no bread an' butter no more!'

'I don't know what to say to it all!' declared Ned, his own eye moist as he turned and walked a few steps with his head down; then regarded them again point blank. From the child escaped troubled breaths and silently welling[25] tears.

'Want some bread and butter, do 'ee?' he said, with factitious hardness.

'Ye – e – s!'

'Well, I daresay I can get 'ee a bit! Naturally, you must want some. And you, too, for that matter, Car'line.'

'I do feel a little hungered. But I can keep it off,' she murmured.

'Folk shouldn't do that,' he said gruffly[26] . . . 'There, come along!' He caught up the child, as he added, 'You must bide here tonight, anyhow, I s'pose! What can you do otherwise? I'll get 'ee some tea and victuals; and as for this job, I'm sure I don't know what to say! This is the way out.'

They pursued their way, without speaking, to Ned's lodgings, which were not far off. There he dried them and made them comfortable, and prepared tea; they thankfully sat down. The ready-made household of which he suddenly found himself the head imparted a cosy aspect to his room, and a paternal one to himself. Presently he turned to the child and kissed her now blooming cheeks; and, looking wistfully at Car'line, kissed her also.

'I don't see how I can send 'ee back all them miles,' he growled, 'now you've come all the way o' purpose to join me. But you must trust me, Car'line, and show you've real faith in me. Well, do you feel better now, my little woman?'

The child nodded, her mouth being otherwise occupied.

'I did trust you, Ned, in coming; and I shall always!'

Thus, without any definite agreement to forgive her, he tacitly acquiesced in the fate that Heaven had sent him; and on the day of their marriage (which was not quite so soon as he had expected it could be, on account of the time necessary for banns[27]) he took her to the Exhibition when they came back from church, as he had promised. While standing near a large mirror in one of the courts devoted to furniture, Car'line started, for in the glass appeared the reflection of a form exactly resembling Mop Ollamoor's – so exactly, that it seemed impossible to believe anybody but that artist in person to be the original. On passing round the objects which hemmed in Ned, her, and the child from a direct view, no Mop was to be seen. Whether he were really in London or not at that time was never known; and Car'line always stoutly denied that her readiness to go and meet Ned in town arose from any rumour that Mop had also gone thither; which denial there was no reasonable ground for doubting.

And then the year glided away, and the Exhibition folded itself up and became a thing of the past. The park trees that had been enclosed for six months were again exposed to the winds and storms, and the sod grew green anew. Ned found that Car'line resolved herself into a very good wife and companion, though she had made herself what is called cheap to him; but in that she was like another domestic article, a cheap tea-pot, which often brews better tea than a dear one. One autumn Hipcroft found himself with but little work to do, and a prospect of less for the winter. Both being country born and bred, they fancied they would like to live again in their natural atmosphere. It was accordingly decided between them that they should leave the pent-up London lodging, and that Ned should seek out employment near his native place, his wife and her daughter staying with Car'line's father during the search for occupation and an abode of their own.

Tinglings of pleasure pervaded Car'line's spasmodic little frame as she journeyed down with Ned to the place she had left two or three years before, in silence and under a cloud. To return to where she had once been despised, a smiling London wife with a distinct London accent, was a triumph which the world did not witness every day.

The train did not stop at the petty roadside station that lay nearest to Stickleford, and the trio went on to Casterbridge. Ned thought it a good opportunity to make a few preliminary inquiries for employment at workshops in the borough where he had been known; and feeling cold from her journey, and it being dry underfoot and only dusk as yet, with a moon on the point of rising, Car'line and her little girl walked on toward Stickleford, leaving Ned to follow at a quicker pace, and pick her up at a certain half-way house, widely known as an inn.

The woman and child pursued the well-remembered way comfortably enough, though they were both becoming wearied. In the course of three miles they had passed Heedless-William's Pond, the familiar landmark by Bloom's End, and were drawing near the Quiet Woman Inn, a lone roadside hostel on the lower verge of the Egdon Heath,[28] since and for many years abolished. In stepping up towards it Car'line heard more voices within than had formerly been customary at such an hour, and she learned that an auction of fat stock had been held near the spot that afternoon. The child would be the better for a rest as well as herself, she thought, and she entered.

The guests and customers overflowed into the passage, and Car'line had no sooner crossed the threshold than a man whom she remembered by sight came forward with a glass and mug in his hands towards a friend leaning against the wall; but, seeing her, very gallantly offered her a drink of the liquor, which was gin-and-beer hot, pouring her out a tumblerful and saying, in a moment or two: 'Surely, 'tis little Car'line Aspent that was – down at Stickleford?'

She assented, and, though she did not exactly want this beverage, she drank it since it was offered, and her entertainer begged her to come in farther and sit down. Once within the room she found that all the persons present were seated close against the walls, and there being a chair vacant she did the same. An explanation of their position occurred the next moment. In the opposite corner stood Mop, rosining his bow and looking just the same as ever. The company had cleared the middle of the room for dancing, and they were about to dance again. As she wore a veil to keep off the wind she did not think he had recognized her, or could possibly guess the identity of the child; and to her satisfied surprise she found that she could confront him quite calmly – mistress of herself in the dignity her London life had given her. Before she had quite emptied her glass the dance was called, the dancers formed in two lines, the music sounded, and the figure began.

Then matters changed for Car'line. A tremor quickened itself to life in her, and her hand so shook that she could hardly set down her glass. It was not the dance nor the dancers, but the notes of that old violin which thrilled the London wife, these having still all the witchery that she had so well known of yore, and under which she had used to lose her power[29] of independent will. How it all came back! There was the fiddling figure against the wall; the large, oily, mop-like head of him, and beneath the mop the face with closed eyes.

After the first moments of paralyzed reverie the familiar tune in the familiar rendering made her laugh and shed tears simultaneously. Then a man at the bottom of the dance, whose partner had dropped away, stretched out his hand and beckoned to her to take the place. She did not want to dance; she entreated by signs to be left where she was, but she was entreating of the tune and its player rather than of the dancing man. The saltatory tendency which the fiddler and his cunning instrument had ever been able to start in her was seizing Car'line just as it had done in earlier years, possibly assisted by the gin-and-beer hot. Tired as she was she grasped her little girl by the hand, and plunging in at the bottom of the figure, whirled about with the rest. She found that her companions were mostly people of the neighbouring hamlets and farms – Bloom's End, Mellstock, Lewgate, and elsewhere; and by degrees she was recognized as she convulsively danced on, wishing that Mop would cease and let her heart rest from the aching he caused, and her feet also.

After long and many minutes the dance ended, when she was urged to fortify herself with more gin-and-beer; which she did, feeling very weak and overpowered with hysteric emotion. She refrained from unveiling, to keep Mop in ignorance of her presence, if possible. Several of the guests having left, Car'line hastily wiped her lips and also turned to go; but, according to the account of some who remained, at that very moment a five-handed reel was proposed, in which two or three begged her to join.

She declined on the plea of being tired and having to walk to Stickleford, when Mop began aggressively tweedling 'My Fancy-Lad',[30] in D major, as the air to which the reel was to be footed. He must have recognized her, though she did not know it, for it was the strain of all seductive strains which she was least able to resist – the one he had played when she was leaning over the bridge at the date of their first acquaintance. Car'line stepped despairingly into the middle of the room with the other four.

Reels were resorted to hereabouts at this time by the more robust spirits, for the reduction of superfluous energy which the ordinary figure-dances were not powerful enough to exhaust. As everybody knows, or does not know, the five reelers stood in the form of a cross, the reel being performed by each line of three alternately, the persons who successively came to the middle place dancing in both directions. Car'line soon found herself in this place, the axis of the whole performance, and could not get out of it, the tune turning into the first part without giving her opportunity. And now she began to suspect that Mop did know her, and was doing this on purpose, though whenever she stole a glance at him his closed eyes betokened obliviousness to everything outside his own brain. She continued to wend her way through the figure of 8 that was formed by her course, the fiddler introducing into his notes the wild and agonizing sweetness of a living voice in one too highly wrought; its pathos running high and running low in endless variation, projecting through her nerves excruciating spasms, a sort of blissful torture. The room swam, the tune was endless; and in about a quarter of an hour the only other woman in the figure dropped out exhausted, and sank panting on a bench.

The reel instantly resolved itself into a four-handed one. Car'line would have given anything to leave off; but she had, or fancied she had, no power, while Mop played such tunes; and thus another ten minutes slipped by, a haze of dust now clouding the candles, the floor being of stone, sanded. Then another dancer fell out – one of the men – and went into the passage, in a frantic search for liquor. To turn the figure into a three-handed reel was the work of a second, Mop modulating at the same time into 'The Fairy Dance', as better suited to the contracted movement, and no less one of those foods of love[31] which, as manufactured by his bow, had always intoxicated her.

In a reel for three there was no rest whatever, and four or five minutes were enough to make her remaining two partners, now thoroughly blown, stamp their last bar, and, like their predecessors, limp off into the next room to get something to drink. Car'line, half-stifled inside her veil, was left dancing alone, the apartment now being empty of everybody save herself, Mop, and their little girl.

She flung up the veil, and cast her eyes upon him, as if imploring him to withdraw himself and his acoustic magnetism from the atmosphere. Mop opened one of his own orbs, as though for the first time, fixed it peeringly upon her, and smiling dreamily, threw into his strains the reserve of expression which he could not afford to waste on a big and noisy dance. Crowds of little chromatic subtleties, capable of drawing tears from a statue, proceeded straightway from the ancient fiddle, as if it were dying of the emotion which had been pent up within it ever since its banishment from some Italian city where it first took shape and sound. There was that in the look of Mop's one dark eye which said: 'You cannot leave off, dear, whether you would or no!' and it bred in her a paroxysm of desperation that defied him to tire her down.

She thus continued to dance alone, defiantly as she thought, but in truth slavishly and abjectly, subject to every wave of the melody, and probed by the gimlet-like gaze of her fascinator's open eye; keeping up at the same time a feeble smile in his face, as a feint to signify it was still her own pleasure which led her on. A terrified embarrassment as to what she could say to him if she were to leave off, had its unrecognized share in keeping her going. The child, who was beginning to be distressed by the strange situation, came up and said: 'Stop, mother, stop, and let's go home!' as she seized Car'line's hand.

Suddenly Car'line sank staggering to the floor; and rolling over on her face, prone she remained. Mop's fiddle thereupon emitted an elfin shriek of finality; stepping quickly down from the nine-gallon beer-cask which had formed his rostrum, he went to the little girl, who disconsolately bent over her mother.

The guests who had gone into the back-room for liquor and change of air, hearing something unusual, trooped back hitherward, where they endeavoured to revive poor, weak Car'line by blowing her with the bellows and opening the window. Ned, her husband, who had been detained in Caster-bridge, as aforesaid, came along the road at this juncture, and hearing excited voices through the open casement, and to his great surprise, the mention of his wife's name, he entered amid the rest upon the scene. Car'line was now in convulsions, weeping violently, and for a long time nothing could be done with her. While he was sending for a cart to take her onward to Stickleford Hipcroft anxiously inquired how it had all happened; and then the assembly explained that a fiddler formerly known in the locality had lately revisited his old haunts, and had taken upon himself without invitation to play that evening at the inn.

Ned demanded the fiddler's name, and they said Ollamoor.

'Ah!' exclaimed Ned, looking round him. 'Where is he, and where – where's my little girl?'

Ollamoor had disappeared, and so had the child. Hipcroft was in ordinary a quiet and tractable fellow, but a determination which was to be feared settled in his face now. 'Blast him!' he cried. 'I'll beat his skull in for'n, if I swing for it tomorrow!'

He had rushed to the poker which lay on the hearth, and hastened down the passage, the people following. Outside the house, on the other side of the highway, a mass of dark heath-land rose sullenly upward to its not easily accessible interior, a ravined plateau, whereon jutted into the sky, at the distance of a couple of miles, the fir-woods of Mistover backed by the Yalbury coppices[32] – a place of Dantesque gloom at this hour, which would have afforded secure hiding for a battery of artillery, much less a man and a child.

Some other men plunged thitherward with him, and more went along the road. They were gone about twenty minutes altogether, returning without result to the inn. Ned sat down in the settle, and clasped his forehead with his hands.

'Well – what a fool the man is, and hev been all these years, if he thinks the child his, as a' do seem to!' they whispered. 'And everybody else knowing otherwise!'

'No, I don't think 'tis mine!' cried Ned hoarsely, as he looked up from his hands. 'But she is mine, all the same! Ha'n't I nussed her? Ha'n't I fed her and teached her? Ha'n't I played wi' her? O, little Carry – gone with that rogue – gone!'

'You ha'n't lost your mis'ess, anyhow,' they said to console him. 'She's throwed up the sperrits, and[33] she is feeling better, and she's more to 'ee than a child that isn't yours.'

'She isn't! She's not so particular much to me, especially now she's lost the little maid! But Carry's everything!'

'Well, ver' like you'll find her tomorrow.'

'Ah – but shall I? Yet he *can't* hurt her – surely he can't! Well – how's Car'line now? I am ready. Is the cart here?'

She was lifted into the vehicle, and they sadly lumbered on

toward Stickleford. Next day she was calmer; but the fits were still upon her; and her will seemed shattered. For the child she appeared to show singularly little anxiety, though Ned was nearly distracted. It was nevertheless quite expected that the impish Mop would restore the lost one after a freak of a day or two; but time went on, and neither he nor she could be heard of, and Hipcroft murmured that perhaps he was exercising upon her some unholy musical charm, as he had done upon Car'line herself. Weeks passed, and still they could obtain no clue either to the fiddler's whereabouts or the girl's; and how he could have induced her to go with him remained a mystery.[34]

Then Ned, who had obtained only temporary employment in the neighbourhood, took a sudden hatred toward his native district, and a rumour reaching his ears through the police that a somewhat similar man and child had been seen at a fair near London, he playing a violin, she dancing on stilts, a new interest in the capital took possession of Hipcroft with an intensity which would scarcely allow him time to pack before returning thither. He did not, however, find the lost one, though he made it the entire business of his over-hours to stand about in by-streets in the hope of discovering her, and would start up in the night, saying, 'That rascal's torturing her to maintain him!' To which his wife would answer peevishly, 'Don't 'ee raft yourself so, Ned! You prevent my getting a bit o' rest![35] He won't hurt her!' and fall asleep again.

That Carry and her father had emigrated to America was the general opinion; Mop, no doubt, finding the girl a highly desirable companion when he had trained her to keep him by her earnings as a dancer. There, for that matter, they may be performing in some capacity now, though he must be an old scamp verging on three-score-and-ten, and she a woman of four-and-forty.

# AN IMAGINATIVE WOMAN

When William Marchmill had finished his inquiries for lodgings at a well-known watering-place[1] in Upper Wessex, he returned to the hotel to find his wife. She, with the children, had rambled along the shore, and Marchmill followed in the direction indicated by the military-looking hall-porter.

'By Jove, how far you've gone! I am quite out of breath,' Marchmill said, rather impatiently, when he came up with his wife, who was reading as she walked, the three children being considerably further ahead with the nurse.

Mrs Marchmill started out of the reverie into which the book had thrown her. 'Yes,' she said, 'you've been such a long time. I was tired of staying in that dreary hotel. But I am sorry if you have wanted me, Will?'

'Well, I have had trouble to suit myself. When you see the airy and comfortable rooms heard of, you find they are stuffy and uncomfortable. Will you come and see if what I've fixed on will do? There is not much room, I am afraid; but I can light on nothing better. The town is rather full.'

The pair left the children and nurse to continue their ramble, and went back together.

[2]In age well-balanced, in personal appearance fairly matched, and in domestic requirements conformable, in temper this couple differed, though even here they did not often clash, he being equable, if not lymphatic, and she decidedly nervous and sanguine. It was to their tastes and fancies, those smallest, greatest particulars, that no common denominator could be applied. Marchmill considered his wife's likes and inclinations somewhat silly; she considered his sordid and material. The

husband's business was that of a gunmaker in a thriving city northwards, and his soul was in that business always; the lady was best characterized by that superannuated phrase of elegance 'a votary of the muse'. An impressionable, palpitating creature was Ella, shrinking humanely from detailed knowledge of her husband's trade whenever she reflected that everything he manufactured had for its purpose the destruction of life. She could only recover her equanimity by assuring herself that some, at least, of his weapons were sooner or later used for the extermination of horrid vermin and animals almost as cruel to their inferiors in species as human beings were to theirs.

She had never antecedently regarded this occupation of his as any objection to having him for a husband. Indeed, the necessity of getting life-leased at all cost, a cardinal virtue which all good mothers teach, kept her[3] from thinking of it at all till she had closed with William, had passed the honeymoon, and reached the reflecting stage. Then, like a person who has stumbled upon some object in the dark, she wondered what she had got; mentally walked round it, estimated it; whether it were rare or common; contained gold, silver, or lead; were a clog or a pedestal, everything to her or nothing.

She came to some vague conclusions, and since then had kept her heart alive by pitying her proprietor's obtuseness and want of refinement, pitying herself, and letting off her delicate and ethereal emotions in imaginative occupations, day-dreams, and night-sighs, which perhaps would not much have disturbed William if he had known of them.

Her figure was small, elegant, and slight in build, tripping, or rather bounding, in movement. She was dark-eyed, and had that marvellously bright and liquid sparkle in each pupil which characterizes persons of Ella's cast of soul,[4] and is too often a cause of heart-ache to the possessor's male friends, ultimately sometimes to herself. Her husband was a tall, long-featured man, with a brown beard; he had a pondering regard; and was, it must be added, usually kind and tolerant to her. He spoke in squarely shaped sentences, and was supremely satisfied with a condition of sublunary things which made weapons a necessity.

Husband and wife walked till they had reached the house

they were in search of, which stood in a terrace facing the sea, and was fronted by a small garden of wind-proof and salt-proof evergreens, stone steps leading up to the porch. It had its number in the row, but, being rather larger than the rest, was in addition sedulously distinguished as Coburg House by its landlady, though everybody else called it 'Thirteen, New Parade'. The spot was bright and lively now; but in winter it became necessary to place sandbags against the door, and to stuff up the keyhole against the wind and rain, which had worn the paint so thin that the priming and knotting showed through.

The householder, who had been watching for the gentleman's return, met them in the passage, and showed the rooms. She informed them that she was a professional man's widow, left in needy circumstances by the rather sudden death of her husband, and she spoke anxiously of the conveniences of the establishment.

Mrs Marchmill said that she liked the situation and the house; but, it being small, there would not be accommodation enough, unless she could have all the rooms.

The landlady mused with an air of disappointment. She wanted the visitors to be her tenants very badly, she said, with obvious honesty. But unfortunately two of the rooms were occupied permanently by a bachelor gentleman. He did not pay season prices, it was true; but as he kept on his apartments all the year round, and was an extremely nice and interesting young man, who gave no trouble, she did not like to turn him out for a month's 'let', even at a high figure. 'Perhaps, however,' she added, 'he might offer to go for a time.'

They would not hear of this, and went back to the hotel, intending to proceed to the agent's to inquire further. Hardly had they sat down to tea when the landlady called. Her gentleman, she said, had been so obliging as to offer to give up his rooms for three or four weeks rather than drive the new-comers away.

'It is very kind, but we won't inconvenience him in that way,' said the Marchmills.

'O, it won't inconvenience him, I assure you!' said the land-lady eloquently. 'You see, he's a different sort of young man from most – dreamy, solitary, rather melancholy – and he cares more to be here when the south-westerly gales are beating against the door, and the sea washes over the Parade, and there's not a soul in the place, than he does now in the season. He'd just as soon be where, in fact, he's going temporarily, to a little cottage on the Island opposite,[5] for a change.' She hoped therefore that they would come.

The Marchmill family accordingly took possession of the house next day, and it seemed to suit them very well. After luncheon Mr Marchmill strolled out towards the pier, and Mrs Marchmill, having despatched the children to their outdoor amusements on the sands, settled herself in more completely, examining this and that article, and testing the reflecting powers of the mirror in the wardrobe door.

In the small back sitting-room, which had been the young bachelor's, she found furniture of a more personal nature than in the rest. Shabby books, of correct rather than rare editions, were piled up in a queerly reserved manner in corners, as if the previous occupant had not conceived the possibility that any incoming person of the season's bringing could care to look inside them. The landlady hovered on the threshold to rectify anything that Mrs Marchmill might not find to her satisfaction.

'I'll make this my own little room,' said the latter, 'because the books are here. By the way, the person who has left seems to have a good many. He won't mind my reading some of them, Mrs Hooper, I hope?'

'O dear no, ma'am. Yes, he has a good many. You see, he is in the literary line himself somewhat. He is a poet – yes, really a poet – and he has a little income of his own, which is enough to write verses on, but not enough for cutting a figure, even if he cared to.'

'A poet! O, I did not know that.'

Mrs Marchmill opened one of the books, and saw the owner's name written on the title-page. 'Dear me!' she continued; 'I know his name very well – Robert Trewe[6] – of course I do; and his writings! And it is *his* rooms we have taken, and *him* we have turned out of his home?'

Ella Marchmill, sitting down alone a few minutes later, thought with interested surprise of Robert Trewe. Her own latter history will best explain that interest. Herself the only daughter of a struggling man of letters, she had during the last year or two taken to writing poems, in an endeavour to find a congenial channel in which to let flow her painfully embayed emotions, whose former limpidity and sparkle seemed departing in the stagnation caused by the routine of a practical household and the gloom of bearing children to a commonplace[7] father. These poems, subscribed with a masculine pseudonym, had appeared in various obscure magazines, and in two cases in rather prominent ones. In the second of the latter the page which bore her effusion at the bottom, in smallish print, bore at the top, in large print, a few verses on the same subject by this very man, Robert Trewe. Both of them had, in fact, been struck by a tragic incident reported in the daily papers, and had used it simultaneously as an inspiration, the editor remarking in a note upon the coincidence, and that the excellence of both poems prompted him to give them together.

After that event Ella, otherwise 'John Ivy', had watched with much attention the appearance anywhere in print of verse bearing the signature of Robert Trewe, who, with a man's unsusceptibility on the question of sex, had never once thought of passing himself off as a woman. To be sure, Mrs Marchmill had satisfied herself with a sort of reason for doing the contrary in her case; that nobody might believe in her inspiration if they found that the sentiments came from a pushing tradesman's wife, from the mother of three children by a matter-of-fact small-arms manufacturer.

Trewe's verse contrasted with that of the rank and file of recent minor poets in being impassioned rather than ingenious, luxuriant rather than finished. Neither *symboliste* nor *décadent*,[8] he was a pessimist in so far as that character applies to a man who looks at the worst contingencies as well as the best in the human condition. Being little attracted by excellences of form and rhythm apart from content, he sometimes, when feeling outran his artistic speed, perpetrated sonnets in the loosely rhymed Elizabethan fashion, which every right-minded reviewer said he ought not to have done.

With sad and hopeless envy, Ella Marchmill had often and often scanned the rival poet's work, so much stronger as it always was than her own feeble lines. She had imitated him, and her inability to touch his level would send her into fits of despondency. Months passed away thus, till she observed from the publishers' list that Trewe had collected his fugitive pieces into a volume, which was duly issued, and was much or little praised according to chance, and had a sale quite sufficient to pay for the printing.

This step onward had suggested to John Ivy the idea of collecting her pieces also, or at any rate of making up a book of her rhymes by adding many in manuscript to the few that had seen the light, for she had been able to get no great number into print. A ruinous charge was made for costs of publication; a few reviews noticed her poor little volume; but nobody talked of it, nobody bought it, and it fell dead in a fortnight – if it had ever been alive.

The author's thoughts were diverted to another groove just then by the discovery that she was going to have a third child, and the collapse of her poetical venture had perhaps less effect upon her mind than it might have done if she had been domestically unoccupied. Her husband had paid the publisher's bill with the doctor's, and there it all had ended for the time. But, though less than a poet of her century, Ella was more than a mere multiplier of her kind, and latterly she had begun to feel the old afflatus once more. And now by an odd conjunction she found herself in the rooms of Robert Trewe.

She thoughtfully rose from her chair and searched the apartment with the interest of a fellow-tradesman. Yes, the volume of his own verse was among the rest. Though quite familiar with its contents, she read it here as if it spoke aloud to her, then called up Mrs Hooper, the landlady, for some trivial service, and inquired again about the young man.

'Well, I'm sure you'd be interested in him, ma'am, if you could see him, only he's so shy that I don't suppose you will.' Mrs Hooper seemed nothing loth to minister to her tenant's curiosity about her predecessor. 'Lived here long? Yes, nearly two years. He keeps on his rooms even when he's not here: the soft air of this place suits his chest, and he likes to be able to come back at any time. He is mostly writing or reading, and doesn't see many people, though, for the matter of that, he is such a good, kind young fellow that folks would only be too glad to be friendly with him if they knew him. You don't meet kind-hearted people every day.'

'Ah, he's kind-hearted . . . and good.'

'Yes; he'll oblige me in anything if I ask him. "Mr Trewe," I say to him sometimes, "you are rather out of spirits." "Well, I am, Mrs Hooper," he'll say, "though I don't know how you should find it out." "Why not take a little change?" I ask. Then in a day or two he'll say that he will take a trip to Paris, or Norway, or somewhere; and I assure you he comes back all the better for it.'

'Ah, indeed! His is a sensitive nature, no doubt.'

'Yes. Still he's odd in some things. Once when he had finished a poem of his composition late at night he walked up and down the room rehearsing it; and the floors being so thin – jerry-built houses, you know, though I say it myself – he kept me awake up above him till I wished him further . . . But we get on very well.'

This was but the beginning of a series of conversations about the rising poet as the days went on. On one of these occasions Mrs Hooper drew Ella's attention to what she had not noticed before: minute scribblings in pencil on the wall-paper behind the curtains at the head of the bed.

'O! let me look,' said Mrs Marchmill, unable to conceal a rush of tender curiosity as she bent her pretty face close to the wall.

'These,' said Mrs Hooper, with the manner of a woman who knew things, 'are the very beginnings and first thoughts of his verses. He has tried to rub most of them out, but you can read them still. My belief is that he wakes up in the night, you know, with some rhyme in his head, and jots it down there on the wall lest he should forget it by the morning. Some of these very lines you see here I have seen afterwards in print in the magazines. Some are newer; indeed, I have not seen that one before. It must have been done only a few days ago.'

'O yes! . . .'

Ella Marchmill flushed without knowing why, and suddenly

wished her companion would go away, now that the information was imparted. An indescribable consciousness of personal interest rather than literary made her anxious to read the inscription alone; and she accordingly waited till she could do so, with a sense that a great store of emotion would be enjoyed in the act.

Perhaps because the sea was choppy outside the Island, Ella's husband found it much pleasanter to go sailing and steaming about without his wife, who was a bad sailor, than with her. He did not disdain to go thus alone on board the steamboats of the cheap-trippers, where there was dancing by moonlight, and where the couples would come suddenly down with a lurch into each other's arms; for, as he blandly told her, the company was too mixed for him to take her amid such scenes. Thus, while this thriving manufacturer got a great deal of change and sea-air out of his sojourn here, the life, external at least, of Ella was monotonous enough, and mainly consisted in passing a certain number of hours each day in bathing and walking up and down a stretch of shore. But the poetic impulse having again waxed strong, she was possessed by an inner flame which left her hardly conscious of what was proceeding around her.

She had read till she knew by heart Trewe's last little volume of verses, and spent a great deal of time in vainly attempting to rival some of them, till, in her failure, she burst into tears. The personal element in the magnetic attraction exercised by this circumambient, unapproachable master of hers was so much stronger than the intellectual and abstract that she could not understand it. To be sure, she was surrounded noon and night by his customary environment, which literally whispered of him to her at every moment; but he was a man she had never seen, and that all that moved her was the instinct to specialize a waiting emotion on the first fit thing that came to hand did not, of course, suggest itself to Ella.

In the natural way of passion under the too practical conditions which civilization has devised for its fruition,[9] her husband's love for her had not survived, except in the form of fitful friendship, any more than, or even so much as, her own for him; and, being a woman of very living ardours, that required sustenance of some sort, they were beginning to feed on this chancing material, which was, indeed, of a quality far better than chance usually offers.

One day the children had been playing hide-and-seek in a closet, whence, in their excitement, they pulled out some clothing. Mrs Hooper explained that it belonged to Mr Trewe, and hung it up in the closet again. Possessed of her fantasy, Ella went later in the afternoon, when nobody was in that part of the house, opened the closet, unhitched one of the articles, a mackintosh, and put it on, with the waterproof cap belonging to it.

'The mantle of Elijah!'[10] she said. 'Would it might inspire me to rival him, glorious genius that he is!'

Her eyes always grew wet when she thought like that, and she turned to look at herself in the glass. *His* heart had beat inside that coat, and *his* brain had worked under that hat at levels of thought she would never reach. The consciousness of her weakness beside him made her feel quite sick. Before she had got the things off her the door opened, and her husband entered the room.

'What the devil—'

She blushed, and removed them.

'I found them in the closet here,' she said, 'and put them on in a freak. What have I else to do? You are always away!'

'Always away? Well . . .'

That evening she had a further talk with the landlady, who might herself have nourished a half-tender regard for the poet, so ready was she to discourse ardently about him.

'You are interested in Mr Trewe, I know, ma'am,' she said; 'and he has just sent to say that he is going to call tomorrow afternoon to look up some books of his that he wants, if I'll be in, and he may select them from your room?'

'O yes!'

'You could very well meet Mr Trewe then, if you'd like to be in the way!'

She promised with secret delight, and went to bed musing of him.

Next morning her husband observed: 'I've been thinking of

what you said, Ell: that I have gone about a good deal and left you without much to amuse you. Perhaps it's true.[11] Today, as there's not much sea, I'll take you with me on board the yacht.'

For the first time in her experience of such an offer Ella was not glad. But she accepted it for the moment. The time for setting out drew near, and she went to get ready. She stood reflecting. The longing to see the poet she was now distinctly in love with overpowered all other considerations.

'I don't want to go,' she said to herself. 'I can't bear to be away! And I won't go.'

She told her husband that she had changed her mind about wishing to sail. He was indifferent, and went his way.

For the rest of the day the house was quiet, the children having gone out upon the sands. The blinds waved in the sunshine to the soft, steady stroke of the sea beyond the wall; and the notes of the Green Silesian band, a troop of foreign gentlemen hired for the season, had drawn almost all the residents and promenaders away from the vicinity of Coburg House. A knock was audible at the door.

Mrs Marchmill did not hear any servant go to answer it, and she became impatient. The books were in the room where she sat; but nobody came up. She rang the bell.

'There is some person waiting at the door,' she said.

'O no, ma'am! He's gone long ago. I answered it.'

Mrs Hooper came in herself.

'So disappointing!' she said. 'Mr Trewe not coming after all!'

'But I heard him knock, I fancy!'

'No; that was somebody inquiring for lodgings who came to the wrong house. I forgot to tell you that Mr Trewe sent a note just before lunch to say I needn't get any tea for him, as he should not require the books, and wouldn't come to select them.'

Ella was miserable, and for a long time could not even re-read his mournful ballad on 'Severed Lives',[12] so aching was her erratic little heart, and so tearful her eyes. When the children came in with wet stockings, and ran up to her to tell her of their adventures, she could not feel that she cared about them half as much as usual.

*

'Mrs Hooper, have you a photograph of – the gentleman who lived here?' She was getting to be curiously shy in mentioning his name.

'Why, yes. It's in the ornamental frame on the mantelpiece in your own bedroom, ma'am.'

'No; the Royal[13] Duke and Duchess are in that.'

'Yes, so they are; but he's behind them. He belongs rightly to that frame, which I bought on purpose; but as he went away he said: "Cover me up from those strangers that are coming, for God's sake. I don't want them staring at me, and I am sure they won't want me staring at them." So I slipped in the Duke and Duchess temporarily in front of him, as they had no frame, and Royalties are more suitable for letting furnished than a private young man. If you take 'em out you'll see him under. Lord, ma'am, he wouldn't mind if he knew it! He didn't think the next tenant would be such an attractive lady as you, or he wouldn't have thought of hiding himself, perhaps.'

'Is he handsome?' she asked timidly.

'*I* call him so. Some, perhaps, wouldn't.'

'Should I?' she asked, with eagerness.[14]

'I think you would, though some would say he's more striking than handsome; a large-eyed thoughtful fellow, you know, with a very electric flash in his eye when he looks round quickly, such as you'd expect a poet to be who doesn't get his living by it.'

'How old is he?'

'Several years older than yourself, ma'am; about thirty-one or two, I think.'

Ella was, as a matter of fact, a few months over thirty herself; but she did not look nearly so much. Though so immature in nature, she was entering on that tract of life in which emotional women begin to suspect that last love may be stronger than first love; and she would soon, alas, enter on the still more melancholy tract when at least the vainer[15] ones of her sex shrink from receiving a male visitor otherwise than with their backs to the window or the blinds half down. She reflected on Mrs Hooper's remark, and said no more about age.

Just then a telegram was brought up. It came from her husband, who had gone down the Channel as far as Budmouth[16] with his friends in the yacht, and would not be able to get back till next day.

After her light dinner Ella idled about the shore with the children till dusk, thinking of the yet uncovered photograph in her room, with a serene sense of something ecstatic to come. For, with the subtle luxuriousness of fancy in which this young woman was an adept, on learning that her husband was to be absent that night she had refrained from incontinently rushing upstairs and opening the picture-frame, preferring to reserve the inspection till she could be alone, and a more romantic tinge be imparted to the occasion by silence, candles, solemn sea and stars outside, than was afforded by the garish afternoon sunlight.

The children had been sent to bed, and Ella soon followed, though it was not yet ten o'clock. To gratify her passionate curiosity she now made her preparations, first getting rid of superfluous garments and putting on her dressing-gown, then arranging a chair in front of the table and reading several pages of Trewe's tenderest utterances. Then she fetched the portrait-frame to the light, opened the back, took out the likeness, and set it up before her.

It was a striking countenance to look upon. The poet wore a luxuriant black moustache and imperial, and a slouched hat which shaded the forehead. The large dark eyes, described by the landlady, showed an unlimited capacity for misery; they looked out from beneath well-shaped brows as if they were reading the universe in the microcosm of the confronter's face, and were not altogether overjoyed at what the spectacle portended.[17]

Ella murmured in her lowest, richest, tenderest tone: 'And it's *you* who've so cruelly eclipsed me these many times!'

As she gazed long at the portrait she fell into thought, till her eyes filled with tears, and she touched the cardboard with her lips. Then she laughed with a nervous lightness, and wiped her eyes.

She thought how wicked she was, a woman having a husband and[18] three children, to let her mind stray to a stranger in this unconscionable manner. No, he was not a stranger! She knew his thoughts and feelings as well as she knew her own; they were, in fact, the self-same thoughts and feelings as hers, which her husband distinctly lacked; perhaps luckily for himself, considering that he had to provide for family expenses.

'He's nearer my real self, he's more intimate with the real me than Will is, after all, even though I've never seen him,' she said.

She laid his book and picture on the table at the bedside, and when she was reclining on the pillow she re-read those of Robert Trewe's verses which she had marked from time to time as most touching and true. Putting these aside, she set up the photograph on its edge upon the coverlet, and contemplated it as she lay. Then she scanned again by the light of the candle the half-obliterated pencillings on the wall-paper beside her head. There they were – phrases, couplets, *bouts-rimés*, beginnings and middles of lines, ideas in the rough, like Shelley's scraps,[19] and the least of them so intense, so sweet, so palpitating, that it seemed as if his very breath, warm and loving, fanned her cheeks from those walls, walls that had surrounded his head times and times as they surrounded her own now. He must often have put up his hand so – with the pencil in it. Yes, the writing was sideways, as it would be if executed by one who extended his arm thus.

These inscribed shapes of the poet's world,

> 'Forms more real than living man,
> Nurslings of immortality,'[20]

were, no doubt, the thoughts and spirit-strivings which had come to him in the dead of night, when he could let himself go and have no fear of the frost of criticism. No doubt they had often been written up hastily by the light of the moon, the rays of the lamp, in the blue-grey dawn, in full daylight perhaps never. And now her hair was dragging where his arm had lain when he secured the fugitive fancies; she was sleeping on a poet's lips, immersed in the very essence of him, permeated by his spirit as by an ether.

While she was dreaming the minutes away thus, a footstep

came upon the stairs, and in a moment she heard her husband's heavy step on the landing immediately without.

'Ell, where are you?'

What possessed her she could not have described, but, with an instinctive objection to let her husband know what she had been doing, she slipped the photograph under the pillow[21] just as he flung open the door, with the air of a man who had dined not badly.

'O, I beg pardon,' said William Marchmill. 'Have you a headache? I am afraid I have disturbed you.'

'No, I've not got a headache,' said she. 'How is it you've come?'

'Well, we found we could get back in very good time after all, and I didn't want to make another day of it, because of going somewhere else tomorrow.'

'Shall I come down again?'

'O no. I'm as tired as a dog. I've had a good feed, and I shall turn in straight off. I want to get out at six o'clock tomorrow if I can[22] ... I shan't disturb you by my getting up; it will be long before you are awake.' And he came forward into the room.

While her eyes followed his movements, Ella softly pushed the photograph further out of sight.[23]

'Sure you're not ill?' he asked, bending over her.

'No, only wicked!'

'Never mind that.' And he stooped and kissed her.

Next morning Marchmill was called at six o'clock; and in waking and yawning she heard him muttering to himself: 'What the deuce is this that's been crackling under me so?' Imagining her asleep he searched round him and withdrew something.[24] Through her half-opened eyes she perceived it to be Mr Trewe.

'Well, I'm damned!' her husband exclaimed.

'What, dear?' said she.

'O, you are awake? Ha! ha!'

'What *do* you mean?'

'Some bloke's photograph – a friend of our landlady's, I suppose. I wonder how it came here; whisked off the table by accident perhaps when they were making the bed.'

'I was looking at it yesterday, and it must have dropped in then.'

'O, he's a friend of yours? Bless his picturesque heart!'

Ella's loyalty to the object of her admiration could not endure to hear him ridiculed. 'He's a clever man!' she said, with a tremor in her gentle voice which she herself felt to be absurdly uncalled for. 'He is a rising poet – the gentleman who occupied two of these rooms before we came, though I've never seen him.'

'How do you know, if you've never seen him?'

'Mrs Hooper told me when she showed me the photograph.'

'O; well, I must up and be off. I shall be home rather early. Sorry I can't take you today, dear. Mind the children don't go getting drowned.'

That day Mrs Marchmill inquired if Mr Trewe were likely to call at any other time.

'Yes,' said Mrs Hooper. 'He's coming this day week to stay with a friend near here till you leave. He'll be sure to call.'

Marchmill did return quite early in the afternoon; and, opening some letters which had arrived in his absence, declared suddenly that he and his family would have to leave a week earlier than they had expected to do – in short, in three days.

'Surely we can stay a week longer?' she pleaded. 'I like it here.'

'I don't. It is getting rather slow.'

'Then you might leave me and the children!'

'How perverse you are, Ell! What's the use? And have to come to fetch you! No: we'll all return together; and we'll make out our time in North Wales or Brighton a little later on. Besides, you've three days longer yet.'

It seemed to be her doom not to meet the man for whose rival talent she had a despairing admiration, and to whose person she was now absolutely attached.[25] Yet she determined to make a last effort; and having gathered from her landlady that Trewe was living in a lonely spot not far from the fashionable town on the Island opposite, she crossed over in the packet from the neighbouring pier the following afternoon.

What a useless journey it was! Ella knew but vaguely where the house stood, and when she fancied she had found it, and ventured to inquire of a pedestrian if he lived there, the answer returned by the man was that he did not know. And if he did live there, how could she call upon him? Some women might have the assurance to do it, but she had not. How crazy he would think her. She might have asked him to call upon her, perhaps; but she had not the courage for that, either. She lingered mournfully about the picturesque seaside eminence till it was time to return to the town and enter the steamer for recrossing, reaching home for dinner without having been greatly missed.

At the last moment, unexpectedly enough, her husband said that he should have no objection to letting her and the children stay on till the end of the week, since she wished to do so, if she felt herself able to get home without him. She concealed the pleasure this extension of time gave her; and Marchmill went off the next morning alone.

But the week passed, and Trewe did not call.

On Saturday morning the remaining members of the Marchmill family departed from the place which had been productive of so much fervour in her. The dreary, dreary train; the sun shining in moted beams upon the hot cushions; the dusty permanent way; the mean rows of wire – these things were her accompaniment: while out of the window the deep blue sea-levels disappeared from her gaze, and with them her poet's home. Heavy-hearted, she tried to read, and wept instead.

Mr Marchmill was in a thriving way of business, and he and his family lived in a large new house, which stood in rather extensive grounds a few miles outside the city wherein he carried on his trade. Ella's life was lonely here, as the suburban life is apt to be, particularly at certain seasons; and she had ample time to indulge her taste for lyric and elegiac composition. She had hardly got back when she encountered a piece by Robert Trewe in the new number of her favourite magazine, which must have been written almost immediately before her visit to Solentsea, for it contained the very couplet she had seen pencilled on the wallpaper by the bed, and Mrs Hooper had declared to be recent. Ella could resist no longer, but seizing a pen impulsively, wrote to him as a brother-poet, using the name of John Ivy, congratulating him in her letter on his triumphant executions in metre and rhythm of thoughts that moved his soul, as compared with her own brow-beaten efforts in the same pathetic trade.

To this address there came a response in a few days, little as she had dared to hope for it – a civil and brief note, in which the young poet stated that, though he was not well acquainted with Mr Ivy's verse, he recalled the name as being one he had seen attached to some very promising pieces; that he was glad to gain Mr Ivy's acquaintance by letter, and should certainly look with much interest for his productions in the future.

There must have been something juvenile or timid in her own epistle, as one ostensibly coming from a man, she declared to herself; for Trewe quite adopted the tone of an elder and superior in this reply. But what did it matter? He had replied; he had written to her with his own hand from that very room she knew so well, for he was now back again in his quarters.

The correspondence thus begun was continued for two months or more, Ella Marchmill sending him from time to time some that she considered to be the best of her pieces, which he very kindly accepted, though he did not say he sedulously read them, nor did he send her any of his own in return. Ella would have been more hurt at this than she was if she had not known that Trewe laboured under the impression that she was one of his own sex.

Yet the situation was unsatisfactory. A flattering little voice told her that, were he only to see her, matters would be otherwise. No doubt she would have helped on this by making a frank confession of womanhood, to begin with, if something had not happened, to her delight, to render it unnecessary. A friend of her husband's, the editor of the most important newspaper in the city and county, who was dining with them one day, observed during their conversation about the poet that his (the editor's) brother the landscape-painter was a friend of Mr Trewe's, and that the two men were at that very moment in Wales together.

Ella was slightly acquainted with the editor's brother. The next morning down she sat and wrote, inviting him to stay at her house for a short time on his way back, and requesting him to bring with him, if practicable, his companion Mr Trewe, whose acquaintance she was anxious to make. The answer arrived after some few days. Her correspondent and his friend Trewe would have much satisfaction in accepting her invitation on their way southward, which would be on such and such a day in the following week.

Ella was blithe and buoyant. Her scheme had succeeded; her beloved though as yet unseen one was coming. 'Behold, he standeth behind our wall; he looketh forth at the windows, showing himself through the lattice,' she thought ecstatically. 'And, lo, the winter is past, the rain is over and gone, the flowers appear on the earth, the time of the singing of birds is come, and the voice of the turtle is heard in our land.'[26]

But it was necessary to consider the details of lodging and feeding him. This she did most solicitously, and awaited the pregnant day and hour.

It was about five in the afternoon when she heard a ring at the door and the editor's brother's voice in the hall. Poetess as she was, or as she thought herself, she had not been too sublime that day to dress with infinite trouble in a fashionable robe of rich material, having a faint resemblance to the *chiton* of the Greeks, a style just then in vogue among ladies of an artistic and romantic turn, which had been obtained by Ella of her Bond Street dressmaker when she was last in London. Her visitor entered the drawing-room. She looked towards his rear; nobody else came through the door. Where, in the name of the God of Love, was Robert Trewe?

'O, I'm sorry,' said the painter, after their introductory words had been spoken. 'Trewe is a curious fellow, you know, Mrs Marchmill. He said he'd come; then he said he couldn't. He's rather dusty. We've been doing a few miles with knapsacks, you know; and he wanted to get on home.'

'He – he's not coming?'

'He's not; and he asked me to make his apologies.'

'When did you p-p-part from him?' she asked, her nether lip starting off quivering so much that it was like a *tremolo*-stop opened in her speech. She longed to run away from this dreadful bore and cry her eyes out.

'Just now, in the turnpike-road yonder there.'

'What! he has actually gone past my gates?'

'Yes. When we got to them – handsome gates they are, too, the finest bit of modern wrought-iron work I have seen – when we came to them we stopped, talking there a little while, and then he wished me goodbye and went on. The truth is, he's a little bit depressed just now, and doesn't want to see anybody. He's a very good fellow, and a warm friend, but a little uncertain and gloomy sometimes; he thinks too much of things. His poetry is rather too erotic and passionate, you know, for some tastes; and he has just come in for a terrible slating from the — *Review* that was published yesterday;[27] he saw a copy of it at the station by accident. Perhaps you've read it?'

'No.'

'So much the better. O, it is not worth thinking of; just one of those articles written to order, to please the narrow-minded set of subscribers upon whom the circulation depends. But he's upset by it. He says it is the misrepresentation that hurts him so; that, though he can stand a fair attack, he can't stand lies that he's powerless to refute and stop from spreading. That's just Trewe's weak point. He lives so much by himself that these things affect him much more than they would if he were in the bustle of fashionable or commercial life. So he wouldn't come here, making the excuse that it all looked so new and monied – if you'll pardon—'

'But – he must have known – there was sympathy here! Has he never said anything about getting letters from this address?'

'Yes, yes, he has, from John Ivy – perhaps a relative of yours, he thought, visiting here at the time?'

'Did he – like Ivy, did he say?'

'Well, I don't know that he took any great interest in Ivy.'

'Or in his poems?'

'Or in his poems – so far as I know, that is.'

Robert Trewe took no interest in her house, in her poems, or in their writer. As soon as she could get away she went into the nursery and tried to let off her emotion by unnecessarily kissing the children, till she had a sudden sense of disgust at being reminded how plain-looking they were, like their father.

The obtuse and single-minded landscape-painter never once

perceived from her conversation that it was only Trewe she wanted, and not himself. He made the best of his visit, seeming to enjoy the society of Ella's husband, who also took a great fancy to him, and showed him everywhere about the neighbourhood, neither of them noticing Ella's mood.

The painter had been gone only a day or two when, while sitting upstairs alone one morning, she glanced over the London paper just arrived, and read the following paragraph:–

### 'SUICIDE OF A POET

'Mr Robert Trewe, who has been favourably known for some years as one of our rising lyrists, committed suicide at his lodgings at Solentsea on Saturday evening last by shooting himself in the right temple with a revolver. Readers hardly need to be reminded that Mr Trewe has recently attracted the attention of a much wider public than had hitherto known him, by his new volume of verse, mostly of an impassioned kind, entitled "Lyrics to a Woman Unknown", which has been already favourably noticed in these pages for the extraordinary gamut of feeling it traverses, and which has been made the subject of a severe, if not ferocious, criticism in the — Review. It is supposed, though not certainly known, that the article may have partially conduced to the sad act, as a copy of the review in question was found on his writing-table; and he has been observed to be in a somewhat depressed state of mind since the critique appeared.'

Then came the report of the inquest, at which the following letter was read, it having been addressed to a friend at a distance:–

'DEAR—, – Before these lines reach your hands I shall be delivered from the inconveniences of seeing, hearing, and knowing more of the things around me. I will not trouble you by giving my reasons for the step I have taken, though I can assure you they were sound and logical. Perhaps had I been blessed with a mother, or a sister, or a female friend of another sort tenderly devoted to me, I might have thought it worth while to continue my present existence. I have long dreamt of such an unattainable creature, as you know; and she, this undiscoverable, elusive one, inspired my last volume; the imaginary woman alone, for, in spite of what has been said in some quarters, there is no real woman behind the title. She has continued to the last unrevealed, unmet, unwon. I think it desirable to mention this in order that no blame may attach to any real woman as having been the cause of my decease by cruel or cavalier treatment of me. Tell my landlady that I am sorry to have caused her this unpleasantness; but my occupancy of the rooms will soon be forgotten. There are ample funds in my name at the bank to pay all expenses.

R. TREWE.'

Ella sat for a while as if stunned, then rushed into the adjoining chamber and flung herself upon her face on the bed.

Her grief and distraction shook her to pieces; and she lay in this frenzy of sorrow for more than an hour. Broken words came every now and then from her quivering lips: 'O, if he had only known of me – known of me – me! ... O, if I had only once met him – only once; and put my hand upon his hot forehead – kissed him – let him know how I loved him – that I would have suffered shame and scorn, would have lived and died, for him! Perhaps it would have saved his dear life! ... But no – it was not allowed! God is a jealous God;[28] and that happiness was not for him and me!'

All possibilities were over; the meeting was stultified. Yet it was almost visible to her in her fantasy even now, though it could never be substantiated–

> 'The hour which might have been, yet might not be,
> Which man's and woman's heart conceived and bore,
> Yet whereof life was barren.'[29]

*

She wrote to the landlady at Solentsea in the third person, in as subdued a style as she could command, enclosing a postal order for a sovereign, and informing Mrs Hooper that Mrs Marchmill had seen in the papers the sad account of the poet's death, and having been, as Mrs Hooper was aware, much interested in Mr

Trewe during her stay at Coburg House, she would be obliged if Mrs Hooper could obtain a small portion of his hair before his coffin was closed down, and send it her as a memorial of him, as also the photograph that was in the frame.

By the return-post a letter arrived containing what had been requested. Ella wept over the portrait and secured it in her private drawer; the lock of hair she tied with white ribbon and put in her bosom, whence she drew it and kissed it every now and then in some unobserved nook.

'What's the matter?' said her husband, looking up from his newspaper on one of these occasions. 'Crying over something? A lock of hair? Whose is it?'

'He's dead!' she murmured.

'Who?'

'I don't want to tell you, Will, just now, unless you insist!' she said, a sob hanging heavy in her voice.

'O, all right.'

'Do you mind my refusing? I will tell you some day.'

'It doesn't matter in the least, of course.'

He walked away whistling a few bars of no tune in particular; and when he had got down to his factory in the city the subject came into Marchmill's head again.

He, too, was aware that a suicide had taken place recently at the house they had occupied at Solentsea. Having seen the volume of poems in his wife's hand of late, and heard fragments of the landlady's conversation about Trewe when they were her tenants, he all at once said to himself, 'Why of course it's he! ... How the devil did she get to know him? What sly animals women are!'

Then he placidly dismissed the matter, and went on with his daily affairs. By this time Ella at home had come to a determination. Mrs Hooper, in sending the hair and photograph, had informed her of the day of the funeral; and as the morning and noon wore on an overpowering wish to know where they were laying him took possession of the sympathetic woman. Caring very little now what her husband or any one else might think of her eccentricities, she wrote Marchmill a brief note, stating that she was called away for the afternoon and evening, but would return on the following morning. This she left on his desk, and having given the same information to the servants, went out of the house on foot.

When Mr Marchmill reached home early in the afternoon the servants looked anxious. The nurse took him privately aside, and hinted that her mistress's sadness during the past few days had been such that she feared she had gone out to drown herself. Marchmill reflected. Upon the whole he thought that she had not done that. Without saying whither he was bound he also started off, telling them not to sit up for him. He drove to the railway-station, and took a ticket for Solentsea.

It was dark when he reached the place, though he had come by a fast train, and he knew that if his wife had preceded him thither it could only have been by a slower train, arriving not a great while before his own. The season at Solentsea was now past: the parade was gloomy, and the flys were few and cheap. He asked the way to the Cemetery, and soon reached it. The gate was locked, but the keeper let him in, declaring, however, that there was nobody within the precincts. Although it was not late, the autumnal darkness had now become intense; and he found some difficulty in keeping to the serpentine path which led to the quarter where, as the man had told him, the one or two interments for the day had taken place. He stepped upon the grass, and, stumbling over some pegs, stooped now and then to discern if possible a figure against the sky. He could see none; but lighting on a spot where the soil was trodden, beheld a crouching object beside a newly made grave. She heard him, and sprang up.

'Ell, how silly this is!' he said indignantly. 'Running away from home – I never heard such a thing! Of course I am not jealous of this unfortunate man; but it is too ridiculous that you, a married woman with three children and a fourth coming, should go losing your head like this over a dead lover! ... Do you know you were locked in? You might not have been able to get out all night.'

She did not answer.

'I hope it didn't go far between you and him, for your own sake.'

'Don't insult me, Will.'

'Mind, I won't have any more of this sort of thing; do you hear?'

'Very well,' she said.

He drew her arm within his own, and conducted her out of the Cemetery. It was impossible to get back that night; and not wishing to be recognized in their present sorry condition, he took her to a miserable little coffee-house close to the station, whence they departed early in the morning, travelling almost without speaking, under the sense that it was one of those dreary situations occurring in married life which words could not mend,[30] and reaching their own door at noon.

The months passed, and neither of the twain ever ventured to start a conversation upon this episode. Ella seemed to be only too frequently in a sad and listless mood, which might almost have been called pining. The time was approaching when she would have to undergo the stress of childbirth for a fourth time, and that apparently did not tend to raise her spirits.

'I don't think I shall get over it this time!' she said one day.

'Pooh! what childish foreboding! Why shouldn't it be as well now as ever?'

She shook her head. 'I feel almost sure I am going to die; and I should be glad, if it were not for Nelly, and Frank, and Tiny.'

'And me!'

'You'll soon find somebody to fill my place,' she murmured, with a sad smile. 'And you'll have a perfect right to; I assure you of that.'

'Ell, you are not thinking still about that – poetical friend of yours?'

She neither admitted nor denied the charge. 'I am not going to get over my illness this time,' she reiterated. 'Something tells me I shan't.'

This view of things was rather a bad beginning, as it usually is; and, in fact, six weeks later, in the month of May, she was lying in her room, pulseless and bloodless, with hardly strength enough left to follow up one feeble breath with another, the infant for whose unnecessary life she was slowly parting with her own being fat and well. Just before her death she spoke to Marchmill softly: –

'Will, I want to confess to you the entire circumstances of that – about you know what – that time we visited Solentsea. I can't tell what possessed me – how I could forget you so, my husband! But I had got into a morbid state: I thought you had been unkind; that you had neglected me; that you weren't up to my intellectual level, while he was, and far above it. I wanted a fuller appreciator, perhaps, rather than another lover —'

She could get no further then for very exhaustion; and she went off in sudden collapse a few hours later, without having said anything more to her husband on the subject of her love for the poet. William Marchmill, in truth, like most husbands of several years' standing, was little disturbed by retrospective jealousies, and had not shown the least anxiety to press her for confessions concerning a man dead and gone beyond any power of inconveniencing him more.

But when she had been buried a couple of years it chanced one day that, in turning over some forgotten papers that he wished to destroy before his second wife entered the house, he lighted on a lock of hair in an envelope, with the photograph of the deceased poet, a date being written on the back in his late wife's hand. It was that of the time they spent at Solentsea.

Marchmill looked long and musingly at the hair and portrait, for something struck him. Fetching the little boy who had been the death of his mother, now a noisy toddler, he took him on his knee, held the lock of hair against the child's head, and set up the photograph on the table behind, so that he could closely compare the features each countenance presented. There were undoubtedly strong traces of resemblance; the dreamy and peculiar expression of the poet's face sat, as the transmitted idea, upon the child's,[31] and the hair was of the same hue.

'I'm damned if I didn't think so!' murmured Marchmill. 'Then she *did* play me false with that fellow at the lodgings! Let me see: the dates – the second week in August . . . the third week in May . . . Yes . . . yes[32] . . . Get away, you poor little brat! You are nothing to me!'

# A CHANGED MAN

The person who, next to the actors themselves, chanced to know most of their story, lived near 'Top o' Town'[1] (as the spot was called) in an old substantially-built house, distinguished among its neighbours by having an oriel window on the first floor, whence could be obtained a raking view of the High Street, west and east, the former including Laura's dwelling, the end of the Town Avenue hard by (in which were played the odd pranks hereafter to be mentioned), the Port-Bredy road rising westwards, and the turning that led to the cavalry barracks where the Captain was quartered. Looking eastward down the town from the same favoured gazebo, the long perspective of houses declined and dwindled till they merged in the highway across the moor. The white riband of road disappeared over Grey's Bridge a quarter of a mile off, to plunge into innumerable straits, windings,[2] and solitary undulations up hill and down dale for one hundred and twenty miles till it exhibited itself at Hyde Park Corner as a smooth bland surface in touch with a busy and fashionable world.

To the barracks aforesaid had recently arrived the—th Hussars, a regiment new to the locality. Almost before any acquaintance with its members had been made by the townspeople, a report spread that they were a 'crack' body of men, and had brought a splendid band. For some reason or other the town had not been used as the headquarters of cavalry for many years, the various troops stationed there having consisted of casual detachments only; so that it was with a sense of honour that everybody – even the small furniture-broker from whom the married troopers hired tables and chairs – received the news of their crack quality.

In those days the Hussar regiments still wore over the left shoulder that attractive attachment, or frilled half-coat, hanging loosely behind like the wounded wing of a bird, which was called the pelisse, though it was known among the troopers themselves as a 'sling-jacket'. It added amazingly to their pictur-esqueness in women's eyes, and, indeed, in the eyes of men also.

The burgher who lived in the house with the oriel window sat during a great many hours of the day in that projection, for he was an invalid, and time hung heavily on his hands unless he maintained a constant interest in proceedings without. Not more than a week after the arrival of the Hussars his ears were assailed by the shout of one schoolboy to another in the street below.

'Have 'ee heard this about the Hussars? They are haunted! Yes – a ghost troubles 'em; he has followed 'em about the world for years.'

A haunted regiment: that was a new idea for either invalid or stalwart. The listener in the oriel came to the conclusion that there were some lively characters among the—th Hussars.

He made Captain Maumbry's[3] acquaintance in an informal manner at an afternoon tea to which he went in a wheeled chair – one of the very rare outings that the state of his health permitted. Maumbry showed himself to be a handsome man of twenty-eight or thirty, with an attractive hint of wickedness in his manner that was sure to make him adorable with good young women. The large dark eyes that lit his pale face expressed this wickedness strongly, though such was the adaptability of their rays that one could think they might have expressed sadness or seriousness just as readily, if he had had a mind for such.

An old and deaf lady who was present asked Captain Maumbry bluntly: 'What's this we hear about you? They say your regiment is haunted.'

The captain's face assumed an aspect of grave, even sad, concern. 'Yes,' he replied, 'it is too true.'

Some younger ladies smiled till they saw how serious he looked, when they looked serious likewise.

'Really?' said the old lady.

'Yes. We naturally don't wish to say much about it.'

'No, no; of course not. But – how haunted?'

'Well; the – *thing*, as I'll call it, follows us. In country quarters or town, abroad or at home, it's just the same.'

'How do you account for it?'

'H'm.' Maumbry lowered his voice. 'Some crime committed by certain of our regiment in past years, we suppose.'

'Dear me . . . How very horrid, and singular!'

'But, as I said, we don't speak of it much.'

'No . . . no.'

When the Hussar was gone, a young lady, disclosing a long-suppressed interest, asked if the ghost had been seen by any of the town.

The lawyer's son, who always had the latest borough news, said that, though it was seldom seen by any but the Hussars themselves, more than one townsman and woman had already set eyes on it, to his or her terror. The phantom mostly appeared very late at night, under the dense trees of the town avenue nearest the barracks. It was about twelve feet[4] high; its teeth chattered with a dry naked sound, as if they were those of a skeleton; and its hip-bones could be heard grating in their sockets.

During the darkest weeks of winter several timid persons were seriously frightened by the object answering to this cheerful description, and the police began to look into the matter. Whereupon the appearances grew less frequent, and some of the boys of the regiment thankfully stated that they had not been so free from ghostly visitation for years as they had become since their arrival in Casterbridge.

This playing at ghosts was the most innocent of the amusements indulged in by the choice young spirits who inhabited the lichened, red-brick building at the top of the town bearing 'W. D.' and a broad arrow[5] on its quoins. Far more serious escapades – levities relating to love, wine, cards, betting – were talked of, with no doubt more or less of exaggeration. That the Hussars[6] were the cause of bitter tears to several young women of the town and country is unquestionably true, despite the fact that the gaieties of the young men wore a more staring colour in this old-fashioned place than they would have done in a large and modern city.

## II

Regularly once a week they rode out in marching order.

Returning up the town on one of these occasions, the romantic pelisse flapping behind each horseman's shoulder in the soft south-west wind, Captain Maumbry glanced up at the oriel. A mutual nod was exchanged between him and the person who sat there reading. The reader and a friend in the room with him followed the troop with their eyes all the way up the street, till, when the soldiers were opposite the house in which Laura lived, that young lady became discernible in the balcony.

'They are engaged to be married, I hear,' said the friend.

'Who – Maumbry and Laura? Never – so soon?'

'Yes.'

'He'll never marry. Several girls have been mentioned in connection with his name. I am sorry for Laura.'

'Oh, but you needn't be. They are excellently matched.'

'She's only one more.'

'She's one more, and more still. She has regularly caught him. She is a born player of the game of hearts, and she knew how to beat him in his own practices. If there is one woman in the town who has any chance of holding her own and marrying him, she is that woman.'

This was true, as it turned out. By natural proclivity Laura had from the first entered heart and soul into military romance as exhibited in the plots and characters of those living exponents of it who came under her notice. From her earliest young womanhood civilians, however promising, had no chance of winning her interest if the meanest warrior were within the horizon. It may be that the position of her uncle's house (which was her home) at the corner of the town[7] nearest the barracks, the daily passing of the troops, the constant blowing of trumpet-calls a furlong from her windows, coupled with the fact that she knew nothing of the inner realities of military life, and hence idealized it, had also helped her mind's original bias for thinking men-at-arms the only ones worthy of a woman's heart.

Captain Maumbry was a typical prize; one whom all surrounding maidens had coveted, ached for, angled for, wept for, had by her judicious management become subdued to her purpose; and in addition to the pleasure of marrying the man she loved, Laura had the joy of feeling herself hated by the mothers of all the marriageable girls of the neighbourhood.

The man in the oriel went to the wedding; not as a guest, for at this time he was but slightly acquainted with the parties; but mainly because the church was close to his house; partly, too, for a reason which moved many others to be spectators of the ceremony: a subconsciousness that, though the couple might be happy in their experiences, there was sufficient possibility of their being otherwise to colour the musings of an onlooker with a pleasing pathos of conjecture. He could on occasion do a pretty stroke of rhyming in those days, and he beguiled the time of waiting by pencilling on a blank page of his prayer book a few lines which, though kept private then, may be given here: –


### At a Hasty Wedding.[8]
#### (*Triolet.*)

If hours be years the twain are blest,
    For now they solace swift desire
By lifelong ties that tether zest
    If hours be years. The twain are blest
Do eastern suns slope never west,
    Nor pallid ashes follow fire.
If hours be years the twain are blest
    For now they solace swift desire.


As if, however, to falsify all prophecies, the couple seemed to find in marriage the secret of perpetuating the intoxication of a courtship which, on Maumbry's side at least, had opened without serious intent. During the winter following they were the

most popular pair in and about Casterbridge – nay in South
Wessex itself. No smart dinner in the county houses of the
younger and gayer families within driving distance of the borough was complete without their lively presence; Mrs Maumbry
was the blithest of the whirling figures at the county ball; and
when followed that inevitable incident of garrison-town life, an
amateur dramatic entertainment, it was just the same. The acting
was for the benefit of such and such an excellent charity –
nobody cared what provided the play were played – and both
Captain Maumbry and his wife were in the piece, having been
in fact, by mutual consent, the originators of the performance.
And so with laughter, and thoughtlessness, and movement, all
went merrily. There was a little backwardness in the bill-paying
of the couple; but in justice to them it must be added that sooner
or later all owings were paid.

## III

At the chapel of ease attended by the troops there arose above
the edge of the pulpit one Sunday an unknown face. This was
the face of a new curate. He placed upon the desk not the
familiar sermon book, but merely a Bible. The person who tells
these things was not present at that service, but he soon learnt
that the young curate was nothing less than a great surprise to
his congregation; a mixed one always, for though the Hussars
occupied the body of the building, its nooks and corners were
crammed with civilians, whom, up to the present, even the least
uncharitable would have described as being attracted thither
less by the services than by the soldiery.

Now there arose a second reason for squeezing into an already
overcrowded church. The persuasive and gentle eloquence of
Mr Sainway operated like a charm upon those accustomed only
to the higher and dryer styles of preaching, and for a time the
other churches of the town were thinned of their sitters.

At this point in the nineteenth century the sermon was the
sole reason for churchgoing among a vast body of religious
people. The liturgy was a formal preliminary, which, like the

Queen's proclamation[9] in a court of assize, had to be got through before the real interest began; and on reaching home the question was simply: Who preached, and how did he handle his subject? Even had an archbishop officiated in the service proper nobody would have cared much about what was said or sung. People who had formerly attended in the morning only began to go in the evening, and even to the special addresses in the afternoon.

One day when Captain Maumbry entered his wife's drawing-room, filled with hired furniture, she thought he was somebody else, for he had not come upstairs humming the most catching air afloat in musical circles or in his usual careless way.

'What's the matter, Jack?' she said without looking up from a note she was writing.

'Well – not much, that I know.'

'O, but there is,' she murmured as she wrote.

'Why – this cursed new lath in a sheet – I mean the new parson! He wants us to stop the band-playing on Sunday afternoons.'

Laura looked up aghast.

'Why, it is the one thing that enables the few rational beings hereabouts to keep alive from Saturday to Monday!'

'He says all the town flock to the music and don't come to the service, and that the pieces played are profane, or mundane, or inane, or something – not what ought to be played on Sunday. Of course 'tis Lautmann who settles those things.'

Lautmann was the bandmaster.

The barrack-green on Sunday afternoons had, indeed, become the promenade of a great many townspeople cheerfully inclined, many even of those who attended in the morning at Mr Sainway's service; and little boys who ought to have been listening to the curate's afternoon lecture were too often seen rolling upon the grass behind the more dignified listeners.

Laura heard no more about the matter, however, for two or three weeks, when suddenly remembering it she asked her husband if any further objections had been raised.

'O – Mr Sainway. I forgot to tell you. I've made his acquaintance. He is not a bad sort of man.'

Laura asked if either Maumbry or some other of the officers

did not give the presumptuous curate a good setting down for his interference.

'O well – we've forgotten that. He's a stunning preacher they tell me.'

The acquaintance developed apparently, for the Captain said to her a little later on, 'There's a good deal in Sainway's argument about having no band on Sunday afternoons. After all, it is close to his church. But he doesn't press his objections unduly.'

'I am surprised to hear you defend him!'

'It was only a passing thought of mine. We naturally don't wish to offend the inhabitants of the town if they don't like it.'

'But they do!'

The invalid in the oriel never clearly gathered the details of progress in this conflict of lay and clerical opinion; but so it was that, to the disappointment of musicians, the grief of out-walking lovers, and the regret of the junior population of the town and country round, the band-playing on Sunday afternoons ceased in Casterbridge barrack-square.

By this time the Maumbrys had frequently listened to the preaching of the gentle curate;[10] for these light-natured, hit-or-miss, rackety people went to church like others for respectability's sake. None so orthodox as your unmitigated worldling. A more remarkable event was the sight to the man in the window of Captain Maumbry and Mr Sainway walking down the High Street in earnest conversation. On his mentioning this fact to a caller he was assured that it was a matter of common talk that they were always together.

The observer would soon have learnt this with his own eyes if he had not been told. They began to pass together nearly every day. Hitherto Mrs Maumbry, in fashionable walking clothes, had usually been her husband's companion; but this was less frequent now. The close and singular friendship between the two men went on for nearly a year, when Mr Sainway was presented to a living in a densely-populated town in the midland counties. He bade the parishioners of his old place a reluctant farewell and departed, the touching sermon he preached on the occasion being published by the local printer. Everybody was sorry to lose him; and it was with genuine grief that his

'There is a good deal in Sainway's argument about having
no band on Sunday.'

Casterbridge congregation learnt later on that soon after his induction to his benefice, during some bitter weather, he had fallen seriously ill of inflammation of the lungs, of which he eventually died.

We now get below the surface of things. Of all who had known the dead curate, none grieved for him like the man who on his first arrival had called him a 'lath in a sheet'. Mrs Maumbry had never greatly sympathized with the impressive parson; indeed, she had been secretly glad that he had gone away to better himself. He had considerably diminished the pleasures of a woman by whom the joys of earth and good company had been appreciated to the full. Sorry for her husband in his loss of a friend who had been none of hers, she was yet quite unprepared for the sequel.

'There is something that I have wanted to tell you lately, dear,' he said one morning at breakfast with hesitation. 'Have you guessed what it is?'

She had guessed nothing.

'That I think of retiring from the army.'

'What!'

'I have thought more and more of Sainway since his death, and of what he used to say to me so earnestly. And I feel certain I shall be right in obeying a call within me to give up this fighting trade and enter the Church.'

'What – be a parson?'

'Yes.'

'But what should I do?'

'Be a parson's wife.'

'Never!' she affirmed.

'But how can you help it?'

'I'll run away rather!' she said vehemently.

'No, you mustn't,' Maumbry replied, in the tone he used when his mind was made up. 'You'll get accustomed to the idea, for I am constrained to carry it out, though it is against my worldly interests. I am forced on by a Hand outside me to tread in the steps of Sainway.'

'Jack,' she asked, with calm pallor and round eyes; 'do you

mean to say seriously that you are arranging to be a curate instead of a soldier?'

'I might say a curate *is* a soldier – of the church militant; but I don't want to offend you with doctrine. I distinctly say, yes.'

Late one evening, a little time onward, he caught her sitting by the dim firelight in her room. She did not know he had entered; and he found her weeping. 'What are you crying about, poor dearest?' he said.

She started. 'Because of what you have told me!'

The Captain grew very unhappy; but he was undeterred.

In due time the town learnt, to its intense surprise, that Captain Maumbry had retired from the——th Hussars, and gone to Fountall Theological College[11] to prepare for the ministry.

## IV

'O, the pity of it! Such a dashing soldier – so popular – such an acquisition to the town – the soul of social life here! And now! . . .

One should not speak ill of the dead, but that dreadful Mr Sainway – it was too cruel of him!'

This is a summary of what was said when Captain, now the Reverend, John Maumbry was enabled by circumstances to indulge his heart's desire of returning to the scene of his former exploits in the capacity of a minister of the Gospel. A low-lying district of the town, which at that date was crowded with impoverished cottagers, was crying for a curate, and Mr Maumbry generously offered himself as one willing to undertake labours that were certain to produce little result, and no thanks, credit, or emolument.

Let the truth be told about him as a clergyman; he proved to be anything but a brilliant success. Painstaking, single-minded, deeply in earnest as all could see, his delivery was laboured, his sermons were dull to listen to, and alas, too, too long. Even the dispassionate judges who sat by the hour in the bar-parlour of the White Hart – an inn standing at the dividing line between the poor quarter aforesaid and the fashionable quarter of

Maumbry's former triumphs, and hence affording a position of strict impartiality – agreed in substance with the young ladies to the westward, though their views were somewhat more tersely expressed: 'Surely, God A'mighty spwiled a good sojer to make a bad pa'son when He shifted Cap'n Ma'mbry into a sarpless!'

The latter knew that such things were said, but he pursued his daily labours in and out of the hovels with serene unconcern.

It was about this time that the invalid in the oriel became more than a mere bowing acquaintance of Mrs Maumbry's. She had returned to the town with her husband, and was living with him in a little house in the centre of his circle of ministration, when by some means she became one of the invalid's visitors. After a general conversation while sitting in his room with a friend of both, an incident led up to the matter that still rankled deeply in her soul. Her face was now paler and thinner than it had been; even more attractive, her disappointments having inscribed themselves as meek thoughtfulness on a look that was once a little frivolous. The two ladies had called to be allowed to use the window for observing the departure of the Hussars, who were leaving for barracks much nearer to London.

The troopers turned the corner of Barrack Road into the top of High Street, headed by their band playing 'The girl I left behind me'[12] (which was formerly always the tune for such times, though it is now nearly disused). They came and passed the oriel, where an officer or two, looking up and discovering Mrs Maumbry, saluted her, whose eyes filled with tears as the notes of the band waned away. Before the little group had recovered from that sense of the romantic which such spectacles impart, Mr Maumbry came along the pavement. He probably had bidden his former brethren-in-arms a farewell at the top of the street, for he walked from that direction in his rather shabby clerical clothes, and with a basket on his arm which seemed to hold some purchases he had been making for his poorer parishioners. Unlike the soldiers, he went along quite unconscious of his appearance or of the scene around.

The contrast was too much for Laura. With lips that now quivered, she asked the invalid what he thought of the change that had come to her.

It was difficult to answer, and with a wilfulness that was too strong in her she repeated the question.

'Do you think,' she added, 'that a woman's husband has a right to do such a thing, even if he does feel a certain call to it?'

Her listener sympathized too largely with both of them to be anything but unsatisfactory in his reply. Laura gazed longingly out of the window towards the thin dusty line of Hussars, now smalling towards Mellstock Ridge. 'I,' she said, 'who should have been in their van on the way to London, am doomed to fester in a hole in Durnover Lane!'[13]

Many events had passed, and many rumours had been current concerning her before the invalid saw her again after her leave-taking that day.

## V

Casterbridge had known many military and civil episodes; many happy times, and times less happy; and now came the time of her visitation. The scourge of cholera had been laid on the suffering country, and the low-lying purlieus of this ancient borough had more than their share of the infliction. Mixen Lane, in the Durnover quarter, and in Maumbry's parish, was where the blow fell most heavily. Yet there was a certain mercy in its choice of a date, for Maumbry was the man for such an hour.[14]

The spread of the epidemic was so rapid that many left the town and took lodgings in the villages and farms. Mr Maumbry's house was close to the most infected street, and he himself was occupied morn, noon, and night in endeavours to stamp out the plague and in alleviating the sufferings of the victims. So, as a matter of ordinary precaution, he decided to isolate his wife somewhere away from him for a while.

She suggested a village by the sea, near Budmouth Regis, and lodgings were obtained for her at Creston,[15] a spot divided from the Casterbridge valley by a high ridge that gave it quite another atmosphere, though it lay no more than six miles off.

Thither she went. While she was rusticating in this place of safety, and her husband was slaving in the slums, she struck up an acquaintance with a lieutenant in the—th Foot,[16] a Mr Vannicock, who was stationed with his regiment at the Budmouth infantry barracks. As Laura frequently sat on the shelving beach, watching each thin wave slide up to her, and hearing, without heeding, its gnaw at the pebbles in its retreat, he often took a walk that way.

The acquaintance grew and ripened. Her situation, her history, her beauty, her age – a year or two above his own – all tended to make an impression on the young man's heart, and a reckless flirtation was soon in blithe progress upon that lonely shore.

It was said by her detractors afterwards that she had chosen her lodging to be near this gentleman, but there is reason to believe that she had never seen him till her arrival there. Just now Casterbridge was so deeply occupied with its own sad affairs – a daily burying of the dead and destruction of contaminated clothes and bedding – that it had little inclination to promulgate such gossip as may have reached its ears on the pair. Nobody long[17] considered Laura in the tragic cloud which overhung all.

Meanwhile, on the Budmouth side of the hill the very mood of men was in contrast. The visitation there had been slight and much earlier, and normal occupations and pastimes had been resumed. Mr Maumbry had arranged to see Laura twice a week in the open air, that she might run no risk from him; and, having heard nothing of the faint rumour, he met her as usual one dry and windy afternoon on the summit of the dividing hill, near where the high road from town to town crosses the old Ridge-way[18] at right angles.

He waved his hand, and smiled as she approached, shouting to her: 'We will keep this wall between us, dear.' (Walls formed the field-fences here.) 'You mustn't be endangered. It won't be for long, with God's help!'

'I will do as you tell me, Jack. But you are running too much risk yourself, aren't you? I get little news of you; but I fancy you are.'

'Not more than others.'

Thus somewhat formally they talked, an insulating wind beating the wall between them like a mill-weir.

'But you wanted to ask me something?' he added.

'Yes. You know we are trying in Budmouth to raise some money for your sufferers; and the way we have thought of is by a dramatic performance. They want me to take a part.'

His face saddened. 'I have known so much of that sort of thing, and all that accompanies it! I wish you had thought of some other way.'

She said lightly that she was afraid it was all settled. 'You object to my taking a part, then? Of course—'

He told her that he did not like to say he positively objected. He wished they had chosen an oratorio, or lecture, or anything more in keeping with the necessity it was to relieve.

'But,' said she, impatiently, 'people won't come to oratorios or lectures! They will crowd to comedies and farces.'

'Well, I cannot dictate to Budmouth how it shall earn the money it is going to give us. Who is getting up this performance?'

'The boys of the—th.'

'Ah, yes; our old game!' replied Mr Maumbry. 'The grief of Casterbridge is the excuse for their frivolity. Candidly, dear Laura, I wish you wouldn't play in it. But I don't forbid you to. I leave the whole to your judgment.'

The interview ended, and they went their ways northward and southward. Time disclosed to all concerned that Mrs Maumbry played in the comedy as the heroine, the lover's part being taken by Mr Vannicock.

# VI

Thus was helped on an event which the conduct of the mutually-attracted ones had been generating for some time.

It is unnecessary to give details. The—th Foot left for Bristol, and this precipitated their action. After a week of hesitation she agreed to leave her home at Creston and meet Vannicock on the ridge hard by, and to accompany him to Bath, where he had secured lodgings for her, so that she would be only about a dozen miles from his quarters.

Accordingly, on the evening chosen, she laid on her dressing table a note for her husband, running thus: –

DEAR JACK, – I am unable to endure this life any longer, and I have resolved to put an end to it. I told you I should run away if you persisted in being a clergyman, and now I am doing it. One cannot help one's nature. I have resolved to throw in my lot with Mr Vannicock, and I hope rather than expect you will forgive me. – L.

Then, with hardly a scrap of luggage, she went, ascending to the ridge in the dusk of early evening. Almost on the very spot where her husband had stood at their last tryst she beheld the outline of Vannicock, who had come all the way from Bristol to fetch her.

'I don't like meeting here – it is so unlucky!' she cried to him. 'For God's sake let us have a place of our own. Go back to the milestone, and I'll come on.'

He went back to the milestone that stands on the north slope of the ridge, where the old and new roads diverge, and she joined him there.

She was taciturn and sorrowful when he asked her why she would not meet him on the top. At last she inquired how they were going to travel.

He explained that he proposed to walk to Mellstock Hill, on the other side of Casterbridge, where a fly was waiting to take them by a cross-cut into the Ivell Road[19] and onward to that town. The Bristol railway was open to Ivell.

This plan they followed, and walked briskly through the dull gloom till they neared Casterbridge, which place they avoided by turning to the right at the Roman Amphitheatre, and bearing round to Durnover Cross. Thence the way was solitary and open to the hill whereon the Ivell fly awaited them.

'I have noticed for some time,' she said, 'a lurid glare over the Durnover end of the town. It seems to come from somewhere about Mixen Lane.'

'The lamps,' he suggested.

'There's not a lamp as big as a rushlight in the whole lane. It is where the cholera is worst.'

By Standfast Corner,[20] a little beyond the Cross, they suddenly obtained an end view of the lane. Large bonfires were burning in the middle of the way, with a view to purifying the air; and from the wretched tenements with which the lane was lined in those days persons were bringing out bedding and clothing. Some was thrown into the fires, the rest placed in wheelbarrows and wheeled into the mead directly in the track of the fugitives.

They followed on, and came up to where a vast copper was set in the open air. Here the linen was boiled and disinfected. By the light of the lanterns Laura discovered that her husband was standing by the copper, and that it was he who unloaded the barrow and immersed its contents. The night was so calm and muggy that the conversation by the copper reached her ears.

'Are there many more loads tonight?'

'There's the clothes o' they that died this afternoon, sir. But that might bide till tomorrow, for you must be tired out.'

'We'll do it at once, for I can't ask anybody else to undertake it. Overturn that load on the grass and fetch the rest.'

The man did so and went off with the barrow. Maumbry paused for a moment to wipe his face, and resumed his homely drudgery amid this squalid and reeking scene,[21] pressing down and stirring the contents of the copper with what looked like an old rolling-pin. The steam therefrom, laden with death, travelled in a low trail across the meadow.

Laura spoke suddenly: 'I won't go tonight after all. He is so tired, and I must help him. I didn't know things were so bad as this!'

Vannicock's arm dropped from her waist, where it had been resting as they walked. 'Will you leave?' she asked.

'I will if you say I must. But I'd rather help too.' There was no expostulation in his tone.

Laura had gone forward. 'Jack,' she said, 'I am come to help!'

The weary curate turned and held up the lantern. 'Oh – what, is it you, Laura?' he asked in surprise. 'Why did you come into this? You had better go back – the risk is great.'

'But I want to help you, Jack. Please let me help! I didn't come by myself – Mr Vannicock kept me company. He will make himself useful too, if he's not gone on. Mr Vannicock!'

The young lieutenant came forward.[22] Mr Maumbry spoke formally to him, adding as he resumed his labour, 'I thought the—th had gone to Bristol.'

'We have. But I have run down again for a few things.'

The two new-comers began to assist, Vannicock placing on the ground the small bag containing Laura's toilet articles that he had been carrying. The barrow-man soon returned with another load, and all continued work for near a half-hour, when a coachman came out from the shadows to the north.

'Beg pardon, sir,' he whispered to Vannicock, 'but I've waited so long on the hill that at last I drove down to the turnpike; and seeing the light, I ran on to find out what had happened.'

Lieutenant Vannicock told him to wait a few minutes, and the last barrow-load was got through. Mr Maumbry stretched himself and breathed heavily, saying, 'There; we can do no more.'

As if from the relaxation of effort he seemed to be seized with violent pain. He pressed his hands to his sides and bent forward.

'Ah! I think it has got hold of me at last,' he said with difficulty. 'I must try to get home. Let Mr Vannicock take you back, Laura.'

He walked a few steps, they helping him, but was obliged to sink down on the grass.

'I am – afraid – you'll have to send for a hurdle, or shutter, or something,' he went on feebly, 'or try to get me into the barrow.'

But Vannicock had called to the driver of the fly, and they waited until it was brought on from the turnpike hard by. Mr Maumbry was placed therein. Laura entered with him, and they drove to his humble residence near the Cross, where he was got upstairs.

Vannicock stood outside by the empty fly awhile, but Laura did not reappear. He thereupon entered the fly and told the driver to take him back to Ivell.

"'I am – afraid – you'll have to send for a hurdle,' he went on feebly'.

# VII

Mr Maumbry had over-exerted himself in the relief of the suffering poor, and fell a victim – one of the last – to the pestilence which had carried off so many. Two days later he lay in his coffin.

Laura was in the room below. A servant brought in some letters, and she glanced them over. One was the note from herself to Maumbry, informing him that she was unable to endure life with him any longer and was about to elope with Vannicock. Having read the letter she took it upstairs to where the dead man was, and slipped it into his coffin. The next day she buried him.

She was now free.

She shut up his house at Durnover Cross and returned to her lodgings at Creston. Soon she had a letter from Vannicock, and six weeks after her husband's death her lover came to see her.

'I forgot to give you back this – that night,' he said presently, handing her the little bag she had taken as her whole luggage when leaving.

Laura received it and absently shook it out. There fell upon the carpet her brush, comb, slippers,[23] and other simple necessaries for a journey. They had an intolerably ghastly look now, and she tried to cover them.

'I can now,' he said, 'ask you to belong to me legally – when a proper interval has gone – instead of as we meant.'

There was languor in his utterance, hinting at a possibility that it was perfunctorily made. Laura picked up her articles, answering that he certainly could so ask her – she was free. Yet not her expression either could be called an ardent response. Then she blinked more and more quickly and put her handkerchief to her face. She was weeping violently.

He did not move or try to comfort her in any way. What had come between them? No living person. They had been lovers. There was now no material obstacle whatever to their union. But there was the insistent shadow of that unconscious one; the thin figure of him, moving to and fro in front of the ghastly[24] furnace in the gloom of Durnover Moor.

Yet Vannicock called upon Laura when he was in the neighbourhood, which was not often; but in two years, as if on purpose to further the marriage which everybody was expecting, the—th Foot returned to Budmouth Regis.

Thereupon the two could not help encountering each other at times. But whether because the obstacle had been the source of the love, or from a sense of error, and because Mrs Maumbry bore a less attractive look as a widow than before, their feelings seemed to decline from their former incandescence to a mere tepid civility. What domestic issues supervened in Vannicock's further story the man in the oriel never knew; but Mrs Maumbry lived and died a widow.

# ENTER A DRAGOON

I lately had the melancholy experience of going[1] over a doomed house with whose outside aspect I had long been familiar – a house, that is, which by reason of age and dilapidation was to be pulled down during the following week. Some of the thatch – brown and rotten as the gills of old mushrooms – had, indeed, been removed before I walked over the building. Seeing that it was only a very small house – what is usually called a 'cottage residence' – situated in a remote hamlet, and that it was not more than a hundred years old, if so much, I was led to think in my progress through the hollow rooms, with their cracked walls and sloping floors, what an exceptional number of abrupt family incidents had taken place therein – to reckon only those which had come to my own knowledge. And no doubt there were many more of which I had never heard.[2]

It stood at the top of a garden stretching down to the lane or street that ran through a hermit group of dwellings in Mellstock parish. From a green gate at the lower entrance, over which the thorn hedge had been shaped to an arch by constant clippings, a gravel path ascended between the box edges of once trim raspberry, strawberry, and vegetable plots, towards the front door. This was in colour an ancient and bleaching green that could be rubbed off with the finger, and it bore a small, long-featured brass knocker covered with verdigris in its crevices. For some years before this eve of demolition the homestead had degenerated, and been divided into two tenements, to serve as cottages for farm-labourers; but in its prime it had indisputable claim to be considered neat, pretty, and genteel.

The variety of incident above alluded to was mainly owing to the nature of the tenure, whereby the place had been occupied by families not quite the kind customary in such spots – people whose circumstances, position, or antecedents were more or less of a critical, happy-go-lucky cast. And of these residents the family whose term comprised the story I wish to relate was that of Mr Jacob Paddock, the market-gardener, who dwelt there for some years with his wife and grown-up daughter.

## I

> 'My old Love came and walked therein,
>     And laid the garden waste.'
>  – O'SHAUGHNESSY[3]

An evident commotion was agitating the premises, which jerked busy sounds into the front plot, resembling those of a disturbed hive. If a member of the household appeared at the door, it was with a countenance of abstraction and concern.

Evening began to bend over the scene, and the other inhabitants of the hamlet came out to draw water, their common well being in the public road opposite the garden and house of the Paddocks. Having wound up their bucketfuls respectively, they lingered, and spoke significantly together. From their words any casual listener might have gathered information of what had occurred.

The woodman, who lived nearest the site of the story, told most of the tale. Selina, the daughter of the Paddocks opposite, had been surprised that afternoon by receiving a letter from her once intended husband, then a corporal, but now a sergeant-major of dragoons, whom she had hitherto supposed to be one of the slain in the battle of the Alma,[4] two or three years before.

'She picked up wi' en against her father's wish, as we know, and before he got his stripes,' their informant continued. 'Not but that the man was as hearty a feller as you'd meet this side o' London. But Jacob, you see, wished her to do better; and one can understand it. However, she was determined to stick to him at that time; and for what happened she was not much to blame, so near as they were to matrimony when the war broke out and spoiled all.'

'Even the very pig had been killed for the wedding,' said a woman, 'and the barrel o' beer ordered in. Oh, the man meant honourable enough. But to be off in two days to fight in a foreign country – 'twas natural of her father to say they should wait till he got back.'

'And he never came,' murmured one in the shade.

'The war ended, but her man never turned up again. She was not sure he was killed, but was too proud, or too timid, to go and hunt for him.'

'One reason why her father forgave her when he found out how matters stood was, as he said plain at the time, that he liked the man, and could see that he meant to act straight. So the old folks made the best of what they couldn't mend, and kept her there with 'em, when some wouldn't. Time has told us, seemingly, that he did mean to act straight, now that he have writ to her that he's a-coming. She'd have stuck to him all through the time, 'tis my belief, if t'other hadn't come along.'

'At the date o' the coortship,' resumed the woodman, 'the regiment was lying in Casterbridge Barracks, and he and she got acquainted by his calling to buy a penn'orth of rathe-ripes off that tree yonder in her father's orchard; though 'twas said he seed *her* over hedge as well as the apples. He declared 'twas a kind of apple he much fancied; and he called for a penn'orth every day till the tree was cleared. It ended in his calling for her.'

' 'Twas a thousand pities they didn't jine up at once, and ha' done wi' it!'

'Well, better late than never, if so be he'll have her now. But, Lord, she'd that faith in en that she'd no more belief he was alive, when 'a didn't come, than that the undermost man in our churchyard was alive. She'd never have thought of another but for that – oh no!'

' 'Tis awkward, altogether, for her now.'

'Still, she hadn't married wi' the new man. Though, to be sure, she would have committed it next week, even the licence being got, they say, for she'd have no banns this time, the first being so unfortunate.'[5]

'Perhaps the sergeant-major will think he's released, and go as he came.'

'Oh, not as I reckon. Soldiers baint particular, and she's a tidy piece o' furniture still. What will happen is that she'll have back her soldier, and break off with the master-wheelwright, licence or no – daze me if she won't!'

In the progress of these desultory conjectures the form of another neighbour arose in the gloom. She nodded to the people at the well, who replied, 'G'night, Mrs Stone,' as she passed through Mr Paddock's gate towards his door. She was an intimate friend of the latter's household, and the group followed her with their eyes up the path and past the windows, which were now lighted up by candles inside.

## II

'And shall I see his face again,
And shall I hear him speak?'[6]

Mrs Stone paused at the door, knocked, and was admitted by Selina's mother, who took her visitor at once into the parlour on the left hand, where a table was partly spread for supper. On the 'bowfitt'[7] against the wall stood probably the only object which would have attracted the eye of a local stranger in an otherwise ordinarily furnished room: a great plum cake, guarded, as if it were a curiosity, by a glass shade of the kind seen in museums – square, with a wooden back, like those enclosing stuffed specimens of rare feather or fur. This was the mummy of the cake intended in earlier days for the wedding-feast of Selina and the soldier, which had been religiously and lovingly preserved by the former as a testimony to her intentional respectability in spite of an untoward subsequent circumstance which will be mentioned. This relic was now as dry as a brick, and seemed to belong to a pre-existent civilization. Till quite recently Selina had been in the habit of pausing before it daily, and recalling the accident whose consequences had thrown a shadow over her life ever since – that of which the

water-drawers had spoken – the sudden news one morning that
the Route had come for the —th Dragoons, two days only being
the interval before departure; the hurried consultation as to
what should be done, the second time of asking the banns being
past, but not the third; and the decision by her father that it
would be unwise to solemnize matrimony in such haphazard
conditions, even if it were possible in the time, which was
doubtful.

Before the fire the young woman in question was now seated
on a low stool, in the stillness of reverie, and a toddling boy
played about the floor around her.

'Ah, Mrs Stone!' said Selina, rising slowly. 'How kind of you
to come in. You'll bide to supper? Mother has told you the
strange news, of course?'

'No. But I heard it outside: that is, that you'd had a letter
from Mr Clark – Sergeant-major Clark, as they say he is now –
and that he's coming to make it up with 'ee.'

'Yes; coming tonight – all the way from the north of England,
where he's quartered. I don't know whether I'm happy or –
frightened at it! Of course I always believed that if he were alive
he'd come and keep his solemn vow to me. But when it is printed
that a man is killed – what can you think?'

'It *was* printed?'

'Why, yes! After the battle of the Alma the book of names of
the killed and wounded was nailed up against Casterbridge
Town Hall door. 'Twas on a Saturday, and I walked there o'
purpose to read and see for myself, for I'd heard that his name
was down. There was a crowd of people round the book, looking
for the names of relations, and I can mind that when they saw
me they made way for me – knowing that we'd been just going
to be married – and that, as you may say, I belonged to him.
Well, I reached up my arm and turned over the farrels of the
book, and under the "killed" I read his surname, but instead of
"John" they'd printed "James", and I thought 'twas a mistake,
and that it must be he. Who could have guessed there were two
nearly of one name in one regiment?'

'Well – he's coming to finish the wedding of 'ee, as may be
said; so never mind, my dear. All's well that ends well.'

'That's what he seems to say. But then – he has not heard yet about Mr Miller; and that's what rather terrifies me. Luckily, my marriage with him next week was to have been by licence, and not banns, as in John's case; and it was not so well known on that account. Still, I don't know what to think.'

'Everything seems to come just 'twixt cup and lip with 'ee, don't it now, Miss Paddock? Two weddings broke off – 'tis odd! How came you to accept Mr Miller, my dear?'

'He's been so good and faithful! Not minding about the child at all; for he knew the rights of the story. He's dearly fond o' Johnny, you know – just as if 'twere his own – isn't he, my duck? Do Mr Miller love you or don't he?'

'Iss! An' I love Mr Miller,' said the toddler.

'Well, you see, Mrs Stone, he said he'd make me a comfortable home, and thinking 'twould be a good thing for Johnny, Mr Miller being so much better off than we, I agreed at last, just as a widow might do – which is what I have always felt myself, ever since I saw what I thought was John's name printed there. I hope John will forgive me!'

'So he will forgive 'ee, since 'twas no manner of wrong to him. He ought to have sent 'ee a line, saying 'twas another man.'

Selina's mother entered. 'We've not known of this an hour, Mrs Stone,' she said. 'The letter was brought up from Lower Mellstock post-office by one of the school-children only this afternoon. Mr Miller was coming here this very night to settle about the wedding doings. Hark! is that your father? Or is it Mr Miller already come?'

The footsteps entered the porch; there was a brushing on the mat, and the door of the room swung back to disclose a rubicund man about thirty years of age, of thriving master-mechanic appearance and obviously comfortable temper. On seeing the child, and before taking any notice whatever of the elders, the comer made a noise like the crowing of a cock, and flapped his arms as if they were wings, a method of entry which had the unqualified admiration of Johnny.

'Yes – it is he,' said Selina, constrainedly advancing.

'What – were you all talking about me, my dear?' said the genial young man when he had finished his crowing and resumed human manners. 'Why – what's the matter?' he went on. 'You look struck all of a heap.' Mr Miller spread an aspect of concern over his own face, and drew a chair up to the fire.

'Oh, mother, would you tell Mr Miller, if he don't know?'

'*Mister* Miller! And going to be married in six days!' he interposed.

'Ah – he don't know it yet!' murmured Mrs Paddock.

'Know what?'

'Well . . . John Clark – now Sergeant-major Clark – wasn't shot at Alma, after all. 'Twas another of almost the same name.'

'Now that's interesting! There were several cases like that.'

'And he's home again; and he's coming here tonight to see her.'

'What ever shall I say, that he may not be offended with what I've done!'

'But why should it matter if he be?'

'Oh, I must agree to be his wife, if he forgives me – of course I must!'

'Ah! But why not say nay, Selina, even if he do forgive 'ee?'

'Oh no! How can I, without being really wicked? You were very, very kind, Mr Miller, to ask me to have you; no other man would have done it after what had happened; and I agreed, even though I did not feel half so warm as I ought. Yet it was entirely owing to my believing him in the grave, as I knew that if he were not he would carry out his promise; and this shows that I was right in trusting him.'

'Yes . . . He must be a goodish sort of fellow,' said Mr Miller, for a moment so impressed with the excellently faithful conduct of the sergeant-major of dragoons that he disregarded its effect upon his own position. He sighed slowly and added: 'Well, Selina, 'tis for you to say. I love you, and I love the boy; and there's my chimney-corner and sticks o' furniture ready for 'ee both.'

'Yes, I know! But I mustn't hear it any more now,' murmured Selina, quickly. 'John will be here soon. I hope he'll see how it all was, when I tell him. If so be I could have written it to him in a letter, it would have been better.'

'You think he doesn't know a single word about our having been on the brink o't. But perhaps it's the other way? He's heard of it, and that may have brought him.'

'Ah – perhaps he has!' she said, brightening. 'And already forgives me.'

'If not, speak out straight and fair, and tell him exactly how it fell out. If he's a man, he'll see it.'

'Oh, he's a man true enough. But I really do think I sha'n't have to tell him at all, since you've put it to me that way!'

As it was now Johnny's bedtime he was carried up stairs, and when Selina came down again her mother observed, with some anxiety, 'I fancy Mr Clark must be here soon if he's coming; and that being so, perhaps Mr Miller wouldn't mind – wishing us good night? – since you are so determined to stick to your sergeant-major.' A little bitterness bubbled amid the closing words. 'It would be less awkward, Mr Miller not being here – if he will allow me to say it.'

'To be sure; to be sure,' the master-wheelwright exclaimed, with instant conviction, rising alertly from his chair. 'Lord bless my soul!' he said, taking up his hat and stick, 'and we to have been married in six days! But, Selina – you are right. You do belong to him,[8] since he's alive. I'll try to make the best of it.'

Before the generous Miller had got further there came a knock to the door, accompanied by the noise of wheels.

'I thought I heard something driving up!' said Mrs Paddock.

They heard Mr Paddock, who had been smoking in the room opposite, rise and go to the door, and in a moment a voice familiar enough to Selina was audibly saying: 'At last I am here again – not without many interruptions! How is it with 'ee, Mr Paddock? And how is she? Thought never to see me again, I suppose?' A step with a clink of spurs in it struck upon the entry floor.

'Danged if I baint catched!' murmured Mr Miller, forgetting company speech. 'Never mind – I may as well meet him here as elsewhere; and I should like to see the chap, and make friends with en, as he seems one o' the right sort.' He returned to the fireplace just as the sergeant-major was ushered in.

# III

'Yet went we not still on in constancy?'
   – DONNE[9]

He was a good specimen of the long-service soldier of those days: a not unhandsome man, with a certain undemonstrative dignity, which some might have said to be partly owing to the stiffness of his uniform about the neck, the high stock being still worn.[10] He was much stouter than when Selina had parted from him. Although she had not meant to be demonstrative, she ran across to him directly she saw him, and he held her in his arms and kissed her. Then in much agitation she whispered something to him, at which he seemed to be much surprised.

'He's just put to bed,' she continued. 'You can go up and see him. I knew you'd come if you were alive! But I had quite gi'd you up for dead! You've been home in England ever since the war ended?'

'Yes, dear.'

'Why didn't you come sooner?'

'That's just what I ask myself! Why was I such a sappy as not to hurry here the first day I set foot on shore! Well, who'd have thought it – you are as pretty as ever!'

He relinquished her to step up[11] stairs a little way, where by looking through the balusters he could see Johnny's cot just within an open door. On his stepping down again Mr Miller was preparing to depart.

'Now – what's this? I am sorry to see anybody going the moment I've come,' expostulated the sergeant-major. 'I thought we might make an evening of it. There's a nine-gallon cask o' Three-Mariners' beer[12] outside in the trap, and a ham, and half a rawmil' cheese; for I thought you might be short o' forage in a lonely place like this: and it struck me we might like to ask in a neighbour or two. But perhaps it would be taking a liberty?'

'Oh no – not at all,' said Mr Paddock, who was now in the room, in a judicial, measured manner. 'Very thoughtful of 'ee. Only 'twas not necessary; for we had just laid in an extry stock of eatables and drinkables, in preparation for the coming event.'

' 'Twas very kind, upon my heart,' said the soldier, 'to think me worth such a jocund preparation, since you could only have got my letter this morning.'

Selina gazed at her father to stop him, and exchanged embarrassed glances with Miller. Contrary to her hopes, Sergeant-major Clark plainly did not know that the preparations referred to were for something quite other than his own visit.

The movement of the horse outside, and the impatient tapping of a whip-handle upon the vehicle, reminded them that Clark's driver was still in waiting. The provisions were brought into the house, and the cart dismissed. Miller, with very little pressure indeed, accepted an invitation to supper, and a few neighbours were induced to come in to make up a cheerful party.

During the laying of the meal, and throughout its continuance, Selina, who sat beside her first-intended husband, tried frequently to break the news to him of her engagement to the other – now terminated so suddenly, and so happily for her heart, and her sense of womanly virtue. But the talk ran entirely upon the late war; and, though fortified by half a horn of the strong ale brought by the sergeant-major, she decided that she might have a better opportunity when supper was over of revealing the situation to him in private.

Having supped, Clark leaned back at ease in his chair, and looked around.

'We used sometimes to have a dance in that other room after supper, Selina dear, I recollect. We used to clear out all the furniture before beginning. Have you kept up such goings-on?'

'No – not at all!' said his sweetheart, sadly.

'We were not unlikely to revive it in a few days,' said Mr Paddock. 'But howsomever, there's seemingly many a slip, as the saying is –'

'Yes, I'll tell John all about that by-and-by!' interposed Selina; at which, perceiving that the secret which he did not like keeping was to be kept even yet, her father held his tongue with some show of testiness.

The subject of a dance having been broached, to put the thought in practice was the feeling of all. Soon after the tables and chairs were borne from the opposite room to this by zealous hands, and two of the villagers sent home for a fiddle and tambourine, when the majority began to tread a measure well known in that secluded vale. Selina naturally danced with the sergeant-major – not altogether to her father's satisfaction, and to the real uneasiness of her mother, both of whom would have preferred a postponement of festivities till the rashly anticipated relationship between their daughter and Clark in the past had been made fact by the Church's ordinances. They did not, however, express a positive objection, Mr Paddock remembering, with self-reproach, that it was owing to his original strongly expressed disapproval of Selina's being a soldier's wife that the wedding had been delayed, and finally hindered – with worse consequences than were expected; and ever since the misadventure brought about by his government he had allowed events to steer their own courses.

'My tails will surely catch in your spurs, John!' murmured the daughter of the house, as she whirled around upon his arm with the rapt soul and look of a somnambulist. 'I didn't know we should dance, or I would have put on my other frock.'

'I'll take care, my love. We've danced here before. Do you think your father objects to me now I've risen in rank? I fancy he's still a little against me.'

'He has repented, times enough!'

'And so have I! If I had married you then, 'would have saved many a misfortune. I have sometimes thought it might have been possible to rush the ceremony through somehow before I left; though we were only in the second asking, weren't we? And even if I had come back straight here when we returned from the Crimea, and married you then, how much happier I should have been!'

'Dear John, to say that! Why didn't you?'

'Oh, dilatoriness, and want of thought, and a fear of facing your father after so long. I was in hospital a great while, you know. But how familiar the place seems again! What's that I saw on the bowfitt in the other room? – it never used to be there – a sort of withered corpse of a cake – not an old bride-cake, surely?'

'Yes, John. Ours. 'Tis the very one that was made for our wedding three years ago.'

'Sakes alive! How time shuts up together, doesn't it, and all between then and now seems not to have been! What became of that wedding-dress that they were making – in this room, I remember – a bluish, whitish, frothy thing?'

'I have that, too.'

'Really! . . . Why, Selina –'

'Yes?'

'Why not put it on now?'

'Wouldn't it seem – And yet, oh, how I should like to! It would remind them all, if we told them what it was, how we really meant to be married on that bygone day!' Her eyes were again laden with wet.

'Yes . . . The pity that we didn't – the pity!' Moody mournfulness seemed to hold silent awhile one not naturally taciturn. 'Well – will you?' he said.

'I will – the next dance – if mother don't mind.'

Accordingly, just before the next figure was formed, Selina disappeared, and speedily came down stairs in a creased and box-worn but still airy and pretty muslin gown, which was indeed the very one that had been meant to grace her as a bride three years before.

'It is dreadfully old-fashioned,' she apologized.

'Not at all. What a grand thought of mine! Now let's to't again.'

She explained to some of them, as he led her to the second dance, what the frock had been meant for, and that she had put it on at his request. And again athwart and around the room they went.

'You seem the bride!' he said.

'But I couldn't wear this gown to be married in *now*!' she replied, ecstatically, 'or I shouldn't have put it on and made it dusty. It is really too old-fashioned, and so folded and fretted out, you can't think. That was with my taking it out of my box so many times to look at. I have never put it on since fitting it – never – till now!'

'Selina – I am thinking of giving up the army. Will you

emigrate with me to New Zealand? – I've an uncle out there, doing well; and he'd soon help me to making a large income. The English army is glorious, but it ain't altogether enriching.'

'Of course – anywhere that you decide upon. Is it healthy there for Johnny?'

'A lovely climate. And I shall never be happy in England … Hah!' he concluded again, with a bitterness of unexpected strength; 'would to Heaven I had come straight back here!'

As the dance brought round one neighbour after another, they were thrown into juxtaposition with Bob Heartall, among the rest who had been called in, one whose chronic expression was that he carried inside him a joke on the point of bursting with its own vastness. He took occasion now to let out a little of its quality, shaking his head at Selina as he addressed her in an undertone:

'This is a bit of a topper to the bridegroom – ho, ho! 'Twill teach en the liberty you'll expect when you've married en!'

'What does he mean by a "topper"?' the sergeant-major asked, who, not being of local extraction, despised the venerable local language, and also seemed to suppose 'bridegroom' to be an anticipatory name for himself. 'I only hope I shall never be worse treated than you've treated me tonight!'

Selina looked frightened. 'He didn't mean you, dear,' she said as they moved on. 'We thought perhaps you knew what had happened – owing to your coming just at this time. Had you – heard anything about what I intended?'

'Not a breath – how should I? – away up in Yorkshire. It was by the merest accident that I came just at this date to make peace with you for my delay.'

'I was engaged to be married; yes; to Mr Bartholomew Miller. That's what it is! I would have let 'ee know by letter, but there was no time, only hearing from you this afternoon … You won't desert me for it, will you, John? Because, as you know, I quite supposed you, dead, and – and –' Her eyes were full of tears of trepidation, and he might have felt a sob heaving within her.

# IV

'And their souls wer a-smote wi' a stroke,
As the lightnen do vail on the oak,
And the things that were bright all around 'em
Seem'd dim . . .'
      – W. BARNES.[13]

The soldier was silent during two or three double bars of the
tune. 'When were you to have been married to the said Mr
Bartholomew Miller?' he inquired.

'Quite soon.'

'How soon?'

'Next week – Oh yes – just the same as it was with you and
me! There's a strange fate of interruption hanging over me, I
sometimes think. He had bought the licence, which I preferred,
so that it mightn't be like – ours. But it made no difference to
the fate of it.'

'Had bought the licence! The devil!'

'Don't be angry, dear John. I didn't know!'

'No – no – I'm not angry.'

'It was so kind of him, considering!'

'Yes . . . I see, of course, how natural your action was – never
thinking of seeing me any more! Is it the Mr Miller who is in
this dance?'

'Yes.'

Clark glanced round upon Bartholomew, and was silent again
for some little while; and she stole a look at him, to find that he
seemed changed. 'John, you look ill!' she almost sobbed. 'It isn't
me, is it?'

'Oh dear no. Though I hadn't somehow, expected it, I can't
find fault with you for a moment – and I don't . . . This is a
deuce of a long dance, don't you think? We've been at it twenty
minutes if a second. And the figure doesn't allow one much rest.
I'm quite out of breath.'

'They like them so dreadfully long here. Shall we drop out?
Or I'll stop the fiddler.'

'Oh no, no. I think I can finish. But although I look healthy enough, I have never been so strong as I formerly was, since that long illness I had in the hospital at Scutari.'[14]

'And I knew nothing about it!'

'You couldn't, dear, as I didn't write. What a fool I have been, altogether!' ... He gave a twitch, as of one in pain. 'I won't dance again when this figure is over. The fact is I have travelled a long way today, and it seems to have knocked me up a bit.'

There could be no doubt that the sergeant-major was unwell, and Selina made herself miserable by still believing that her story was the cause of his ailment. Suddenly he said in a changed voice, and she perceived that he was paler than ever,

'I must sit down.'

Letting go her waist, he went quickly to the other room. She followed, and found him in the nearest chair, his face bent down upon his hands and arms, which were resting on the table.

'What's the matter?' said her father, who sat there dozing by the fire.

'John isn't well ... We are going to New Zealand when we are married, father. A lovely country! ... John, would you like something to drink?'

'A drop o' that Schiedam of old Owlett's[15] that's under stairs, perhaps?' suggested her father. 'Not that nowadays 'tis much better than licensed liquor.'

'John,' she said, putting her face close to his and pressing his arm, 'will you have a drop of spirits, or something?'

He did not reply, and Selina observed that his ear and the side of his face were quite white. Convinced that his illness was serious, a growing dismay seized hold of her. The dance ended; her mother came in, and learning what had happened, looked narrowly at the sergeant-major.

'We must not let him lie like that; lift him up,' she said. 'Let him rest in the window-bench on some cushions.'

They unfolded his arms and hands as they lay clasped upon the table, and on lifting his head found his features to bear the very impress of death itself. Bartholomew Miller, who had now come in, assisted Mr Paddock to make a comfortable couch in the window-seat, where they stretched out Clark upon his back.

Still he seemed unconscious. 'We must get a doctor,' said Selina. 'Oh, my dear John, how is it you be taken like this?'

'My impression is that he's dead! murmured Mr Paddock. 'He don't breathe enough to move a tomtit's feather.'

There were plenty to volunteer to go for a doctor, but as it would be at least an hour before he could get there, the case seemed somewhat hopeless. The dancing party ended as unceremoniously as it had been begun; but the guests lingered round the premises till the doctor should arrive. When he did come the sergeant-major's extremities were already cold, and there was no doubt that death had overtaken him almost at the moment that he had sat down.

The medical practitioner quite refused to accept the unhappy Selina's theory that her revelation had in any way induced Clark's sudden collapse. Both he, and the coroner afterwards, who found the immediate cause to be heart failure, held that such a supposition was unwarranted by facts; they asserted that a long day's journey, a hurried drive, and then an exhausting dance, were sufficient for a fatal result upon a heart enfeebled by the privations[16] of a Crimean winter and other trying experiences, the coincidence of the sad event with any disclosure of hers being a pure accident.

This conclusion, however, did not dislodge Selina's opinion that the shock of her statement had been the immediate stroke which had felled a constitution so undermined.

## V

'For Love's sake kiss me once again!
I long, and should not beg in vain.'
                    – BEN JONSON.[17]

At this date the Casterbridge Barracks were cavalry quarters, their adaptation to artillery having been effected some years later. It had been owing to the fact that the —th Dragoons, in which John Clark had served, happened to be lying there that

Selina made his acquaintance. At the time of his death the barracks were occupied by the Scots Greys, but when the pathetic circumstances of the sergeant-major's end became known in the town, the officers of that regiment offered the services of their fine reed and brass band, that he might have a funeral marked by due military honours. His body was accordingly removed to the barracks, and carried thence to the church-yard[18] on the following afternoon, one of the Greys' most ancient and docile chargers being blacked up to represent Clark's horse on the occasion.

Everybody pitied Selina, whose story was well known. She followed the corpse as the only mourner, Clark having been without relations in this part of the country, and a communication with his regiment having brought none from a distance. She sat in a little shabby brown-black mourning carriage, squeezing herself up in a corner to be as much as possible out of sight during the slow and dramatic march through the town to the tune from *Saul*.[19] When the interment had taken place, the volleys been fired, and the return journey begun, it was with something like a shock that she found the military escort to be moving at a quick march to the lively strains of 'Off she goes',[20] as if all care for the sergeant-major were expected to be ended with the late discharge of the carbines. It was, by chance, the very air to which they had been footing when he died, and unable to bear its notes, she hastily told her driver to drop behind. The band and military party diminished up the High Street, and Selina turned over the bridge and homeward to Mellstock.

Then recommenced for her a life whose incidents were precisely of a suit with those which had preceded the soldier's return: but how different in her appreciation of them! Her narrow miss of the recovered respectability they had hoped for from that tardy event worked upon her parents as an irritant, and after the first week or two of her mourning her life with them grew almost insupportable. She had impulsively taken to wear the weeds of a widow, for such she seemed to herself to be, and clothed little Johnny in sables likewise. This assumption of a moral relationship to the deceased, which she asserted to be only not a legal one through two most unexpected accidents, led the old people to indulge in sarcasm at her expense, whenever they beheld her attire, though all the while it cost them more pain to utter than it gave her to hear it. Having become accustomed by her residence at home to the business carried on by her father, she surprised them one day by going off with the child to Chalk-Newton,[21] in the direction of the town of Ivell – and opening a miniature fruit and vegetable shop, attending Ivell market with her produce. Her business grew somewhat larger, and it was soon sufficient to enable her to support herself and the boy in comfort. She called herself 'Mrs John Clark' from the day of leaving home, and painted the same on her sign-board.[22]

By degrees the pain of her state was forgotten in her new circumstances; and getting to be generally accepted as the widow of a sergeant-major of dragoons, an assumption which her modest and mournful demeanour seemed to substantiate, her life became a placid one, her mind being nourished by the melancholy luxury of dreaming what might have been her future in New Zealand with John, if he had only lived to take her there. Her only travels now were a journey to Ivell on market-days, and once a fortnight to the churchyard in which Clark lay, there to tend, with Johnny's assistance, as good widows are wont to do, the flowers she had planted upon his grave.

On a day about eighteen months after his unexpected decease Selina was surprised in her lodging over her little shop by a visit from Bartholomew Miller. He had called on her once or twice before, on which occasions he had used without a word of comment the name by which she was known.

'I've come this time,' he said, 'less because I was in this direction than to ask you, Mrs Clark, what you mid well guess. I've come o' purpose, in short.'

She smiled. ''Tis to ask me again to marry you?'

'Yes; of course. You see, his coming back for 'ee proved what I always believed of 'ee, though others didn't. There's nobody but would be glad to welcome 'ee to our parish again, now you've showed your independence, and acted up to your trust in his promise. Well, my dear, will you come?'

'I'd rather bide as Mrs Clark, I think,' she answered. 'I am not ashamed of my position at all; for I am John's widow in the eyes of Heaven.'

'I quite agree – that's why I've come. Still, you won't like to be always straining at this shopkeeping and market-standing, and 'twould be better for Johnny if you had nothing to do but tend him.'

He here touched the only weak spot in Selina's resistance to his proposal – the good of the boy. To promote that there were other men she might have married off-hand without loving them, if they had asked her to; but though she had known the worthy speaker from her youth, she could not for the moment fancy herself happy as Mrs Miller.[23]

She said something about there being far better women than she, and other natural commonplaces, but assured him she was most grateful to him for feeling what he felt, as indeed she sincerely was. He went away after taking tea with her, without discerning much hope for him in her goodby.

## VI

'Men are as the time is.'
– KING LEAR.[24]

After that evening she saw and heard nothing of him for a great while. Her fortnightly journeys to the sergeant-major's grave were continued whenever weather did not hinder them; and Mr Miller must have known, she thought, of this custom of hers. But though the churchyard was not nearly so far from his homestead as was her shop at Chalk-Newton, he never appeared in the accidental way that lovers use.

An explanation was forth-coming in the shape of a letter from her mother, who casually mentioned that Mr Bartholomew Miller had gone away to the other side of Shottsford – Forum[25] to be married to a thriving dairyman's daughter that he knew there, his chief motive, it was reported, being less one of love than a wish to provide a companion for his aged mother.

Selina was practical enough to know that she had lost a good, and possibly her only, opportunity of settling in life after what had happened, and for a moment she regretted her independence. But she became calm on reflection, and to fortify herself in her course of fidelity started that afternoon to tend the sergeant-major's grave, in which she took the same sober pleasure as at first.

On reaching the churchyard and turning the corner towards the spot as usual, she was surprised to perceive another woman, also apparently a respectable widow, and with a little boy by her side, bending over Clark's turf, and spudding up with the point of her umbrella some ivy roots that Selina had reverently planted there to form an evergreen mantle over the mound.

'What are you digging up my ivy for?' cried Selina, rushing forward so excitedly that Johnny tumbled over a grave with the force of the tug she gave his hand in her sudden start.

'Your ivy?' said the respectable woman.

'Why, yes! I planted it there – on my husband's grave.'

'*Your* husband's!'

'Yes. The late Sergeant-major Clark. Anyhow, we were going to be married in a few days – twice over!'[26]

'Indeed. But who may be my husband, if not he? I am the only Mrs John Clark, widow of the late sergeant-major of dragoons, and this is his only son and heir.'

'How can that be?' faltered Selina, her throat seeming to close up as she just began to perceive its possibility. 'He had been – going to marry me twice – and we were going to New Zealand.'

'Ah – I remember about you,' returned the legitimate widow calmly and not unkindly. 'You must be Selina; he spoke of you now and then, and said that his relations with you would always be a weight on his conscience. Well, the history of my life with him is soon told. When he came back from the Crimea he became acquainted with me at my home in the north, and we were married within four weeks of first knowing each other. Unfortunately after living together a few months we could not agree; and after a particularly sharp quarrel, in which perhaps I was most in the wrong – as I don't mind owning here by his grave-side, poor man! – he went away from me, declaring he would get his discharge and emigrate to New Zealand; and

'What are you digging up my ivy for?'

never come back any more. The next thing I heard was that he had died suddenly at Mellstock at some low carouse; and as he had left me in such anger, to live no more with me, I would not come down to his funeral, or do anything in relation to him. 'Twas temper, I know; but that was the fact . . . Even if we had parted friends it would have been a serious expense to travel three hundred miles to get here, for one who wasn't left so very well off . . . I am sorry I pulled out your ivy roots; but that common sort of ivy is considered a weed in my part of the country.'

# Notes

These notes offer two distinct kinds of assistance: clarification of obscurities and indication of noteworthy textual variants. They do not include definition of words, which may be found in the accompanying Glossary. Angled brackets (< >) indicate material deleted in manuscript.

Biblical quotations are taken from the King James version of 1611. Shakespeare quotations are taken from *The Riverside Shakespeare*, ed. G. Blakemore Evans (Boston: Houghton Mifflin, 1974).

## 'THE MELANCHOLY HUSSAR OF THE GERMAN LEGION'

1. *the downs*: Hardy identified these as Bincombe Down (*Collected Letters*, II, 131), on the high chalk ridge north of Weymouth.
2. *King's German Legion*: Various regiments were posted to Dorset during the early years of the nineteenth century for coastal protection when invasion by Napoleon was feared. The story is based on oral and journalistic accounts of an event that took place in 1801 (see Introduction). Hardy's interchangeable references to the 'King's German Legion' and the 'York Hussars' are inaccurate. While both consisted mainly of Hanoverians, they were separate regiments, and the York Hussars, raised in 1794, were disbanded in June 1802, the year before the King's German Legion was founded. For these and other details of the distinction between them, see George Lanning, 'Hardy and the Hanoverian Hussars', *Thomas Hardy Journal* 6 (1990), 69–73. In 1890 *BT* and again in 1912 *WT* Hardy avoided some of the potential confusions by making the story's title simply 'The Melancholy Hussar', excising 'of the German Legion'.
3. *A divinity still hedged kings*: Cf. 'There's such divinity doth hedge

a king/ That treason can but peep to what it would' (Shakespeare, *Hamlet*, IV.v.124–5).

4.  *sea-side watering-place a few miles to the south*: George III's visits to the spa and port town of Weymouth, on the Dorset coast eight miles south of the county town of Dorchester, began in 1789, when he visited there to convalesce from illness. For more than fifteen years he was a regular summer visitor, staying at Gloucester Lodge. The association is commemorated in the statue of him erected on the seafront in 1809 and his giant equestrian figure carved out on a nearby chalk down, as well as in the 'Regis' designation attached to 'Budmouth', Hardy's fictional name for Weymouth. Unlike 1894 *LLI*, 1890 *BT* refers to Weymouth by name a number of times.

5.  *trimming the box-tree borders*: An early three-page draft indicates only that Grove trimmed the bushes 'for tidiness'. In the MS submitted for 1890 *BT*, Hardy added several details emphasizing a culpable self-absorption in Grove, including the later reference to his 'taste for lonely meditation over metaphysical questions' (see Ray, 26).

6.  *her father's acquaintance*: One of several details emphasizing Phyllis's respectability that appear in the MS used for 1890 *BT*, but not in an earlier three-page draft MS. The later MS also has Matthäus Tina telling Phyllis 'you will not fly alone with me' because Christoph will accompany them, and Tina's homesickness is intensified, as Ray suggests, 'to mitigate his desertion from the army' (Ray, 27).

7.  *The spot was . . . on the west*: Added for 1894 *LLI*. The 'Isle of Portland', the actual name of the long rocky island south of Weymouth, became in 1912 *WT* 'Portland – the Isle of Slingers', its fictional name in the novel *The Pursuit of the Well-Beloved*. St Aldhelm's Head is the Wessex name for St Alban's Head, a high headland between Weymouth and Bournemouth. The Start is Start Point, west of Weymouth on the south Devon coast.

8.  *Like Desdemona*: Shakespeare's Othello describes Desdemona falling in love with him while hearing of his military adventures: 'She lov'd me for the dangers I had pass'd,/ And I lov'd her that she did pity them' (I.iii.167–8). This sentence, added for 1890 *BT* at the proof stage (Ray, 30), invokes another ill-fated love affair across national boundaries.

9.  *Saarbrück*: A German town close to the French border. It is rendered as 'Sarrbruk' ('Sarsbruk' in 1890 *BT*) in the transcription from the burial register at the end of the story.

10. *this home-woe, as he called it in his own tongue*: *Heimweh*, the German word for 'homesickness', is a conflation of the words for 'home' and 'woe'.

11. *made anything like intimacy difficult*: Revised in MS from the less accurate 'prevented anything like intimacy' (for further details, see Ray, 28).

12. *'Love me little, love me long'*: Proverbial but also incorporated into an anonymous Elizabethan lyric (*c.* 1569–70) whose opening couplet and refrain read: 'Love me little, love me long,/ Is the burden of my song' (see *Elizabethan Lyrics from the original Texts*, ed. Norman Ault (New York: Capricorn Books, 1960), pp. 61–2).

13. *my country is by the Saar*: 'my country is Bavaria by right' (1890 *BT*). 'Bavaria' was revised in MS from 'Prussia'. It is important to Tina's moral characterization as a deserter that he is not a Hanoverian and, like his Alsatian friend Christoph, comes from an area not at war with France. Both have homes near the French border.

14. *passionate longing for his country, and mother, and home*: In MS 'longing' replaced 'admiration', and the reference to Tina's mother was added (see Ray, 27). This is again designed to make his actions seem motivated by overwhelming attachment to country and family, and therefore less culpable.

15. *the Nothe*: Promontory jutting out into the sea east of Weymouth. This lookout point's military associations subsequently became more pronounced with the building in 1860 of a major fort for coastal defence.

16. *Cleopatra of Egypt*: At the Battle of Actium, Cleopatra's flight causes her lover, Mark Antony, to follow, granting victory to their opponent, Octavius Caesar (see Shakespeare, *Antony and Cleopatra*, III.x).

17. *camp of the Assyrians*: The image is of total annihilation: 'And it came to pass that night, that the angel of the Lord went out, and smote in the camp of the Assyrians an hundred fourscore and five thousand: and when they arose early in the morning, behold, they were all dead corpses' (2 Kings 19.35. See also Isaiah 37.36).

18. *down*: All previous printed versions have the typographical error 'dawn', despite the clear MS reading 'down'. A similar substitution from MS spelling, 'eyes starting' instead of 'eyes staring', has been made for this edition two paragraphs down to correct another typographical error occurring in all former printed versions. See Ray, 29–30.

19. *On the open green ... levelled carbines*: Many of the execution
details are based on an account from the *Morning Chronicle*,
4 July 1801, which Hardy summarized in the 'Trumpet-Major
Notebook' (containing research notes collected in 1878–9 in the
British Museum in preparation for writing *The Trumpet-Major*,
Hardy's 'Napoleonic' novel). However, this report does not refer
to the two coffins or contain the earlier description of farmers
heading to town for market. The latter jarring allusion to everyday
life may have been suggested by two notes in the 'Trumpet-Major
Notebook': 'June 30.1801, was on a Tuesday' and 'Tuesday? Tu.
was chief market day.' The quoted entries from the registry of
burials at the end of the story give 30 June as the date of the
interments, though the newspaper says that the executions took
place on Wednesday morning (*Personal Notebooks*, 124–5). In a
diary note of 27 July 1877, Hardy records the following eyewitness account: 'James Bushrod of Broadmayne saw the two
German soldiers [of the York Hussars] shot [for desertion] on
Bincombe Down in 1801. It was in the path across the down, or
near it. James Selby of the same village thinks there is a mark'
(*Life*, 119).

  This 1894 *LLI* description of the execution differs from 1890
*BT* in a number of details. In 1890 *BT*, the regiments are drawn up
'in a square' rather than 'in line', and the 'melancholy procession
entered the square'. The change was presumably made because
Hardy recognized the potential hazard to onlookers in his original
conception of the scene. The serial makes no mention of 'a mourning coach', shows the condemned men accompanied by 'a clergyman' not 'two priests', and has a firing-party comprised of only
twelve men.

20. *regiments wheeled ... When the survey*: 'regiments were marched
past the spot, and when the survey' (1890 *BT*).

21. *Jersey*: In the 'Trumpet-Major Notebook' entry (see n. 19), the
deserters are said to have been caught in Guernsey.

22. *the soldiers lie*: The soldiers were buried in the south-east corner
of Bincombe churchyard, and the parish burial register containing
the record of their interment survives (see Kay-Robinson, 133;
and Lea, 148).

## 'A TRAGEDY OF TWO AMBITIONS'

1. *Halborough*: May derive from the name of a former rector at West
Coker (one of the story's settings), whose name was Halberton

(Kay-Robinson, 204). The substitution of 'borough' for 'berton' underlines the brothers' attempts to leave their rural roots for an urban, middle-class milieu. MS reveals that Hardy originally contemplated foregrounding the family name in the story's title: 'The Shame of the Halboroughs' was rejected in favour of the existing title. (See Introduction.)

2. *Homeric blows and knocks, Argonautic voyaging, or Theban family woe*: The brothers are not reading classical literature – Homer's epics, Apollonius Rhodius' *Argonautica*, or Sophocles' tragedies – but rather studying in preparation for ordination into the Church of England. When Hardy worked as an architect's apprentice he used to read the Greek Testament in order to engage in theological disputes with his fellow pupil Henry Bastow. But when Bastow moved to Tasmania, 'Hardy, like St Augustine, lapsed from the Greek New Testament back again to pagan writers' (*Life*, 36).

3. *The Dog-day sun in its decline*: During the hot days between early July and early September, Sirius, the Dog Star, rises and sets with the sun.

4. *light drab clothes of an old-fashioned country tradesman*: MS shows '<white> light clothes of a <miller> country tradesman'. Other earlier MS references show 'millwright' substituted for '<miller>' as the father's occupation. For fuller details of MS variants, see Ray, 195–7.

5. *to get their waggons wheeled*: 'to get their leaze-corn ground' MS/1888 *UR*. The change for 1894 *LLI* makes all details of the father's occupation consistent.

6. *Donnegan's Lexicon*: James Donnegan's *A New Greek and English Lexicon* (1826) was an outdated text by 1888, when the story is presumably set. 'Liddell and Scott', Hardy's 1898 poem about the *Greek–English Lexicon* (1843) by Henry George Liddell (1811–98) and Robert Scott (1811–87), has Liddell recalling that he had been tempted to give up the project, 'But feared a stigma/ If I succumbed, and left old Donnegan/ For weary freshmen's eyes to con again' (*Poetical Works*, III, 177).

7. *nine hundred pounds*: 'seven hundred pounds' (MS/1888 *UR*). Description of the loss of this money as 'the sharp thorn of their crown' implicitly compares their suffering with Christ's (see Introduction).

8. *a term of years as national schoolmasters . . . despised licentiates*: National Schools, under the auspices of the National Society for Promoting the Education of the Poor in the Principles of the

Church of England (founded in 1811), were the main providers
of elementary education before the 1870 Education Act made
primary education compulsory. Training in a theological college
would allow ordination without a university degree (the surplice
without a hood). Wells (Fountall) Theological College was
founded in 1838 to offer further clerical training to graduates,
but began to accept non-graduates during the 1870s. For fuller
details of the ecclesiastical context, see Owen Chadwick, *The
Victorian Church*, Parts I and II (Oxford: Oxford University
Press, 1966, 1970).

9.  *'heard his days before him'*: The speaker of Tennyson's 'Locksley
    Hall' (1842) looks back to the time before he had been rejected
    in love, asking the 'Mother-Age' to 'Make me feel the wild
    pulsation that I felt before the strife,/ When I heard my days
    before me, and the tumult of my life' (ll. 109–10). The passage
    associates Joshua with the frenzy and self-absorption of Tenny-
    son's speaker.

10. *Sandbourne*: Based on Bournemouth, a coastal resort about thirty
    miles east of Weymouth, associated by Hardy with somewhat
    tawdry *nouveau riche* opulence. It is the location of the lodging-
    house in which Alec D'Urberville is living with Tess at the time
    of his murder (*Tess of the D'Urbervilles*).

11. *whom they loved more ambitiously than they loved themselves*:
    MS adds 'if that were possible' (see Ray, 197).

12. *Paley's Evidences*: William Paley's *A View of the Evidences of
    Christianity* (1794), a standard argument-from-design justifica-
    tion of Christianity, was required reading for all Cambridge
    graduates, but became increasingly outmoded during the Vic-
    torian period. The volumes that Joshua is working through,
    Edward Bouverie Pusey's *Library of the Fathers of the Holy
    Catholic Church, anterior to the division of the East and West*
    (1836–85), of which Pusey edited only the first, are associated
    with the Oxford Movement and High Church Anglicanism.

13. *Archbishop Tillotson was the son of a Sowerby clothier, but he
    was sent to Clare College*: John Tillotson (1630–94), son of a
    dissenting cloth-worker and graduate of Clare Hall, Cambridge,
    became Archbishop of Canterbury in 1691.

14. *Binegar Fair*: Binegar was the actual location of a horse fair until
    the 1950s (see Kay-Robinson, 194).

15. *To succeed in the Church ... soul and strength*: This list of
    ecclesiastical desiderata was expanded for 1894 *LLI*; 1888 *UR*
    has only 'as a gentleman'.

16. *Narrobourne*: Based on West Coker, near Yeovil (see Kay-Robinson, 200–203). The fictional name evokes both the restrictive circumstances into which the Halborough brothers are born and the culvert (where 'the stream suddenly narrowed to half its width') in which their father's body is trapped.

17. *'O Lord, be thou my helper!'*: In this song of dedication for the house of David (Psalms 30.10), the Psalmist praises the Lord for having hidden his face and thus for eliciting the quoted supplication. Joshua is incapable of the humility enjoined by the biblical passage he invokes for his sermon.

18. *a Dorcas, or Martha, or Rhoda*: Names often associated with rustic women (cf. Rhoda Brook, the milkmaid in the title-story of *Withered Arm*). MS originally read 'a Dorcas, Rhoda, or Tryphena', the last the name of a cousin to whom the young Hardy may have been engaged (see Ray, 196).

19. *cloud no bigger than a man's hand*: Ahab and the Israelites, having turned from God to the worship of Baal, endure drought, from which they are rescued by Elijah, whose servant sees from Mount Carmel 'a cloud, small as a man's hand, rising from the sea', presaging torrential rain (1 Kings 18.44). While Hardy presumably wanted to suggest the emergence of a momentous event from apparently trivial origins, the invocation of an entirely propitious cloud resonates inappropriately with the threat inherent in the father's return.

20. *Ivell*: Yeovil. This MS substitution for 'Sherton' clearly establishes Narrobourne as the Wessex version of West Coker – as does the insertion a few paragraphs later (for 1894 *LLI*) of the actual name 'Hendford Hill' (Ray, 196). According to Kay-Robinson, the weir into which the elder Halborough falls is located in 'the hamlet of Holywell, between West and North Coker' (203).

21. *'He has fallen in!'*: MS originally preceded this statement with '<Just God>'. In the same scene, it deleted the following statement by one of the brothers: 'To think he should just have been resolved upon ruining us all, should have pronounced my disgrace with such exultation' (see Ray, 196).

22. *as they stood breathless ... their bare branches waved to and fro*: 1912 *LLI* adds the following unequivocal indication of the brothers' culpability in their father's death: 'In their pause there had been time to save him twice over'. 1894 *LLI* had also changed the father's desperate cries from 'feeble' to 'gurgling' words, thus emphasizing how close he is to drowning. The brothers' failure to save their father also recalls the opposite response of Mr Barnet

in 'Fellow-Townsmen' (see *Withered Arm*) and the drowning of Grandcourt in George Eliot's *Daniel Deronda* (1876), where Gwendolyn Harleth momentarily pauses before throwing a rope to her drowning husband, whom she hates. When this connection was observed by Samuel Chew in 1922, Hardy protested that 'kindred incidents are common to hundreds of novels' (*Collected Letters*, VI, 156).

23. *Joshua had tolled and read himself in at his new parish*: A new minister would officially announce his arrival by tolling the church bell, reading publicly the Thirty-Nine Articles of Faith, and making the Declaration of Assent.

24. *To tell the truth, the Church*: Substituted in MS for '<Damn the Church, she>' (see Ray, 196).

25. *'Why see – it was there . . . and they walked away*: This whole episode of the growing walking-stick was added in 1894 *LLI*. (See Introduction.)

26. *Τπέμεινε σταυϱὸν, αἰσχύνης καταφϱονήσας*: The sons' filial and human failures are tacitly contrasted with the greatness of Jesus, 'who for the joy that was set before him endured the cross, despising the shame' (Hebrews 12.2).

## 'THE FIRST COUNTESS OF WESSEX'

1. *By the Local Historian*: Absent from 1889 *H*, as are subsequent references to the narrator. These were added for 1891 *GND*, in which 'The First Countess of Wessex' opens a series of stories told by members of the Wessex Field and Antiquarian Club. Along with 'Barbara of the House of Grebe' (see next story), 'The Marchioness of Stonehenge' and 'Lady Mottisfont', it is placed under the heading ' PART I *BEFORE DINNER*'. 1891 *GND* also removed the Roman numerals designating each of the story's eight sections, leaving merely an extra line space to indicate the transitions. This edition omits 'Dame the First' and 'Dame the Second', the designations inserted in 1891 *GND* above the title lines for 'The First Countess of Wessex' and 'Barbara of the House of Grebe' respectively.

2. *King's-Hintock Court*: Wessex name for Melbury House, eight miles north-west of Dorchester; owned in Hardy's day by the Earls of Ilchester (see Appendix II for information on Hardy's relationship to this family's history).

3. *Blackmoor or Blakemore Vale*: Hardy's 'Vale of Little Dairies' lies south-east of Sherborne and south-west of Shaftesbury, in the

north of Dorset. 1889 *H* had 'White-Hart or Blackmore Vale', but for 1891 *GND*, published little more than a month before the first instalment of the serialization of *Tess of the D'Urbervilles*, Hardy removed the allusion to the legend of the white hart, which receives extensive treatment in the novel.

4. *last century*: 'eighteenth century' (1912 *GND*) in order to date the story for the twentieth-century reader. Hardy forgot to make the analogous change to the story's final paragraph, which refers to 'Barbara, who lived towards the end of the last century'.

5. *twelve or thirteen*: 'thirteen or fourteen' (1889 *H*). The change more accurately reflects the age of the historical original. For 1891 *GND*, Hardy also changed the age of Phelipson, whose characterization has no factual basis, from sixteen to fifteen, and made him two years Betty's senior rather than three.

6. *his father... at Court*: This detail only approximately corresponds to the situation of Reynard's historical original, Stephen Fox. The father, Sir Stephen Fox, was highly placed in the royal court after the Restoration, as was a son, Charles, by his first marriage. But by the mid-1730s, when this conversation supposedly occurs, both had long since died (in 1716 and 1713 respectively). Only Fox's younger brother, Henry, later first Lord Holland, had continued court influence (see Giles Stephen Holland Fox-Strangways, sixth Earl of Ilchester, *Henry Fox, First Lord Holland, His Family and Relations*, vol. I (London: John Murray, 1920), pp. 9–16).

7. *monstrous*: 'absurd' (1889 *H*).

8. *Falls-Park*: Based on Mells Park in Somerset, owned by the Horner family.

9. *Its classic front, of the period of the second Charles*: 'Its Palladian front, of the period of the first Charles' (1912 *GND*).

10. *battlemented ... could not eclipse*: In a further refinement of architectural detail, 1912 *GND* changed 'battlemented' to 'many gabled'. '[C]ould not eclipse' formerly read 'decidedly lacked' (1889 *H*). Hardy may have made the change to phrasing less judgemental of King's-Hintock as part of his attempt to placate the fifth Earl of Ilchester.

11. *so heavily upon his gelding*: 'fifteen stone upon his mare' (1889 *H*).

12. *deceased friend*: In changing the plot of 1889 *H*, in which Phelipson dies in a fall from the ladder at Betty's window, Hardy failed to notice that both Phelipson's parents pack him off to sea after he has abandoned Betty. This contradiction appears in all post-1889 *H* editions.

13. *Quixotic*: Given to romantic delusions, like the central character

of *Don Quixote de la Mancha* (1605, 1615), a picaresque novel
by Spain's Miguel de Cervantes (1547–1616).

14. *Ivell*: Based on Yeovil, just north of Blackmoor Vale. Melchester
and Evershead are based, respectively, on Salisbury and Evershot.

15. *the carouse decided upon*: 'this decided upon' (1889 *H*).

16. *Baxby of Sherton Castle*: Based on the Digby family of Sherborne
Castle. This particular Baxby takes his place among the other
somewhat disreputable members of his family created by Hardy,
including the philandering husband in 'Anna, Lady Baxby'
(*GND*) and Edred Fitzpiers of *The Woodlanders*, who is
descended from the Baxbys on his mother's side.

17. *Reynard*: 1912 *GND* restores the un-capitalized 'reynard' from
1889 *H*, thereby emphasizing the predatory relationship to 'ewe
lamb' and evoking beast-fable resonances.

18. *basin-full of blood*: The drawing of blood – using a leech, knife
or cupping-dish – was standard medical treatment for many ailments as late as the nineteenth century.

19. *items*: 'particulars' (1889 *H*). The change was presumably made
because Hardy noticed the repetition of 'particular' in the next
paragraph.

20. *A child not yet thirteen!*: Added for 1891 *GND* and changed to
'just gone thirteen' for 1912 *GND*.

21. *at the nearest church within half-an-hour*: Added for 1891 *GND*.

22. *title*: 1912 *GND* specifies 'peerage'.

23. *Sow-and-Acorn*: The inn where Philip Hall gives his sister's dress
to his wife in the story 'Interlopers at the Knap' (see *Withered
Arm*). Its original is the Acorn Inn in Evershot, whose photograph
appears in Lea (213).

24. *Elm-Cranlynch*: Kay-Robinson (200) associates this with the
manor at Corfe Mullen near Wimborne, held by a Charles Phelips,
whose name is close to the fictional 'Charles Phelipson'.

25. *Rosalind*: In male disguise, Rosalind of Shakespeare's *As You
Like It* teaches Orlando, the object of her own secret affections,
how to love.

26. *Candlemas*: Feast of the Purification of the Virgin Mary, now
celebrated on 2 February. But before England accepted the Greg-
orian calendar (1752), Candlemas Day was 14 February, which
is also Valentine's Day. Hardy may well have been consciously
conflating virginal and carnal associations here to give ironic
appropriateness to Dornell's apparently arbitrary choice of date,
which also happens to be that of the main hiring-fair of the
agricultural year.

27. *Necessary*: Beginning with 1891 *GND*, a greater period flavour was added to Susan Dornell's letter by the use of eighteenth-century conventions of capitalization and the substitution of the antiquated phrases 'be like to' for 'probably' and 'warrant ye' for 'guarantee'.

28. *'He is coming ... Well, yes'*: Absent from 1889 *H*, which begins the next sentence: 'She had hastily'.

29. *To lock her up*: 'To lock the door upon her' (1889 *H*). Greater confinement is suggested from 1891 *GND* on, when the mother's bedchamber is made 'a passage-room to the girl's apartment'. In 1889 *H*, the two rooms are merely opposite each other, so that Susan can only keep watch by leaving her door ajar.

30. *Nanny Priddle*: This name is close to that of Retty Priddle, one of the milkmaids in *Tess of the D'Urbervilles*, who is descended from an aristocratic family.

31. *Betty had looked so wild ... from her wilfulness*: This whole section was added in 1891 *GND* as part of the radical modification to the plot of the serial version.

32. *wench*: 'my girl' (1889 *H*).

33. *still extant in King's-Hintock church*: Hardy took this couplet verbatim from the description of Stephen Fox's monument in Hutchins, 679. In the story's conclusion, he also accurately paraphrased Hutchins's account of Betty's epitaph for her husband. The monument still stands in Melbury Sampford Church (Kay-Robinson, 108).

34. *Mendip Hills*: A range of hills running across North Somerset, extending south-east below Bristol and Bath.

35. *the child Betty's*: 'little Betty's' (1889 *H*).

36. *she'll have a reason for not waiting for him*: 1912 *GND* has the more precise 'whom my illness will hinder waiting for him'.

37. *kill the Squire*: 1889 *H* then had: 'If, on the other hand, Tupcombe could carry out the sick man's wish and cheat the coming husband, the incident might have a wonderful effect upon the Squire, and he might live.' For subsequent details deleted for 1891 *GND* see Appendix II.

38. *While pausing ... young Phelipson*: Tupcombe's observation of Phelipson's arrival and the subsequent elopement are, of course, absent from 1889 *H*. Tupcombe simply sees a great-coat on the ladder, which he takes to be Reynard's; hence his decision to destabilize the ladder.

39. *an ungenteel death*: 1889 *H* had the less ironic 'a terrible death-bed'. Dornell's last words are the same in 1889 *H*, although

uttered in response to his wife's telling him not of an elopement
but of 'the scenes which had been enacted at King's-Hintock that
night'. Since those scenes include the death of Phelipson, his dear
friend's son, Dornell's jubilation at Betty's vindication of her
father's choice – 'She vowed that my man should win!' – sounds
maliciously ironic. Its inappropriateness as the response of a
doting father may indicate that the serial version was a bowdlerization of the original MS version and 1891 *GND* a restoration
of the original rather than a rewriting. But, as Ray observes (82),
in the absence of a surviving MS 'it is impossible to determine
whether Hardy restored the text as it appeared in the manuscript
or whether he re-wrote the story for the collected edition' (see
n. 47).

40. *Long-Ash Lane*: The road between Dorchester and Yeovil, featured also in 'Interlopers at the Knap' (see *Withered Arm*).

41. *you can't be mine whilst he's alive*: See Introduction for Angel
Clare's similar logic for rejecting Tess on their wedding night.

42. *Cunigonde in Schiller's ballad*: In Schiller's 'The Glove: A Tale',
Cunigonde dares the knight Delorges to bring back her glove
from a den containing a lion, tiger and two leopards. Delorges
performs the dangerous task, but then leaves the lady in retaliation
for her having made such a demand. Hardy owned Edward
Bulwer Lytton's 1857 translation of *The Poems and Ballads of
Schiller* (*Literary Notebooks*, entry 1133n). He wrote the poem
'After Schiller' in 1889 (*Biography*, 302).

43. *the only constant attribute of life is change*: Cf. 'Nothing is
permanent but change, nothing constant but death. Every pul-
sation of the heart inflicts a wound, & life would be an endless
bleeding were it not for Poetry' (*Literary Notebooks*, I, 179).
Björk cannot identify 'Börne', the source for this quotation, but
notes (392) that Hardy uses it again to characterize Pierston's
perception of the ideal woman in *The Well-Beloved*. Reynard's
later reflection that 'In a few years her very flesh would change –
so said the scientific; – her spirit, so much more ephemeral, was
capable of changing in one' is also adapted from one of Hardy's
literary notes, taken from 'Mr Justice Fry on Materialism' in the
*Spectator* 55 (20 May 1882): 'He felt it a striking fact that he,
like others, was conscious of the same personality, the same
individual consciousness now, that he had 30 yrs. ago, although
meanwhile, according to the physiologists, the material portion
of his being had completely changed every 7 years. Hence there
was to be experienced a being within us separate from matter'

(*Literary Notebooks*, I, 147–8). In both cases, Reynard's cool and worldly attitude conflicts with the spirit of the quotation.

44. *nothing finite*: The sentiment would be more logical if these words, which appear in all printings, were 'something finite' or 'nothing infinite'.

45. *speck*: 1912 *GND* has the more graphic 'pit'.

46. *formerly combated strenuously*: In 1889 *H*, Susan's devotion to her husband's memory takes the form – as it later does here – only of rebuilding King's-Hintock Church and establishing charities in all the Hintock villages rather than, somewhat implausibly, becoming a convert to his views on early marriage.

47. *packed off to sea by his parents*: Hardy has seemingly forgotten that Phelipson is the son of Dornell's 'dear deceased friend'. This may indicate that the serial version, in which the young Phelipson dies, reflects the original MS (for counter-evidence, see n. 39), with Hardy not noticing the contradiction created by a revision.

48. *I cannot state*: 'cannot be stated' (1889 *H*). The change foregrounds the presence of a narrator in the collected edition. In 1889 *H*, this paragraph begins with the sentence 'What could a poor girl do?'

49. *an errant passion ... its bearings*: 'an offence which he might with some reason have denounced as unforgivable, however cruel her position had been in view of herself as an entrapped child' (1889 *H*).

50. *she were willing for him to come soon*: 'she thought it would be safe for him to repeat the experiment which had failed so egregiously at the former date' (1889 *H*).

51. *was struck by her child's figure*: Betty's seeing of Reynard surreptitiously, and the pregnancy to which it has led, do not occur in 1889 *H*.

52. *Casterbridge*: Wessex name for Dorchester. The other two places where the pair met, Abbot's-Cernel and Melchester, are Cerne Abbas and Salisbury respectively, both north-east of Dorchester. Salisbury's Red Lion also appears in *The Hand of Ethelberta* and *Jude the Obscure*.

53. *dozen times*: 1912 *GND* adds '– I mean quite alone, and not reckoning'. Betty also adds that the meeting at Abbot's-Cernel was 'in the ruined chamber over the gatehouse', namely the entrance porch to the abbot's hall, which still stands (see Kay-Robinson, 99–100). Her mother's repetition of the word 'accident' is italicized to indicate her incredulity.

54. *The little white frock ... great unhappiness*: Added for 1891
    GND. 1912 GND has 'figured' for 'white'. This more accurately
    describes the actual dress which, according to Kay-Robinson
    (108), is 'flowered' and still preserved in Melbury House.

55. *Wessex Field and Antiquarian Clubs*: Based on the Dorset Natural
    History and Antiquarian Field Club, of which Hardy was a
    member, and which met at the Dorset County Museum.

56. *the shaking ... made the dry bones move*: In a valley of dry bones,
    God tells Ezekiel to: 'Prophesy upon these bones, and say unto
    them, O ye dry bones, hear the word of the Lord.' When the
    prophet has done so, 'there was a noise, and behold a shaking,
    and the bones came together, bone to his bone' (Ezekiel 37.4
    and 7).

57. *best of all possible worlds*: 'All is for the best in the best of possible
    worlds' is the governing precept of the philosopher Pangloss in
    *Candide* (1759), the satire on the optimism of Rousseau and
    Leibniz by Voltaire (1694–1778).

## 'BARBARA OF THE HOUSE OF GREBE'

1. *Lord Uplandtowers'*: Based on Anthony Ashley-Cooper, fifth
   Earl of Shaftesbury (1761–1811), who in 1786 married Barbara
   Webb (1762–1819), daughter of Sir John Webb, whose baronetcy
   had been created in 1640 (see Hutchins, III, 298; Brady, 88; and
   Ray, 87–8). Hardy used pedigrees and dates from Hutchins (see
   Appendix II), but appears to have invented most of the plot.

2. *turnpike-road connecting Havenpool and Warborne with the
   city of Melchester*: Road connecting Poole and Wimborne with
   Salisbury. Built in 1755, it would eventually be one of the first
   macadamized roads in southern England, although this could not
   have been before 1819, when the paving process was invented
   (Kay-Robinson, 79).

3. *Chene Manor*: Based on Canford Manor, east of Wimborne. A
   1786 engraving of the kitchen where, later in the text, breakfasts
   are said to have been cooked for John of Gaunt, looks 'very much
   as it does today' (Kay-Robinson, 78). John of Gaunt (1340–99),
   son of Edward III, was the Duke of Lancaster.

4. *Hundred of Cockdene*: A 'Hundred' is an ancient subdivision of
   a county, having its own moot (a court for dealing with local
   legal and administrative matters). An actual counterpart for
   'Cockdene' has not been identified.

5. *Drenkhards*: Based on the Trenchards, an old Dorset family. Sir George Drenghard is the first husband of the Lady Penelope in the story of the same name from *A Group of Noble Dames*. In *Tess of the D'Urbervilles*, they are a declined family, like Tess's own. On the occasion of his being presented with the Freedom of the Borough of Dorchester (16 November 1910), Hardy regretted the loss, among other Dorchester buildings, of 'the fine mansion of the Trenchards at the corner of Shirehall Lane' (*Life*, 379).

6. *Lornton Inn*: Located in Horton, between Wimborne and Cranborne, and later described as 'between the Forest and the Chase', that is, between the New Forest and Cranborne Chase (see Kay-Robinson, 78).

7. *French horns and clarionets, the favourite instruments of those days at such entertainments*: Before the advent of relatively low-priced pianos and organs in the mid-nineteenth century (as reflected in Hardy's *Under the Greenwood Tree*, set *c.* 1840), bands of musicians playing portable instruments were common, especially in rural areas.

8. *devil*: 'deuce' (1890 G). 1891 *GND* generally restores the less bowdlerized language of MS and 1890 *HW*, while 1912 *GND* makes the language more explicit still, for example printing 'God' and 'Damn' in full.

9. *Shottsford-Forum*: Wessex name for Blandford Forum, north-east of Dorchester. MS had first made Willowes a landscape painter and then a 'hopeful yeoman', while his father had been variously a curate attracted to non-conformity, a farmer and a music teacher (see Ray, 88, who suggests that the decision to make Willowes the descendant of a glass-painter renders Barbara's marriage especially 'unsuitable'). A later reference to Willowes adds 'plebeian' for 1891 *GND*.

10. *six weeks*: MS originally showed six months (see Ray, 89). Presumably the change was made to be more appropriate to the later comment about a 'descending scale' of marital happiness, calibrated in weekly divisions.

11. *tinctures of Maundeville ... York, and Lancaster*: The historical Barbara Webb's maternal grandmother happened to have been a Talbot (see Ray, 87). But the choice of noble names here, culminating in the royal houses of Plantagenet, York and Lancaster, presumably has little specific significance, the arbitrary list merely carrying the ironic implication that Barbara is related to virtually all the British aristocracy.

12. *Her fair young face … puce gown*: James Laver notes that after 1780 'there was a rage for ostrich feathers' on 'formal hats' in imitation of a portrait of the Duchess of Devonshire by Gainsborough and women wore shoes open 'a couple of inches behind the toes'. After 1778, women wore 'richly ornamented' underskirts and the 'two skirts were frequently of contrasting colours' (*English Costume of the Eighteenth Century*, drawings by Iris Brooke (1931; London: Adam & Charles Black, 1964), pp. 74, 76 and 68).

13. *Yewsholt*: Yewsholt Lodge is the Wessex name for Farrs House, north-east of Corfe Mullen. Kay-Robinson notes that Hardy exaggerated its smallness (77). The original name in MS had been 'Wood Park'.

14. *sedan-chair*: 'sentry-box' (MS/1890 G/1890 HW).

15. *Pisa*: 'Florence' in MS. Ray speculates (89) that the change was made to remove an overly melodramatic connection between the origin of the statue and the location of Barbara's death.

16. *Carnival*: Half-week or week before Lent, a time of revelry in Roman Catholic countries.

17. *Italian comedy*: During the eighteenth century, Carlo Goldoni (1707–93) reformed Italian comedy, substituting comedy of character for the improvisational conventions of traditional *commedia dell'arte*.

18. *After long weeks*: 'In due time' (1890 G/1890 HW). Other 1891 GND changes from these earlier versions substituted 'appalling' for 'grievous', 'Slowly' for 'Thus', and 'seventeen months' for 'sixteen months', all with the effect of emphasizing Willowes's suffering.

19. *A quick spasm … looked aside and shuddered*: For the bowdlerized 1890 G, this whole passage was excised, as were 'hideous' (which became 'dreadful' in 1912 GND) and Willowes's later inquiry 'Can you bear such a thing of the charnel-house near you?' 1891 GND restores the MS/1890 HW version, but with revisions that increase the horror and sense of Barbara's distance from Willowes: 'parted lips' becomes 'ashy lips', she sinks down beside 'her chair' rather than 'his knees', 'impulsive devotion' becomes 'momentary devotion', and 'this human fragment' becomes 'this human remnant, this *écorché*'.

20. *Adonis*: 'Apollo' (MS/1890 G/1890 HW). Adonis, the handsome youth loved by Aphrodite and killed by a boar, evokes primarily physical beauty, while Phoebus-Apollo, the Greek god of light, is

associated with intellectual and moral beauty, as manifest in the arts, medicine and prophecy. Uplandtowers later likens, perhaps ironically, the sculptured representation of Willowes to Phoebus-Apollo.

21.  *loathe*: The bowdlerized 1890 *G* had 'know', and also deleted 'horrified' from Barbara's dialogue. Before 1891 *GND*, in this same paragraph 'fancy' read 'realize'.

22.  *new and terrible form*: 'other terrible form' (1890 *G*/1890 *HW*). Earlier in the same sentence, 'that figure' formerly read 'he' (1890 *G*) and 'the figure' (1890 *HW*).

23.  *poor husband*: 'poor', another detail that heightens sympathy for Willowes, was added for 1891 *GND*.

24.  *It was something like this*: Added for 1891 *GND*.

25.  *forbidding*: 'repulsive' (1890 *HW*). The bowdlerized 1890 *G* has no adjective here. The italicization of 'human' and 'divine' in the letter was added for 1891 *GND*.

26.  *You will see me again*: MS cancellation indicates that Willowes originally said he would never return: 'The revision means that he can eventually be presumed dead when he fails to return as promised, thus allowing Barbara to marry Uplandtowers' (Ray, 89).

27.  *it was doubted*: 'she doubted' (1890 *G*/1890 *HW*).

28.  *nearly all churches have been made to look like new pennies*: Hardy disapproved of the Victorian movement to renovate and restore churches, in which he participated as a young architect. In 'Memories of Church Restoration' (1906), he celebrates those 'few – very few – old churches, diminishing in number every day, as chance to be left intact owing to the heathen apathy of their parson and parishioners in the last century' (*Public Voice*, 253). The 'lion-and-unicorn' in the list of unwanted votive offerings are the heraldic English lion and Scottish unicorn that support the Royal Coat of Arms.

29.  *that lopped and mutilated form*: 'lopped and' added for 1891 *GND*. The bowdlerized 1890 *G* deleted 'mutilated'.

30.  *as awake as seven sentinels*: The image is from the Apocrypha: 'And heed the counsel of your own heart, for no one is more faithful to you than it is. For our own mind sometimes keeps us better informed than seven sentinels sitting high on a watchtower' (Ecclesiasticus (Sirach) 37.13–14). In relation to the predatory Uplandtowers, there is ironic appropriateness in this invocation of heart truths.

31. *Knollingwood Hall*: Based on St Giles's House, Wimborne St Giles, near Cranborne, north of Chene Manor, Yewsholt Lodge and the Lornton Inn (see Kay-Robinson, 78).

32. *sweet-pea or with-wind natures which require a twig of stouter fibre than its own to hang upon and bloom*: The similarly infantile Car'line Aspent of 'The Fiddler of the Reels' (see this volume) is also 'limp as withy-wind', always yearning for 'something to cling to'. 'With-wind' (also 'withywind') is the now dialect word for bindweed.

33. *socially*: 'abstractedly' (1890 G); 'abstractly' (1890 HW).

34. *The heir-presumptive . . . no promise of this*: Deleted from 1890 G but retained in 1890 HW; 'and asked her what she was good for' was added for 1891 GND.

35. *passionate*: 'gentle' (1890 G/1890 HW).

36. *love*: 'tenderness' (1912 GND).

37. *stammered*: 'said' (1890 G/1890 HW).

38. *mouth*: 'lips' (1890 HW).

39. *infidelity!*: 'fickleness' (1890 G). This would appear to be further bowdlerization for the English serial, since 1890 HW retains 'infidelity'.

40. *This is . . . ha, ha!*: This is a restoration of the more explicit MS version, emphasizing the socio-sexual consequences for Uplandtowers of Barbara's infatuation with her marmoreal lover. 1890 G bowdlerized the sentence into 'This is treachery to the living!' Even 1890 HW, usually more explicit than its English counterpart, merely adds to the 1890 G version 'this is where my hopes are wrecked', primly leaving the nature of the hopes non-specific.

41. *disfigured head*: 'dead man' (1890 G). 1890 G also deleted the subsequent 'Neither nose nor ears!' 1912 GND, by contrast, compounded the disfigurement by adding 'nor lips scarcely'.

42. *It was a fiendish disfigurement . . . after the wreck*: Deleted for 1890 G; 'rendered still more shocking by being' was added for 1891 GND.

43. *predilection*: 'solicitude' (1890 G).

44. *When she was in her bed-chamber*: Beginning here, the bowdlerized 1890 G deletes the description of Barbara's three encounters with the statue, returning to the story at 'It was a long time before the Countess came to herself.' 1891 GND makes only minor modifications, noted below, to the unbowdlerized 1890 HW version.

45. *when they were in the dark*: Added for 1891 GND.

46. *cropped and distorted*: 'mutilated' (1890 *HW*).
47. *inflicted*: 'initiated' (1890 *HW*). 1891 *GND* also added 'horrid' to the next sentence.
48. *there was silence, and*: Added for 1891 *GND*. In the same paragraph, 1890 *HW* reads 'put her gently on the floor' for 'took her gently to the window'.
49. *considerable change seemed to have taken place in her emotions*: 'complete reversal of emotion seemed to have taken place in her' (1890 *G*/1890 *HW*). The serial versions also have 'impulsively kissed' for 'with gasps of fear abjectly kissed'. 1890 *HW* adds the sentence 'His cruelty had not brought forth hatred, but love,' at the end of this paragraph.
50. *begged*: 'sobbed' (1890 *G*/1890 *HW*).
51. *cried the poor Countess slavishly*: Added for 1891 *GND*, as was the passage from ' "Never," said he' to 'late husband's memory'. 1890 *G* deleted 'how could I ever be so depraved!' and the later passage from 'How fright could have effected' to 'his sight for a moment'. 1890 *HW* retained these, but had 'reversional' for 'reactionary' and 'slavishly' for 'tightly'.
52. *enervated*: 'beautiful' (1890 *G*/1890 *HW*).
53. *Little personal events ... eight following years*: 'She bore him several children in the eight following years' (1890 *G*); 'She bore him no less than ten children in the eight following years' (1890 *HW*). 1890 *G* deletes 'but half of them came prematurely into the world, or died a few days old'. In both serial versions, the phrasing of the previous sentence is 'was one of slavery to her own obsequious amativeness for a perverse and cruel man'.
54. *D'Almaine*: 'Welland' (1890 *G*/1890 *HW*); 'd'Almaine' (1912 *GND*). Ray notes that the daughter of Barbara Webb married the Honourable Mr Ponsonby, later Lord de Mauley, and suggests that the change was possibly 'to echo the Norman sound of the historical title' (87).
55. *brutal*: 'selfish' (1890 *G*).
56. *sensuous love for a handsome form*: 'love of the form' (1890 *G*); 'love through the eyes' (1890 *HW*).
57. *The company thanked*: These last two paragraphs serve both as commentary on 'Barbara' and preparation for the next story in *A Group of Noble Dames*, which is not included in this edition.
58. *latent, true affection*: 1890 *G* and 1890 *HW* precede this phrase with 'an uninterrupted'.

## 'FOR CONSCIENCE' SAKE'

1.  *the utilitarian or the intuitive theory of the moral sense*: Hardy
    had great admiration for John Stuart Mill (1806–73), remem-
    bering him in May 1906, on the centenary of his birth, as 'one of
    the profoundest thinkers of the last century' whose 'On Liberty'
    'we students of that date knew almost by heart' (see *Life*, 355–6).
    For Mill's complex ruminations on the counter-claims of utilit-
    arianism and intuitive imagination, see his famous *Westminster
    Review* essays on Jeremy Bentham (1748–1832) and Samuel
    Taylor Coleridge (1772–1834) in F. R. Leavis, ed. *Mill on Ben-
    tham and Coleridge* (London: Chatto & Windus, 1962). Hardy's
    *Literary Notebooks* contain numerous references to Mill.

2.  *a familiar and quiet London street*: 'Sherton Street' (1891 *FR*).
    In MS/1891 *FR* 'Sherton Street, W.' is also given as the location
    for the first section, 'High Street, Exonbury' for the second, and
    'London Again' for the third.

3.  *Bindon*: See Introduction, n. 30. MS shows that early on in the
    composition of the story, Hardy changed the doctor's name from
    'Benton', and Leonora's surname from 'Falkland'.

4.  *real gravity*: 'importance' (1891 *FR*).

5.  *Toneborough*: Based on Taunton. Leonora and Frances Frank-
    land live in Exonbury (Exeter), and Revd Percival Cope moves to
    Ivell (Yeovil). In 1891 *FR*, 'Outer Wessex' was 'Lower Wessex'.
    As Gary Alderson has pointed out (Thomas Hardy Association
    Forum, 1 September 2002), Hardy appears not to have noticed
    the discrepancy that has Millborne, earlier declared to be aged at
    least fifty, claiming in his conversation with Bindon to have
    broken his promise and departed for London only twenty years
    ago, at the age of 'one-and-twenty'.

6.  *specimen of the heap of flesh called humanity*: 'specimen of
    humanity' (1891 *FR*).

7.  *bewildering happy savages . . . country*: 'making happy savages
    miserable, and other such enthusiasms of this Christian country'
    (1891 *FR*).

8.  *silver broth-basin . . . Cathedral*: In 1891 *FR*, Walker is 'vicar-
    choral' and receives a 'silver pitch-pipe' for his 'faithful and
    arduous ministry'.

9.  *at any hour between sunrise and sunset*: Added for 1894 *LLI*.

10. *passively*: 'promptly' (1891 *FR*); 'by the servant' was added for
    1894 *LLI*.

11. *I have no wish to marry*: 1891 *FR* follows this with 'I remember no such promise of yours.' Hardy may have felt that this made Leonora seem too culpable in undergoing a sexual falling in which a promise of marriage was not a major factor.

12. *scantly-whiskered*: 'smoothly-shaven' (1891 *FR*).

13. *St John's, Ivell*: An actual church 'of some prestige' in Yeovil located, as in the story, on St Peter's Street (Kay-Robinson, 204). In 1891 *FR*, Percival Cope was formerly merely living, rather than 'doing duty', in Exonbury, and Ivell was fifty miles 'away', not 'up the line'. The rephrasing reduces the sense of distance by emphasizing the directness of the railway connection.

14. *Percival Cope*: Ironic combination of the Christian name of an Arthurian knight renowned for his purity (which makes him fit companion for Bors and Galahad in their quest for the Holy Grail) with a surname evoking an ecclesiastical ceremonial cloak. 1891 *FR* specifies Cowes as the Isle of Wight watering-place.

15. *peculiarities to radical distinctions*: '*nuances* to distinctions of tribal intensity' (1891 *FR*). Hardy's fascination with heritable physical traits is reflected throughout his work, most notably in *The Well-Beloved* and the poem 'Heredity' (*Poetical Works*, II, 166–7), which begins 'I am the family face;/ Flesh perishes, I live on.'

16. *a stereotyped expression and mien*: 'regulation lines and curves' (1891 *FR*).

17. *father and his child*: 'man and girl' (1891 *FR*).

18. *fastidious*: Added for 1894 *LLI*.

19. *apple of discord*: The mythological referent is the golden apple, thrown by Eris (Discord) before the gods. It falls to Paris's lot to award this prize to the most beautiful of three goddesses, Hera, Aphrodite and Athene. After she promises him the fairest woman in the world, Paris awards the apple to Aphrodite, a choice which leads to the abduction of Helen and the Trojan War.

20. *of her irregular birth?*: Added for 1894 *LLI*.

21. *the spectre to their intended feast of Hymen*: The image probably derives from Matthew Gregory Lewis's ballad 'Alonzo the Brave and the Fair Imogine' in his Gothic novel *The Monk* (1796). Imogine vows, as her beloved Alonzo departs to fight in a distant land, that she will remain true 'if ye be living, or if ye be dead'. But barely a year later, she marries a rich baron. A helmeted stranger arrives at the wedding feast, and when Imogine asks him to share in the celebration, he unveils his skeletal head, identifies

himself as Alonzo, claims his faithless bride, and sinks with her 'through the wide-yawning ground'. In 1891 *FR*, 'irritation' in the previous sentence read 'desolation'.

22. *conscience*: 'honour' (1891 *FR*).

23. *celibate's*: Added for 1894 *LLI*.

24. *cry about*: 'sense of' (1891 *FR*).

25. *and notice it*: Added for 1894 *LLI*; 'insisted' in the next sentence was formerly 'supposed'.

26. *heavy thought . . . laxity*: The ill-fated daughter of Oedipus and Jocasta and subject of a play by Sophocles, Antigone embodies the conflict between observance of a religious obligation and submission to secular authority. By observing funeral rites for her brother, Polyneices, she offends against King Creon's command that he be left unburied, thereby herself suffering the fate of being buried alive. The Antigone reference was incorporated for 1891 *FR*. In MS, Millborne is initially burdened with 'weariness of life', but Hardy deleted 'life' and added 'his fellow creatures – ever answering negatively, as he sat and smoked among men, the inquiry in the *Hippolytus*: "What reserved person is not hateful? – and in the sociable is there any charm?"' (see Ray, 189). The change was presumably made because Antigone's situation has less ambiguous application to Millborne than Hippolytus', since not only does Hippolytus assert that there is indeed charm in the sociable but he is also unlike Millborne in being chaste: a devotee of the virginal Artemis, he incurs the wrath of Aphrodite, the goddess of sexual love. In 1891 *FR*, 'heavy' read 'bitter'.

## 'THE SON'S VETO'

1. *if somewhat barbaric*: Added for 1891 *ILN*. The effect is presumably 'barbaric' in not only the braiding of the hair but also the fur and feathers of the hat. Hardy was particularly sensitive to the killing of wildlife for mere sport or ornament. See, for example, 'The Puzzled Game-Birds' (*Poetical Works*, I, 185–6); 'Compassion: An Ode in Celebration of the Centenary of the Royal Society for the Prevention of Cruelty to Animals' (*Poetical Works*, III, 147–8); or the scene depicting the plight of wounded pheasants in *Tess of the D'Urbervilles* (Chapter XLI).

2. *hat and jacket . . . public school*: The distinctiveness of the jacket would suggest England's best-known public school, Eton College, which has given its name to both a collar and a jacket style. This

is partly confirmed by the later mention of the cricket match at Lord's (see n. 23).

3.  *'Has, dear mother – not have!'*: Cross-generational self-consciousness occasioned by dialect speech is recurrently used by Hardy to signal class-based embarrassment. See, for example, Michael Henchard's attack on Elizabeth-Jane for saying 'Bide where you be' (*The Mayor of Casterbridge*, Chapter XX), or Mr Melbury's concern that his boarding-school educated daughter Grace will 'sink down to our level again, and catch our manners and way of speaking' (*The Woodlanders*, Chapter XI).

4.  *North Wessex ... Aldbrickham*: North Wessex encompasses primarily the county of Berkshire, south of Oxford, and Aldbrickham ('Oldbrickham' in 1891 *ILN*) is based on Reading. This is Hardy's only use of Aldbrickham outside its central bleak role in *Jude the Obscure*. Gaymead (not mentioned by name at this point in 1891 *ILN*) remains elusive of definition, although Kay-Robinson's identification (161) with Sulhampstead or Sulhampstead Abbots, about three miles south of Theale, is the most convincing.

5.  *reverend*: Added for 1894 *LLI*.

6.  *had been done that could be done*: 'was over' (1891 *ILN*).

7.  *Sam*: 'Ned' (1891 *ILN*). Hardy may have made the change because he decided to use 'Ned' in the later story 'The Fiddler of the Reels', which was also collected for 1894 *LLI*.

8.  *college living*: An ecclesiastical benefice in the bestowal of an Oxford or Cambridge college. The vicar lives in seclusion because of the absence of resident landowners, who as his class equals would provide intellectual and social companionship. In the previous sentence, 'just' was added for 1894 *LLI*.

9.  *and continuous*: Added for 1894 *LLI*.

10.  *his lips upon her cheek*: 'his lips upon hers' (1891 *ILN*). This is one of the rare occasions when the periodical phrasing is more sexually charged than the book version. Later in this paragraph, 'reverend and' was added for 1894 *LLI*.

11.  *and wasted hours ... faintest*: 'and her once cherry cheeks grew lily-pale' (1891 *ILN*).

12.  *Randolph*: Charlotte M. Yonge's *History of Christian Names* (1863, 1884), which Hardy owned (*Biography*, 350), translates 'Randolph' as 'House wolf', a fitting term for his ability to destroy Sophy's chance of domestic happiness.

13.  *well-packed cemetery ... great city*: 'well-packed' added for 1894

*LLI*, in which 'great city' replaced 1891 *ILN*'s 'Metropolis'. By the end of the nineteenth century, nearly fifty municipal cemeteries had been opened in South London alone, of which the two earliest were Norwood (1837) and Nunhead (1840). The National Society for the Abolition of Burial in Towns (1845) had attempted to address the problem of overcrowded and unhealthy churchyard burial sites, and the Cemeteries Clauses Act (1847) and the Burial Act (1852) pioneered the establishment of commercial cemeteries. As Hardy suggests here, this inevitable change from local churchyard burial to centralized cemeteries made the context for interment more impersonal, particularly by comparison with the familial and community continuities still embodied in rural churchyard burial. For the latter, see Hardy's poem 'Transformations' (*Poetical Works*, II, 211–2), with its reflection on the comfort in knowing that 'Portion of this yew/ Is a man my grandsire knew', or 'Voices from Things Growing in a Churchyard' (ibid., 395–7).

14. *drab*: 'tawny' (1891 *ILN*).

15. *with which he, like other children ... herself*: 'with which she had been born and which she had loved in him' (1891 *ILN*); 'further and further' in the next sentence formerly read 'farther and farther'.

16. *waggon after waggon ... privileged to rest*: This is much expanded from 1891 *ILN*, which reads 'cabbages, carrots, turnips, built up in pyramids and frustums with such skill that a rope was sufficient to secure the whole load'. In 1891 *ILN*, this paragraph's final sentence read only 'Wrapped in a cloak, it was soothing to watch them when depression and nervousness hindered rest.' The passage is based upon a diary memory recorded in *Life*: 'July 7 [1888]. One o'clock a.m. I got out of bed, attracted by the never-ending procession ... as seen from our bedroom windows Phillimore Place. Chains rattle, and each cart cracks under its weighty pyramid of vegetables' (219). Developing gradually from its inception in 1640, Covent Garden Market expanded throughout the Victorian period, remaining down to its closure in 1974 London's major wholesale fruit, vegetable and flower market.

17. *moving in an urban atmosphere*: Added for 1894 *LLI*, along with other minor modifications designed to heighten the urban/rural contrast (see, for example, n. 18). Perhaps because of the use of 'vehicles' in this sentence, Sam's 'old-fashioned vehicle' (1891 *ILN*) became an 'old-fashioned conveyance' in 1894 *LLI*.

18. *in South London*: Added for 1894 *LLI*, as was 'in dear old North
    Wessex' in the next sentence.
19. *Not in one of these wretched holes!*: Added for 1894 *LLI*.
20. *sidling*: While MS shows 'sliding' (which to Ray (182) 'seems a
    much more appropriate term', indicating that all print versions
    contain an overlooked misprint), 'sidling', with its suggestion of
    obliqueness and uncertainty, is arguably intentional and more
    appropriate to the lame Sophy. Hardy may even have initially
    intended 'sliding' and then noticed the other, more athletic, reson-
    ances potentially evoked by a slide downstairs with the aid of a
    handrail. This edition therefore retains 'sidling'. In the next two
    sentences, 'on his strong arm' and 'ever-waiting' were added for
    1894 *LLI*.
21. *notwithstanding . . . at one time*: Added for 1894 *LLI*.
22. *though everything I possess would be lost to me by marrying
    again*: This is not simply a reference to social status but to financial
    resources. Though the Married Woman's Property Act of 1882
    would have allowed Sophy to inherit her husband's money, his
    will has put most of it in trust and presumably dictates that it will
    be lost to her in the event of a second marriage.
23. *cricket-match . . . public schools*: The first Eton v. Harrow cricket
    match, still a major social and sporting event held every June,
    took place at Lord's cricket ground in 1805, with Byron playing
    on the Harrow side. Lord's, the home of the Marylebone Cricket
    Club (ultimate arbiter of all matters relating to cricket), moved
    to its present site in North London in 1814. The next sentence
    was added for 1894 *LLI*.
24. *and all around . . . like her*: 'and the proud fathers and mothers
    on the coaches around; but never a mother like her' (1891 *ILN*).
    Combined with the 1894 *LLI* addition to the next sentence of
    'had not cared exclusively for the class they belonged to', this
    expansion heightens the sense of arrogant profligacy in the class
    to which Randolph aspires.
25. *timidly*: 'firmly' (1891 *ILN*). In the same paragraph, for 1894
    *LLI*, 'The youth's' replaced 'His' and 'flushed' was added.
26. *It was dropped . . . peremptoriness*: 'It was dropped for three
    years' (1891 *ILN*).
27. *and finally taking . . . and swear*: 'and finally made her swear
    before a little cross and shrine in his bed-room' (1891 *ILN*). The
    addition of the ironic 'private devotions' and the forcing of Sophy
    to kneel heightens the sense of Randolph's manipulative hypocrisy

in making a selfish social imperative masquerade as a spiritual and filial obligation.

28. *whose eyes were wet*: Added for 1894 *LLI*. In 1891 *ILN*, the 'young smooth-shaven priest in a high waistcoat' is just a 'young cleric'.

## 'ON THE WESTERN CIRCUIT'

1. *Western Circuit*: A circuit judge presides over provincial county or crown courts, travelling from place to place to hear cases. The Western Circuit covers the south-western English counties.

2. *Melchester*: Based on Salisbury, whose cathedral is invoked in the next sentence. For another Hardyan view of Salisbury Cathedral, see 'A Cathedral Façade at Midnight' (*Poetical Works*, III, 9).

3. *eighth chasm of the Inferno ... Homeric heaven*: *Inferno*, the first book of the *Divina Commedia* by Dante Alighieri (1265–1321), puts frauds in the fiery eighth chasm of the Inferno. Homer's heaven is notably rumbustious: see, for example, the end of Book I of *The Iliad*.

4. *architecture*: 'ecclesiology' (1891 *EIM*/1891 *HW*). In the next sentence, 'his hat on one side and' was added for 1894 *LLI*.

5. *holiday-game*: 'fair-day-game' (1891 *EIM*). This is one of several occasions on which 1891 *HW*, which shows 'holiday-game', is closer in phrasing to 1894 *LLI* than 1891 *EIM*.

6. *black cape, grey skirt ... brown hat and brown gloves*: 'brown cape, crimson skirt, light gloves and – no, not even she, but the one behind her; she with the black skirt, grey jacket, black and white hat and white cotton gloves' (1891 *EIM*). 1891 *HW* again shares the phrasing of 1894 *LLI*. In the next paragraph, both serials read 'her each brief transit' for 'each of her brief transits'.

7. *mirrors ... pause and silence*: 'revolving mirrors, steam trumpets, drums, cymbals, cornets, dulcimers, and other kinds of music to pause and silence' (1891 *EIM*/1891 *HW*). In the same sentence, both serials have 'intervening scenes' for 'intervening forms'.

8. *Great Plain*: Salisbury Plain, evocative for Hardy of both austere remoteness and mystery, largely because of its association with Stonehenge. In *Tess of the D'Urbervilles*, also published in 1891, Hardy's most famous vulnerable country girl is arrested at Stonehenge for her seducer's murder, after flight across the plain.

9. *a young lady*: 'a young widow-lady' (1891 *EIM*); 'a young widow lady' (1891 *HW*). This change is central to the substantial bowdlerizing undergone by the serial versions, in an attempt to

make Edith Harnham's infatuation with Raye less culpable. Later in this paragraph, the serial versions reveal that she has been a widow for fifteen months (a comfortably respectable period) and that she has an uncle living temporarily with her; there is no mention of the fact that she 'did not care much' about her husband. Subsequent textual changes necessitated by this serial plot modification will not be noted individually unless they have particular significance. Harnham is a name with many Salisbury associations: Harnham Gate, one of the surviving medieval entrances to the Cathedral Close, leads to Harnham Bridge and ultimately the villages of West and East Harnham, one and a half miles south-west of the city.

10. *Wintoncester*: Based on Winchester, the old Saxon capital of Wessex.

11. *to passion*: 'to such passion' (1891 *EIM*/1891 *HW*). Both serials lack the terminal 'despair', concluding instead with 'as none can foretell'. 1891 *EIM* has 'discontent' for 'content'.

12. *Wintoncester ... Bar at Lincoln's-Inn*: Winchester College, founded in 1382, is England's oldest public school. Lincoln's Inn is one of the four London Inns of Court (Inner Temple, Middle Temple and Gray's Inn being the other three) that have the authority to call to the bar those who are qualified to be barristers. Both institutions give Raye a social status that his pipe and clothes belie.

13. *with sensitive lips*: 'mobile-lipped' (1891 *EIM*/1891 *HW*). In the next sentence, both serials have 'brusquely entered' for 'sauntered', and the man in question is 'Uncle Stephen' (see n. 9).

14. *very wicked and nice*: 'very nice' (1891 *EIM*/1891 *HW*). In both serials the next sentence begins, 'She was so greatly struck with the young barrister's manner, voice, with the fascination of his touch ...'

15. *well-bred*: 'highly qualified' (1891 *EIM*/1891 *HW*). In the next sentence, the serials read only 'touch' for 'touch of her hand'.

16. *occupying her eyes with*: 'occupied with' (1891 *EIM*/1891 *HW*). In the serials, this paragraph refers to both the maidservant and Edith Harnham as 'young'. The excision was probably made to avoid repetition, since the adjective is used again in 'end-of-the-age young man', which specifically associates youth with the sexual adventurousness of the *fin de siècle*.

17. *business*: In the serials, Casterbridge (Dorchester) has no 'concern' for Raye.

18. *grey wig, curled in tiers, in the best fashion of Assyrian bas-reliefs*:

Hardy is comparing barristers' long curled wigs to the stylized hair of the sculpted figures in ancient Assyrian bas-reliefs, many of which he would have seen in the British Museum.

19. *Thoughts of unpremeditated conduct . . . dissatisfied depression*: 'Thoughts of a frivolous flirtation, on which a week earlier he would not have believed himself capable of wasting his time, threw him into a state of dissatisfaction' (1891 *EIM*/1891 *HW*). The change makes Raye's impulses marginally less casual.

20. *won her, body and soul*: 'won her heart entirely' (1891 *EIM*); 'won her heart' (1891 *HW*). MS has 'won her entirely', suggesting the sexual falling that the serials elide and that 'body and soul' makes specific.

21. *given way so unrestrainedly to a passion for an artless creature . . . in his hands*: 'given way [play, 1891 *HW*] so unrestrainedly to a passing fancy for a young creature so charmingly inexperienced, who had placed herself so trustingly in his hands' (1891 *EIM*/1891 *HW*). The change partially restores the MS reading 'harmful passion'. In the serials 'a passing desire' in the next sentence read 'kisses [1891 *EIM*/a kiss 1891 *HW*] upon her red lips'.

22. *He could not desert her now*: Not in serials, where the next sentence's 'unintentional connections' were 'unpremeditated attachments'.

23. *trusting*: 'simple' (1891 *EIM*/1891 *HW*).

24. *that live on expectation*: 'who live without working' (1891 *EIM*/ 1891 *HW*).

25. *the epistle, and in truth did not begin to read it*: 'the epistle, and as a matter of fact did not read it' (1891 *EIM*/1891 *HW*). Hardy presumably noticed the repetition of 'fact' from the previous sentence. Later in the same paragraph, he changed 'epistle' to 'missive', again presumably because he noticed that he had already used 'epistle' in this sentence. In the serials, 'passionate' in this sentence read 'affectionate'.

26. *a few lines written across*: To save postal expense at a time when rates were dependent on the number of sheets sent, additional lines were frequently superimposed at right angles to text already written.

27. *he would write*: Added for 1894 *LLI*, when 'he asked for another letter' was also added to the next paragraph. The effect of emphasizing this mutual solicitation of letters is to give greater weight from the outset to the misleading epistolary base of the relation-

ship. In the serials, 'some near day' read just 'some day', making Raye's dealings with Anna again rather more offhand.

28. *even in days of national education*: The 1870 Elementary Education Act provided national elementary education in England and Wales, and in 1880 education was made compulsory until the age of ten.

29. *From some words . . . suspicions*: Added for 1894 *LLI*, although in MS also Edith has had 'a sad suspicion' about Anna's 'actual relations with the young man'. Other minor phrasing changes in this paragraph – such as 'resulted so seriously' for 'so unsettled', and 'poor little creature in her charge' for 'pretty little creature' – emphasize that Edith's confirmed suspicions are of Anna's dangerous physical intimacy with (rather than mere emotional vulnerability to) Raye. This suggests that Edith's readiness to comply with Anna's deceit is due in part to a sense of class guilt over failure adequately to protect a servant from the predations of a gentleman.

30. *That he had been able . . . she-animal*: Added for 1894 *LLI*. Not only is Anna's seduction made explicit here but also Edith's own sexual fascination with Raye.

31. *There was a strange anxiety . . . state of affairs*: These two paragraphs restore the situation, although not the precise phrasing, of MS, making explicit again the pregnancy that had been bowdlerized from the serial versions.

32. *'I wish it was mine – I wish it was!'*: For 'it' both serial versions have 'he', relocating the focus from child to lover as part of the expunging throughout this section of all reference to Anna's pregnancy.

33. *the cottage on the Plain*: In the serials, Anna goes to the cottage only because of illness brought on by 'damps of winter, aggravated, perhaps, by her secret heart-sickness at her lover's non-appearance'.

34. *She expresses herself . . . elementary schools?*: Added for 1894 *LLI*. In the serials, Anna seems 'fairly ladylike' rather than 'fairly educated', and 'bright-minded' rather than 'bright in ideas'. Although the changes make Anna appear more educated to the sister, they ironically underline the specifically educational aspects of the chasm between Anna and Raye, since Miss Raye's speculations are incorrect and Anna has attended no schools (see n. 28).

35. *don't bear his child!*: 'have no child' (MS); 'have neither lover nor

child' (1891 *EIM*); 'have no lover' (1891 *HW*). Bowdlerization makes mention of a child in 1891 *EIM* something of a *non-sequitur*. The absence of the pregnancy also makes Raye's offer to marry Anna considerably more altruistic.

36. *rise to the woolsack*: Become Lord Chancellor, whose seat in the House of Lords consists of a square sack of wool, a reminder of the traditional source of England's wealth.

37. *married already*: 'in mourning for your husband' (1891 *EIM*/ 1891 *HW*).

38. *or rather ratification of a previous union*: Present in MS (with 'the' before 'ratification') but excised for serials. In 1891 *EIM* the suburb is 'cheap' rather than 'new'.

39. *Knollsea*: Based on Swanage. In MS and serials the honeymoon is to take place in Tunbridge Wells, a fashionable Kentish spa town, close to London, that had enjoyed royal patronage since before the Civil War. The resonances of Knollsea/Swanage are far more demotic and provincial.

40. *and with the ideas of a goose*: Added for 1894 *LLI*, as a further underlining of Anna's educational inadequacies (see n. 34).

41. *abjectly*: 'passionately' (1891 *EIM*/1891 *HW*). 1894 *LLI* also adds 'raised her' in the next sentence. The two minor modifications emphasize both Anna's subordination to Raye and his instinctive attempt to counteract it.

42. *wan*: 'sad' (1891 *EIM*/1891 *HW*).

43. *in her anguish*: Added for 1894 *LLI*, as were the later 'devoted lovers' and 'O my cruel one'.

44. *that showed ... had come*: 'depicting her miserable sense of the end of her impassioned dream' (1891 *EIM*/1891 *HW*). In the serials, the force of the ending is much diminished by the uncle's taking the place, in both station and drawing-room, of the excised husband.

45. *Anna is married*: MS reveals that originally the story ended here. The subsequent description of the newly married couple was added at a late stage of the MS's evolution (see Ray, 204).

46. *dreary*: 'dry' (1891 *EIM*/1891 *HW*).

## 'THE FIDDLER OF THE REELS'

1. *Great Exhibition of 1851*: The story first appeared in a *Scribner's Magazine* special number (May 1893) commemorating the Chicago World's Fair. This invocation of the first world's fair, the 1851 Great Exhibition, is therefore particularly appropriate.

2. *the Conquest*: The imposition of Norman rule on England after the victory of William the Conquerer over Harold II at the Battle of Hastings in 1066.

3. *led us onward to talk*: 'led me onward to think' (1893 *SM*). The removal for 1894 *LLI* of first-person singular pronouns from this point on gives a markedly more impersonal tone to the narrative voice, suggesting a story founded in folk history rather than firsthand narratorial experience (see n. 5).

4. *Stickleford, Mellstock, and Egdon*: Based respectively on Tincleton, the three hamlets of Stinsford, Lower Bockhampton and Higher Bockhampton (in the last of which Hardy was born), and the Puddletown Heath area. Later in this story 'Lewgate' refers specifically to the Higher Bockhampton part of Mellstock parish. Mellstock forms the background for *Under the Greenwood Tree*, while the heathland provides the dominant setting for *The Return of the Native*.

5. *whom the seniors in our party had known well*: Added for 1894 *LLI*, as was 'they said' in the next sentence. This generational distancing further emphasizes the mythic element in the tale (see n. 3). In 1893 *SM*, Ollamoor is merely first in 'order' rather than in 'prominence'.

6. *perhaps a little repulsive at times*: 'perhaps not repulsive; merely, in his better moments, tolerable' (1893 *SM*). The change would seem to make Ollamoor more repellant, rather than, as Ray suggests (224), less.

7. *Greenhill Fair*: Based on the annual September fair held at Woodbury Hill, near Bere Regis (Kingsbere). In *Far from the Madding Crowd*, Sergeant Troy (a ladies' man even more destructive than Wat Ollamoor) plays the beguiling highwayman Dick Turpin in a travelling circus at Greenhill Fair.

8. *Paganini*: More than musical facility associates Ollamoor with the legendary violinist and composer Nicolo Paganini (1782–1840). Superstitious contemporaries attributed Paganini's uncanny skills, which included the ability to move his audience to tears, to diabolic influence, and he had a reputation for predatorily manipulative relationships with women.

9. *jigs, reels, ... quadrilles and gallops*: England's traditional country-dances eventually gave way in the nineteenth century to more fashionable cosmopolitan imports, such as the quadrille and gallop.

10. *the old Mellstock quire-band ... disbanded as ecclesiastical functionaries*: The disbanding, based on the 1842 demise of the

Stinsford Church quire in which Hardy's grandfather, father and uncle had played, is central to the plot of *Under the Greenwood Tree*, whose characters include the Dewy family and Michael Mail.

11. *Wold Hundredth*: The 'Old Hundredth', one of Hardy's favourite church tunes, is a setting for the Tate and Brady metrical form of Psalm 100, better known as the hymn 'All People That on Earth Do Dwell'.

12. *Aspent*: The name suggests 'aspen', a tree whose leaves, attached to the stem by long stalks, quiver in the wind. The association evokes Car'line's convulsive responsiveness to Ollamoor's playing. In the next sentence, 1893 *SM* has 'soul-stealing' for 'heart-stealing', suggesting a more diabolic power.

13. *to instrumentation*: Added for 1894 *LLI*.

14. *Moreford*: Based on Moreton. In 1893 *SM*, Moreford is six miles eastward.

15. *convulsively towards the ceiling*: 'convulsively several times' (1893 *SM*).

16. *The railway to South Wessex was in process of construction*: The Wilts, Somerset & Weymouth Line opened in September 1848. Ned's stay in London lasts approximately from 1847 to 1851.

17. *huge glass-house*: Ned would have been one of more than two thousand men who worked from September 1850 to February 1851 to complete construction of the Crystal Palace in time for the Great Exhibition opening date (1 May). Designed on the principles of a greenhouse by Sir Joseph Paxton (1801–65), former head gardener for the Duke of Devonshire, this gigantic iron-and-glass structure was later moved from Hyde Park to Sydenham, in South London. It was destroyed by fire on 30 November 1936.

18. *little*: Added for 1894 *LLI*.

19. *at the core*: 'to the core' (1893 *SM*). Though slight, this prepositional modification radically reduces Car'line's supposed goodness.

20. *excursion-trains*: To make the Exhibition accessible to as many people as possible, modestly priced (and modestly equipped) excursion trains revolutionized working-class travel, bringing people to London from all over England. By the time the Exhibition closed, it had received six million visitors.

21. *tender face*: 'features' (1893 *SM*).

22. *'Your own child?' 'Yes!' 'Well – as God's in—'*: '"Well – upon my —"' (1893 *SM*). 1912 *LLI* adds after ' "Yes!" ': ' "But who's

the father?" "The young man I had after you courted me." ' In
the next sentence, 1893 *SM* has 'mention' for 'name'.

23. *'I hope you'll excuse it . . . many miles!'*: ' "I hope you'll excuse
it, dear Ned, now I have come so many miles" ' (1893 *SM*). The
plaintive optimism of 'this once' and the additional 'many' add
an almost comically wheedling note to Car'line's characterization.
In the next sentence, 1893 *SM* has 'steadily' for 'palely', while
'with a start' is added for 1894 *LLI*.

24. *the first time*: Added for 1894 *LLI*, as were 'beginning to sob
outright' and ' "What the devil can I do!" Hipcroft groaned.' In
1893 *SM*, Car'line 'sighed' rather than 'gasped'. The changes
heighten the emotional tension between the two. 1912 *LLI*
expands to 'the first time he took advantage o' me'.

25. *silently welling*: 'concealed' (1893 *SM*). Hardy presumably
noticed the contradiction between 'concealed' and the earlier 'the
tears rolled down her chubby cheeks'. In the next sentence, 1893
*SM* has 'preoccupied hardness of utterance' for 'factitious
hardness'.

26. *he said gruffly*: Added for 1894 *LLI*, as was ' "I s'pose" ', both
giving a more grudging tone to Hipcroft's expressions of concern.

27. *time necessary for banns*: The calling of banns in the parish
churches of the engaged couple on three consecutive Sundays
before the wedding is the customary prelude to an Anglican
marriage service.

28. *Heedless-William's Pond . . . Bloom's End . . . Quiet Woman Inn
. . . Egdon Heath*: This is the landscape of *The Return of the
Native*, in which Damon Wildeve is the landlord of the Quiet
Woman and Mrs Yeobright lives at Blooms End, sometimes
associated with Hardy's birthplace but more generally applied to
the valley west of Egdon Heath. The Quiet Woman is also the
Travellers' Rest of the poem 'Weathers' (*Poetical Works*, II, 326).
For Heedless William, see Introduction.

29. *her power*: 'all power' (1893 *SM*). Hardy presumably noticed the
repetition of 'all', in both this sentence and the next.

30. *'My Fancy-Lad'*: Also known as 'Johnny's Gone to Sea', this was,
like 'The Fairy Dance' mentioned later, one of 'the endless jigs,
hornpipes, reels, waltzes, and country-dances that his [Hardy's]
father played of an evening in his early married years, and to
which the boy danced a *pas seul* in the middle of the room' (*Life*,
19). Both tunes are also mentioned in 'The Dance at the Phoenix'
(*Poetical Works*, I, 57–62), in which another woman with a
doubtful past and in thrall to music dances to her death.

31. *those foods of love*: Cf. Orsino's opening words in Shakespeare's *Twelfth Night*: 'If music be the food of love, play on' (I.i.1).

32. *fir-woods of Mistover backed by the Yalbury coppices*: In *The Return of the Native*, Mistover Knap, the location of the Vye home, is north of Blooms End. The 'Yalbury coppices' are based on Yellowham Wood, between Dorchester and Puddletown. Their 'Dantesque gloom' invokes the threatening shades of Dante's *Inferno*.

33. *She's throwed up the sperrits, and*: Added for 1894 *LLI*.

34. *and how he could . . . a mystery*: Added for 1894 *LLI*.

35. *You prevent my getting a bit o' rest!*: Added for 1894 *LLI*, at which time 'peevishly' was substituted for the more sympathetic 'plaintively'.

## 'AN IMAGINATIVE WOMAN'

1. *watering-place*: 1912 *LLI* restores the MS deletion 'of Solentsea' (based on Southsea, adjacent to Portsmouth, in Hampshire) after 'watering-place'. For the association of this location with Florence Henniker, and hence Hardy's possible reasons for the deletion, see Ray, 172–4. Deletions on the first page of MS reveal that 'Marchmill' originally read 'Marchfold', and that the story's original title was 'A Woman of Imagination'.

2. In 1894 *PMM*, this paragraph begins 'They were less distinctly an ill-assorted than an unassorted couple.'

3. *life-leased at all cost . . . kept her*: 'life-leased, at all cost to heart or conscience, which well-trained young women of moral and enlightened countries are duly taught by their high-principled mothers, kept her' (1894 *PMM*). A life-lease on a property expired only with the death of the signatory tenant.

4. *Ella's cast of soul*: 'that volatile cast of soul' (MS). No published version has this reading.

5. *the Island opposite*: The Isle of Wight, which is separated from the mainland by a stretch of water known as the Solent, the source of Hardy's fictional name for Southsea.

6. *Trewe*: In MS the poet's name is 'Crewe'. Ray (173) suggests that the name was changed in all printed versions to disguise possible associations with Florence Henniker, whose uncle's name was Lord Crewe. As likely a cause for modification is the unpoetic resonance of this name of a major northern industrial town, best known for steel manufacture and a railway junction linking together Manchester, Birmingham and Liverpool.

7.   *a commonplace*: 'an uncongenial' (MS). No published version has this reading.

8.   *symboliste nor décadent*: The fashionable poetic modes of the 1890s. The description of Trewe's verse in this paragraph applies equally to Hardy's.

9.   *In the natural way . . . fruition*: 'In the natural course of passion, under conditions which the wit of civilization has ingeniously devised for its extinction' (1894 *PMM*).

10.  *'The mantle of Elijah!'*: See I Kings 19.19, in which Elijah casts his mantle on Elisha, who follows him, and II Kings 2.7–15, in which on Elijah's ascent to heaven Elisha takes up his mantle and is seen by other prophets to have assumed Elijah's role.

11.  *Perhaps it's true*: Added for 1896 *WT*.

12.  *'Severed Lives'*: Presumably suggested by Dante Gabriel Rossetti's 'Severed Selves' (1871), subsequently incorporated as Sonnet 40 into *The House of Life* (1881). For a discussion of the associations between Trewe and Rossetti see Joan Rees, *The Poetry of Dante Gabriel Rossetti: Modes of Self-Expression* (Cambridge: Cambridge University Press, 1981), pp. 197–8. For similarities between Rossetti and Hardy as poets, see Pauline Fletcher, 'Rossetti, Hardy, and the "hour which might have been"', *Victorian Poetry* 20 (1982), 1–13.

13.  *Royal*: Added for 1896 *WT*, as was 'Royalties' in the next paragraph. This underlining of the royal status of the Duke and Duchess adds plausibility to Ray's suggestion (172) that the photograph is intended to be of the Duke of York (later George V) and his bride, Princess May of Teck (later Queen Mary), who were married on 6 July 1893, just before Hardy began work on this story.

14.  *eagerness*: 'childish eagerness' (1894 *PMM*). While this change apparently lessens Ella's immaturity, it is counteracted a little later when what formerly read 'youthful in nature' is revised for 1896 *WT* to 'immature in nature'.

15.  *vainer*: 'more sensitive' (1894 *PMM*). MS also has 'vainer', making the less judgemental serial reading a unique one.

16.  *Budmouth*: Marchmill's voyage has been a substantial one. Budmouth, based on Weymouth, is more than sixty miles west of Southsea.

17.  *The poet wore . . . spectacle portended*: The claim has recurrently been made that Hardy based this description of Trewe on Holman Hunt's famous portrait of the young Dante Gabriel Rossetti (see, for example, Rees, *The Poetry of Dante Gabriel Rossetti*, p. 198).

Certainly there are numerous photographs showing Rossetti in a slouch hat.

18. *a husband and*: Added for 1896 *WT*.

19. *Shelley's scraps*: The notebooks (Bodleian Library, Oxford) that Shelley left on his death include numerous fragments of poetry.

20. *'Forms more real ... immortality'*: From Shelley's 'Prometheus Unbound', I.748–9. The same poem is invoked again later, when Ella sees herself as 'sleeping on a poet's lips': cf. 'On a poet's lips I slept/ Dreaming like a love-adept' ('Prometheus Unbound', I. 737–8). The introductory phrase 'inscribed shapes of the poet's world' was added for 1896 *WT*.

21. *under the pillow*: 'into the bed' (1894 *PMM*). The serial reading is the last surviving printed evidence of MS deletions that originally had the photograph hidden in the bed itself rather than merely under the pillow (see n. 23). In MS, this paragraph also originally had Ella experiencing 'almost a guilty sense that she had the poet actually present with her'. While this was deleted in MS, other less charged references to the actual bed (Marchmill's inquiry 'Not in bed yet?' and his observation 'I didn't know you had gone to bed so soon') survive in MS, only to be deleted for 1894 *PMM*. The scene, originally heavily imbued with sexual suggestiveness, was thus progressively bowdlerized.

22. *if I can*: In MS this is followed by:

> He passed through into the <adj> dressing-room communicating, & she cd. hear him pulling off his clothes. She wondered which of the <bed> rooms he was going to occupy, & finding that he showed no sign of withdrawing she said,
>
> 'That is a comfortable little bed in the <other> upper room, isn't it? <I am rather fatigued.>'
>
> <Is it?> 'O yes,' he replied. 'Well no, it isn't. It is so beastly narrow. I shan't disturb you by my getting up: it will be long before you are awake.' And he <chose> returned to the room she was in.

See Ray, 175.

23. *While her eyes ... photograph further out of sight*: 'While her eyes ... photograph under the pillow' (MS). This sentence replaces a longer MS deletion that read:

> There <u>would</u> <might> have been nothing remarkable in his finding the photograph lying on the table or <outside the> bed, but it might have struck him as odd to find it inside: at any rate <she> Ella in her

sensitiveness fancied so; \<accordingly she\> & she softly drew up her
foot, & pushed the \<pho\> picture down as far as she could reach
with her toes.

The next three lines (' "Sure you're not ill?" . . . kissed her'), added
for 1894 *PMM*, do not appear in MS. 1912 *LLI* adds ' "I wanted
to be with you tonight" ' after 'kissed her'. Brady speculates (101)
that this is the night on which the new baby is conceived. See Ray,
178.

24.  *'What the deuce . . .' . . . withdrew something*: ' "What the deuce is
this that's been bothering me so?" Imagining her asleep, he lifted
the edge of the bedclothes, and withdrew something' (1894 *PMM*).
MS also has 'bothering', but 'devil' for 'deuce' and 'coverlet' for
'bedclothes'. In the next sentence, 1894 *PMM* has 'Mr Trewe's
portrait' for the more suggestive 'Mr Trewe' (MS 'Mr Crewe').

25.  *to whose person she was now absolutely attached*: 'for whose
person she was now absolutely love-sick' (1894 *PMM*). The
'fashionable town on the Island opposite' is presumably Ryde.

26.  *'Behold, he standeth . . . heard in our land'*: See Song of Solomon
2.9 and 11–12. 1896 *WT* has the misprint (corrected here)
'looked' for 'looketh'. MS deletion originally had the beloved
coming 'leaping upon the mountains, skipping upon the hills'
from Song of Solomon 2.8.

27.  *published yesterday*: Given the other Rossetti associations, Hardy
may have had in mind Robert Buchanan's famous attack in 'The
Fleshly School of Poetry: Mr D. G. Rossetti' (*Contemporary
Review*, October 1871). Hardy himself was particularly sensitive
to adverse reviews, as evidenced in his response to the devastating
*Spectator* notice of his first novel, *Desperate Remedies*: 'He
remembered, for long years after, how he had read this review as
he sat on a stile leading to the eweleaze he had to cross on his way
home to Bockhampton. The bitterness of that moment was never
forgotten; at the time he wished that he were dead' (*Life*, 507).

28.  *God is a jealous God*: See Exodus 20.5.

29.  *'The hour . . . life was barren'*: From Dante Gabriel Rossetti's
'Stillborn Love', Sonnet 55 of his *The House of Life*.

30.  *which words could not mend*: Added for 1896 *WT*. MS lacks
everything from 'under the sense' to 'could not mend'.

31.  *the dreamy . . . the child's*: Added for 1896 *WT*. 1912 *LLI*
further expands the first part of this sentence: 'By a known but
inexplicable trick of Nature there were undoubtedly strong traces
of resemblance to the man Ella had never seen.'

32.  *'Then she did ... yes*: Bowdlerized from 1894 *PMM*. MS and 1894 *PMM* both have the narratorial aside '(he never did before, by the way)' after 'murmured Marchmill'.


## 'A CHANGED MAN'

1.  *'Top o' Town'*: The town in question is Casterbridge (Dorchester), whose 'Top o' Town' is a westernmost crossroads formed by the intersection of High West Street, and the roads north to Ivell (Yeovil), west to Port Bredy (Bridport), and south to Budmouth (Weymouth). It is also the intersection of two of the tree-lined walks (collectively referred to here as 'the Town Avenue') surrounding much of Dorchester. The house with the oriel window is supposedly 51 High West Street and Laura's house the last one on the same (north) side (see Kay-Robinson, 13). 1913 *CM* has 'just below' for 'near'.

2.  *straits, windings*: 'rustic windings, shy shades' (1913 *CM*). The actual distance from Top o' Town to Grey's Bridge is more than half a mile. The bridge is first mentioned by name in 1900 *S* (1900 *C* has 'the stone bridge').

3.  *Maumbry's*: The name evokes one of Casterbridge's bleakest locations, Maumbury Rings, a neolithic henge monument (and later Roman amphitheatre) recurrently associated by Hardy with the town's darker history, including executions and blood sports. Its most allusive Hardyan role, as a locale for clandestine meetings fraught with destructive secrets, comes in *The Mayor of Caster-bridge*. The name is not obviously appropriate to Maumbry's beneficent and self-sacrificing nature, nor even to the faithless Laura Maumbry (who ultimately remains loyal to her husband's memory). It may, therefore, have been suggested simply by the Rings' location at the south-west extremity of town, about half a mile below the barracks at the north-west corner.

4.  *twelve feet*: 'ten feet' (1913 *CM*). As Ray suggests (270), Hardy presumably decided that ten feet was a more realistic height for a ghost created by one soldier sitting on another's shoulders.

5.  *'W. D.' and a broad arrow*: The initials and emblem stamped on all War Department property.

6.  *the Hussars*: 1913 *CM* adds: ', Captain Maumbry included,'.

7.  *corner of the town*: 'corner of West Street' (1913 *CM*).

8.  *AT A HASTY WEDDING*: The poem is Hardy's own, subsequently collected for *Poems of the Past and the Present* (1902 (1901)). While l.3 was then changed to read 'By bonds of every bond the

best', and 'suns' (l.5) became 'stars' (*Collected Poems*, I, 179), Hardy retained the original phrasing for 1913 *CM* and other editions of the story.

9.   *Queen's proclamation*: 'Royal proclamation' (1913 *CM*). The proclamation was the required preliminary to the court's being declared in sitting.

10.  *gentle curate*: 'gentle if narrow-minded curate' (1913 *CM*). 'None so orthodox as your unmitigated worldling' was added for 1900 *S*.

11.  *Fountall Theological College*: Based on Wells Theological College (see 'A Tragedy of Two Ambitions', n. 8).

12.  *'The girl I left behind me'*: With words sometimes attributed to the Irish novelist and song-writer Samuel Lover (1797–1868), set to a traditional melody also known as 'Brighton Camp', 'The Girl I Left Behind Me' was routinely played as a march at times of troop departure. In *The Dynasts* (Part Third, Vi.iv), Hardy mentions the tune, by both names, as the accompaniment to troops marching out of Brussels towards the field of Waterloo (*Poetical Works*, V, 184–5 and 358). The tune is in the manuscript music books of Hardy's father and grandfather. Far from being 'now nearly disused', it still has current military resonances on both sides of the Atlantic.

13.  *Durnover Lane*: Durnover is based on Fordington, the eastern section of Dorchester, part of which encompassed the low-lying slum area centring on Mixen (Mill) Lane, most famously evoked in *The Mayor of Casterbridge*.

14.  *the man for such an hour*: Maumbry's Herculean humanitarian work during the cholera outbreak is based upon the comparable labours in 1854 of Henry Moule (1801–80), vicar of St George's, Fordington, and father of Hardy's friend Horace Moule. In a 1919 letter to another son, Handley Moule, Bishop of Durham, Hardy describes Henry Moule's work in ways similar to the subsequent description here of Maumbry's selfless efforts:

> The study of your father's life (too short really) has interested me much. I well remember the cholera-years in Fordington: you might have added many details. For instance, every morning a man used to wheel the clothing and bed-linen of those who had died in the night out into the mead, where the Vicar had a large copper set. Some was boiled there, and some burnt. He also had large fires kindled in Mill-Street to carry off infection. An excellent plan I should think. (*Life*, 423; also *Collected Letters*, V, 315)

For Hardy's relationship with the Moule family, see *Biography*, particularly 64–70 and 153–6.

15. *Creston*: Based on Preston, beneath the crest of the downs north-east of Weymouth.

16. *—th Foot*: '—st Foot' (1913 *CM*). The change was presumably made to accentuate the distinctness of Vannicock's regiment from the '—th Hussars', Maumbry's former regiment.

17. *long*: Added for 1900 *S*.

18. *Ridge-way*: Seemingly here the road that runs east–west along the crest of the downs between Dorchester and Weymouth. Sometimes Hardy uses it to refer to the old Dorchester–Weymouth Road itself, here said to be crossing the Ridgeway at right angles. Hardy provided his own sketch of the Ridgeway to accompany his poem 'The Alarm' in the first edition of his 1898 volume *Wessex Poems* (*Poetical Works*, I, 46–51).

19. *Mellstock Hill ... Casterbridge ... Ivell Road*: This is a remarkably circuitous route, taking them eastwards around the south side of Casterbridge to pick up a fly to take them back westwards around the north side, and hence to the Ivell (Yeovil) road. Presumably the route is dictated solely by the plot need for Laura to encounter her husband in Durnover. The Yeovil to Bristol railway opened in 1853 (see Ray, 271).

20. *Standfast Corner*: Standfast Corner, a short distance north of the major Durnover Cross intersection, is close to Standfast Bridge, which will take the couple across the river and up to Mellstock Hill on the town's east side. In 1913 *CM*, 'mead' later in this paragraph becomes the bleaker 'moor'.

21. *amid this squalid and reeking scene*: Added for 1900 *S*.

22. *came forward*: 'came forward reluctantly' (1913 *CM*).

23. *slippers*: 1913 *CM* adds 'nightdress' to this list.

24. *ghastly*: Added for 1900 *S*.

## 'ENTER A DRAGOON'

1. *I lately had the melancholy experience of going*: 'I lately had a melancholy experience (said the gentleman who is answerable for the truth of this story). It was that of going ...' (1913 *CM*). As Ray observes (290), the addition avoids any confusion between a narratorial and an authorial voice.

2. *of which I had never heard*: Hardy was recurrently fascinated by the domestic history to which a house of any age has been witness, and makes it the burden of a number of poems: see, for example,

'The Self-Unseeing' (*Poetical Works*, I, 206); 'Old Furniture', 'The Strange House', 'A House with a History' (*Poetical Works*, II, 227–8, 346–7, 419–20); and 'Concerning His Old Home' (*Poetical Works*, III, 194). The cottage described here bears some resemblances to Hardy's birthplace in Higher Bockhampton.

3.   *My old Love came ... O'SHAUGHNESSY*: The epigraph comprises the last two lines of the opening stanza of 'Song' ('I made another garden, yea') by Arthur O'Shaughnessy (1844–81). Anticipating the story's central situation, the poem describes the destruction of a new love by the return of an old. Hardy removed all six epigraphs for 1913 *CM*. All are identified and discussed by Ray (287–9).

4.   *Alma*: The Battle of Alma (20 September 1854) was the first major British victory in the Crimean War (1854–6). Hardy's friend Augustus Lane Fox Pitt-Rivers (1827–1900), the soldier and archaeologist, had been present at the battle.

5.   *licence ... unfortunate*: Marriage by either banns or licence would be legal, but a licence, which would be more expensive, would not only avoid the wait required for banns to be read on three successive Sundays but also afford greater privacy.

6.   *'And shall I see ... speak?'*: From 'The Sailor's Wife' by William Julius Mickle (1735–88), a minor Scottish poet in whom Hardy once expressed much interest (see *Collected Letters*, VI, 266).

7.   *'bowfitt'*: ' "beaufet" ' (1913 *CM*). OED recognizes 'beaufet' (but not 'bowfitt') as a variant of buffet, in the sense of sideboard.

8.   *him*: 'the child's father' (1913 *CM*).

9.   *'Yet went we not ...' DONNE*: From 'Elegy 12. His Parting from Her' by John Donne (1572–1631). As Ray observes (288), while the line itself 'anticipates the renewal of love', the title presages Clark's death.

10.  *the high stock being still worn*: This style of stiff neckcloth or collar, fashionable in the eighteenth century, survived in military and clerical dress long after its discontinuance in civilian circles. In less austere form, it can still be seen in modern riding habits and clerical collars.

11.  *step up*: 'peep up' (1913 *CM*). Presumably Hardy bothered with this minor adjustment because he noticed the repetition in 'stepping down' a little later.

12.  *Three-Mariners' beer*: ' "Phoenix" beer' (1913 *CM*). The change may have been made not only because of the military associations of the Phoenix (' "The Faynix" has always been favoured by the soldiery of the barracks for their convivial gatherings' (Lea, 264)

but also because of Hardy's association of the Phoenix with excessive, and ultimately fatal, dancing (see 'The Dance at the Phoenix', *Poetical Works*, I, 57–62). Neither the Phoenix nor the Three Mariners survive as inns, but the buildings (albeit in the case of the Three Mariners a late nineteenth-century replacement of the earlier Elizabethan building) can still be seen opposite each other in Dorchester's High East Street.

13. *And their souls ... BARNES*: From the opening stanza of 'Bad News', from *Poems of Rural Life in the Dorset Dialect* (1879), by Hardy's mentor and friend the Dorset dialect poet William Barnes (1801–86). In the poem (unlike the story), the rumour of bad news proves false.

14. *Scutari*: After the Battle of Alma, conditions in the British military hospital at Scutari, Constantinople, were so appalling that *The Times* (12 October 1854) appealed to its readers to try to ameliorate the situation. By the first week in November, Florence Nightingale was in Scutari with a team of thirty-eight nurses. For an eyewitness account of Scutari, see Robert G. Richardson, ed. *Nurse Sarah Anne. With Florence Nightingale at Scutari* (London: John Murray, 1977), an edition of the diary kept during the winter of 1854–5 by Sarah Anne Terrot, one of the nurses who worked with Nightingale at the hospital. Also E. T. Cook, *The Life of Florence Nightingale*, 2 vols. (London: Macmillan, 1913).

15. *old Owlett's*: For the smuggler Jim Owlett, see 'The Distracted Preacher' (*Withered Arm*); at the end of this story, set in the 1830s, Owlett escapes to America. Since 'Enter a Dragoon' is set around 1857, this must be another member of the smuggling family. As Selina's father ruefully observes, 'licensed liquor', on which duty has been paid, was formerly deemed inferior in quality to contraband.

16. *for a fatal result ... privations*: 'for such a result upon a heart enfeebled by fatty degeneration after the privations' (1913 CM).

17. *For Love's sake ... JONSON*: From Lyric seven, 'Begging Another, on Colour of Mending the Former', from 'A Celebration of Charis in Ten Lyrical Pieces' by Ben Jonson (1572–1637).

18. *churchyard*: 1913 CM adds 'in the Durnover quarter', associating the burial with St George's, Fordington (see 'A Changed Man', nn. 13 and 14).

19. *Saul*: The famous Dead March comes in Act III of the oratorio *Saul*, by George Frederick Handel (1685–1759).

20. *'Off she goes'*: A traditional British jig tune, best known as the accompaniment to the nursery rhyme 'Humpty Dumpty'.

21. *Chalk-Newton*: Based on Maiden Newton.
22. *sign-board*: 1913 CM adds ' – no man forbidding her'.
23. *Mrs Miller*: At this point 1913 CM adds a substantial paragraph elaborating on Bartholomew Miller's motivations in renewing his suit: 'mother is growing old, and I am away from home a good deal, so that it is almost necessary there should be another person in the house with her besides me'. In the next paragraph, 1913 CM adds a penultimate sentence: 'However, Selina would not consent to be the useful third person in his comfortable home – at any rate just then.'
24. *'Men are as the time is.'* – *KING LEAR*: The words are Edmund's, delivered to the Captain along with a note that orders the deaths of Lear and Cordelia: the quotation (V.iii.31–3) continues 'to be tender-minded/ Does not become a sword'. Duplicitous as Clark is, the association with the homicidal Edmund seems a touch hyperbolic.
25. *Shottsford-Forum*: Based on Blandford Forum.
26. *'Anyhow … twice over!'*: ' "Anyhow, as good as my husband, for he was just going to be" ' (1913 CM).

# Appendix I
# History of the Short Story Collections

Most of Hardy's short stories first appeared in periodicals and then were collected in volumes: *Wessex Tales: Strange, Lively, and Commonplace* (London: Macmillan, 1888); *A Group of Noble Dames* (London: Osgood, McIlvaine, 1891); *Life's Little Ironies: A Set of Tales with Some Colloquial Sketches Entitled A Few Crusted Characters* (London: Osgood, McIlvaine, 1894); and *A Changed Man, The Waiting Supper, and Other Tales, Concluding with The Romantic Adventures of a Milkmaid* (London: Macmillan, 1913).

The 1888 two-volume first edition of *Wessex Tales* contained 'The Three Strangers' (*Longman's Magazine*, March 1883), 'The Withered Arm' (*Blackwood's Edinburgh Magazine*, January 1888), 'Fellow-Townsmen' (*New Quarterly Magazine*, April 1880), 'Interlopers at the Knap' (*English Illustrated Magazine*, May 1884), and 'The Distracted Preacher' (*New Quarterly Magazine*, April 1879). Macmillan also printed a one-volume edition of *Wessex Tales* in 1889. When Hardy reprinted the collection for the 1896 Osgood, McIlvaine edition of his novels, he added a new story, 'An Imaginative Woman' (*Pall Mall Magazine*, April 1894), which he placed first. For the definitive 1912 Wessex Edition of his novels, Hardy then moved 'An Imaginative Woman' to *Life's Little Ironies* and shifted two stories, 'A Tradition of Eighteen Hundred and Four' and 'The Melancholy Hussar of the German Legion', from *Life's Little Ironies* to *Wessex Tales*.

The 1891 first edition of *A Group of Noble Dames* contained ten stories loosely connected by a storytelling framework in which the narrators were presented as members of the Wessex Field and Antiquarian Club who are confined by stormy weather and pass the time by telling stories about seventeenth- and eighteenth-century Wessex women (some are loosely based on historical figures from John Hutchins's *History and Antiquities of the County of Dorset*[1]). These narratives are 'The First Countess of Wessex' (*Harper's New Monthly Magazine*, December 1889); 'Barbara of the House of Grebe', 'The

Marchioness of Stonehenge', 'Lady Mottisfont', 'The Lady Icenway', 'Squire Petrick's Lady' and 'Anna, Lady Baxby' (all as 'A Group of Noble Dames', *Graphic*, Christmas Number, 1 December 1890); 'The Lady Penelope' (*Longman's Magazine*, January 1890); 'The Duchess of Hamptonshire' ('The Impulsive Lady of Croome Castle', *Light*, April 1878); and 'The Honourable Laura' ('Benighted Travellers', *Bolton Weekly Journal*, December 1881). *A Group of Noble Dames* was reprinted for the 1896 Osgood, McIlvaine Edition and the 1912 Wessex Edition.

The 1894 first edition of *Life's Little Ironies* included eight stories: 'The Son's Veto' (*Illustrated London News*, Christmas number, December 1891); 'For Conscience' Sake' (*Fortnightly Review*, March 1891); 'A Tragedy of Two Ambitions' (*Universal Review*, December 1888); 'On the Western Circuit' (*English Illustrated Magazine*, December 1891); 'To Please His Wife' (*Black and White*, June 1891); 'The Melancholy Hussar of the German Legion' (*Bristol Times and Mirror*, January 1890); 'The Fiddler of the Reels' (*Scribner's Magazine*, May 1893); 'A Tradition of Eighteen Hundred and Four' (*Harper's Christmas*, December 1882). The volume concluded with a series of sketches entitled 'A Few Crusted Characters' ('Wessex Folk', *Harper's New Monthly Magazine*, March–June 1891). *Life's Little Ironies* was reprinted for the 1896 Osgood, McIlvaine edition and for the 1912 Wessex Edition of Hardy's novels (see above for changes to its contents).

After Hardy had rearranged the narratives in *Wessex Tales* and *Life's Little Ironies* for the 1912 Wessex Edition, the first three volumes of stories could be seen to have distinctive principles of organization: *Wessex Tales* consisted of stories that imitated traditional regional narratives, all of them set some decades back in the nineteenth century; *A Group of Noble Dames* consisted of stories about aristocratic Wessex women of the seventeenth and eighteenth centuries; *Life's Little Ironies* – like *Jude the Obscure*, published a year later – consisted chiefly of stories with a contemporary setting and context. *A Changed Man*, however, which Hardy assembled in 1913 in conjunction with the 1912 Wessex Edition, simply brought together the remaining uncollected stories, new and old, that Hardy considered worthy of republication; it does not display, therefore, a discernible pattern in subject matter or technique. The volume contains 'A Changed Man' (*Sphere*, April 1900); 'The Waiting Supper' (*Murray's Magazine*, January and February 1888); 'Alicia's Diary' (*Manchester Weekly Times*, October 1887); 'The Grave by the Handpost' (*St James's Budget*, Christmas Number, November 1897); 'Enter a Dragoon' (*Harper's Monthly Magazine*,

December 1900); 'A Tryst at an Ancient Earthwork' (*Detroit Post*, March 1885); 'What the Shepherd Saw' (*Illustrated London News*, Christmas Number, December 1881); 'A Committee-Man of "The Terror"' (*Illustrated London News*, Christmas Number, November 1896); 'Master John Horseleigh, Knight' (*Illustrated London News*, Summer Number, June 1893); 'The Duke's Reappearance' (*Saturday Review*, Christmas Supplement, December 1896); 'A Mere Interlude' (*Bolton Weekly Journal*, October 1885); and 'The Romantic Adventures of a Milkmaid' (*Graphic*, Summer Number, June 1883).

Several stories remained uncollected: 'How I Built Myself a House' (*Chambers's Journal*, March 1865); 'Destiny and a Blue Cloak' (*New York Times*, 4 October 1874); 'The Thieves Who Couldn't Stop Sneezing' (*Father Christmas*, December 1877); 'An Indiscretion in the Life of an Heiress' (*New Quarterly Magazine*, July 1878); 'The Doctor's Legend' (*Independent*, March 1891); 'Our Exploits at West Poley' (*Household*, November 1892–April 1893); and 'Old Mrs Chundle' (unpublished during Hardy's lifetime, MS in the Dorset County Museum). Hardy also collaborated with Florence Henniker in the composition of 'The Spectre of the Real' (*To-Day*, November 1894). This official collaboration, along with two stories by his second wife that were influenced and corrected by Hardy ('Blue Jimmy: The Horse Stealer', published in the 1911 *Cornhill* under the name F. E. Dugdale, and the unpublished 'The Unconquerable'), has been joined with the uncollected stories in the only full scholarly edition of any of Hardy's short fiction: Pamela Dalziel's *Thomas Hardy: The Excluded and Collaborative Stories* (Oxford: Clarendon Press, 1992).

## NOTE

1. Hutchins's *History* dates back to the eighteenth century, but Hardy owned a copy of the four-volume 3rd edition, published 1861–73 (*Biography*, 582n).

# Appendix II
# Hardy's Use of History in 'The First Countess of Wessex'

'The First Countess of Wessex' is broadly based on events documented in John Hutchins's immense four-volume *History and Antiquities of the County of Dorset*, an eighteenth-century work of which Hardy proudly owned a Victorian third edition.[1] King's-Hintock Court is the Wessex name for Melbury House, thirteen kilometres north-west of Dorchester, which was inherited in 1729 by Susannah Strangways, who in 1713 had married Squire Thomas Horner of Mells Park, Somerset, a man below her in his possessions and style of life. These historical originals for the parents of Betty Dornell likewise had one daughter – Elizabeth Strangways-Horner, born in 1723 – who at the age of thirteen, under pressure from her mother, married Stephen Fox, later Lord Ilchester (1741) and then the first Earl of Ilchester (1756); like Betty Dornell, she did not live with her husband until some years after her marriage.[2] In 1893, Hardy told an interviewer that his attention was first drawn to these historical personages by 'the only fact which can be learned from the records': 'that the child was married at that age'.[3] He presumably then followed the procedure he described in his Preface to *A Group of Noble Dames*, where 'The First Countess of Wessex' was collected in 1891, of 'raising images' from genealogies by 'unconsciously filling into the framework the motives, passions, and personal qualities which would appear to be the single explanation possible of some extraordinary conjunction in times, events, and personages'.[4] Hardy freely fabricated some facts, in other words, for his own imaginative purposes. There is no evidence in Hutchins or elsewhere, for example, that Elizabeth Strangways-Horner was attracted to another man after her marriage to Fox, a detail that appears in both the 1889 periodical version of the story and its volume appearance two years later. Neither is there any known basis for two plot elements introduced in 1891: that the daughter was rejected by a lover after contracting smallpox and that the mother, guilt-stricken after her husband's death, then tried to discourage the daughter from living with her husband.

Hardy's relationship to the story, however, is not so distant or dispassionate as such a process of historical fantasizing would imply, for he also wrote to Lord Lytton in July 1891 that the stories in *A Group of Noble Dames* came from 'the lips of aged people in a remote part of the country, where traditions of the local families linger on, & are remembered by the yeomen & peasantry long after they are forgotten by the families concerned'.[5] As Michael Millgate has suggested, one of those aged sources for 'The First Countess of Wessex' was 'almost certainly' Hardy's mother, Jemima Hand Hardy (1813–1904). As a young Melbury Osmond woman in destitute circumstances, she had worked as a cook for two relatives of the third Earl of Ilchester, and through her mother, the former Betty Swetman (1778–1847), she descended from a family that had once possessed property near Melbury House. According to Millgate, 'the Swetmans had been small landowners – or, as Hardy was fond of saying, "yeomen" – for generations, farming land subsequently absorbed into the Melbury House estates of the Earls of Ilchester. The land had been theirs, Hardy once told a friend, at a time "when the Ilchesters were at plow"'. The implication in this statement that the rise of the Ilchesters coincided with the decline of the Swetmans is roughly consistent with Hardy's family tradition that his mother's ancestors were 'ruined' at the time of the 1685 Monmouth Rebellion, when the illegitimate son of the beheaded Charles I led an abortive insurrection against James II.[6] Hardy reported in the *Life* that the Swetmans 'seem to have been involved in the Monmouth rising' and that one of them 'was probably transported', which 'seems to have helped to becloud the family prospects of the maternal line of Hardy's ancestry'. Hardy had also been told that two of the Swetman daughters narrowly escaped being raped by victorious loyalist soldiers.[7] The ancestors of the Ilchesters were on the opposing side. Indeed, during the Parliamentary Revolution (1649–60), Stephen Fox's father – of yeoman stock and originally in service at the court of Charles I – had curried the favour of the dead King's legitimate son, thus building a fortune and ensuring a place for himself as Paymaster of the Forces in the courts of Charles II and James II after the Restoration.[8] It is not surprising, then, that the *Life* pointedly describes the former Swetman house as 'now in the possession of the Earl of Ilchester'.[9] Just a year before he wrote 'The First Countess of Wessex', Hardy had made a sketch of that house, noting on the back that this was 'where G. [Granny] Melbury & her father were born'.[10]

Nor was Melbury House and its environs the only property in which Hardy invested such emotional and imaginative interest. 'The First Countess of Wessex' also features the manor at Corfe Mullen near

Wimborne (called Elm-Cranlynch in the story and occupied by Charles Phelipson), which, as Hutchins reports, had dwindled to cottages after it had been lost by the Phelips family.[11] And in August of 1888, Hardy visited Woolcombe, once owned by a family to which he thought he was related; he then made this mansion the setting for the honeymoon scenes in *Tess of the D'Urbervilles*, a novel that dwells on the decline of families.[12] In the case of 'The First Countess of Wessex', the focus on houses extended even to its illustrations, for in December 1888 Hardy requested of James Ripley Osgood, the London agent for *Harper's New Monthly Magazine*, that the story's artist have 'a special skill' in delineating not only period costume but also 'old English manor-house architecture, & woodland scenery'. Hardy proposed the name of one artist who was 'fairly good at architecture', mentioned a drawing of Melbury House in the British Museum, and offered to entertain the chosen artist for a few days in order to 'accompany him to the scenes'. A month later, the painter Alfred Parsons did make such a trip,[13] and the result was two contrasting sets of pictures. The American illustrator C. S. Reinhart provided four illustrations featuring the story's human characters, while Parsons furnished the architectural and landscape drawings: a headpiece showing Melbury House seen from a neighbouring hill, plus full-page pictures of Mells Park seen from its avenued approach, of Squire Dornell and Tupcombe driving through a hilly countryside towards Bristol, and of the entrance gate to the Ilchester estate at Melbury Park. Most intriguing is the last of these, which features close to its edge on the right a mustachioed man who does not appear in the narrative and who resembles Hardy himself as he looked in the late 1880s. Significantly, this mysterious figure is leaving the estate, not by the main gate, but by climbing the stile to its side, and he is carrying over his shoulder, tramp-style, a sack tied to a stick; he is not dressed as a rustic, however, but rather wears a respectable suit and hat. It is tempting to think that Hardy gave Parsons instructions for the details of this illustration – perhaps even that he posed for it – and that the presence of the genteel tramp on the stile is linked to his own ambivalent feelings about the lost property and house on the outskirts of Melbury Park.[14]

In any case, it is indisputable that Hardy felt a hereditary tie with the very property that the fictional Stephen Reynard so deftly makes his own by becoming the husband of the heiress Betty Dornell.[15] And while she, in turn, by marrying him, becomes the future 'First Countess of Wessex', it is Hardy himself who is slyly implicated in Reynard's justification for the choice of title. Paraphrasing Reynard in his letter to Betty when he seeks to win her heart, Hardy's narrator reports that, when mentioning his expected peerage, Reynard tells her he 'thought the title of Wessex would be eminently suitable, considering the position of much of their property'. This focus on the 'position' of the Ilchester property – the word could imply more than location – has a double effect. On the one hand, it draws attention to the wiliness of Reynard, whose marriage with his child-wife has already brought him the 'enormous estates' which had made possible his promised peerage. At the same time, however, Reynard's letter establishes an imaginative identification between Hardy and the house of Ilchester.[16] For here the intellectual property of 'Wessex' – to which he had begun so prominently to lay claim – gives its name to the titled family that owns the land and house his maternal family had lost many generations before. To tell the story passed down by his 'yeomen' ancestors and to make it central to the history of Wessex is thus to reclaim their propertied past: Hardy himself, in the person of Reynard, playfully becomes the first Earl of Wessex and the father of that house's multiple (fictional) progeny.[17]

This fanciful tinkering with the history of an eminent family still living at Melbury House was potentially damaging for the Hardy who, as a renowned novelist, had begun to socialize in élite circles, and he eventually learned that the fifth Earl of Ilchester had been angered by the story. What is not known, however, is which version the Earl was responding to. Was it the 1889 *Harper's* version, published in the United States with the illustrations of his property, or the 1891 volume version, significantly different from the first and published, without pictures, in England? There is also no evidence indicating when – before or after the decision to offer the changed version of 1891 – Hardy heard of Ilchester's annoyance. In either case, even the possibility that the Earl might be offended could have provided the reason for Hardy to alter the story for its volume publication, when for the first time it would be reviewed inside England. For although Martin Ray suggests that the plot for *Harper's* was probably a bowdlerization, there is no evidence that the journal called for any changes to the original manuscript or that the 1891 version was written first. It is quite possible, then, that the second publication is the bowdlerized one, a response to the known or anticipated sensitivity, not of an editor, but of the Ilchesters.[18] For the book version, while it introduces, as Ray points out, an elopement, a kiss, secret meetings and a pregnancy,[19] also makes respectable the relationship between the Earl and Countess by removing the strong implication that she was not a virgin when she finally yielded to her husband.

In the periodical, Phelipson dies from a fall because Tupcombe, thinking it is Reynard who has entered Betty's bedroom, destabilizes the ladder at the window. Phelipson is repeatedly described as the 'lover' of Betty, and when, immediately after the fatal fall, her mother finds her lying 'in a dead swoon' and wearing only a 'night-gown', the narration explicitly suggests the aftermath of a sexual assignation:

> Before going near her daughter she quickly pushed the door behind her, put the room in order, and gently closed the window, which was a little open, though this had been unobserved from below. She then wrapped a dressing-gown round Betty, called in the house-steward, and told him that her daughter had seemingly run to the window and fainted at sight of the accident outside.

At a later stage in this first version, the narrator also volunteers that 'Mrs Dornell had reason to think that the night on which the rash young fellow had lost his life was not the only occasion of his surreptitiously visiting King's-Hintock Court,' and Reynard's cool logic at learning the circumstances of Phelipson's death is summarized in language that implies a recognition of distinctly sexual misconduct: 'How would it matter what the old Eve had been, if the new Eve's mind veered in a direction favourable to him?'[20]

In accepting what has happened, Reynard makes his most cunning move in the wooing of his young wife. But the implication that Betty (and thus the first Countess of Ilchester) had committed adultery – not to mention that she finally developed an affection for her husband only because of his expected peerage – could well have been part of what provoked anger in the fifth Earl of Ilchester. In any case, the Betty of the later version is given a less ambiguous history. Carried from her room by Phelipson immediately after he has arrived and warned of Reynard's impending arrival (significantly, she did not know that he was coming, and there is no time for lovemaking), she then feels 'much misgiving' after their escape. The introduction of the smallpox incident, which replaces the fatal fall in the periodical version, then exposes Phelipson as a shallow suitor and reveals that Reynard, with his daring kiss, is the one who truly loves Betty. In this version, there are indeed sexual assignations, but they involve the man who is already her legal husband rather than a lover who tries to displace him. The volume publication, in short, removes the potentially scandalous aspects of Betty Dornell's sexual history, and although it retains the characterization of Reynard as a clever strategist, it none the less establishes him as a chivalrous lover who is prepared to risk his life to prove his devotion to his young wife. Betty may shock her mother with the revelation of her pregnancy, but the child she is carrying is both legitimate and the offspring of the only man she has ever slept with.

Whether or not these changes of 1891 were a direct response to objections by the Earl of Ilchester, Hardy's reluctance to offend members of the old family is obvious in his revisions for the 1895 Osgood, McIlvaine edition of *The Woodlanders*, which move Little-Hintock, the village of the seductive Felice Charmond, a respectable distance from Melbury House – a decision that was anticipated, as F. B. Pinion has pointed out, in the 1891 addition to 'The First Countess of Wessex' of a reference to Little-Hintock as 'several miles' east of King's-Hintock.[21] Though Hardy's reasons for both these sets of changes were obviously practical, there may also have been an emotional motivation, for he had still another tie to the history of the Ilchesters: Lady Susan Fox-Strangways, the daughter of Stephen Fox and Elizabeth Strangways-Horner, who eloped in 1764 with the well-known Irish actor William O'Brien, lived with her husband for many years in Stinsford House, near Hardy's own home at Bockhampton, and both were buried in a vault built by Hardy's paternal grandfather. Hardy reported in the *Life* that this connection 'lent the occupants of the little vault in the chancel a romantic interest' in his mind 'at an early age', and he described the 1892 destruction of Stinsford House by fire as 'a bruising of tender memories for me'. He felt especially drawn to the O'Briens, moreover, because Lady Susan 'caused such scandal in aristocratic circles' by marrying an artist without title or property. Twice in the *Life*, Hardy challenges Horace Walpole's judgement that she had 'stooped' in this marriage to a talented actor and dramatist, and he mentions proudly that both his grandmothers had seen O'Brien perform and that his great-grandfather and grandfather 'had known him well'. He also quotes the reminiscences of a local labourer who had praised Lady Susan for her generosity and concludes the entry with a fond epithet: 'A kind-hearted woman, Lady Susan.'[22] In sum, although Hardy may have seen the marriage of the first Earl of Ilchester as made partly for reasons of convenience, he also viewed the elopement of the Earl's daughter as a love match, an overcoming of rigid class divisions. What emerges from such tangled associations, then, is a complex and sometimes contradictory response by Hardy to family traditions about the house of Ilchester: filtered through both his mother's and his father's sides, these stories of property lost and gained, of arranged and forbidden marriages, fed into his abiding preoccupation with sexual desire across class lines.

It is hardly a coincidence, then, that the literary text most clearly linked to 'The First Countess of Wessex' is Sir Walter Scott's *The Bride of Lammermoor* (1819), a work Hardy praised in his 1888 essay, 'The Profitable Reading of Fiction'.[23] For *The Bride of Lammermoor* also features an ambitious heiress who has married below her own rank and who then forces her young daughter, against the will of the father, to marry a man of her mother's choosing. In addition to having similar plots, both love stories serve as vehicles for an exploration of political change. In Scott's novel, the class differences repeat the historical conflict between a declining aristocracy and the aspiring middling classes at the time of the Union. In Hardy's story, the background to the marriage is the conferral of noble titles on Stephen Fox because he is a 'favourite at Court' – one of several indirect allusions to the well-known association of both Stephen and his brother, Henry (father of Whig leader Charles James Fox), with Robert Walpole's Whig politics. The success of the brothers, moreover, had depended on the previous rise in the Tory Party of their yeoman father (see n. 8). The Fox family, in short, was notorious for its strategies of political expediency, and it is this aspect of the historical Stephen Fox that Hardy foregrounds in his fictional character: Reynard is successful in wooing the young heiress precisely because he is a 'diplomatist' who knows that 'the only permanent attribute of life is change'. His cleverness is presented as tact, his opportunism as patience, and his understanding of Betty's past infatuation as something that can be changed is simply a domestic application of a political principle that he has always embraced. This wry transformation in 'The First Countess of Wessex' of the fox from beast-fable tradition into the fairy-tale prince – especially prominent in the less cynical 1891 version – is accomplished by the story's comic method and form, which reverses the tragic outcome of Scott's novel: where Lucy Ashton had escaped her mother's manipulations only by violently attacking her new bridegroom and then dying, Betty Dornell defies Susannah first by fleeing from Reynard and then by recognizing his authority over her mother's: ' "But, my dearest mamma, you made me marry him!" ' she exclaims with a logic worthy of her diplomatic husband, ' "and of course I've to obey him more than you now!" ' So the story can end happily, with the future Earl triumphant in his property, his wife and the prospect of numerous offspring. And this is Hardy's whimsical triumph as well: Wessex – the imaginative place whose ownership he had fully claimed in the recent collection of stories entitled *Wessex Tales* – had acquired its presiding aristocrat, one with intimate ties to Hardy's own fantasies about his ancestral past.

'The First Countess of Wessex' in its two versions can finally be seen, then, as a revealing example of a tendency in Hardy – not unlike that in his character Angel Clare – both to resent and to romanticize aristocratic privilege. This doubleness, which became increasingly apparent during the 1890s as Hardy's growing fame put him in social contact with people of wealth and title, emerged again in his subsequent relationship with the Ilchester family. When the fifth Earl of Ilchester died in 1905, Hardy wrote in elegiac tones to his friend Florence Henniker that 'Our county has lately lost a noble lord – its Lr Lieutenant', and for a few days in November 1915 he was a guest of Lady Ilchester at Melbury House, after which he sent her the manuscript of a poem he had written 'in Melbury Park years and years ago'.[24] That poem, dated 1901 in *Time's Laughingstocks* (1909), is 'Autumn in King's-Hintock Park', spoken in the voice of an old woman meditating, as she rakes leaves, on the passage of time. Though she sees 'Lords' ladies pass in view', she is not one of these noble dames (a variant title was 'Autumn in My Lord's Park'); rather, she occupies the perspective of Hardy's mother and grandmother, who knew the Ilchester estate only from the outside. So Hardy – now the famous creator of 'Wessex', but also still the son of a woman who cooked for relations of the Ilchesters – could pay tribute to this aristocratic family, now his friends, even as he reminded them of who lived outside their gates. Indeed, more than thirty years after the periodical publication of 'The First Countess of Wessex', some of the mischief in the genteel tramp at the entrance to Melbury Park (if one can presume that this figure is meant to be Hardy) may have intruded on a happy social occasion at Max Gate. In February 1919, Florence Hardy wrote to Sydney Cockerell,

> T. H. is very well and very cheerful. He had a visit yesterday from Lady Ilchester and her daughter and we were quite a noisy party – shouts of laughter, such as I had not heard here for many months. He insisted upon telling that awful story of the burning of Mary Channing, with all its gruesome details. I tried in vain to stop him, for the daughter turned white – she is only fifteen.[25]

So Hardy continued to tell stories to the Ilchesters, parts of which they did not want to hear. At the same time, however, by marrying his Wessex to their Dorset, he also had become part of their social set: like the Foxes, Hardy the descendant of yeomen had entered the world of the aristocracy.

## NOTES

1.  *Biography*, 4. Hardy invented the 'Wessex' title, although fiction became reality in 1999 when, at the time of his marriage, Prince Edward, Elizabeth II's youngest son, assumed the title of Earl of Wessex, his bride thereby becoming an actual first Countess of Wessex. One assumes that those responsible for the choice were not sufficiently familiar with Hardy to be aware of the less conventional episodes in the fictional couple's marital odyssey.

2.  See John Hutchins, *The History and Antiquities of the County of Dorset*, vol. II (Westminster: J. B. Nicols, 1861; repr. East Ardsley: E. P. Publishing, 1973), pp. 663–79; Giles Stephen Holland Fox-Strangways, sixth Earl of Ilchester, *Henry Fox, First Lord Holland, His Family and Relations*, vol. I (London: John Murray, 1920), pp. 44–7; Brady, 85–6; and Ray, 79–81.

3.  Quoted in Ray, 80.

4.  See *Personal Writings*, 24.

5.  *Collected Letters*, I, 239–40.

6.  *Biography*, 317, 13, 9 and 12.

7.  *Life*, 10–11. John Symonds Udal notes that the Monmouth Rebellion 'never fails to stir the hearts of West Dorset folk' (*Dorsetshire Folk-Lore*, 2nd edn (1922; repr. Guernsey: Toucan Press, 1970), p. 150), and in 'The Duke's Reappearance', his 1896 story featuring the ancestral house, Hardy draws on another Swetman tradition, that the family was visited by 'one of Monmouth's defeated officers' (*Life*, 11).

8.  On the career of Sir Stephen Fox, father of the first Earl of Ilchester, see Ilchester, *Henry Fox*, pp. 4–16; and *The Home of the Hollands, 1605–1820* (London: John Murray, 1937), pp. 32–5.

9.  *Life*, 11.

10. *Biography*, 279.

11. Millgate (*Biography*, 191) notes that the 'decline' of this house is described in Hutchins.

12. *Biography*, 293.

13. *Collected Letters*, I, 181–2.

14. Six of the seven Parsons and Reinhart illustrations, plus the headpiece, appeared again in the 1891 publication by Harper & Brothers of *A Group of Noble Dames*, and the 1896 Osgood, McIlvaine edition featured a frontispiece by Henry Macbeth Raeburn entitled 'King's-Hintock Court' (Ray, 75–6).

15. Squire Dornell described Reynard as 'poor', but the historical Fox

had considerable property and money. His estates, however, had been purchased by his father, while the Strangways were, according to the sixth Earl of Ilchester, 'a family of ancient descent', and their property in southern England dated back to the early fifteenth century (Ilchester, *Henry Fox*, p. 31).

16. The name 'Betty' may be a veiled reference to Betty Swetman; Elizabeth Strangways-Horner is not referred to in the diminutive in Hutchins or other published sources.

17. In his 1890 poem, 'The Rhyme of the Three Captains', Rudyard Kipling ironically calls Hardy 'Lord of the Wessex coast and all the lands thereby' (quoted in *Biography*, 308).

18. Hardy had completed the volume version of *A Group of Noble Dames*, a job that included adding 'The First Countess of Wessex' and three other stories to the six that already comprised the periodical printings of 'A Group of Noble Dames', in early 1891. By this point, not long after he had spent months bowdlerizing the manuscripts of 'A Group of Noble Dames' and of *Tess of the D'Urbervilles* for their appearances in the *Graphic*, Hardy had become adept at anticipating what might be objectionable in his fiction and at finding cynical ways of getting around those objections. It is unlikely, before the multiple rejections of *Tess* at the end of 1889 and the difficult negotiations with the *Graphic* during 1890, that Hardy would have felt the need to bowdlerize the original version of 'The First Countess of Wessex', which he had sent to *Harper's* late in 1888.

19. See Ray, 78 and 81.

20. 1891 *GND* also replaced 'an offence which he might with some reason have denounced as forgivable' with the milder 'an errant passion which he might with some reason have denounced'.

21. *Thomas Hardy: His Life and Friends* (New York: St Martin's Press, 1992), p. 213. Since this detail was added in 1891, it could indicate that Ilchester's response to 'First Countess' prompted the later changes to the novel.

22. *Life*, 14, 264, 13 and 170.

23. *Personal Writings*, 121.

24. *Collected Letters*, III, 190 and V, 134.

25. *Letters of Emma and Florence Hardy*, ed. Michael Millgate (Oxford: Clarendon Press, 1996), p. 157.

# Appendix III
# A Note on the Illustrations

Eight of the eleven stories selected for this volume were accompanied in their original periodical issue by illustrations (for details, see A Note on the History of the Texts). This edition includes all the illustrations that appeared with three of those stories: 'The First Countess of Wessex', 'A Changed Man' and 'Enter a Dragoon'.

The headpiece and three outdoor or architectural drawings by Alfred Parsons (1847–1920) and the four character drawings by Charles Stanley Reinhart (1844–96) prepared for the appearance of 'The First Countess of Wessex' in *Harper's New Monthly Magazine* have been included not only for their innate interest, as examples of work by two of the most accomplished illustrators of their time, but also because in their different ways both artists have something of a special place in the illustration of Hardy's short fiction. Six years earlier, Reinhart, already recognized as one of America's best illustrators, had provided four drawings to accompany the 1883 publication of 'The Romantic Adventures of a Milkmaid' in the *Graphic*, three of which were also used for this story's American periodical appearance in *Harper's Weekly* (see *Withered Arm*, Appendix II). He is thus the only artist other than Parsons to have provided illustrations for more than one of Hardy's short stories, Parsons's second contribution being limited to a headpiece illustration of Dorchester High Street to accompany 'Wessex Folk' (subsequently collected as 'A Few Crusted Characters' for 1894 *LLI*) in *Harper's New Monthly Magazine* (March–June 1891).

There is no evidence that Hardy was involved in the choice of Reinhart for 'The First Countess of Wessex' commission. This would have resulted naturally from the artist's lengthy association with Harper's, for whom he had worked exclusively from 1870 to 1877 and to whom he was again contracted until 1890. He had illustrated various works by Tennyson, Longfellow, Dickens, Wilkie Collins and, most recently, Henry James, who was to write an encomiastic essay about Reinhart for *Harper's Weekly* (14 June 1890), which he later collected for inclusion in his *Picture and Text* (New York: Harper, 1893), a volume that coincidentally also contained James's essay on Alfred Parsons. The 'First Countess' drawings show clearly Reinhart's penchant for the stylized dramatic moment, developed during his evolution in the 1870s and 1880s as a genre painter, although paradoxically the most inherently melodramatic situation, Mrs Dornell's discovery of Betty collapsed in a swoon after Phelipson's fatal fall (a scene excised from 1891 *GND*), generates the most static and flaccid of his four contributions.

Hardy played an active role in both suggesting Alfred Parsons as a possible illustrator and hosting him at Max Gate during his visit to Dorset.[1] Parsons had already emerged as what Hardy referred to as 'one of the most promising painters of the English landscape school',[2] and he went on in his later years to become President of the Royal Society of Painters in Water Colours. The verisimilitude of his rendering of Mells Park ('Falls-Park') may have contributed to the current Earl of Ilchester's reputed unease with the periodical appearance of the story (see Appendix II).[3] But the perspectival subtlety of all his drawings, and particularly the wide-angle expansiveness of the view of Squire Dornell and Tupcombe riding off 'in the direction of Bristol' (reminiscent as it is of the fascination with expanding lines of sight that Hardy recurrently displays in the narrative viewpoints of his fiction), must have appealed to Hardy's still-sharp architect's eye, and more than justified his confidence in Parsons's suitability for the project.[4]

The other illustrations included in this edition are those for the two stories for which the copy-text is an illustrated periodical version. The two half-page drawings that precede the individual parts of the *Sphere* printing of 'A Changed Man' are by Archibald Standish Hartrick (1864–1950), who, like Alfred Parsons, went on to a distinguished career as a painter and illustrator.[5] He had begun working in London as an illustrator in the late 1880s, and there is no evidence that either he or his work was known to Hardy. Relative to the sophistication and precise match to textual circumstance of the Reinhart and Parsons illustrations, Hartrick's work seems somewhat casual and possibly rushed, the choice of scene depicted almost arbitrary, with the result that the drawings become more of an adjunct to the story than a genuine complement. Facial features are perfunctorily rendered and body-lines awkward to the point of distortion, contributing little to Hardy's characterization.

Rather more successful is A. Hayman's full-page engraving that closed the *Harper's Monthly Magazine* publication of 'Enter a Dragoon'. Here the choice of moment depicted seems as inevitable as the drawing's terminal location, immediately after the devastating curtain-line, 'that common sort of ivy is considered a weed in my part of the country'. The louring churchyard clutter and the harrowing cross-grave confrontation of the two women draped in widow's weeds provides a genuine pictorial enlargement of Hardy's textual situation. Unfortunately, the fuller identity of this Harper's staff artist remains unknown.

Since for the rest of the stories this edition uses as copy-text first collected versions that were not accompanied by illustrations, the decision was made not to include them. Readers interested in seeing all the illustrations that accompanied magazine versions of Hardy's short stories can find them on the web page maintained by Martin Ray under the auspices of the Thomas Hardy Association (http://www.yale.edu/hardysoc). Of particular interest may be the four drawings accompanying 'On the Western Circuit' (1891 *EIM*) prepared by Walter Paget (1863–1935), who in the same year had been George Newnes's intended choice of illustrator for the *Strand* magazine appearances of Arthur Conan Doyle's Sherlock Holmes short stories. In error the commission went to his older brother, Sidney, ensuring that Walter would go on to even greater familiarity as a model than as an artist: Sidney based the most famous and enduring image of the detective on his handsome younger brother.

# NOTES

1. *Collected Letters*, I, 181; and *Biography*, 286.
2. *Collected Letters*, I, 187.
3. Carl J. Weber, *Rebekah Owen and Thomas Hardy* (Waterville: Colby College Library, 1939), p. 74; and Ray, 79.
4. There is a quite striking similarity between the viewpoints adopted by Parsons and those taken up by Hardy himself in the drawings that he made to accompany some of the poems in his first volume of verse, *Wessex Poems* (1898); compare particularly Hardy's second sketch for 'Her Death and After' and Parsons's view of Falls-Park, and Hardy's sketch for 'My Cicely' and Parsons's view of the route to Bristol (*Poetical Works*, I, 56 and 67).
5. See A. S. Hartrick, *A Painter's Pilgrimage through Fifty Years* (Cambridge: Cambridge University Press, 1939).

# Glossary

In the case of words that have various meanings, the definitions given here relate only to the specific contexts in which they are used in these stories.

## Abbreviations

**adj.** adjective
**adv.** adverb
**dia.** dialect
**interj.** interjection
**obs.** obsolete
**phr.** phrase
**p. p.** past participle
**pron.** pronoun
**pr. t.** present tense
**sb.** substantive
**sb. pl.** substantive plural
**vb.** verb

*afflatus*, **sb.** creative inspiration
*alma mater*, **sb.** one's college or university (Latin for 'bountiful mother')
*barony*, **sb.** the rank of a baron, the lowest inheritable title
*bowfitt*, **sb.** buffet, sideboard
*bouts-rimés*, **sb. pl.** rhymed endings (French)
*boys'-love*, **sb.** popular name for southernwood, an aromatic worm-wood shrub
*by Jerry*, **oath** euphemism for 'by God' or 'by Jesus'
*canonical*, **adj.** generally accepted
*Carrara marble*, **sb.** finest Italian marble, named for the town in Tuscany

*Cercle*, sb. when capitalized, used to mean a group of friends, or club (French for 'circle')

*chapel of ease*, sb. small chapel built for use of those living at some distance from a main parish church

*chiton*, sb. ancient Greek tunic ($\chi\iota\tau\omega\nu$)

*chok' it all*, vb. phr. a mild oath, probably from 'may I be choked'

*clinker*, sb. hard brick or cinder

*close*, sb. cathedral, college or school precinct; an enclosure adjacent to a building

*curricle-phaeton*, sb. a curricle (two-wheeled) and a phaeton (four-wheeled) are both open carriages drawn by two horses. This unusual hybrid of the two would suggest a four-wheeled carriage built for speed and sportiness

*daze me*, oath damn me

*deal shaving*, sb. fir or pine timber, sawn into standard-sized boards

*désinvolture*, sb. a free manner, with overtones of insolence (French)

*drab*, sb. linen or woollen cloth, often of a grey, dull brown or natural undyed colour

*dragoon*, sb. mounted infantryman

*dung-mixen*, sb. dung-hill

*écorché*, sb. something flayed, wounded, or otherwise deformed (French)

*e'en*, adv. when prefixed to verbs, a colloquial and antiquated meaning for 'just' or 'nothing else but'

*embayed*, p. p. enclosed

*farrel*, sb. binding, cover of a book

*fault*, sb. a fracture in geological strata that brings rocks of different periods into contact with each other

*float-board*, sb. one of the boards of a water-wheel

*fly*, sb. light, one-horse covered carriage

*fretted*, p. p. worn away

*frustums*, sb. pl. drums of a column or stones of a pier (architectural)

*glebe*, sb. land that provides part of a clergyman's living

*grass-bents*, sb. pl. long stiff grass or rushes

*hussar*, sb. member of a light cavalry regiment

*impedimenta*, sb. pl. baggage, especially of an army (Latin)

*imperial*, sb. small tufted beard popularized by and named for the Emperor Napoleon III

*jerry-built*, adj. cheaply and carelessly built

*journey-work*, sb. work done as a day labourer for hire

*kerseymere*, sb. fine twilled woollen cloth

*knotting*, sb. decorative knotted lace, used to make borders or fringes *licentiate*, sb. person licensed to perform a professional function without a formal degree

*limpidity*, sb. transparency, clarity

*lingual*, adj. having the quality of language

*lymphatic*, adj. lacking energy

*meine Liebliche*, sb. 'my beloved' (German)

*mésalliance*, sb. marriage with a social inferior (French)

*midden-heaps*, sb. pl. heaps of refuse or dung

*mind*, vb., dia. remember

*murrey*, adj. purplish-red, like the mulberry

*naphtha*, sb. petroleum-based fuel

*nonage*, sb. minority, or youth generally

*oi*, dia. aye, yes

*Old Tom*, sb. strong gin

*Ooser*, sb. mask with grim jaws, put on with a cow's skin to frighten people

*oriel window*, sb. projecting polygonal window

*packet*, sb. mail-boat

*pea-jacket*, sb. short wool overcoat, originally worn by sailors

*penates*, sb. pl. Roman household gods

*pillion*, sb. cushion attached to rear of saddle to accommodate a second rider

*pis aller*, sb. last resort (French for 'worst course')

*poll*, sb. back part of the head, neck

*post-chaise*, sb. travelling carriage hired from stage to stage or drawn by horses so hired

*psalmody*, sb. the art of singing psalms or setting them to music

*rackety*, adj. boisterous, socially lively

*raft*, vb. rouse, upset

*rathe-ripes*, sb. pl. early-ripening Dorset apples

*rawmil*, adj. made from 'raw' (i.e., unskimmed) milk

*repoussé*, adj. referring to a method of creating ornamental metal work by hammering into relief from the reverse side (French for 'pushed back')

*rococo-work*, sb. elaborate ornamentation

*route*, sb. in a military sense, the order to march, depart

*sakes alive*, phr., dia. exclamation of surprise

*saltatory*, adj. pertaining to dancing or jumping

*sang froid*, sb. composure in unsettling circumstances (French for 'cold blood')

*sappy*, sb. simpleton

*Schiedam*, sb. Dutch gin, named for its town of origin

*serpent*, **sb.** bass wind instrument coiled back on itself like a snake

*slack-twisted*, **adj.** inactive, lazy

*slouched hat*, **sb.** soft, broad-brimmed hat (more usually 'slouch hat')

*sprigged-laylock*, **adj., obs. dia.** decorated with a lilac-sprig design

*stuff-gownsman*, **sb.** one who wears the woollen gown of a junior barrister who has not taken silk (i.e., become a Queen's/King's Counsel)

*tails*, **sb. pl.** lower edges of a skirt

*tesserae*, **sb. pl.** small blocks used in mosaic work

*tie-beam*, **sb.** horizontal beam that prevents two roof rafters from separating

*tippet*, **sb.** cape or muffler covering shoulders

*topper*, **sb.** something hard to beat, or that comes as a surprise or blow

*totties*, **sb. pl.** feet (usually of little children)

*tranter*, **sb.** carrier, bearer of people or goods

*trap*, **sb.** wheeled vehicle

*tremolo-stop*, **sb.** organ stop designed to create vibrating effect on a single note

*trump*, **sb.** colloquial term for a person of courage or generosity

*upping-stock*, **sb.** stepped block for use in mounting a horse

*volte-face*, **sb.** a turning round, especially a complete change of argumentative position (French)

*wideawake*, **sb.** low-crowned, wide-brimmed felt hat

*with-wind, withy-wind*, **sb.** bindweed

*Zounds*, **interj.** archaic conflation of 'God's wounds', evoking Christ's crucifixion.

# PENGUIN (Ⓟ) CLASSICS

## *The Classics Publisher*

'Penguin Classics, one of the world's greatest series' JOHN KEEGAN

'I have never been disappointed with the Penguin Classics. All I have read is a model of academic seriousness and provides the essential information to fully enjoy the master works that appear in its catalogue' MARIO VARGAS LLOSA

'Penguin and Classics are words that go together like horse and carriage or Mercedes and Benz. When I was a university teacher I always prescribed Penguin editions of classic novels for my courses: they have the best introductions, the most reliable notes, and the most carefully edited texts' DAVID LODGE

'Growing up in Bombay, expensive hardback books were beyond my means, but I could indulge my passion for reading at the roadside bookstalls that were well stocked with all the Penguin paperbacks ... Sometimes I would choose a book just because I was attracted by the cover, but so reliable was the Penguin imprimatur that I was never once disappointed by the contents.

Such access certainly broadened the scope of my reading, and perhaps it's no coincidence that so many Merchant Ivory films have been adapted from great novels, or that those novels are published by Penguin' ISMAIL MERCHANT

'You can't write, read, or live fully in the present without knowing the literature of the past. Penguin Classics opens the door to a treasure house of pure pleasure, books that have never been bettered, which are read again and again with increased delight' JOHN MORTIMER

# CLICK ON A CLASSIC

## www.penguinclassics.com

### *The world's greatest literature at your fingertips*

Constantly updated information on over 1600 titles, from Icelandic sagas to ancient Indian epics, Russian drama to Italian romance, American greats to African masterpieces

•

The latest news on recent additions to the list, updated editions and specially commissioned translations

•

Original scholarly essays by leading writers: Elaine Showalter on Zola, Laurie R. King on Arthur Conan Doyle, Frank Kermode on Shakespeare, Lisa Appignanesi on Tolstoy

•

A wealth of background material, including biographies of every classic author from Aristotle to Zamyatin, plot synopses, readers' and teachers' guides, useful web links

•

Online desk and examination copy assistance for academics

•

Trivia quizzes, competitions, giveaways, news on forthcoming screen adaptations

•

eBooks available to download

# READ MORE IN PENGUIN

In every corner of the world, on every subject under the sun, Penguin represents quality and variety – the very best in publishing today.

*For complete information about books available from Penguin – including Puffins and Penguin Classics – and how to order them, write to us at the appropriate address below. Please note that for copyright reasons the selection of books varies from country to country.*

**In the United Kingdom:** *Please write to* Dept EP, Penguin Books Ltd, Bath Road, Harmondsworth, West Drayton, Middlesex UB7 0DA

**In the United States:** *Please write to* Consumer Services, Penguin Putnam Inc., 405 Murray Hill Parkway, East Rutherford, New Jersey 07073-2136. *VISA and MasterCard holders call 1-800-631-8571 to order Penguin titles*

**In Canada:** *Please write to* Penguin Books Canada Ltd, 10 Alcorn Avenue, Suite 300, Toronto, Ontario M4V 3B2

**In Australia:** *Please write to* Penguin Books Australia Ltd, 487 Maroondah Highway, Ringwood, Victoria 3134

**In New Zealand:** *Please write to* Penguin Books (NZ) Ltd, Private Bag 102902, North Shore Mail Centre, Auckland 10

**In India:** *Please write to* Penguin Books India Pvt Ltd, 11, Community Centre, Panchsheel Park, New Delhi 110017

**In the Netherlands:** *Please write to* Penguin Books Netherlands bv, Postbus 3507, NL-1001 AH Amsterdam

**In Germany:** *Please write to* Penguin Books Deutschland GmbH, Metzlerstrasse 26, 60594 Frankfurt am Main

**In Spain:** *Please write to* Penguin Books S. A., Bravo Murillo 19, 1ºB, 28015 Madrid

**In Italy:** *Please write to* Penguin Italia s.r.l., Via Vittoria Emanuele 45Ia, 20094 Corsico, Milano

**In France:** *Please write to* Penguin France, 12, Rue Prosper Ferradou, 31700 Blagnac

**In Japan:** *Please write to* Penguin Books Japan Ltd, Iidabashi KM-Bldg, 2-23-9 Koraku, Bunkyo-Ku, Tokyo 112-0004

**In South Africa:** *Please write to* Penguin Books South Africa (Pty) Ltd, P.O. Box 751093, Gardenview, 2047 Johannesburg

# TOLSTOY

# Anna Karenina

*'Everything is finished . . . I have nothing but you.*
*Remember that'*

Anna Karenina seems to have everything, but she feels that her life is empty until the moment she encounters the impetuous officer Count Vronsky. Their subsequent affair scandalizes society and family alike, and soon brings jealousy and bitterness in its wake. Contrasting with this tale of love and self-destruction is the vividly observed story of Levin, who strives to find contentment and a meaning to his life – and also a self-portrait of Tolstoy himself.

This new translation has been acclaimed as the definitive English version. The volume contains an introduction by Richard Pevear and a preface by John Bayley.

'Pevear and Volokhonsky are at once scrupulous translators and vivid stylists of English, and their superb rendering allows us, as perhaps never before, to grasp the palpability of Tolstoy's "characters, acts, situations"' JAMES WOOD, *New Yorker*

*Translated by* RICHARD PEVEAR *and*
LARISSA VOLOKHONSKY
*With a preface by* JOHN BAYLEY